PRAISE FOR *MERCY OF A RUDE STREAM*

REQUIEM FOR HARLEM

"[Roth] is still a formidable storyteller. His chronicle is fueled with a raw octane that drives the plot with relentless energy. He has the knack of making us turn the page."
–Jack Schwartz, *The Forward*

"Roth's novel is the redeeming legacy of a troubled man who was touched by 'that unique, unutterable afflatus of creativity.'"
–Steven G. Kellman, *Atlanta Journal-Constitution*

"The powerful conclusion to an amazing series of autobiographical novels."
–*Kirkus Reviews* (starred review)

"Henry Roth's genius lay in his spontaneity–that, and his ability to recall how it felt to be young…. In *Requiem for Harlem* there is storm and stress and Roth makes it very real, filled with ambiguity."
–Barbara Holliday, *Detroit Free Press*

FROM BONDAGE

"Surely nothing like this series has been written before, nor will be again…. *Mercy of a Rude Stream* will be looked upon as a landmark of the American literary century."
–David Mehegan, *The Boston Globe*

"Extraordinary…clearly indispensable to the appreciation of Roth's unique life and work as a whole."
–Frank Kermode, *The New York Times Book Review*

"*From Bondage* is a monumental literary achievement."
–Jonathan Kirsch, *Los Angeles Times*

"A wondrous, disturbing, and ruthlessly honest chronicle of the complex and often wrenchingly twisted process of assimilation. The sheer dynamism generated by the writer's act of memory and confession is awe-inspiring."
–Hedy Weiss, *Chicago Sun*

A DIVING ROCK ON THE HUDSON

"*A Diving Rock on the Hudson* has the verisimilitude only a few rare works of fiction manage to achieve."
–Joan Smith, *San Francisco Examiner*

"As provocative as anything in the chapters of St. Augustine or Rousseau."
–Stefan Kanfer, *Los Angeles Times Book Review*

"Rises to impressive heights. Roth is the monarch of all he conveys."
–Paul West, *The Washington Post Book World*

"Applies a torque to the mind's geometry that literary events rarely do."
–Marc Shechner, *Chicago Tribune*

A STAR SHINES OVER MT. MORRIS PARK

"Roth creates his own *Portrait of the Artist as a Young Man*–a marvelously poetic chronicle."
–*Chicago Sun-Times*

"An extraordinary and provocative work...One of the great literary comebacks of the century."
–*San Francisco Chronicle*

"An extraordinary work, one arguably unparalleled in American letters."
–*Philadelphia Inquirer*

"Mr. Roth's innovative use of language...is both beautiful and highly realistic.... Although there is no style called Rothian, there should be."
–*The New York Times Book Review*

Mercy of a Rude Stream

Also by Henry Roth

Call It Sleep
Shifting Landscape
Mercy of a Rude Stream: Volume I
    A Star Shines over Mt. Morris Park
Mercy of a Rude Stream: Volume II
    A Diving Rock on the Hudson
Mercy of a Rude Stream: Volume III
    From Bondage

Volume IV: Mercy of a Rude Stream

R E Q U I E M   F O R   H A R L E M

H E N R Y   R O T H

PICADOR
ST. MARTIN'S PRESS
NEW YORK

This is a work of fiction. Although some characters were inspired by people whom the author knew, the narrative is not intended in any way to be
a depiction of any real events. This novel is certainly not an autobiogra-
phy, nor should it be taken as such.

MERCY OF A RUDE STREAM, VOLUME IV: REQUIEM FOR HARLEM. Copyright © 1998
by The Literary Estate of Henry Roth. Editor's Afterword copyright © 1998
by Robert Weil. All rights reserved. Printed in the United States of America.
No part of this book may be used or reproduced in any manner whatsoev-
er without written permission except in the case of brief quotations embod-
ied in critical articles or reviews. For information, address Picador
175 Fifth Avenue, New York, N.Y. 10010.

Picador® is a U.S. registered trademark and is used by St. Martin's Press
under license from Pan Books Limited.

For information on Picador Reading Group Guides, as well as order-
ing, please contact the Trade Marketing department at St. Martin's Press.
Phone: 1-800-221-7945 extension 488
Fax: 212-677-7456
E-mail: trademarketing@stmartins.com

Interior photographs courtesy of Archive Photos

Library of Congress Cataloging-in-Publication Data

Roth, Henry.
    Requiem for Harlem / Henry Roth.
      p.   cm.   — (Mercy of a rude stream ; v. 4)
    ISBN 0-312-20205-9
    1. Jews in New York (State) — New York — Fiction. 2. Harlem (New
York, N.Y.) — Fiction. I. Title. II. Series: Roth, Henry. Mercy of a rude
stream; v. 4.
[PS3535.0787M47   1994 vol. 4 1999]
813'.52—dc21
                                                                    98-31435
                                                                        CIP

First published in the United States by St. Martin's Press

First Picador Paperback Edition: January 1999

D10 9 8 7 6 5 4 3 2

For Roz and Bill Targ,
Paragons of Loyalty

THE FAMILY OF IRA STIGMAN

Ira's Mother's Family Tree

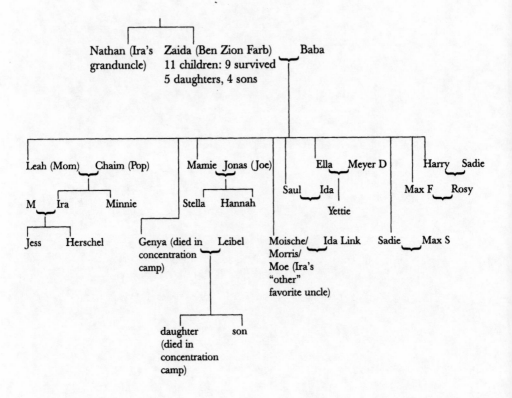

Nathan (Ira's granduncle)   Zaida (Ben Zion Farb) 11 children: 9 survived 5 daughters, 4 sons   Baba

Leah (Mom) Chaim (Pop)   Mamie Jonas (Joe)   Ella Meyer D   Harry Sadie

M Ira Minnie   Stella Hannah   Saul Ida   Max F Rosy

Jess Herschel   Genya (died in concentration camp) Leibel   Yettie

Moische/ Morris/ Moe (Ira's "other" favorite uncle)   Ida Link   Sadie Max S

daughter (died in concentration camp)   son

⌣ Married

┬ Children

THE FAMILY OF IRA STIGMAN

Ira's Father's Family Tree

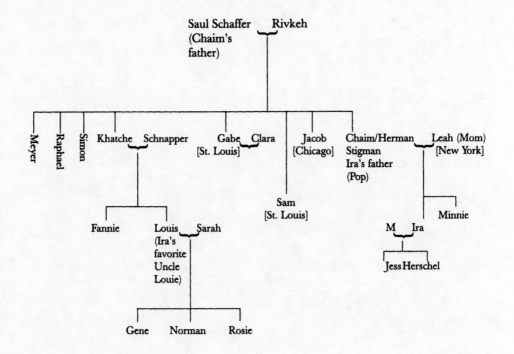

Saul Schaffer (Chaim's father) — Rivkeh

Meyer | Raphael | Simon | Khatche — Schnapper | Gabe [St. Louis] — Clara | Jacob [Chicago] | Chaim/Herman Stigman Ira's father (Pop) — Leah (Mom) [New York]

Sam [St. Louis]

Fannie | Louis (Ira's favorite Uncle Louie) — Sarah

M — Ira | Minnie

Jess Herschel

Gene | Norman | Rosie

⌣ Married

┬ Children

CONTENTS

Without Haste, Without Rest.
Not thine the labour to complete,
And yet thou art not free to cease!

לֹא עָלֶיךָ הַמְלָאכָה לִגְמוֹר
וְלֹא אַתָּה בֶּן חוֹרִין לְבָטֵל מִמֶּנָּה

—*The Mishnah,*
   Abot, 2:16 I
   Translated by Rabbi Isidore Myers

PART ONE

|

Ira Stigman's legs were weary, legs and feet and instep, but the long march was well worth its fatigue. He had hiked and hiked, past Grand Central Station and 42nd Street, past all the crosstown trolley lines, at 34th, at 23rd, at 14th, at 10th, and then he turned west to 8th Street. Gut and innards were at peace, head was clear. He had traveled over a hundred city blocks from the red brick tenement, counting the jog west from Lexington to Fifth Avenue. Nearly six miles, according to accepted reckoning. Ahead of him, a block away, loomed two figures of George Washington, either side of the arch named in his honor, heroic in size and monumentally calm. And behind the arch, Washington Square Park spread out in a rectangle of grass and trees still verdant despite the October chill, paved walks and a fountain flourishing at the center. From the slant of sun and hint of chill in the shadows, Ira judged the time must be approaching five o'clock, though Sunday strollers were still numerous in the park, and benches well occupied. Luxuriously, negligent with liberation from acute discomfort, he considered his next step—literally. He could go into the park, find a space on a bench and sit down, rest his weary shanks awhile, and then walk east again, a few blocks past NYU to Astor Place, and take the Lexington Avenue subway home. Sunday, he'd be sure to have a seat. But he had another option: he had the keys to Edith's apartment in his pocket.

If Edith was home, he could rest while he visited; if she wasn't home, he could stretch out on the couch; could relieve his bladder in privacy, though it wasn't too distended: perspiration had taken care of that. No, it would be better to piss right here in the men's toilet in the park and be done with it, in case Edith was home. Right. He made his way across the park to the men's toilet, relieved himself against the slate, holding his hand cupped over his cock, a trick he had learned from an obvious gentleman next to him once, learned it eagerly because he was always a little apprehensive that he didn't stack up so well against other guys.

He exited—and now what? The walk to the pissoir had brought him a few blocks nearer Edith's. He felt renewed. What were a few blocks more? She would be transported with mirth when he regaled her with an account of his gastronomic adventures with Leo, whom he had just finished tutoring. He could already hear the peal of her laughter as he described the waning of the bowling ball within him— to the tune of "Tramp, tramp, tramp, the boys are marching."

Three helpings of pasta with lovely little meatballs he had consumed earlier that afternoon, with collateral slices of bread, washed down with dago red wine. "Wow!" he had told Leo as he put down his fork. "Boy, am I ever full. I'm stuffed."

He was indeed—and more: sated to stupefaction—arms hanging down, stultified. "Hey, Leo, I got to lie down," Ira had told his friend after they had finished.

"No kiddin'? There's a sofa in the front room. Or you want to go in my bedroom?"

"No. Just to lie down for a few minutes. I guess I ate too much."

Leo had led the way. The front-room windows above the sofa looked out on Lexington Avenue. Early-afternoon sunlight, which had warmed the black horsehair of the sofa, had fallen on Ira as he stretched out on top. Lethean Lexington Avenue traffic three stories below, volleys of Italian from the dining room, clink-clank of dishes and utensils being washed in the kitchen—Ira fell into a slumber like a coma. When he awoke, he felt a huge, gross lump of undigested feast inside his stomach that pressed against his abdomen like a bowling ball. He wasn't sure he'd survive. Panicky, he got to his feet, tottered, plopped back on the sofa again, and sat there, unable even to slump, rubbing the bowling ball in his belly. "Wow!"

Leo had heard him, and had come in, faithful Leo, snub nose and thick lips awry with concern. "Whatsa matter?"

"Ow, I ate too much." Ira massaged his bloated paunch and lamented. "Jesus, I ate too much."

"You're not gonna be sick or nothin'?"

"No. It's all in there. What a bellyache."

"You didn't eat so much. You're pregnant," Leo grinned.

"Aw, cut out the shit. Jesus, I hurt."

"Waddaye wanna do? You wanna lay down some more?"

"No, no. Jesus Christ."

"You don't wanna puke, do you? I can get you some o' my mother's bakin' soda."

"No, no. Don't say anything."

"What d'you wanna do?"

"Lay an egg. Wow!"

Leo cackled.

"I'm not kidding."

"You ain't?"

"No. Wooh! Did you ever see an aepyornis egg?"

"A who?"

"That's what I got in my gut. Go to the Museum of Natural History. I gotta walk."

"Is that where you goin'?"

"No, I'm just going to walk, walk, walk. Get me my hat and jacket, will you? I don't want them to see me, you know what I mean?"

"I'll go with you."

"No, I'll just go in and say goodbye. Get the hat and jacket." Only the most heroic kind of locomotion could help him in the fix he was in, Ira was sure. "Wow!"

He was grateful to Leo for helping him into the jacket. He grimaced over suppressed groans, and with a smile like a plaster cast on his face, went into the kitchen and thanked Leo's mother, then into the dining room, where the three cooks were playing cards. He said something about a great fiesta, and now he had to walk it off, and made for the door and the stairs. Leo, who insisted on following Ira down into the street, to make sure he was all right, again offered to accompany him, but Ira shook hands with him at the stoop and waved his pupil away. "Good luck. I'll see you after the exam. I got to get goin'. Boy," he grunted. "Thanks. So long." And he headed downtown.

Ow, bowling ball, bowling ball. Why did he have to do it? He'd have to churn it up, and churn it up, and churn it down to size. Knead it and knead it back again into the dough it was supposed to be. Oh, bastinado it, drub it, rubadubdub it. No hungry generations tread thee down. O-o-o-h. Jumpin' Jesus, how do you tenderize a bowling ball? Walk. Hoof it, man, hoof it.

He had first wheeled toward Park Avenue, tramped a block west, and there wheeled south. Forget it, if you can at least get by the side of the Grand Central ramp on 102nd Street; look at the blocks of glittery mica schist and gneiss. Watch the afternoon sun glint off the rock as you knead down the rock in your belly. He groaned.

He strode south; and thought of the kid exploring here a seeming thousand years ago, catapulted to Harlem from the Lower East Side just thirteen years ago, a thousand years ago, a geologic age. There were then pirates skulking in that railroad ramp, do you remember? Buccaneers with booty, wassailing with tankards and cutlass. Oh, jolly good ale and old they swigged. Stride, stride. There. It was a little easier, wasn't it? By the shores o' Gitchee Goomie, there I sat down and wept, remembering thee, O Zion. Keep goin'.

Heading south, ramp and ground intersect, the best-laid plans, and the best lays too gang aft agley, by-by, ol' granity pal. O-o-o-h. Median strip, see? Full of grass and flowers and shrubs. Charming, ain't it, when one was affluent? And resided in sedate townhouses on either side of wide, wide Park Avenue, with a butler or a footman visible through the glass door. Ah, hear ye, magnates, hear ye: how the trains down below rumbled softly through the vents among the marigolds, rumble obsequiously, w-o-o-o. Keep up the footwork, bud. Once more into the breech, O Peristalsis, and yet once more. Marvelous! It's only a croquet ball now. . . .

He hadn't seen Edith since that famous night when he escorted her with Lewlyn to the Hoboken pier, last spring, months ago now. He could have seen her last night, with her old loverboy Larry—but no, this was going to be so much better, total independence. And she liked his independence much better. Now heading west, further refreshed by his lightened load, he left the park and headed for Sixth Avenue under the El.

He could not wait to tell her about the orgy at Leo's: three cooks, three plates of pasta, two loaves of Italian bread, bumpers of wine—if that wasn't hilarious, despite the pain.

Quickening his steps, he reached Sixth Avenue in the fine shadow of a late Indian summer, passed under the El, followed familiar diagonal shortcuts to Seventh and Morton. Around the gas station, and under the leaves of sidewalk trees, he reached house number 32, got out the key to the house door—no, no, he'd better ring. He did. No buzzer sounded in return. Then she *wasn't* home. Exactly the alternate contingency he had thought of. He could stretch out on that couch—just what his knees prayed for, answer to his knees' needs—ah, a quarter hour, half hour, and if she came home meanwhile—so what if he fell asleep?

Up the two flights of carpeted stairs, silently ascended. And just to make doubly sure, and be doubly polite, he knocked on the door . . . waited. No answer. Okay. He separated her apartment door key from the house door key, groped for the slot, inserted.

And as he did, he heard, he thought he heard, no, he heard the slightest commotion on the other side of the door, and he hesitated—

Just in time to hear Edith's voice, unmistakably Edith's, hurried: "Just a minute, Ira!"

Had she been asleep, had he wakened her? Oh, God! Ira withdrew the key.

A second later, two seconds later, the door swung open, and into the electric-lighted hall stepped Edith, pulling the door after her. "Ira," she said. "I thought it was you."

"Yeah, it's me." He retreated in utter confusion. "Excuse me! Gee, Edith. I rang the buzzer—I—I'm sorry!"

"I wasn't in a position to receive callers." The Professora's eyes were bright, bright and roguish; and her voice high-pitched, on the verge of shrillness. "It's quite all right, Ira." She was wearing a new dark green bathrobe with black trefoils on it. Not merely wearing it,

7

but by the way she held the garment at her throat, bunching the cloth together with tiny fist, by the intimate way her form swelled the cloth with contour, there could be no escaping the perception: the body her bathrobe enveloped was nude. "Ira, can you wait a few minutes? You can wait in my neighbor Amelia's room. She's gone for the weekend, and I have her keys. Please wait," she appealed.

"Oh, no. What a dope I am. Gee."

"I'm glad you came over. I'll get her keys. Just one minute."

"No, I was only walking. I'll come again. It's all right."

"You're sure? Will you call me?"

"Yeah, I just happened to eat too much macaroni—I mean pasta— and I—" Keys still in hand, Ira began making his way toward the stairs. "I was walking it off."

"I'm so sorry," Edith said. "Are you all right?"

"Oh, sure. It's all eased up, shrunk."

As he spoke, he took the first step down. Solicitously watching him descend, Edith opened the door behind her, and from deep inside the room, a dry, sandy chuckle emanated.

"You'll call?" Edith's voice followed Ira down the steps.

"Yeah. In a couple o' days. All right?"

"I'm so sorry."

"It's nothing. G'bye."

"Goodbye, Ira."

He heard the apartment door close above him . . . walked carefully, deliberately down the stair treads, as if his doing so helped to obliterate his blunder, as if quiet would eliminate his mistake—as if it never happened. . . . What a sap. Hand slid on banister to newel post. He jingled the two keys on the ring; he could almost have flung them out into the gutter when he opened the house door, so great was his chagrin. He pocketed them instead, and stepped out onto the side-walk.

What a dope! What an imbecile! He turned back toward Seventh Avenue. Yeah, but all those tears, all that sound and fury, storm and stress, that wracking taxi ride last spring with Edith so distraught, those floods of woe—they didn't mean a thing; there she was in bed with Lewlyn again. The same guy she had renounced, denounced, heaped with scorn! Hey, wait a minute—and now his knees began to ache with renewed pang—couldn't he get it through his thick head that ladies wanted to be laid? Yeah, ladies wanted to be laid, just like gentlemen wanted to lay them?

It was the same feeling of disappointment he had had six weeks before, just as his senior year of CCNY had begun, when, keeping pace with the scattering of fellow students traveling downhill, he had caught sight of Larry about a half block ahead: Larry accompanied by someone else: yes, sociology professor Lewlyn, still fleeing his unfaithful wife, Marcia Meede . . . how operatic it all did sound . . . had returned from England. Ira made no effort to catch up with the two, but kept his distance, until he saw them enter Wentworth Hall. Something to meditate on, watching the pair, the younger and the elder, instructor and student, Larry gesturing with large, white hands, Lewlyn listening benignly. Something to ponder on, with Edith the unseen despairing apex of the triangle. So much meaning inhered in it, so much meaning in this transient configuration, but what was it? Irony, irony was easy to discern—he was a *mevhin* of irony. But the immense, positive shape of meaning escaped him, the meaning that all this irony declared about human life. It was way beyond the mere sexual involvement of student and instructor with the same woman. What was human life striving after? If he could only discover that larger significance, that larger affirmation. Maybe there wasn't any, though it seemed there was. He had thought he was then nothing but a big fool and a wretched sinner too.

The feeling persisted still, not a week after Yom Kippur, his unobservant atonements all for naught, as he rounded the small gas station at Seventh Avenue again. Maybe he was wrong. What the hell did he know about love? Maybe Lewlyn was now all finished with that British spinster he hoped would free him from Marcia's net. Or maybe Lewlyn had come back to Edith again. No wonder she looked that way: droll, wanton, impish. *'Tis done, 'tis done, I've won, I've won, quoth she and whistles thrice.* Yeah, but why had she wanted Ira to come over again, almost imploring him? No, he was wrong again. Nothing had changed. He could bet on that.

He had to get to a subway seat and sit down before his legs caved in. Get on at Christopher, transfer at 42nd. In the scarce remaining light from the west, Ira broke into a trot, and as he passed the news kiosk on Seventh he picked up speed, from trot to run. He tore down the stairs, in twilight's gloom, plunked a token in the slot, for once, and breathless, he boarded the uptown train; he'd dropped his jitney into the hopper.

Ira sat with thumbs hooked in belt. Had he painted himself into a corner? Probably. But he had to keep going to keep from falling down. He tried to think back, scanned an older yellow typescript to his right: *I felt baffled; I felt bitter; with this first line, the next chapter had begun. No use denying it to myself any longer, slurring the matter over as I did about so much else in life, habitually permitting connotations to blur, and thus obviate a decisive response.* It was true, Ira meditated, he had a knack for being at the wrong place at the wrong time. He had already begun to hope, more and more articulately, that Edith would lose Lewlyn, irrevocably. And with Larry clearly diminishing to a mere indulgence, one depending on a propitious moment to terminate, he, Ira himself, heir apparent, somehow, sometime soon would become Edith's lover.

Ira bolted up and suddenly addressed himself consciously to the little chips of the time when he was alive, alive, twenty-one, and entering that senior year at CCNY. Chips, he called them, noting he had used a singular instead of a plural verb. Well, chips of the time—considered as a unit. In a more illustrative way of speaking, they weren't really chips, these notations he had beside him on the collapsible steel typing table; they were a few of the anchor points in the world he lived in, and to which the web of his existence was connected, loosely connected mostly, remotely connected. They and millions of other events like them made up the ever-changing content of his days. In this particular case, these events—the start of class, the Yankees World Series win, those agonizing fifteen seconds of the Tunney-Dempsey fight, the "slow count," were all part, all chips, of the year 1927, nearing the end of October.

For a while, after what he had seen—and heard—that Sunday afternoon in October, his hopes seemed to him fatuous, fatuous and untenable. How could she so reverse herself, when she had hardened her mind against Lewlyn as a duplicitous and perfidious person—and weak—as one who had made it appear that he was undecided in his choice of wife, whose indecision she was gullible enough to take at face value? Was he still undecided, or was he still playing her for a fool? Which? These were difficult, nay, impossible judgments for the young and anything but acute Ira to make. According to Edith's version in later years, Lewlyn had come back from England in the same uncertain frame of mind as he had gone, and she had resumed the relationship with him upon his return, because Lewlyn still ostensibly hadn't made up his mind. He was still in a state of uncertainty, but Edith tended to fabricate. Ira came to learn that, to learn it by his own relationship with her, and its aftermath. It was the same thing he had discerned, intuitively, about Edith from the beginning: her trait of making herself the heroine of a tragedy in which she was enmeshed and made to suffer because others took advantage of her innate goodness. And just as she had admitted in the midst of her sobs and tears, the night Ira escorted her home from the ship, that she had been deceiving herself with regard to Lewlyn's choice of permanent mate, so she did when he came back from England—came back, according to him, to Lewlyn, with vows of marriage already exchanged between himself and Cecilia. That he entered into a sexual transaction with Edith, that was another matter. An entire year of continence, or celibacy, was too much to expect of any man, as Ira found out when he nearly went mad in Los Angeles during his six months of separation from M in '38—too much to ask of any man, and yet not too much to ask of a woman, as M bore witness, as Cecilia bore witness, and how many myriads of women over the centuries bore witness? Anyway, this last sequel of the sterile affair Edith evidently entered into in a spirit of play—consciously—or in that Greek spirit that Lewlyn esteemed so greatly: wherein friendship between the sexes reached its greatest intimacy via intercourse.

October was in its third week when in the afternoon's mail delivery Ira recognized the single letter showing through the scroll in the dented brass letterbox as Edith's: inside her unmistakable envelope was her typed note, single-spaced as was her wont, helter-skelter, and dashed-off. PLEASE! PLEASE! Her letter appeared almost hysterical. Would he telephone her as soon as he could? She was very much concerned at not hearing from him. She had telephoned the drugstore, Biolov's, but they told her nobody answered the door. Please, would he call her as soon as he received this. Ira had refused to come along to visit Edith, Larry had told her. She thought she knew why, but not hearing from him so long, she was deeply upset. She had something terribly important she wanted to tell him—and only him.

Ira had sulked awhile. Was that "something important" just an inducement? Was he wrong about Lewlyn? And what if he was wrong? And Lewlyn and Edith had just made shift to while away the time until Lewlyn could marry elsewhere. They played the two-backed beast in the meantime, as Shakespeare called it, expediently and amicably franfreluquied—how did Quarles spell it? So there was still Lewlyn. And there was Larry still. So he would kind of squeeze in between them, if he ever did. Make up a *troika*. Nah. And he wouldn't know how to break down the barrier anyway. If he couldn't when he lay next to her in the same bed, when would he have the gumption? All he had about a career as a writer was just a bunch of hallucinations, his usual muzzy fantasies. Leaving his briefcase on the kitchen table of Mom's empty kitchen, he tripped lightly down the dingy stairs. Fishing the nickel out of his pocket, he crossed the street, entered Biolov's, twirled his hand in greeting at Joey Shapiro behind the counter. Joe was the younger son of Mrs. Shapiro on the same floor, and now a longtime Biolov's unlicensed pharmacy assistant. Ira opened the telephone booth's folding wooden doors and called Edith's number.

"Ira, is that you? Heavens, I'm dreadfully sorry about what happened. I didn't offend you, I hope. I wouldn't offend you for the world."

"Oh, no. It's just a—" He shrugged at the transmitter. "It wasn't your fault. If I barge in like that."

"You're always welcome. You know that. I was hoping you'd be with Larry when he came over. I don't know how I could have made amends. Or somehow—indicated—I was with Lewlyn."

"I know. I heard him."

"You did? One of those utterly meaningless things still continuing. You must have gone away thinking I'm a perfect fool."

"No. I just figured."

"I'd made up my mind I wasn't going to break my heart a second time. And just when I do, wouldn't you know this silly thing renews— only it's far from silly."

"What do you mean?"

"Oh. Can you come over? I miss not being able to talk to you terribly, Ira."

"What d'you mean? When?"

"This afternoon, for a few minutes."

"Today?"

"Yes. Can you? I've gotten so dependent on you."

"Well, if you want me to."

"Very much."

"All right. I'm in the street already. I'll take the subway."

"You're a treasure."

Utterly meaningless. Ira mulled over her words as he directed his purposeful stride toward Lexington Avenue. At the corner of Lexington, he turned right to 116th Street. Less of a walk. What did utterly meaningless signify? It meant that she didn't expect anything to come of this, what d'you call it? Liaison. That was what it meant. What the hell, he laid Stella every chance he got; he wasn't going to marry her. It was what he was telling himself a couple of weeks ago—that Surfeit Sunday, he could call it, the way *goyim,* gentiles, called a certain Tuesday—before Lent? After Lent? No, before Lent, Mardi Gras, Fat Tuesday, Schmaltzy Tuesday. And what else? Maundy Thursday. What the hell was Maundy?

How the stores had all proliferated along the avenue, now that there was a subway station on 116th Street. It was just Pop's bad luck that he had invested in a delicatessen on 116th near Lexington too soon, before the subway was built. He might have prospered afterward.

Ira descended the subway stairs, wedged his jitney into the slot, and bulled through the turnstile to the platform. What he should be thinking about was Edith's saying meaningless—meaningless what? Meaningless pastime—oh, no, she didn't say that; she said utterly meaningless. That was it. It could only mean one thing: it was just pastime, just as she had said. Lewlyn was betrothed, fancy word, to the other woman in England. That was what it meant. So the way was open. Wow. He entered the uncrowded downtown train. So he wasn't wrong. Destiny was destiny. Jesus, how would he do it then? She said he was a treasure. So what should he do? Lie to her? Say he had never done it, but wanted to do it with her. He liked her, dearest person he knew. She was so fond of him too, valued his friendship, she said. So he—he needed, like Lewlyn, like Lewlyn's Greek idea of intimacy consummating. Ah, hell, he couldn't. He was sure she would, but he couldn't. Jesus Christ. Edith pulling up her knees, drawers off, pussy out, bare-ass. He couldn't. He couldn't think of her that way. Delicate, refined, Ph.D., professor of English literature, a professor. That was the trouble. . . .

II

Open-mouthed, aware momentarily that he had lapsed into total unawareness, he listened to Edith.

She had suspected she might be in for trouble, Edith said, when she was four days overdue. She had always been so regular. But now she was certain, after the examination by Dr. Teragan. There could be no doubt about it: she was definitely pregnant. "It's so strange," she said. "I feel so blithe, and yet I'm terribly concerned. Abortions are no joke, Ira, and it looks as if I may have to go through one."

"Why?" he asked numbly.

She had tried everything else, she explained. Everything that might bring on menstruation, camomile, angelica, even castor oil. Of course, what she was really trying to do was to bring on miscarriage, but nothing had worked. She was lavish with particulars; feminine and arcane, they agitated rather than edified: there might be all sorts of complications from an abortion. Even with the best of them, when one had money enough to have them done by a doctor, they were illegal, and abortionists risked their licenses to perform them. Also because of the pressure on the physician, and the conditions of secrecy under which he performed the operation, sterility might be neglected; hemorrhaging and infections might result, and often did. With lagging and uneasy attention, Ira interrupted only once: that was when she said, "I can imagine how risky these back-alley ones must be."

"What are back-alley ones?" he asked.

"When they're done by midwives or other nonprofessionals." She laughed ruefully. "What women have to go through." And because the doctor did risk his license, the fee he charged for an abortion was high. And that brought on another round of problems, problems centering on money, or the lack of it, and why: "I can ill afford the expense of an abortion right now," she said. "It comes at such a dreadful time. I ought to send my sister something for the child's birthday. Something, now that she's divorced. Her husband is deliberately delaying alimony. He has plenty of money. He was law partner of Woodrow Wilson's secretary. But that's his way of getting back at Leona. And of course, she's a fool when it comes to managing her affairs. Father is in a terrible fix. He can't help her. He needs help himself. He's hardly able to carry on his own law practice. And Mother's life insurance payments are due." Still, oddly enough, despite all the difficulties and obligations she enumerated, she was animated in feature and in movement, and she laughed—quite gaily for Edith. "If I could, if it weren't that kind of a male-dominated world, I'd be tempted to go through with it. I really think I would, for the sake of the sensation of well-being. I don't imagine it lasts."

"Go through with what?" God, his mouth was wet enough, he had to run the back of his hand over his lips.

"Have the child."

"You would?"

"Oh, yes. Can you imagine the shock I'd give the head of the English department? Can't you just see Professor Watt's face when I became unmistakably pregnant—walked into our faculty office, big with child!" She was jesting, something she almost never did, deliberately breaking out of her patina of solemnity with witticism of her own making. "In some societies one could. I'm sure I could have my own child if I so wished in modern-day Russia, without benefit of a marriage license. But alas, it's our own sanctimonious America, and I'll have to have an abortion, and an illegal one too, as if even a legal one were fun. And I'll have to find the money to pay for it. And that's going to be a great, great nuisance, to say the least. And I'll have to find an abortionist. I don't know any. And I'll have to turn to Lewlyn. It is *his* child."

Ira felt as if all his past worries, worries and anxieties—and memories of anguish—effectively dammed the flow of even simpleminded inference. "So if it is?"

"I think I know exactly the day. I thought it was one of my safe ones." Her little hands, locked negligently in her lap, tightened. "Oh, I understand. I don't have the money. Can you imagine what would happen if I didn't have an abortion—in the impossible event I didn't? Lewlyn would regard that as willful, deliberate entrapment, do you understand, Ira? As if I were compelling him to marry me. I wouldn't stoop to that, it goes without saying." Her brown eyes held steady in determination, and she added: "I no longer want him to marry me."

"No? I didn't think of it that way." How could he tell her in what way he thought of these things? What these things were to him that she dwelled on so freely, things that to him were snarled into such knots and tangles of wrongdoing he could never hope to loosen them. So she was pregnant. Pregnancy pointed toward abortion, abortion to abortionist, abortionist to his fee, to money. That was how it went. He frowned with downcast eyes at the stylized corn symbol on the gray Navajo blanket at his feet. That was how it went, how it ought to go, diagrammatic, honest. His mind felt so caught in its own coils—no, struggling with its own coils, trying to free itself, to see, see what? Objectively, no, more than that: see himself oppositely, from the woman's point of view—Edith's view—his mirror image in his own head. "Does Lewlyn know?" he groped.

"Not yet."

"No?"

"I wasn't certain myself until I wrote you."

"No." Again, Ira felt compelled to resort to the back of his hand against his moist lips. "I don't know how it goes. I just feel scared."

"You're very sweet," she said. Voice and feature combined in endearment. "I knew I could turn to you. No, it's not all that dangerous," she reassured. "There's always a chance of infection, of course. And bleeding. The nastiest thing is the illegality of the whole business. And that's not very comforting. But most people walk out of the doctor's office after a few hours' rest not too much the worse for the experience. I suppose because I've never had an abortion I'm less fearful about it than perhaps I should be. What worries me most at the moment is the financial aspect of it. As I say, Lewlyn will have to take financial responsibility for that, or part of it. I don't expect there will be any trouble on that score. Marcia and her friends can undoubtedly put him in touch with a competent abortionist." Seated on the gunny-sack-cloth-covered couch, with her back to the wall as always, she tugged absently at the ash-gray hem of her skirt, toward trim, silk-smooth calves. And as absent as her act, her mien: "Irony is, I no longer care."

"No? When we came back from the ship, last spring, I asked you, why did you have to do it? You explained. Love was that way. You wouldn't be denied the beauty of its ending. Something like that. You said you were—you weren't wise." Ira gesticulated. "So why did you begin again?"

"I can't resist another's need." She smiled placatingly.

"But everybody needs."

"I do too. I need to be reassured in my insecurity with men. I mentioned Louise Bogan to you, I remember. I have a feeling of inadequacy with the typical masculine male, the kind of thing she doesn't have. I have to shore up the feeling that haunts me of not being entirely—not being properly a woman."

The perplexity on Ira's countenance must have been graphic; her delicate lips formed into tender sympathy. "I don't suppose I make too much sense."

"Not yet, but that's probably me."

She laughed outright.

"No, I don't mean that," Ira hastened to amend. "I mean, I'll think about it. That's how I figure things out. I go over what somebody said. Over and over. And then there's a kind of message comes out of it."

"I know. You're remarkable. I'm going to tell you something," she said after a brief pause. "Something I've never told anyone else. It's something in the nature of a confession. It's the other side of what I just said about not being able to resist another's need. It needs to be said, so you won't think I'm all magnanimity, I'm all altruism. In other words, I have my wicked side."

"You? You have a wicked side, Edith?"

"Why did I begin again? It's my secret way of evening scores. With Marcia, with Cecilia. I guess Marcia would see it in her typically anthropological way. We're all apes, you know. It's a female's way of evening scores, and not a very nice one. I'm going to have to pay for it too."

"I just hope it comes out all right."

"Yes. But I'm much tougher than I seem."

"I hope so, Edith. I hope I can help, but I don't know how."

"You have already. A great deal. As long as you don't become impatient with me."

"No. Gee."

"You'll call me? Often. Do you have enough money?"

"Enough? A whole nickel?"

"I don't want you to go without. Ira, you're very dear to me." She slid forward, and pretty above the knees too, stood up.

Ira did too.

"I guess I'll go."

"I won't let you go unless you let me help you—for all the help you've given me."

He was all too familiar with the maneuver. "I haven't! I haven't given you any help," he protested—pro forma. "You're gonna need the money yourself."

"Not to that extent. I need you more. Please. I know how little allowance you get." She extracted a five-dollar greenback from her purse, tendered it.

"You keep tempting me, Edith, and I can't resist."

"Don't. You'll hurt my feelings."

She could look so winning at some moments, moments like these, the gleam on her olive skin, her brown eyes appealing, she'd get him started, when it was the furthest thing from his mind: maternal, that was it: she wanted to take care of him. Maybe because she was pregnant. He took the five dollars from her, guiltily, yet with a sense of sheepish inevitability. Rumors of the future could petrify you where you stood between the dark piano and the dark tapa on the door. "Thanks, Edith."

"How are courses going, Ira?"

"Huh? 'Orful,' as Mom would say. The only thing I get anything out of is Milton."

"Do you?"

"Yeah. What vowels: *Ophiucus huge.* Makes you drool."

"I may get to work on an anthology of modern poetry—after this is all over."

"Oh, yeah?"

"It's Professor Watt's idea, his and the publishers. They believe I ought to have a textbook for my course. You can see why." She inclined her head pertly. "I'll get very little out of it, either in money or glory. Do you think you'd care to help? I have a feeling I could use your help once it really begins to take shape."

"Me? How? I can spull good, that's all." He chortled.

"Indexing, acknowledgments, and other chores. How's your cold, by the way? You seem to have recovered."

"I did. I got over it a long time ago." He moved, self-conscious and awkward again, reached for the doorknob, fell silent a second peering at the dark tapa. "I wish your troubles didn't amount to more than my cold."

"I'd be glad if they didn't. Unfortunately it's not one of those things that goes away by itself." She extended her hand.

And for the first time in his life, he felt like kissing somebody's hand. She was so kind, so fond, so brave in the midst of trial, you had to bow before her. It didn't seem artificial, lifting her tiny hand to his lips. It seemed as if the act were already presaged, preformed in space. She raised her other hand toward her bosom. . . .

He glanced at the top of his yellow typescript, his notes, prepared years before. Nearly two decades ago he had attempted a first draft, on his Olivetti manual, with much prompting from dear friends, when his hands could still stand the impact of the keys. Now he knew he would never finish. Fortunately, the holy sages of his people relieved him of the obligation: "You are not required to finish," ran the Talmudic dictum (as if it could be otherwise). A posthumous novel that might never see publication, floppy disks that might never be printed into paper copies.

His thoughts returned to Edith. *And when I crumble who will remember the lady of the west country.* Who could remember now, so many years after, decades after, why he had paid a visit to Mamie's so late in the evening? Had he also been to Edith's? Had he just left Edith's, and on impulse on the way home gotten off at the 110th Street station on the Lenox Avenue line? Or had he just gone mad with craving for a piece of ass, vulgar as he thought of it, burning within? Need, desire, lust that had driven him out of the house and along the tract from 119th and Park Avenue to 112th west of Fifth. Skip to my loo, my darling. Memory held a kind of detritus, an intimation, that he was coming from somewhere, perhaps Edith's, keeping him informed of the latest developments of her pregnancy, or the steps being taken to abort it, the appointment made for her by Lewlyn with the abortionist, the place, the fee. Was it twenty-five dollars? Or was that some figure that merely stuck in his mind for some reason? Still, twenty-five bucks was no mean sum in those days, a week's pay (after all, Ira had earned about twenty-seven dollars for a fifty-six-hour work week in the subway repair barn). It would be ironic if his vestigial memory was correct: if he had actually come from a visit to Edith's to Mamie's—and hence called on Mamie so much later than usual. Ha, where the hell *had* he come from?

He had sought the answers to some of these questions with Marcia over twenty years ago at a luncheon in New York. "Once in the evening at Edith's . . ." Ira lunged heavily into the subject, hesitated for lack of preamble, and tacked into generalities. "I want to point this out first, the shock the uninitiated receives simply because he was unacquainted with the nuances, or hadn't yet learned the—" he gesticulated erratically—"the amenities of the culture into which he was being inducted."

"The manners?" Marcia sipped her martini.

"All right, the manners," he acquiesced. "You and Edith were engaged in a tête-à-tête, when I came calling—unannounced and inopportunely, as I realized as soon as she opened the door. Do you remember that?"

Marcia gazed at him steadily from the other side of the table. Basilisk, the fearful alertness of the blue eyes behind her eyeglasses. "I'm not sure."

"Then it doesn't matter. I wouldn't be able to restore the situation for you. It was way back in the twenties. So there's no point to the question I wanted to ask you."

"I remember being at Edith's one evening with you and Lewlyn and your friend Larry."

"No, Marcia, that must have been some other evening. Before this. I re-call one of Edith's soirées when you had just heard Heisenberg's lecture on his theory of indeterminacy. You gave us the benefit of what you had heard."

"I believed it implied the existence of free will in the universe. And gave indirect proof of Christian theology. It implied the Christian concept of a deity—"

"But that's not what I'm coming at," Ira wrenched himself loose. "The occasion I'm referring to was when you and Edith were alone. Or you had been until I arrived. And you just said something to Edith—as you were pulling on your gloves—about her having enjoyed Lewlyn while she could."

"I remember reminding her that he was irrevocably pledged to Cecilia."

"Was that it?" Ira prompted.

"Just to make sure she had no illusions her possible childbearing would alter the situation. I don't think she did. I believe she said, 'I'm going to miss him. He's such a wonderful lover.' And I said, 'France is full of wonderful lovers, Edith.' And she answered with a kind of pretend wistfulness: 'But I'm not in France.' Is that what you mean?"

"Ah, that's what I remember! Her saying to you with a smile: 'But I'm not in France.' It seemed so apt."

"Were you in the apartment at the time?"

"Inconspicuously. Behind a book or a magazine."

"Strange. I don't remember. I don't have any blocks in my memory ei-ther. Lewlyn does. But I don't."

"Lewlyn does?"

"Oh, yes. Many."

"I'm sorry to hear that. I hope to see him soon."

"I warn you, be careful. His memory has become very patchy. Do you have his address?"

"Yes, thanks. Anyway, there you both were speaking so casually, so lightly, as if over a trifling matter. Do you remember what you said to her on leaving?"

"Not exactly." Marcia paused long enough for the waitress to set down the bowl of steak tartar she had been ordered to bring for her, and the omelette for Ira. "I may have said I'm afraid this will have the opposite effect: of terminating the interim affair."

"Ah, then you did! That's my point about different cultural nuances, the shock they transmit to the uninitiated on recognition." Ira wagged his finger at her, conscious of the irony of seeming to enlighten the most celebrated social critic of their time. "Do you know what Edith did as soon as you said goodbye, and closed the door behind you? She burst into tears. I was never so surprised in my life. I felt as if I were profaning a rite—or being initiated into one. In my tradition, when feelings got wrought up to that pitch, imprecations were exchanged, insults hurled, sometimes blows. Here, antagonisms were so rarefied I never sensed them. Cultivated spoofing, I thought."

Marcia's countenance betrayed rue—not penitence—rue, that she might have caused undue distress to one who nevertheless merited reproof then, but was now dead. Marcia said nothing for a moment, but sank her fork into the rubicund mound of steak tartare before her. "I may have been a little forthright," she said. "That's quite possible. I'm not ashamed to admit I never did approve of Edith's dealings with men. They were anything but restrained. In fact, very nearly, well, very, promiscuous. I suppose my resentment showed. We used to say that sex with Edith was an extension of hospitality."

"You did?" Ira grinned at the neatness of Marcia's epigram. Trust Marcia; she could epitomize things more pithily than anyone else. "I was once crude enough to recite to her a list of her lovers. She burst into tears. Boorish of me."

"Why, she even seduced my younger brother," Marcia said in a tone bordering on vehemence.

"Oh, she did?" Ira congratulated himself that his guile had paid off.

"It didn't hurt him any. But I was furious at the time."

Ira addressed himself to his omelette. "I must say that he wasn't on my list."

III

It was a raw, sodden afternoon in November when Ira left the shelter of the Christopher Street subway kiosk—and left behind the more prudent passengers, lingering on the top steps, anxiously studying the lowering outlook for some sign of abatement of the rain. He set out as fast as he could toward Morton Street and Edith's apartment, driving himself through cold, slant flurries, and over street rill and puddle, yet he still arrived with shoes soggy and dripping, and topcoat drenched through to the jacket shoulder. Just as well he had decided to stow his briefcase in his locker for the day; would have been one more thing to lug through the rain. Tomorrow was Friday anyway, and he had only one class that day, Culture and Education. He would read the damned assignment sometime in the morning. Or try to. Enough to get by.

It was actually interesting stuff, if he gave it a chance, but he didn't. He let his brain turn to concrete when he opened a text in education. He didn't give a damn. How the hell was it that Larry could stand up in class and palaver with Professor Elkins minutes on end, as if the rest of the class didn't exist, or was an audience, about the effect on the Renaissance of Vittorino da Feltre's theories of education—with a bewitched Professor Elkins? Just the reverse of the way things had been in that elocution class long ago—everything seemed long ago.

In black-and-white herringbone skirt, and finely knit black sweater, a wanly smiling Edith admitted Ira into the apartment. But no sooner had she done so than she sat down with an air of constraint, hastily, in her usual place on the gunny-cloth-covered couch, her back to the wall. Perhaps it was the black sweater that made her look paler than usual, or it may have been after she told him about her condition that he thought so in a kind of instant retrospect. She was her considerate, solicitous self: "Heavens, Ira, you didn't tell me when you called you had no umbrella and no rubbers. You're soaking. You'd better take off as many layers of those wet clothes as you can. And your shoes and stockings."

"I wear socks." Dripping fedora in hand, he stood raptly before the fire in the steel basket of the fireplace. "Boy, you got a fire going, Edith. That's really nice." He removed his topcoat, approached the hearth. "Gee."

"You're sopping wet. Ira, please take off your shoes, dear. You'll catch your death."

"Yeah? I don't mind." He sat down on the wicker armchair—which snapped disconcertingly under his weight. "I mean, I don't mind taking off my shoes . . . my socks too. . . . What d'you call that kind of coal, those big chunks, do they have a name?"

"Cannel coal."

"Cannel coal?" He looked from fluttering flame to Edith, and back at flame appreciatively. "I wonder why?"

"I had the janitor bring them from the man across the street. It's such a dreary day. I've been so cold."

"Yeah? It's so cozy. Only thing is, it's expensive, I bet."

"Moderately. But on occasion—" Smiling, in obvious discomfort, she thrust her legs out stiffly over the edge of the couch. "I thought I'd splurge."

"Yes?" Shoes in one hand, socks in the other, Ira stood up. "Mind if I spread these on the radiator for a while? I bet they'll start steaming too."

"Please don't stand on ceremony—after all these years. You can take your trousers off and dry them if you want to."

"Oh, no! I just want to dry the socks. The shoes—" He flapped his hands in token of hopelessness. "They'll take all night."

"Yes? As long as that?" Again, there was no mistaking the stiffness with which her back slid up erect against the wall behind her—and the way her neck became rigid. "I had no business letting you come in all this weather. But I did desperately want to talk to you—" She laughed weakly. "As always."

"That's all right." Ira sat down, tried rubbing toes together. "In front of this fire, after wading through all that rain, it's like a re-ward—" He turned to look at Edith again, and stopped: something about her appearance he wasn't taking into account, something amiss. He could feel his brow furrow as his gaze became intent. "You all right, Edith?"

"Not at the moment, I'm afraid." She grimaced uncharacteristi-cally, more in annoyance with herself than in pain. Still, the way she shifted her body on the couch bespoke extreme discomfort.

"What's the matter?"

"I've had the abortion."

"When?"

"This morning. At about half past ten."

"Pete's sake, you let me talk about socks and shoes, and you've had an abortion? Doesn't it hurt?"

"Oh, yes. I've canceled classes. Tomorrow too probably. I called up the secretary of the English department—"

"What does the doctor give you? Does he know?"

"She."

"All right, she. Does she know?"

"I'm to see her tomorrow morning again. It's bearable. I'm sorry I'm so—conspicuously uncomfortable." She grimaced again. "The doctor scrapes the inside of the uterus, scrapes the embryo off. It's like an induced miscarriage—"

"I know. You told me."

"Of course, there's some internal hemorrhaging—"

"And as much pain as that?"

"That's what worries me."

"No wonder you keep moving around."

"I just hope there are no complications. Infections and that sort of thing."

"No." Ira was silent, his own helplessness manifest. "Can I do something? Can I get you something to eat?"

"Oh, no. Thanks. I'll have a cup of canned soup later. I'm not altogether helpless; I just feel awful." She smiled bravely. "I'm sorry. I must look like something the cat dragged in."

"Oh, no. What's the difference?" Ira felt oppressed by the sheer gravity of the event, oppressed, compelled to undivided focus. "Infections. That's something to worry about."

"Oh, I'll be all right, I'm sure. There may be a few more complications than usual."

"I hope you're wrong. Anybody with you? Anybody coming? I mean Lewlyn."

"No."

"No?"

His fists struck both thighs. Thoughts slipped one past the other in his mind, rendering all opaque. Jesus, he could pass judgment—or he could feel disapproval—freely about Lewlyn. Real indignant. The night the Yankees won the series, he and Stella, Murderers' Row, all right.

"You're an angel to bear with me this way," said Edith.

"Oh, no! Gee whiz."

"You are. You're the only one I care to see." Her small hands in her lap, slack torso against the wall, brown eyes very large in the sallowness of pallid olive skin. "I've finished with all my lovers, I'm glad to say."

All? Ira made no attempt to reply. The word *all* bulked in his mind, too unwieldy to budge.

"To make matters worse, Larry was here yesterday. That was quite a session."

"Yesterday? He didn't say anything to me."

"Hardly surprising." Nuances never found him prepared: *Hardly surprising.* "He came to resolve certain doubts he had about his mistress. About me— Are you in a draft?"

He had sneezed. The current of air flowing close to the floor had cooled his bare feet. He eased his sopping pants cuffs away from his shins.

"I'm all right."

"Here, put this cushion over them."

"No, it's okay."

"Please, lad, I don't want you catching another cold. I have a blanket somewhere—"

"That'll be fine. That's enough." He got up with forestalling haste and took the cushion she proffered, went back to the wicker armchair, and snuggled his toes under the velvety cover.

"That's plenty."

"You sure? I can't tell you how guilty I felt about your last cold."

"Nah."

"Larry felt that our relationship was no longer the same as it had been, that I no longer loved him, that he was no longer as dear to me as he had been. I no longer gave him the kind of encouragement I once had. He sensed my indifference. He sensed all kinds of changes had taken place between us—all of which was true. And then he asked me point-blank: was I having an affair with Lewlyn?" Edith straightened her back again. "I said I was—"

"Yeah, but—" Ira interrupted impulsively, mechanically. "You said it was over."

"I said I was—deliberately. I might have added 'had been,' but I didn't."

"No?" How complex the form of those delicate lips in the face across the room now seemed.

"On the eve of an abortion, I no longer felt like coddling him. Perhaps I was a little hardhearted. But he seemed to have recovered very well from that one incident involving his heart, and it was time he knew the truth. He didn't own me; he couldn't possibly own me. I didn't tell him he'd become too commonplace for words. I did tell him I was pregnant—there was no possibility in the world the child was his. Not the least. And for very obvious reasons. For very obvious reasons."

Ira's attention sheered away. There it was again: the cramped synopsis of cat on the wall, and the shriek, and the bunny-hugging—

"Cruel of me to tell him, because he would certainly know as much. I told him I was sure the child was Lewlyn's. Oh, we had quite a session. I didn't tell him how much I would rather have the child than go through an abortion. I didn't want to hurt him any more than I could help. Good heavens, if only there were a man who saw fit to marry me and give the child color of legitimacy—" Her pallor increased, her large brown eyes became protuberant and her countenance resentful.

"I wonder what I would have done if I were a man who loved, or thought I loved, a woman who was pregnant by another man—would I feel enough protectiveness to overcome my jealousy or vanity? I wonder. I think I would. I did as much for a friend once with much less at stake. But I really shouldn't complain. I was fortunate."

"Fortunate!" Ira could hear his own Yiddish intonation.

"Larry ranted at me: I was promiscuous, I was loose. I was unfaithful. All sorts of rubbish. Fie on thee, I thought: I told him I was due to have an abortion tomorrow."

"Tomorrow?" Ira felt the momentary throb of headache, as if he had gulped down too much ice cream. "You mean today?"

"Yes, of course. Just what I expected happened. He was through with me. I didn't deserve *his* love." She found solace in a deep breath. "Thank heavens he won't be too hurt. He won't hurt himself. At least, I'm sure of that: the one thing I was so afraid of. What a relief that is!"

Her pallor had increased, ashy; her solemn brown eyes bulged; her shoulders drooped. He wasn't following her.

"Maybe you shouldn't talk anymore," Ira pleaded. "Listen, I'll stay around till you go to bed. Whatever you want."

"No, I'd rather forget the pain. Please. If you don't mind."

"Yeah, but maybe it's no good for you."

"Oh, no. It is. Wait till you hear why: he slammed the door when he left. Larry actually slammed the door. I knew then he had protected his ego. He was safe."

"Oh."

Ira turned his chilly feet toward the fire for a second or two. Tongues of flame rising from the blocks of coal inaudibly mulled the thought in warmth and color: so that was how she knew: the guy slammed the door. The guy was sore, so he slammed the door. He slammed the door, so he was safe. The gray rain pattered hard against the window when Ira faced Edith again.

"So he's through with you?"

"Oh, yes, he's through." She spoke with such animated disdain it approached derision. "His undefiled love for me is at an end—poof! But what I've been through—what I'm going through this minute—is nothing."

"You hurt?"

"I hurt like fury."

"I'm so sorry, Edith."

She laughed—and wept. Ira sat quietly, wondering what to do next. Pity, he heard a block of coal shift in the basket grate behind him: pity. The fire somehow felt good at his back. Pity was consumed into comfort, oxidized into warmth. *Why, let the stricken deer go weep; the hart ungalled play.* Yeah, he had willed it all. But what could he do? . . . Just sit there, socks drying, woman weeping, *Bulluc sterteth, bucke verteth, murie sing cuccu.* In a little while, the rain would let up a little maybe, but it wouldn't matter if it didn't. He couldn't console her, he couldn't help her. What it must feel like with your insides scraped— about where would the uterus be in him? Belly-button height, or lower? Imagine it rubbed against a grater, Mom's *riebahsel.* Well, he'd get his socks, and see what she said: whether she wanted him there any longer, or wanted to be alone with her suffering.

He got up from the creaking chair and went to the radiator. Her gaze followed him; drearily, she wiped the copious tears on her cheeks with dainty handkerchief. "I bet you hate the sight of everybody who wears pants," Ira ventured.

"Not quite everybody." She held the damp ball of handkerchief in her lap. "Are you going out in this?"

"I think I better."

"I don't blame you."

"No, it isn't that," he protested the implication of his deserting her. "If you want me to stay—or do something."

"You've borne with me quite long enough."

"Nah."

"I'm a little ashamed of myself, as usual. I ought to be able to stand this, without having to weep on your shoulder."

"It's all right. Boy, these socks are nice and toasty already."

"At least one good thing has come out of the whole sorry mess: a harmless end to a long-drawn-out, silly affair. I don't think you're likely to see Larry here again very soon."

"No," Ira agreed. "I guess not." Curious, how the past coalesced into a kind of opaque introspection that marked the end. "Could I get you a drink, Edith? Would you like something? I think my socks are pretty dry by now. I could go out to a restaurant."

"No. Thanks. I'd like some tea. Would you?"

"Yes, sure. How do you make it? I saw you use a teapot. You just put the tea in it? I mean, at home, Mom makes a kind of essence. It's separate, and you add hot water." Was his garrulity welcome to her, he wondered: she sat so passively enduring pain. "We have tea when we have meat for supper. If you have coffee, you can't have milk in it."

"Really?"

"Yeah, I only learned here you can drink coffee black. So what do I do?"

"There's a teaball in the drawer of the kitchenette. I think I ought to stay quiet."

"Oh, yeah, I'll find it. I'm the champeen finder of teaballs. Which drawer?"

"Usually, it's in the one on the left—unless Dorotheena changed it when she cleaned."

"Then it would have to be on the right. Hmm!" Why did he feel compelled to clown? "My inferences—" he wagged his hand—"nobody can match them. Except when I have to find something. I'll need hot water, right?"

"Yes." Was that a wan smile she tried to retain through a troubled shifting of her body? "About half-fill the copper kettle. And no more tea than half in the teaball. I use much less. I like it weak. I'm afraid you'll have to rummage in the shelf above the sink for the package of tea. Can you find it? I keep it up there with the coffee and the Grape-Nuts."

"Oh, yeh, yeh." He held the copper kettle under the gushing brass faucet in the closet kitchenette. And after he had lit the flame on the two-burner gas stove and set the kettle on it, he hunted for the other articles. He found them also. Finding them was no great trick, since utensils were few, and the place was so small. "You going to want some toast? I see there's slices of package bread here."

"No, thanks, dear, I'd better not. I'll consider myself lucky if the tea stays down."

"Is that so? It hurts that much?" He couldn't help noticing the gray cast over her olive skin. "I'll sit down where I can keep my eye on the kettle."

"Make some toast for yourself, if you like. There's marmalade."

"No, I'll spoil my supper. I've got to have an appetite like a wolf, or I don't eat. And then Mom moans and groans— Wait a minute: you want me to stay? I mean it: I can stay as long as you like."

"No, thanks. It's sweet of you, Ira, but I'll be all right. I've just got to get through the next twenty-four hours. I have some kind of painkiller the doctor gave me if I needed it."

"Well, don't you need it?"

"I hate to take it. It has morphine in it, I'm sure."

"Oh, yeh?" Ira glanced at the kettle.

"It's terribly constipating."

"Well, maybe you'll get dreams, like De Quincey. I read that Coleridge was interrupted in the middle of 'Kublai Khan'—" He chortled at his absurd non sequitur. "I mean somebody interrupted him." She regarded him with patient indulgence. "Another minute. Maybe I put too much water in the kettle. But I got the teaball in the teapot al-

ready. Then I pour about half full of boiling water in the teapot. Is that
the idea?"

"Yes."

"Another minute. My mother never lets me do anything around
the kitchen."

"I'm sure this puts an end to any notion I may have had of having
children," Edith said apathetically, as if at a distance, or talking to herself. "It may not be the worst thing: they take up one's whole life, unless one is rich and can afford a maid to take care of them. And how
often they turn out like some relative one has no use for. Or worse,
perhaps, in this case: like the father. But they *are* adorable as babies."

Slowly, the extent, the numbness of her dolor communicated itself
to him, vacated his masquerade of concentrating on the kettle. He
glimpsed for an instant something outside his ken, the frustration of a
womanly urge, a woman's reality, a woman's woe. And there was nothing to offer in the face of that, only the silence of pity, and nothing
commensurable with it either, only the troubled forcing of fingernails
against the flesh of fingers—even as he listened. So that was an abortion, a bereavement of her body.

"I no longer expect magnanimity from any man," she went on in the
same hopeless, contemplative tone. "The child might have been Larry's.
There was that chance. But you see what *his* reaction was. And Lewlyn's—his was the most truly craven behavior in the whole ugly mess."

"Yes?" She activated all kinds of memories of his own vile behavior,
behavior of a trapped rat. Murder-prone. Yes, but Jesus Christ—swiftly
justification welled up—how did Lewlyn's fix compare to having once
possibly knocked up his own sister? Ira listened with averted eyes,
glowering with inner contention: and where would he have gotten the
dough for an abortion? Whom could he have asked to help him out?
Leo maybe? To whom could he have dared confess he'd knocked up
his sister?

"Lewlyn reminded me it could have been Larry's—about which I
told him there was almost no chance. Or as he said, that other Pales-
tinian—he meant Zvi Benari, the Zionist agronomist friend of Shmuel
Hamberg's, the man I knew at Berkeley. I told him I hadn't seen Zvi in
months." She shook her head. "Lewlyn was sure it wasn't his. In spite
of my own instincts, my own certainty, he refused to believe it was his.

Isn't that revealing? You have no idea of the panic he went into about accepting mere responsibility, as if I would take advantage of him—which I would never dream of doing."

"No."

It was all so grim. While she softly carried on, he thought that he was himself blood brother to Larry in his evasion of responsibility, and to Lewlyn also—though in different, wildly different circumstances. He might have done the same thing—although once again he justified his panicky evasion by rejecting the analogy: how did this compare to the anguish, the murderous anguish, the high school kid had felt that fall afternoon, an afternoon that twisted him past his tolerance to endure any more.

Ira studied the raindrops under the top of the window, each waiting for reserves to swell it out before sliding down the pane. Her acrimony was different from Minnie's, wasn't it, but it was still acrimony. There was no forgiveness if they thought you knocked them up—you were the father, they said—whether you thought you were or not, or whether you knocked them up or no. You were to take care of them, defenseless with child.

Everything he learned, he learned here. A block of coal in the fireplace split, and he turned just in time to see the two interfaces separate, and each half foliate, like thick decks of some kind of black cards. Black cards, blackguards. Life was always in flux, but it always seemed to go to a predetermined end. Why did he think that?

As though she were answering his unspoken question, "You'd believe I was having the abortion solely for his sake," Edith said. "I was to have the abortion to keep *his* skirts clean. I shan't have anything more to do with Lewlyn. You can be sure of that."

To keep *his* skirts clean. She had used that expression before, and he never could visualize it. Men didn't wear skirts, unless she was thinking of Lewlyn, the former priest with black surplice buttoned down to his shoes—and you'd have to be sure the first button matched the first buttonhole—but hell, don't get yourself sidetracked, don't bounce back into woozy orbit again.

There it was: I shan't have anything more to do with Lewlyn. And just before that she had said: You won't see much of Larry around here. Not Larry and not Lewlyn. And he himself, he, the least and the last, here he was, trying to comfort her after an abortion for which the other two might have been responsible. Just as if he had made it up out of whole cloth, as they said, as if he had made the future jump through the hoop of his fantasy. He almost had, hadn't he?

When the hell was that kettle going to boil? Should he raise the flame? There—there went the kettle: Boiling. Steaming. About time.

"I wonder if discolored teakettles take longer to boil." Ira stood up. "Now the hot water goes into the teapot, right?"

"Yes. But be careful of the handle."

"It's not too hot."

"And let the ball steep—oh, a minute will be enough. You can leave it in longer after you've poured mine."

Leave it in a minute longer after he had poured hers. *"And in a minute there is time,"* he said, effacing involuntary smut with a quote as he pressed the teapot cover in place. Too bad to be bent out of whack forever. "You take sugar?"

"No, thanks."

"No? I was in a cafeteria once, and the counterman asked the customer sitting beside me if he wanted tea. The guy said tea with a slice of lemon. And the counterman said no, we don't have any lemon. So the man just shrugged, as if what's the use? It's strange how some things remain in your mind forever."

"You're priceless."

"I don't know about that."

"Oh, you've found the paper napkins too?"

"Oh, yeah."

"I've agreed to do the anthology. I have that to do. And I have a couple of narrative poems in mind—narrative poems have a much better chance of being published than lyrics."

"They do?"

"And I'd love to do them—especially I seem to want to do one about Lewlyn. I have just the right title for it too, I think: 'The Reassembled Man.'"

"Reassembled?" Ira repeated. "You mean he came apart?"

"He *had* come apart," she stressed. "He showed it during my pregnancy. You never saw a man so unhappy. It was as if my pregnancy were the last straw to the breakdown Marcia's rejection of him had begun."

"So why is he—I mean, who's going to reassemble him?"

"It's the English spinster who's going to do that: fit him out with new ideals, with a sense of self-worth. Make a new person of him. He hurried frantically to make all the arrangements—with Marcia's help, you can be sure, to get my pregnancy out of the way. He acted as if his salvation depended on it. And Marcia was only too happy to direct things for him."

"Yeah?"

"She wanted him punished just enough for his mistake in taking me for a mistress, and then to rescue him. And he was only too happy to have her rescue him, as if he were a baby— I think it's steeped long enough for me. He is a baby."

"Yeh? Okay, I'll pour it."

"I had no idea how puerile he was. I know now."

"Yeh? Like that?" Ira brought her tea over. "It looks *shvakh*, so weak."

"Oh, no, that's fine, thanks. You're an angel. I wish I owned a pair of house slippers big enough for you. Would save your traipsing around in your bare feet."

"That's all right. Athlete's foot fungus isn't fussy. You don't want sugar?"

"No, thanks. Just leave the spoon on the saucer." She reached out tiny hands.

"So how can you drink tea without sugar?"

"The taste really comes through better."

"And that's what you want? That's the opposite of the guy who wanted the slice of lemon."

"He wasn't very sophisticated."

"Oh."

"If I can manage to get invitations to Yaddo or Peterboro these next two years, I think I could get both jobs done."

"Which jobs done?"

"The anthology and the narrative poems."

"Oh." He poured his own tea, added sugar. "That's pretty hot, you know. You want me to come over and hold your cup so you can sit up more?"

"Oh, no. I can manage, thanks. I just hate to move at the moment.

Do you think you'll be able to spare Saturdays or weekends to help me with the anthology—once this nonsensical crisis is past? There's been some money allocated for clerical assistance."

"Me? I'd be glad to help. But I told you all I was any good at was proofreading. That's in part because I'm fairly good at spelling."

"That's very important, too. Proofreading this kind of work is very important. But there are a hundred other things you can do, tiresome chores, if you wish, that I resent very much, but devilishly necessary in preparing an anthology—as I said before: writing poets or publishers for permissions, making sure of acknowledgments, checking bibliographies—oh, hundreds of things. Even helping me edit my own writing. I tend to be too hasty these days." She smiled at last. "And discussing ideas with me."

"Yeah? Ideas? You worry me."

"Oh, no. Please, Ira. You have as good a mind as anyone." She sipped cautiously from her teaspoon. "The tea is just right, thanks. I conceive of the book, for whatever worth it will have, as reflecting the realities of city life, and the moods they generate in the poet. And what I badly need, or mainly need, is someone like yourself born and brought up in the city—"

"I was born in Galitzia," Ira groused in demurral. "And I'm not a poet. I'm scared, Edith. Honest."

"Oh, fiddlesticks. You spent your entire life in the city," Edith persisted. "You've already shown your grasp of the city mind in that piece of yours that appeared in your college magazine. You're the ideal person to provide an antidote to the saccharine romanticism of people like myself brought up in the West. I suppose I'm a little better now than I was," she qualified.

"How do you mean?"

"Oh, now, Ira. The city means so much more to you than it does to me. More in nuance, more in evocation, in metaphor. Do you understand? Especially because you're still a student, don't you see? An intelligent and sensitive student."

The first tinge of liveliness heightened her olive skin, gray and lusterless until this moment. "You're not a student in some out-of-the-way, self-contained campus, with its dormitories and fraternities and sororities and small-town stores and meeting places. You're a student in the city, and that's exactly the kind of student I have in my classes at NYU. Jewish mostly. So you can see how useful you could be—because those are the ones the anthology would be addressing: those living within city blocks, not in the country, not under open sky—"

"Yeah, but you got to have taste, you got to have—" He began rotating his shoulder against a sudden itch. "I mean—what do I mean?—discrimination in poetry, modern poetry. The kind of thing you have when you review somebody's book of poems for the *Times* or *The Nation.* You've got that kind of certainty."

"Oh, I'll choose the poems, if that's what's worrying you. Between the textbook publishers and Dr. Watt, they're going to want to get out the anthology on a shoestring. It's only a scheme to put money into their pockets anyway. The anthology, so called, will be required reading in my modern poetry courses."

"I'll be glad to help with the—with the, with the mechanics—"

"No, I'd like your opinion about the poems too—"

"Listen, Edith, I don't have opinions. I like or I don't like. I'm still just the same as a kid. Sure, I can tell you I like Tennyson's 'Tithonus' way ahead of his 'Ulysses,' but that's a hundred years ago, and who cares? I like some of Vachel Lindsey, I like Conrad Aiken's *Senlin,* I like some of Robert Frost. But what's the difference? Everybody knows they're good poems. I learned those from Larry's Untermeyer anthology. But what I'm trying to say is I would never have known Eliot was a great poet except for you, reading him right here: 'Prufrock,' *The Waste Land*—"

"That's more than Larry ever learned."

"Yeah, but Larry's got ideas. He can tell you why he's got his opinion of a poem. I couldn't. You got to have ideas why it's good, why it's bad." Ira raised his voice. "I don't. Gee whiz."

"Well, you do have ideas, of course you do! Far better than his ever were!"

"I don't!"

"Oh, rubbish, Ira. Will you stop that!"

"*Parakutskie,* that's the way I should be drinking," he grumbled.

"What, dear? I'm sorry."

"Well, if I had a lump of sugar, the way they used to break them off a loaf that came wrapped in blue paper on Passover, on the East Side,

I could pour the tea in a saucer and suck it through the sugar. That's *parakutskie.* Maybe I wouldn't get a chance to holler so much—at a sick woman."

"I'm not really sick."

"No?"

"No, I intend to go on living."

"That's good. I'm really happy. Honest, Edith, I am."

"I'm much happier too. Will you take my umbrella with you when you go home?"

"Oh, no, my socks must be bone-dry by now. I'll duck in between the raindrops. I don't want an umbrella, Edith, I'll lose it."

"Then you'll have to take five dollars. I want you to call me Saturday. And have dinner with me."

"It costs only a nickel to call, and you've had a great expense already."

"But your call is easily worth five dollars."

"Oh, yeh? Your five dollars, and my Aunt Mamie's dollar, I'm gonna get rich."

"Silly."

"More tea? There's more."

"No, thanks. I'd appreciate it if you took my cup."

"Oh, yeh, sure."

"Thanks. It distresses me, Ira, to hear you run yourself down so."

"Well, I'm just comparing myself with others."

"And I am too, child."

IV

Hollow . . .

Why he wanted to start the section with that particular word he wasn't quite sure, nor whether it was appropriate. Probably only roughly appropriate. Jess had flown in Thursday evening from a geophysics conference he had attended in Dallas—and stayed until Sunday morning at the Monterey.

Jess had been with his parents from Thursday night until Sunday morning (actually, Saturday night, for he had arranged to take the shuttle bus from the motel to the airport so early Sunday morning they didn't see him off). They had had the pleasure of his company Thursday night, and two whole days. And a pleasure it had been indeed. Their son with them, rangy, charming, distinguished in mind and in person, and graying, graying, alas— their little boy was now forty-five—no matter what had happened before, no matter Jess's now ingrained silences. Perhaps Ira's son no longer knew how to communicate over the entire spectrum of his rich personality—a cause for sorrow rather than animus: who knew how badly hurt he had been by that first ill-fated marriage of his? Anyway, Ira felt himself doting on his son again, as he had when the grown man had been a child.

Ira had never been allowed to be a child, nor had Ira the father allowed his son. Too late in life Ira had tried to redress the situation, do incompetent penance for blame. He and M had gone shopping one day, and he had bought his eldest son, Jess, a gift, remarking when he presented it how damned few times he had bought his children presents (with which M concurred later, when Ira repeated the remark): a combination digital clock and auto compass, marked down from three dollars to two. (And Ira had received a gift in return, bought at the Albuquerque Museum, which Jess and M visited: a book entitled *Pioneer Jews*, by Harriet and Fred Rochlin, about the role and career of Jews in the West and Southwest, full of archival photos and interesting accounts of all sorts of prosaic, mercenary, and picturesque Jewish characters, including even a major general, but mainly of resourceful merchant Jews from Germany who emigrated to America in the latter half of the nineteenth century, amassed fortunes there, and often attained high political office, including, in several cases, governorships of the states or territories they had settled in.)

"Maybe you shouldn't have turned off your word processor," said M on the same occasion, when the two came back into the kitchen after closing the water valve under the mobile home. "But then you may not be able to work anyway."

She was right, to a certain extent: right, write, rite. Damn. Griefs of the mobile home owner. It hadn't occurred to him when Jess was still here, fixing a leak in the little valve in the copper tubing leading to the evaporative cooler—it hadn't occurred to him that the small pilot light in the heat tape, which was wrapped around the water pipe that supplied kitchen and bathroom, might be on, while the tape itself was burned out. Such had apparently been the case. For when he went outdoors first thing in the morning after breakfast to check on whether the job was effective—after a cold night, with the temperature dropping to the low twenties—although he had let a small trickle of water run from the kitchen faucet as additional safeguard and kept a 100-watt lamp burning under the "trailer," he noticed damp semicircles on the cement at places where the skirting at the bottom of the mobile home touched the patio. Evil omen. He hadn't noticed those damp half-moons yesterday, and the night before last had been just as cold. Well, maybe it was just precipitation, cold air coming in contact with the relatively warmer skirting. Ah, man and his fond hopes. So he and M had gone out and raised one of the "hatches" in the skirting in order to ascertain the cause, the origin of the damp places on the cement, in order to verify their hopes that condensation indeed was responsible, and not a break or crack in the water lines.

"No, it doesn't look very hopeful," M had said, when Ira pointed to the cement at the edge of their neighbor's skirting —which seemed bone-dry. If the cause of the wetness had been condensation of cold air on the skirting, why wasn't her patio strung with half-round splotches? Everything pointed in the right direction: the heat tape was shot, burned out, done for. And so it was. And last night, having assured himself everything was in order, 100-watt lamp on, the holes of the nearby ventilation strip in the skirting duly masked with a sheet of plastic, and a slender stream of water flowing in kitchen sink and bathroom lavatory, he had slept as he hadn't slept in many a night, the sleep of the just, and he awoke almost pain-free. Fool's paradise. Well. He had poked his arm into the open hatch, and crooked the elbow so that he could run his fingers along the near edge of the floor, and encountered a kind of shallow channel there, for what reason it was there he didn't know, but moist it was, more than damp: wet. *Hélas!*

V

Hurl'd headlong flaming from th' ethereial sky
With hideous ruin and combustion down
To bottomless perdition, there to dwell
In adamantine chains and penal fire,
Who durst defy th' Omnipotent to Arms.

"Well, where is he?" Mom's voice came to Ira as if across the centuries, from the present to the time Milton wrote *Paradise Lost.* He had finished reading the lesser poems, finished *Comus* and *Lycidas,* and begun reviewing the first six books of *Paradise Lost* for the midterms.

"Who? Pop?" Ira looked up from the page.

"Pop, shkrop, the sire, the shmire," Mom found satisfaction in the pejorative echo. "You can't trust him at all." She opened the kitchen window—on the immediacy of bare wash lines in the cold, darkening backyard. Pushing aside the butter dish and half-full quart bottle of milk in the window box, she brought in the freshly prepared jar of horseradish. Its tarnished metal cap was tightly screwed down over a scrap of brown paper that covered the mouth of the jar. Next she took out of the window box an enameled pot—gefilte fish balls, Ira conjectured—that she had set out in the cold to congeal the sauce into aspic. And finally, she brought into view a glass bowl of fruit compote, prunes and raisins and dried apples. Ingredients of the *Shabbes* supper, of Friday-night fare, they were as familiar as the pair of solid brass candlesticks on the cloth-covered table.

"It grows wintry," Mom remarked as the cold draft from outdoors invaded the close air of the kitchen.

"Yeah, well, it's November, Mom," Ira agreed. He could almost see the cold air coil itself within the humid, prevailing odor of chicken soup issuing from the large kettle on the gas stove.

"It's shivery out. Perhaps I shouldn't have brought the food in yet. Who knows when he'll come?" She set the compote and horseradish on the sink sideboard, shut the window.

"It's still early, isn't it? Not even five." Ira held aloft his notebook

and *Collected Poems of John Milton* while Mom spread the white tablecloth beneath his elbows. He let his eyes wander over the lines he
had just read: *Him the Almighty Power/Hurl'd headlong flaming from th'*
ethereial sky . . . What lingo! It made you hold your breath. "Minnie
isn't even here yet," he said absently.

"Minnie eats at Mamie's on Monday, Wednesday, and Friday.
Three times a week. Have you forgotten?" Mom set the brass candlesticks on the tablecloth. "She goes to your college at night."

"Oh, yeah." Minnie had enrolled in a business course and a
speech course given in the evening at CCNY. And to save shuttling
from west to east from her job, and rushing through supper at home,
and then back again from east to west to CCNY, she had arranged with
Mamie to have supper there the nights she attended classes. Thus she
could stay within easy reach of the West Side subway.

"It's growing dark," Mom said. "It's time for me to *bensht lekht.*" She
planted the pale candles in the candlesticks.

"Go ahead."

Mom was a wavering demi-agnostic: whenever she referred to
God, she invariably added (unless in the presence of Zaida) ". . . if
there is a God." Still she blessed the Sabbath candles, *bensht lekht,* just
as she had been taught to do from girlhood. The practice was too
deeply ingrained to abandon, but there again, she would often finish
the Hebrew prayer by saying: "Why I do this, I don't know." Without
religious faith himself, a self-proclaimed atheist, an *Epikouros,* as Pop
with his manifold superstitions dubbed his son, Ira nevertheless enjoyed the ritual. He found it touching; the balm of candlelight, the
rich, mellow candlesticks, the hush of ceremony awoke in him a remnant of reverence still lingering from childhood. He welcomed the occasion. Maybe it was because it was Mom who officiated at it, and not
Pop, that Ira remained solemn and pensive throughout the short invocation, neither condescending nor snide in witticism, as he invariably was when Pop presided over Jewish festivals, especially those that
were celebrated a second night: the Rosh Hashanah and the Passover.
Above all, he found the second recital of the Passover insufferably te-
dious. To have to sit through a second time the circumstances of the
Exodus from Egypt, a second time consecutively, Pop droning unintel-
ligibly and interminably as he conducted a fuming Ira twice in succes-

sion out of Egypt. "This is the bored of affliction" was Ira's favorite quip, when the *matzah* was displayed, which fortunately only Minnie understood at first, although after a while Pop took umbrage at his son's irreverence. Pop became particularly irritated when Ira insisted on repeating the same remark whenever his father's recitation of the *Haggadah* reached the page which contained the engraving of Moses smiting the recumbent Egyptian: "Boy, think of all the suffering we Jews would have been saved if it was the other way. If the slave driver smote Moses, and we had settled in Egypt like all the rest of Pharaoh's subjects. But no, we have to be different."

Short-throated, her heavy body plodding on swollen, edemic ankles, her bobbed hair thick and graying about her wide, fleshy face, Mom was wearing a freshly laundered, fire-engine-red housedress with white shrimplike curlicues on it and a red bow at the back; she was wearing the freshly laundered housedress *l'kuvet Shabbes*. She took the box of household matches from the top of the green icebox, brought it over to the table, and extracting a match, struck a light against the sandpaper strip on the side. Broad brow knit, her sorrowful eyes intent, she lit the candles one after the other. Then she blew out the flame on the end of the match and placed it in the ashtray near Ira's pipe. Covering her face with her puffy, workaday hands, she recited the traditional prayer under her breath and in scarcely articulate Hebrew, so that all Ira could make out were the long-imbued sounds of the incantation that began all Hebrew benedictions: *"Barukh atah adonoi elohenu melekh ha oylum . . ."* And the terminal words, when she removed her hands from before her face: *"Uhmein seluh."*

> *Nine times the space that measures day and night*
> *To mortal men, he with his horrid crew,*
> *Lay vanquished, rolling in the fiery gulf,*
> *Confounded, though immortal—*

"He could be here an hour ago if he wanted to." Mom's words knit into Milton's printed ones. "How long does it take to clean up after a breakfast-lunch job? To fill the salt and pepper cellars, the ketchup and the mustard bottles, the sugar bowls. He tells me he spends the time in between that and coming home inspecting business prospects. But I know better."

"Yes?" Impatiently Ira skimmed the text for his cue word, found it: *immortal. But his doom/Reserv'd him to more wrath; for now the thought/Both of lost happiness and lasting pain/Torments him—*

"He slips into a movim pickchehr."

"Yeh?" Ira looked up again.

"Me he never takes along. I'm a stock, a block—"

"Mom!"

"Ah, that's right, you're studying."

"Well, what else? I've got a test, a midterm test it's called, and it's being given on Monday."

"Ah, ah. Forgive me. I chatter."

"I don't mind. I'm used to it. But not when you're talking about Pop. You understand?"

"I understend. But my heart overflows."

"Yeah, I know. But you upset me."

"Well, let's talk about something else. Or do you wish to study?"

"I don't know. It all depends," Ira relented. "Just don't talk about Pop."

"When Minnie is home, we have a hundred things to talk about, don't you know, about women's wear, about rags and relatives, what he said and what she said, about cooking and window curtains. But with you, Ira, I have to unburden myself."

"Well, please don't. Or I'll begin studying again. Maybe I better anyway. I've got about a hundred and fifty pages to review—'review' means reading over again what I've already read before." He translated the English word into Yiddish, and was caught off-guard by a yawn. "Go ahead."

"*Noo,* let's talk of other things," Mom said resignedly. She turned off the burner under the frying pan in which she had been frittering croutons in chicken fat. Next to the soup pot was a discolored old bean crock, and after removing the last of the croutons, she drained the chicken *shmaltz* into the crock. He ought not to be watching her, Ira told himself; he had more important things to do. Nor should he be talking to her either. He had learned long ago that the euphoria of

Friday afternoon wasn't as far from the grind of Monday morning as the extravagant mirage of the weekend made it seem. And the midterm on Milton was only the first of the exams coming up. One in Modern European History. At least two more in the ed courses. Blah. Interim quizzes already indicated that at the rate he was going, by the end of the spring term, he'd still be lagging behind a credit or more toward his B.S. degree at graduation.

No, he ought not to be watching her or talking to her, but he felt like taking a break. Strange, though they were whole worlds apart in schooling, in attainment, and—what was the right word?—in milieu, mental milieu as well as environmental, and there was much, much he could no longer share with her, and much he would never dream of sharing with her, abominations that would have grieved and horrified her, still she was Mom. Her brooding temperament meshed with his as it always had, and did even now, despite his advantages, his college education, his cultivated friends.

She still understood him, intuitively, imaginatively, understood him in the realm of feeling. Unknowingly, she had indoctrinated him into tragedy, given him a penchant for it, the tragic outlook. He recognized that fact, now that he had grasped the rudiments of how to form abstractions, to generalize. She was the source of his tragic bent, and that was their bond.

"Let's talk of how people work their way up in the world." Mom took the frying pan to the sink and began wiping the inside with a sheet of Yiddish newspaper. "Agreed?"

"All right," Ira conceded warily.

"There's my sister Mamie. She has a new radio. They already had a phonograph. She has a telephone, hot running water, a large apartment with steam heat—"

"Stimma hitta, hotta watta, alavata, talafana," Ira jeered indulgently out of Joyce.

"What?"

"Oh, I was just joking. So what about Mamie?"

"From a little capmaker, her husband, Jonas, is now a partner in a restaurant. No? And Mamie is a—how do you call it? Superintendent of the house, and gets her rent free."

Mom attacked the frying pan with a liberal salvo of Rokeach's scouring powder. "Sometimes I think they guard themselves from me, for fear I might blight their prosperity with the evil eye. But what, think I. Envy you? Never. You're my sister. Thrive. Prosper."

She flushed the frying pan under the faucet. "It will have to wait until I do the supper dishes. You understend what I'm saying?"

"*Tockin, tockin,*" Ira patronized in Yiddish.

"As cold water flows like icicles from our faucet in winter, so my fate is my fate. Not only to be bitterly poor, but yoked to that lunatic."

"Mom!" Ira warned.

"It's not true?"

"You said you wouldn't talk about Pop. You're going crazy on the subject."

"Crazy? I?"

"Yeah, lately."

"God be my judge if I am crazy."

"All right, then you're not. I just can't stand it!"

"He's crazy!" She had been stung too badly to contain herself. "Who doesn't know his capers? Through the length and breadth of the waiters' union they know it. Boss and busboy, who doesn't know my little Chaim? And patrons too—beyond doubt. This one he will tell, 'If you're in such a hurry, why didn't you come in earlier,' and the other one who points to the tip left on the table, he will say, 'If you didn't take it, nobody else will'—"

"That's his idea of a joke!" Ira countered.

"A joke? May a stroke fell him. Fortunately, his present boss is a *goy,* a Bohemian, a decent man, and the patrons are largely *goyim.* If he had a Jewish boss, and they should come to quarrel, your father would throw crockery at him. Hasn't he already flung a water pitcher through a mirror? But before *goyim* he quakes, so he behaves a little."

"All right! All right, Mom! Save it for some other time."

"The wonder is I'm not crazy," she persisted obdurately. "Who wouldn't go crazy serving such a sentence as I'm condemned to serve living with him? And to the stranger"— she suddenly shifted mien— "he's a model of meekness. Inoffensive. Tender as a mulberry."

"I know!" Ira flared up, shouted: "For Christ's sake, I know!"

He slumped down in his chair, scowled. "If only I'd got away from here and gone to Cornell when I had a chance!"

"*Noo*, it's an old story." It was Mom's turn to pacify. "Pray, pay no attention. It's an old story. Nothing to become distraught over." She came over to the table and sat down.

"No, but you do."

"Pay no attention. Beside, today is the *erev Shabbes*, and on the eve of the Sabbath, serenity and peace should hold sway—don't you know?" Her irony wasn't lost on him.

"Yeah, *erev Shabbes* or not, I could kill the sonofabitch."

"Go, don't be foolish." Mom tried to keep her tone light.

"I could. Not only for what he's done to you, for what he's done to me. Was there ever such a mean, stingy, screwy little louse. I can't figure him out, that's all. You know what? He's a child. He's a lunatic."

"*Noo, tockin, tockin.*" A tremendous sigh shook her. "What can you do? A loafer he is not. A gambler he is not. He works, he provides. On whose earnings would you have gotten this far into college?"

"On your skrimping you mean, on your quarter a day, the stipend of your miserable allowance. I know the guy. He gives and begrudges, he promises and withholds. It's the goddamnedest thing, the way he keeps changing his mind. It's the way he offered to pay my first-year expenses in Cornell, and then reneged. I didn't want to go anyway. So what the hell was the difference? He would have paid Minnie's way through college, though."

"Well, she's his favorite. A father, a daughter, don't you know. But your father he still is."

"Yeah, that's about all. Tell me one thing, will you—before he comes home: why the hell didn't you leave him? Now that I'm old enough to understand these things, it would have been better for all of us, for you, for Minnie, for me. I remember his throwing coffee in your face—I still remember it was coffee with milk in it—*café au lait* it's called in French. Why the hell did you stand for it? And Minnie and I sat under the table crying when you came to blows—on Essex Street or Henry Street, there on the East Side when he was out of work. Why didn't you leave him? What the hell made you hang on to the louse? This is America."

Her face sagged as her heavy fingers stroked the weave of the tablecloth. "Indeed it is America. And I with two children in it, not much more than toddlers. To whom should I turn? Were my father and mother here? No. Nor my kin? Not even one. Not Moe, not Mamie. No one. Believe me, were even Moe here, things would have been different."

Her features changed, almost as if a ripple passed across them, reflecting some kind of inner debate, an envisaging. "A man like Moe— Morris, my stout, hearty brother. But he had still to arrive in the new land. Then to whom would I turn? If I had clasped my children to me and fled, then to whom and where? A word of English I didn't know."

"Well, but it was all Yiddish, all around you. What do you mean?" Ira challenged. "You didn't need English."

"You don't understand. And the shame and the fright? Alone and timid. Well, I had one *landsfrau,* Frieda—I had more, but I knew only the way to Frieda's. Did I know the way through streets? I knew only the way to Frieda's, and she already had consumption. So what other remedy, except to cling to Chaim, to bow the head and cling to my husband?"

"Oh, hell."

"*Verfallen,*" she said. "It's all in the past. Meanwhile I have an *ausgestudierteh* son."

"Yeah, *ausgestudiert.* What I've learned you wouldn't believe. I'd have been a hell of a lot better off, a lot more independent, a lot tougher, if I'd had to go to work like the other kids on the block, after they graduated from public school—"

"But I didn't want that, a crude toiler for a son. Never!" She raised her head in unflinching, indomitable opposition. "When the midwife placed you on my breast, I blessed you, and I vowed I would have a son schooled in the nobility of the mind."

"Yeah?"

"And that was the least he owed me, no? A pittance more to further your education. Minnie's he needed no urging—and as if in spite, fate prevented her. Alas, he's a peculiar man. There's no knowing him: one minute he's proud that you attend college—he brags to the other waiters that he has a son in college—the next minute he chafes at the expense. You're a never-ending burden; you earn nothing; your idleness is fostered at his cost."

"Mmm."

Maybe Freud was all wrong. The confused smattering Ira had

picked up about Freudianism jiggled in conjecture. Freud was wrong with his theory of the father's urge to castrate the son because of sexual rivalry for the mother. The old boy had got it wrong, Ira speculated sardonically. He himself had whet his piece on his sister, had grown up ravening to get in her every chance he had, and even though her dating had made her off limits for several years now, he desired her nonetheless.

It always would hold him, lure his fantasy. Maybe that was the form the Freudian hypothesis about the supposed rivalry of father and son for the mother took. Who the hell knew. Damn. The whole thing was irrelevant anyway, wasn't it? The relevant insight might be the inherent resentment of the son by the father because of economic reasons. The parent had to support his offspring, as in Ira's case, had to provide for him a long time before he could expect a return—maybe never get one. Hence the resentment, which Freud translated into sexual rivalry for the mother.

Oh, it was goofy, both views. What about the female child, the daughter? She had to be supported too, until she could contribute her share to the domestic economy of the family, but she contributed early, and wasn't resented as much—and maybe brought in a fat purchase price at marriage. . . . They could always drown them, as they did in China. Cut the balls off boy infants, drown the girl infants, sell the boy infants as eunuchs.

The West did neither, of course; neither did Jews. So where did that leave him? With aimless moorings, aimless moonings. One could as easily exploit that selfsame economic resentment of father toward son, and the subsequent sense of guilt on the part of the son toward the father, as the seminal, seminal, yeah, as the seed-need for substantiating that guilt by guilty act, really endowing guilt with justification, as you could by Freudian means. Hail Karl Marx. Maybe the guys in the '28 alcove had a point with their economic determinism.

The notion elated him: as if he had made a discovery, like—well, say like Copernicus accounting for the motion of the planets, of the solar system, a damned sight better than old man Ptolemy, more simple, more sensible, too, dispensing with all the swarming, silly epicycles.

Extraordinary! In a kind of golden haze compounded of candle-light and rumination, he watched Mom plodding heavily but quietly about the kitchen. From a large paper bag on the washtub utility table she removed the braided *kholleh,* the appealing Sabbath bread, its ornamental braids on top glistening like sardonyx as she transferred the loaf to a platter. She brought the platter to the dining table near the candlesticks, covered the loaf with a white cloth.

"Everything is becoming so frightfully dear," she said. "A small bunch of soup greens, five cents, an onion three cents, a piece of chuck meat forty cents a pound." She went to the stove, lifted the lid on the pot of simmering chicken soup, looked down disapprovingly at the contents. "I cut off all the fat from the hen, but still the broth has a thick layer of it."

"I don't like it."

"I know. *He* does."

"Well, I don't. It's too damned *shmaltzy.*"

"I know. I know your American tastes, Ira. Yours and Minnie's. Do you remember when you once fought over who was to get the heel of Herbst corn bread with chicken *shmaltz* on it? Chicken *shmaltz* spread on after it was rubbed with garlic."

"Oh, I wouldn't mind it today, but not in soup. And anyway, try to show up among American people with garlic on your breath." He chuckled. "Good old *knubl,*" reverting to the word in Yiddish. "*Knubl, knubl,* toil and trouble."

"For your sake I'll skim off as much as I can." She brought out a large serving spoon and a carving knife from the drawer in the built-in china closet, placed the carving knife on the table, and proceeded to skim the chicken soup. "So why has everything become so frightfully dear?"

"Supply and demand," Ira said tersely.

"And what does that mean?"

"More buyers, fewer sellers."

"And yet I see the same pushcart peddlers when I go shopping on Sunday morning on Park Avenue. The pushcarts are heaped with fruit and vegetables. So much. Still, every housewife with her few dollars stands aghast at the high prices. A cabbage, to make stuffed cabbage, a lowly cabbage, four cents a pound. It's unheard of, Iraleh. I have to ponder every Sunday where best to spend the little money I have. It's the truth. It takes me longer and longer to shop."

"So I've noticed."

"Why?"

"Why what? That I've noticed?"

"No. That everything is so dear."

"Oh." Ira scowled. "There must be a shortage somewhere, Mom," he said testily. "Somebody's cornered the cabbage market. Or all the *Yidlekh* are suddenly dying for *hullupchehs*. Has sour salt gone up too?"

"*Alles!*" Mom said emphatically. "Turn where you will."

"Damned if I know, Mom. Tell you the truth, I never gave a damn about economics. That's what they call this subject in college. It has to do with commerce and trade and profits. And of course, money—*geldt*."

"I know it. A Jew like you is something not to be believed. A Jew without regard for making money—who hates huckstering, haggling, bargaining—he wriggles like a worm when I go shopping with him for secondhand clothes. Did you ever hear of such a thing? Not to strive for wealth. It's something rare, rare. How did you lose out? You're my son. You're Chaim Stigman's son. For success in business, my husband would barter his breath. Had he the judgment to match his craving, believe me he'd be a magnate, but he hasn't. And you care nothing for success. Even Minnie does."

Mom rested the serving spoon in a dish and came over to the table and sat down again. "Well, where is he? Plague take him. He's lost himself in some theater."

She suddenly became spirited and spiteful. "Would he were lost for good. I'd be rid of him. *Gotinyoo!*" she invoked. And was interrupted by Ira's exclamation of warning:

"Mom!"

"Forgive me, *zindle*. I forgot myself. I forgot our agreement." And after a short space of silence, "Do you know the rent goes up two dollars a month beginning December?"

"You told me."

"An Irisher, and for no reason he raises the rent. Talk about Jewish landlords flaying the hide off the tenant. An Irisher. You see? The bleak year take him. He doesn't do the same? Two dollars, on top of the three he already mulcted from us when he tore out a washtub and knocked a doorway through to the toilet and put in electricity. But to paint these decrepit burrows, to daub the kitchen walls with a fresh coat of that green bile, green slop, he calls paint, condemn him to death before he'll do it."

"Yeah?" He forgot himself listening to Mom: who could help but surrender to that contralto richness of feeling in which everything she uttered was steeped?

"And you," her sorrowful brown eyes searched his face, "do you have a few groats on yourself?"

Ira debated with himself for a few seconds while he returned her steady gaze. The last thing he wanted was a donation from Mom. He knew only too well how much and how often she suffered wringing her paltry allowance from Pop.

"I have a few groats, yes."

"You have, yes," she mimicked skeptically.

"I tell you I have!"

"From whence have you? Mamie's alms were a week ago. You don't think I know?"

"Aw, Mom. For Christ's sake!"

"Sinful mother that I am, I mean only if you truly need it. I see you have become a personage. You mingle with higher folk than ever I dreamed you would—than ever *you* dreamed you would. Isn't that true? *Noo,* with empty pockets how can you consort with them—those you've told me about? Somehow your destiny is there. I see." She clasped her hands. "Only speak—I hoard for a Persian lamb coat, you know as well as I do."

"I don't need it. Thanks." Ira nodded in strenuous assurance; less than strenuous Mom wouldn't believe. "I've got almost three dollars in my pocket."

"Verily?"

"Do I have to show you?"

"No, no. *Got sei dank.* From where did you filch three dollars?"

"I didn't filch it. Edith gave it to me."

"The Professora? *Azoy?*"

Ira shrugged—noncommittally.

"Aha. I have a gigolo for a son. Cadger!"

"I'm not a cadger!" He had raised his voice. "I've spent a lot of time with her when she's been in trouble—*tsuris,* you understand? I've listened to her complaining. I've sympathized with her. She feels I've been of service, I've done a great favor, done her a lot of favors. She feels indebted. So what am I going to do? She won't let me go around penniless."

"You don't feel ashamed?"

"I don't know what to feel."

"But you take it. *Noo,* bless her for her generosity. What a fine, noble person she must be."

"She is."

"Woe is me." Mom's sigh would have been stagy in anyone else, but with her, emotion resonated from the depths of her being.

"Why do you say that?" Ira demanded gruffly.

"I already see," she said.

"Oh, you do? You see what?"

"Indeed, my son." A sibylline presence, a sibylline quiescence enveloped her as she spoke. "A woman forsaken is like a vine. She clings to whatever will support her."

"Who says she's forsaken?"

"She's not?"

"You make it sound so Jewish."

"Jewish, *goyish,* regardless." When she meditated, Mom's lips always swelled out in a pout. "How destiny fulfills itself: that you should be on hand, impecunious Jewish youth, out of this poverty, out of this destitute 119th Street, in her need for someone to turn to. Truly, it's something to marvel at."

"Mom, will you cut it out? You're going way, way off. She's an independent woman: she doesn't have to turn to anybody; she doesn't have to lean on anybody. She's just the opposite of you. She's self-reliant, they call it in English. Brave. Self-supporting. You should have seen how brave she was after she had an abortion."

"A what? *Oy, gevald!* She was pregnant?"

"Well, what else?" Ira could scarcely refrain from yelling. "If she had an abortion!"

"Poor woman! He deserves the gibbet, that rascal."

"Oh, boy! The gibbet, no less."

"No? He who toys with a woman's heart deserves the gibbet. And to get her with child beside."

"Listen, he didn't toy with her heart, and he got her an abortionist, it's called, as soon as she found out. He paid for the whole thing. He paid the doctor."

"A great boon." Mom was unimpressed.

"No? You've got a short memory, Mom. Don't be such a saint. You had to lift up your brother Morris. You picked up two-hundred-and-twenty-pound Morris, when you didn't want another baby. You think I don't remember."

"What else could I do with a miser like my husband, tell me?"

"Oh, all right. I wasn't talking about that." They were both silent, vexed with each other.

"Don't forget there were other men around. Larry was there too." Ira buttressed contention with reminder.

"Larry?" Mom dismissed her son's plea. "What was Larry to a grown woman? A boy, a comely boy, nothing more. Could she consider him seriously? Go. This Lewleh you call him, this was an adult. Cholera carry him off, but an adult he was. And he gave her to understend he might marry her. You told me yourself." Mom interspersed words with ominous strokes of double fingers.

"Yeah, but Christ's sake, we weren't talking about that!"

"What were we talking about?"

"We were talking about how she could have been pregnant—*who* made her pregnant."

"You don't have to shout. I understand."

"Yeah, but you're always winding things around." Ira gesticulated vehemently. "I just wanted to tell you that he paid for it all."

"*He* paid. What are you saying?"

"Cash I mean."

"All right. A fine man." Mom halted further discourse in that direction with heavy sarcasm. "Deep into the sod let him go, for my sake."

"Yeah?"

"The man buys a passage to England—last summer you told me. He knows months in advance where his choice lies. His choice lies with another woman. And he returns and toys with her heart. He deludes her into thinking he is still undecided."

"How do you know?"

"You told me, no?"

"Well, *she* knew too. She knew that he had chosen the other woman, the woman in England!" Ira shouted. "She saw a book the other woman gave him: Shakespeare's *Sonnets* they were called. Inscribed—you know what I mean: inscribed 'To our future together'—Ah, what's the use," he growled. "You just live in a different world, that's all."

"*Noo,* I'm a *Dummkopf,* a greenhorn. Not a sophisticate like your Professora. What can I do? I wept these eyes out to enhance your education, to keep you from becoming the common *Dummkopf* that I am."

"Aw, Mom, you're not a *Dummkopf.* I didn't say that. I said you lived in a different world."

"Well, let's talk further." Mom directed her sad, searching gaze at him—in challenge. "Would you like? You can tell me. I'm your mother."

"Like what?" Ira countered guardedly.

"You've seen her fondled by other lovers; you've seen her kissed and cherished and handled by others. She's lost her appeal to you, hasn't she?"

"Oh, is that it? You're back to the clinging vine again."

"Don't sneer." Once more oracular her gravity: "How old is she?"

"Edith? She's thirty-two."

"Undoubtedly thirty-five."

"I said she was thirty-two!" Ira bristled. "*Tsvei'n dreizig!* If I say she's thirty-two, why do you tell me she's thirty-five?"

"Very well, thirty-two. Eleven years older than you are."

"What's that got to do with it?"

"Everything and nothing. I mean only—" Mom groped for words. "Granted she isn't a clinging vine. Today you are her confidant. But tomorrow? The distance between confidant and lover grows ever shorter."

"I never measured it," he sulked.

"No? But I have."

"Yeah? How?"

"You shared the same bed with her."

"But I told you! Nothing happened!" Ira again raised his voice.

"Not this time. But she shed tears before you, did she not?"

"Shed tears before me. Oh, for Christ's sake!"

Mom sighed again. "I wouldn't blame you if you became her lover—in real earnest: you may go and live with her."

"Is that so? Thanks."

"No? What? Live in these gloomy, little crypts, this forlorn cold-water flat of four cells, when you can have better? And in this poverty to have to depend on *him*, tight-fisted and stingy—do I need edify you—when *she* already has shown over and over how bountiful she is, how fond of you, no? What do you prefer? My travails, my tears, his hostility, our dearth, the four of us pent up between narrow walls. Or do you crave trudging for alms to Mamie's on 112th Street once a week? Go to the Professora if you wish. She is kind to you. She is generous. She is refined. That she's a *shiksa* and older? That's nothing, counts for nothing. She would take care of you. I bless her for that. Perhaps she would help you find a path to become someone: a *mensh*. Who knows? Something other than you are now, a *shlemiel*. Still, you're my son."

"Yeah?"

Mom made no answer. In the silence, Ira heard Pop's quick, light step entering the hallway outside—and nodded in signal.

"Me and my deafness." Mom tilted her head in surmise. "Is it he, my paragon?"

"It's your paragon, all right," Ira assured laconically.

"*L'kuvet Shabbes,* my paragon returns. *Noo.*" She stood up. "Shall I take your books off the table?"

"No. I'll put them away myself." Ira arose as the door opened.

VI

Furious with himself. The goddamn drive had locked—wouldn't budge—and locked him out of over an hour's work. And as luck would have it—always ill luck became compounded—he had forgotten to release his timer, which he habitually set to tinkle when an hour had elapsed. So he was stuck.

He had touched some hexed combination of keys, and the accursed cursor had disappeared from the screen. Well, goddamn it again. What had he been up to? It wasn't what he was up to that was primary; it was the mood he was in, the emotional setting of his prose that determined the form of the prose. Well, what the hell good was blowing his top, raving and ranting? The frigging thing was lost, down the tube, down the drain, into the empty set. *A shvartz yur auf is!* Try to repeat what he had said:

Oh, yeah, how well it began—could he recapture it? His introducing first the fact that the sort of backbiting his parents were engaged in was entirely proscribed on *erev Shabbes,* Sabbath eve, time of serenity, when every Jew was a king, a potentate. And God forgive him now because he couldn't forget the deplorable wisecrack he was guilty of making: that Pop was a mashed potentato; mawkish verbal incontinence, responsibility for which he wriggled out of by laying the blame at the foot of Joyce. Sing heavenly muse how Mom had reminded Pop that he had blackened the eyes of the son of the master artisan, before quitting the artisan's employ. And she had gone on to pun that the deed was in keeping with his blacksmith's calling. Her twitting earned her his harassed glare.

Yet again, but in a variegated fashion, Mom told Ira the familiar story of Pop's first trip to America. A few days after Pop fled from his apprenticeship and came home, she recalled, he had purloined a sufficient sum from his father's wallet to pay for steerage passage to America, purloined the cash and absconded with it to Hamburg, port of departure for America. Once in New York, he telegraphed his brother Gabe for additional funds for his fare to St. Louis. Both of these things Pop himself related to Ira years later, laughing at the memory of his youthful misdemeanor. Pop did have a glint of humor—but usually long after the fact. In short, Pop had avoided New York with its sweatshops, its opportunities severely limited to the needle trades, its virulent discrimination against Jews, its crammed tenements, infested with vermin and breeding grounds for tuberculosis and cholera, its teeming Jewish multitudes scrounging and toiling for a living. Instead, he had traveled by railroad coach to the West. The West—where so many Jews in the nineteenth century had already gone, not the hordes of Jews who composed the early-twentieth-century influx from the persecuted, orthodox *shtetls* of East Europe, with their narrow, rabbinically defined horizons, but adventurous, cosmopolitan Jews of German origin, who settled in the West and in many instances made their fortunes there.

The year in which Pop set out, 1899, was almost like a watershed in time, separating the arrival of the German Jews from that of the East European ones. To St. Louis Pop had first gone, and—again with a laugh—he told how he had backed a cart loaded with scrap metal collected from his brother Gabe's junkyard over the dock and into the Mississippi. The two had quarreled.

"Oh, with whom didn't my spouse quarrel?" Mom observed with due redundancy.

Pop had quarreled with his brother, felt sorry for himself, felt neglected, deserted, and lonely. Poor man—he must have been deprived of mother love, youngest in the family, and not regarded as either prudent or shrewd, and he wasn't. Still, the baby of the family—of about eight or nine children—should have been cherished, but he wasn't cherished either. How many times had Ira studied his paternal grandmother Rivkeh's photographic portrait hanging on a wall in the front room: the rigidity, the forbidding rigidity, of her lineaments was such that Ira would think of her later as the Jewish twin of Grant Wood's *American Gothic.* Deprived of mother love, maybe—to do a little homespun psychologizing—not deemed perspicacious, shrewd, a *khukhim,* either with respect to money matters or to study. Again, Ira recalled Mom's saying how delicate in constitution Pop's next-older brother was, Jacob, and devoted entirely to the study of the Talmud—and how Pop had tormented his weaker sibling, even provoked him into a scuffle. He had mauled Jacob so badly that Pop had to go into hiding for a week in order to avoid a paternal caning. Keeping out of sight during the day, he had skulked in the dark at night outside the house, waiting for his mother to circumvent her husband's wrath by surreptitiously providing her wayward son with the leftovers from supper.

Anyway, in America, in the expansive American West, Pop naturally became homesick, and he returned to Galitzia.

* * *

How like his son, Ira reflected, not without bitterness: how like him his son was in hundreds of ways.

If there existed any differences in character between them, Ira and his own execrable father, they probably derived from Mom, and salient among them was that Ira couldn't permit himself the subterfuge to which Pop invariably had recourse, when he sought relief from the consequences of his impetuousness, his folly, his execrable judgment: it was all the fault of the Devil. The Devil always came to Pop's rescue. "The Devil prompted me," Pop invariably said. And so now: "The Devil prompted me. I became homesick. I yearned to see my mother."

And see her he did. He traveled back to Austro-Hungary. He not only saw his mother, but there, alas, he also found Leah, the woman who was to become Ira's mother.

Old story. Still fuming over the fancied lost verve of the prose the computer had robbed him of, old story, Ira told himself. Well, you've patched up the lacuna, after a fashion, bridged the gap, more or less. Get on with the tale, get on with your *erev Shabbes,* goddamn the luck.

VII

"Indeed." The single word seeped irony as Mom leaned over the table to clear the dishes.

"It wasn't so?" Pop looked up at her.

"I said indeed."

"Nag." He goosed her, chirruping genially at the same time, chirruping the way he had urged on his horse when he was a milkman. "Tlkh, tlkh."

"When you're frozen by the past, embarrassed, yes, molest your wife." She bumped his hand away.

"Uh-uh. She's excited." Her reaction never failed to amuse him.

"Spare me your endearments." Mom paused on the way to the sink. "You still owe me two dollars balance from my allowance for the week. I would appreciate receiving that more than your endearments."

"On *erev Shabbes?*" Pop indulged in mock dismay. "The candles are still burning, shedding their holy light. How can you ask me for two dollars? It's a sin. I'm a Jew, no?"

"My pious Jew. Tomorrow is also *Shabbes*. Until evening. And what new excuse will you find then? Yesterday was Thursday. You could have settled the score then. Sunday begins a new week."

"I'll pay you, I'll pay you. I'm not fleeing the country."

"You could flee into your grave."

Pop chuckled. Mom glowered. It was the stock confrontation between them. Too bad Minnie was absent, the only one capable of entreating and cajoling Pop into ending the petty crisis. She had a way with him, softly beseeching and pleading as Ira never could. She probably would persuade him to give Mom the balance of her allowance when she got home—but until she got home, the air of conflict that he hated more than anything else hung about the kitchen: conflict over money, and in particular the tag end of Mom's allowance.

Oh, hell, guilt again: Jesus, had Ira been out working, bringing home a pay envelope, the way the other kids on the street did, how different, how much easier for Mom—having to wrangle with the old bastard for all of two bucks.

He gazed at the candles, trying to make up his mind whether to get his copy of Milton's poems from the shelf under the china closet, or to try to protect Mom, interject some witticism, maybe, divert her fixation on the subject of her allowance. How she tormented herself over it, and how Pop enjoyed prolonging her torment. No, he couldn't lose himself in Milton. Not on *erev Shabbes*. Not with Pop digging his mother's grave before him.

Again, his gaze rested on the wavering light of the candles. Tapers they were called once. Probably because they did taper once. Burned halfway down. Weren't they a measure of time in ancient days? Once they were lit, if you were an Orthodox Jew you weren't allowed to touch them again, or touch the flame. Or relight them if they were blown out. To do so was to perform work. And on *Shabbes* no work was permitted. Wasn't that the silliest goddamn idea? And yet for him this particular observance, this particular manifestation of Judaism, had become an intertwining of rebellion with memory, of erstwhile piety with present disbelief.

Ira was about to get up and go for his book, but paused to listen to Pop reminisce. "To every married couple my father allotted a milk cow," Pop resumed.

"Yeah?"

The expansive little man adjusted his eyeglasses and pushed his stained felt hat back on his head, revealing the deepening coves of his balding brow. "To my brother Sam, who already had two children, he allotted two cows. And to all married pairs, of course, a flock of chickens, a garden plot—and a *goy* to tend it, naturally. Firewood we had, eggs we had, sour cream we had, cottage cheese also."

Ira smirked surreptitiously, diverted in spite of himself by Pop's pronunciation of the English word: *Kaddish* cheese.

"It's true," Pop insisted.

"I believe you, Pop."

"We didn't starve—as they did, the children in her family. That old glutton Zaida took good care of himself, you can be sure of that. He kept food under lock and key. But not so my father. We had an abundance of everything. Even brandy we didn't lack. Schnapps. What, Saul, the superintendent of Count Ustorsky's distillery, should begrudge us a measure of brandy?"

"Then why did you leave Austria, Pop?"

"Why? To go around idle, that's not my nature."

"But your father was the superintendent of a big distillery."

"Hah! Struck the mark." Mom brought up the glass bowl of compote. "My clever son."

"Struck the mark? What do you know about it?" Pop turned on her. "I'm not one to rely on my father."

"Oh."

Ira smacked his lips as Mom set down the compote and went to the sideboard for saucers and a serving spoon. He loved Mom's compote, the variegated prunes, raisins, and dried pears in dark sauce.

"Go tell your grandmother. We've heard your stories." Mom returned and sat down. Her laughter too often held the hint of a jeer, and it did now. "Why do you believe him?"

"It's all right," Ira appeased. Jesus, that goddamn two bucks. She was as implacable as a piranha when he baited her.

"You were too light-witted for that kind of work. To run a large distillery takes judgment. Your father didn't trust you. True?" She picked up a saucer.

"In your addled brain it's true," Pop retorted. "My father didn't want all his sons working at the same trade. My brother Simon was already working there—and Raphael and Meyer and my brother-in-law, Schnapper. The rest of us he wanted to learn a trade."

"Aha."

"No," he mocked in turn. "Look! Look how she serves! A thousand times I told you, don't dump it out of the bowl. Use the serving spoon."

"Chaim," Mom rejoined, "you serve your customers in the restaurant however you wish. I'll serve however I wish at home."

"Even a horse would have learned by now."

"Dine with a horse then, my finical spouse." An angry and constrained silence followed, all too latent with furious quarrel.

"Wow, this is good compote, Mom," Ira said with enthusiasm—that he hoped would allay tension. "It tastes good, so good."

"Ess, ess, zindle."

"With pleasure, Mom. You know that."

"I'll brew some tea."

"Such a compote I could wish on my foes." Pop put down his spoon.

"Sin, what you're saying is sin," Mom warned.

"Aw, c'mon, Pop." Lacking Minnie's tender supplication, Ira tried jollying his father. "It's tasty, Pop."

"Let her next husband eat it." He pushed away his saucer.

"Would the Almighty bless me with one."

"Okay." Ira was determined to avert head-on collision. "What trade did you learn, Pop?"

"None. I never learned a trade." Pop evidently sought to collaborate in keeping the Sabbath peaceful—despite Mom's knowing moue.

"That was my misfortune. That's why I had to come to America. My brother Gabe was here dealing in junk—"

"But you say your father wanted you to learn a trade," Ira interrupted.

"And I didn't want to learn the trade he chose for me— Uh, she's grimacing again!"

"Oh, for Pete's sake! Mom, just let me talk to Pop, will you?"

"Talk. To your heart's content." She couldn't have signaled more clearly that she meant not a word of it.

"My father apprenticed me to an artisan in wrought iron. I wanted to be a fiddler."

"A what? A fiddler?"

"A fiddler."

"You wanted to be a fiddler?" Ira had never heard Pop say that before. He had wanted to be a fiddler. All at once, so much about him appeared to fall into place, could be made explicable: his fits of merriment at times, on weekends or during the summer vacation, when they rode together in the milk wagon, when the strain Pop was under seemed to relax, or his distance from Ira seemed to diminish, when brief, antic interludes of camaraderie slipped out from behind the strict guise of father; those times when he watered the horse at the polished granite watering troughs with other teamsters, and they chaffered, laughed at Pop's comic remarks, joked and bantered. And he joined them, prankish and merry, boyish, waggish, off-guard, hardly Pop, his forbidding aspect in abeyance.

So he had wanted to be a fiddler. If one could but hold that phase of him in mind, consider who he might have been, the impulses that once ruled him—implied in his wanting to be a fiddler. No, it was too late. Too late because of what Pop thought he had to be, strict and aloof toward his son, too late because of Mom, because Ira saw Pop as she saw him, as she had trained Ira to see him.

But here was that glimpse: of an atrophied core, a core that bespoke a latent kinship, also atrophied, scarified, and hardened beyond Ira's reaching.

"I wanted to be where people were enjoying themselves and were happy," Pop said. "Where people danced and had a gay time. At a wedding. At a festival. A party. . . . No, it didn't suit my father: Saul Schaffer, the Count's distillery master, in charge of hundreds of cattle—they were fed mash from the distillery. As good as a veterinarian in the eyes of the peasants—they knew him for miles around. Saul Schaffer's son apprenticed to a common fiddler? The son of distillery master Saul Schaffer to play in a *kletchmer*? Never! That was no trade. He apprenticed me to an artisan in wrought iron. Imagine a stalwart like me working at a forge, with hammer and tool and tong amid flame and soot. And his wife, she provided fare—after what I was accustomed to at home—so may she fare. I ran away. I ran home again."

Ira awakened from his reverie, and felt as if the bottom had dropped out of everything, his work, inspiration, especially his drive, everything else. Strange it happened. It happened to all writers, all artists he was sure: some kind of lapse, the momentary power failure, when fluorescents went out, and had to be relit. Jesus, he knew the plot, the track he had in mind, the bearing—but he could only think of Maine, the time when goose down, plucked early in the fall while flies still abounded, had become a repository for fly eggs—which hatched in the down, after M had made a pillow of it, *his* pillow, in which the maggots soon began a ceaseless crepitation as they devoured the barbules of the feathers, setting up a gruesome ticking within the ticking: a macabre time bomb. No, this story would scarcely do. Nor would the other: about the bags of feathers he had hung up to dry in the attic, right above the kitchen table, on which unaccountably—for a while— maggots dropped out of the electric fixture in the kitchen ceiling. Oh, a jocund time he and M and the kids had of it. But one germane story he might draw on: about the time the warden of the state prison brought two trusties to help dress the several crates of ducks and geese raised in the prison. That might be touching. . . .

But the one thing he wanted to emphasize above all else was that no matter how profitable the business might have been, the business of raising, processing, custom-dressing, and marketing waterfowl, there was nothing unscrupulous about his custom dressing; it was just in the nature of things. How many hand-fed, plump, choice, and most attractive and easily marketable ducks and geese were brought to him by their owners, who had bought them from him as ducklings or goslings, and now pleaded with him that he swap their birds for any birds of his own, usually nothing near so well-fed and select as theirs, the reason being that neither the owner nor his family could bring themselves to eat their pets. Oh, dear, departed days not so dear, just departed. And besides that, there was no one else in the entire state of Maine who did custom dressing of ducks and geese, because no one else had on hand the hundred or so pounds of wax in which to dip the birds after most of the feathers had been removed, thus producing a clean, shiny skin. Waterfowl hunters by the dozen brought him their game birds—in fact, people came from as far away as the neighboring state of New Hampshire to have him dress their ducks and geese. It was amazing the lengths to which people would go to avoid plucking a duck or goose.

So it was very profitable—or should have been, if he had charged enough, and he didn't. Mom had been right after all. But no matter how potentially profitable it all was or would have been, the point to make was that he couldn't take it seriously. There was the rub, the disability: once he had known that unique, unutterable afflatus of creativity, he could never take any other occupation seriously again. He could never quite sever from that pristine rapture again, divorce himself from it though he tried—and thought he had succeeded in doing. That was the whole thing in a nutshell—or an eggshell. The writing of the one novel had gone so deep, he would be forever after haunted by the experience. Some metaphoric vein of precious ore he had struck within the psyche—and he could never ignore, never forget it, do what he might. He had been a precision metal grinder and a gauge maker in toolrooms and machine shops for five years before he raised ducks and geese, and he had been a busy shop steward and active union man all that time, and still the pressure of narrative dialogue and situation and denouement, half-formed shapes of stories and novels, kept intruding into his mind. Some vein of a rare lode of perception he had been fortunate enough to strike within the spirit, a lode he had exposed, kept radiating beyond his control. Thanks to his wife, thanks to longevity, in large part due to her intelligent care, despite infirmities, he could once again prospect within his soul for what seemed to him its luminous treasure. Considering his age, the opportunity extended him couldn't possibly last much longer, but long or short, he had known a moment of grace. He was happy to share it with others, even as he was honored in the privilege his readers accorded him of making it possible for him to share his happiness with them.

VIII

It would seem that Ira's paternal grandfather, devout Jew with ear-locks, and in the portrait hanging in the Stigman front room only a lit-tle less Gothic than his wife, had relented in his attitude toward Pop, after Ira was born. Mom affirmed that the old man had become very fond of Ira, dandled him on his knee. "And the night before we left for America, he leaned on his stick and watched you dance: you danced so prettily, the tears came to his eyes, the eyes of Saul, distillery foreman of Tysmenicz." He had relented so far as to put a stake in, to "bankroll" Pop so he could set himself up as a horse trader. Pop, in ad-dition to loving the fiddle, loved horses; he loved horses the way young people of a later generation loved automobiles. However, love was not enough when it came to trading horses: he was outwitted time and again, and in short order he went bankrupt.

"So what was there to do?" Pop asked rhetorically. "To wander about in idleness, and depend on my father again? *Nisht b'mutchkeh.* I borrowed the money from my father, and I came to America once more."

"You did? You were already a citizen."

"Of course. They put me in jail when I came back to Austria, be-cause I didn't answer the call to serve in the army." Pop chuckled. "For a few days only, before they let me go. There were other prisoners in the same cell. And one fellow could fart whenever he wanted to. Hup hup! Another one." Pop laughed heartily. "'Stefyan, fart for us': Hup. Hup. A report. He married a girl in Czechoslovakia, and when he picked up his bride to carry her through the door, the way the *goyim* do, he ripped out a fart you could hear all over Prague."

"That *is* funny." Ira grinned appreciatively.

"When it comes to that he's adept," Mom agreed, derogatively. "He can always spin you a funny tale."

"Here she comes," Pop derided.

Mom seemed ever impelled to blight budding amiability between father and son. "You know that means I was a citizen born abroad. Like an ambassador's son. Isn't that true?"

"In those days, what else?"

"And you weren't really a citizen yourself. Boyoboy, nothing has ever gone regularly with me," Ira reflected.

"Now you're worrying? You voted already."

"I know. It's just that, technically, I'm not supposed to be here."

"And if it weren't for Saul, the superintendent, you wouldn't be here," said Mom.

"You mean that he loaned Pop the money to come over again?"

"Loaned? He gave. You didn't borrow the money," Mom addressed Pop.

"She knows I borrowed the money."

"Mom, will you let him tell his story!" Ira chided.

"His father *gave* him the money."

"In her addled brain, my father gave me the money."

"Then when did you repay him? Did you have money to repay him?"

"Afterward. He wrote me that he forgave me the debt."

"When?"

"When I was already in America. Before I brought you and Ira over. To use the money I owed him to bring you here."

Mom grimaced—in hopeless disbelief so intense it was indistinguishable from an affront.

"As if I weren't there." She turned to Ira. "I see the old man standing before me as if it were yesterday. 'Chaim,' he said, 'the first time you stole a way to America. This time, go like a man. I don't want you to disgrace yourself. You have a wife and child. Here's the passage money to America. Go with my blessings.'"

"Away, madwoman!"

"What the hell's the difference, Mom?" Ira burst out.

"The truth is nothing to you? That's how I brought you up?" By his silence, she knew she had her son at a disadvantage. "Do you want me to teach you how to catch a liar?"

"I don't want to know."

"Ask him to repeat his story a week from now. Two weeks from now."

"Leah, if you're seeking for something untoward to darken your fate, you haven't far to search."

"I'm seeking the two dollars coming to me, if you want to know what I seek."

"In spite, no?"

"Be consumed in my spite."

"A man comes home from work on Friday night," Pop said bitterly. "He comes home from pikers and from stiffs who don't leave him even a dime for a tip. From *nudnicks* and from pests. Waiter, the coffee is cold. Waiter, the rolls are stale. Waiter, you call this borsht? Waiter, I came in ahead of her. It's *erev Shabbes*. He looks for peace and quiet. What awaits him? A shrew. A nag. A plague. Right away, money. In front of the lighted candles, she holds up her bag, and wants her husband, tired from a day's work, to fill it up."

"Fill up my bag," Mom scoffed with equal bitterness. "Fill up a grave! Fill up my bag on eleven miserable dollars a week. Who buys the scouring powder for the pots and pans? And the Bon Ami for the windows? I'm out of cockroach powder, and the *goya* below us on the ground floor never powders. Who buys the kerosene to burn the bedbugs out of the bedsprings? Who pays the line-up man when the washline breaks?—a whole quarter. And a quarter five days a week for Ira—"

"Go tell it to your granny. You think I don't know Minnie contributes to your purse five dollars every week?"

"Fortunately. Or there would be chaos here. You would go shop for your own horseradish, you would go shop for your own carp and pike for gefilte fish on Friday."

"And you wouldn't sport a new rag every other week."

"And what if I do? And if I do, why do I? In a rag is my consolation for the wretched husband I have. In a rag I conceal my sorrows from my neighbors."

"Mom, will you cut it out, for Christ's sake! Let's have some more tea. Why don't you do the dishes? Anything! Please!"

"A *hivnuh!*" Mom snapped at Ira. "A fine son I have."

"Now you can see what she's like. What a fine mother you have. What a fine wife I have—"

"Yeah? Why the hell don't you give her the lousy two dollars?"

"Oh, you're becoming a cracker, too?" Pop retorted. "So easily said. Let's see you give her two dollars."

"All right. I will, goddamn it." Ira jumped up, dug his hand into his pocket.

"Sit down!" Mom flared at him. "I don't need your charity."

"Oh, Jesus." Ira flopped down into his chair.

"You see she doesn't need it," Pop baited. "She doesn't need the two dollars. What will she do with them tonight? Where will she spend them? She does it to provoke me. To mar a Sabbath."

"I'll lend them to *you*. Give them to her. We'll have some peace."

"Wipe your ass with them."

No one spoke. It was as though vituperation had brought them so close to explosion that no one wanted to risk the angry word of detonation.

"I have some honey cake left." Mom brought Ira a second cup of tea. "Would you like? It's good."

"A very small piece, Mom," Ira obliged.

"It's very filling." She brought the leftover slab of dark-brown, solid loaf, *hunik-lekekh,* as it was called, made with crystallized honey, and served Ira with a slice to accompany his second glass of tea. "You're still not taking any sugar?"

"No, Mom. The cake's enough."

"Chaim?" she offered equably. He waved her away. She went to the sink, stacked the dishes in the enameled basin, and then went to the stove for the steaming, speckled blue pot on the gas flame, returned to the sink, and moderated the cold water gushing from the brass faucet with the hot water decanted from the pot. She began washing dishes. Midway, she wiped her eyes, blew her nose into her hand, and rinsed it under the other faucet.

"Immediately, she starts piddling with her eyes," Pop remarked.

"If your head roared like mine," Mom said expressionlessly, "you'd know what it is to weep."

"Is it bad?" Ira asked.

"Tonight, the engineer is in a frenzy. The train roars like mad."

"Yeah? Did they have anything new to say at the clinic?"

"Chronic catarrh and again chronic catarrh. At the Harlem Hospital especially they tell you nothing. Each word costs them too much. I would need slaves, like Titus, to pound on anvils to drown out the roaring in my head."

"Is that what he did? You mean the Roman emperor Titus."

"So your Zaida told me. The Almighty punished him for destroying the holy temple in Eretz Yisrael."

"Yeah? What did *you* do?" Ira said. She laughed.

"My clever son." Pop had gotten *Der Tag* from the top of the icebox meanwhile, spread it on the table, and begun perusing it.

"*Noo,* Chaim," Mom persisted in patient, appeasing tone of voice. "What do you think? Will the French judges let him go free?"

"I'm not a prophet," was Pop's curt reply.

"Who's that?" Ira asked.

"Schwartzbart."

"Oh, the guy who shot Simon Petlyura?"

"The bastard who killed as many Jews as he could in Galitzia. A thousand deaths that beast deserved, not one," Mom intoned. "The Almighty has a special fire for him."

"Yeah? Trouble is all it takes is one bullet."

"Sometimes it's a great pity. A bloodthirsty, cold-blooded brigand like that. Ai, yi, all the Jews he killed and maimed: in the tens of thousands. And, I'm sure, many of our own *mishpokha.*" Mom turned around partly from the sink. "A Ukrainian murderer and his cossacks destroy a world of Jews, our world of Jews, and he can live unscathed in Paris. Let one Jew, a Russian Jew at that, a student, avenge their deaths, and it's an outrage. And your gentile papers call him a patriot. How is that?"

"I don't know, Mom. You just wonder whether it's worth it, that's all. The guy is dead. Killing him doesn't bring the Jews to life that *he* killed. So what the hell's the use?"

"Then what would you do? Schwartzbart, is he that much different from you, a student like you, an immigrant?"

"I don't know." Ira frowned, nibbling meditatively on the edge of the dense *hunik-lekekh,* so unlike American cakes, unglamorous, barely sweetened—so Jewish. . . .

It occurred to him suddenly there had been a time when he hadn't realized the cake was Jewish. It was simply *hunik-lekekh.* He was an urchin on 9th Street skipping down the tenement stairs to the untidy grocery across the street to buy five cents' worth of crystallized honey for Mom, viscous, sluggish stuff scooped from an open keg into a speckled wax-paper cone. "I don't know, Mom. That's the trouble."

"*Noo*, could you take him to court? If the Jews he slew were in Russia, and he and his marauders are in Paris? In what court could you accuse him? In a French court? He's in Paris, and he committed his crimes in Russia. And who cares about *Yidlekh* anyway? Hanging would have been a better end for the dog. It would have taken a few minutes longer—"

"*Chibeggeh, chibeggeh, chibeggeh.*" Pop shuffled his newspaper while he mocked. "She talks."

Mom was stung: "My sage. Then you speak."

"I have better things to do. I'm reading."

She took a deep breath, was mute.

How often conversation was aborted that way, ended that way, in the Stigman household—with a thud of silence. Only when Minnie was home was there a little more give and take, chatter, debate. Pop welcomed his daughter's opposition, often laughed at it, at her sharp disagreements and impertinences. She overrode his opinions, and he enjoyed her doing so—all the things he wouldn't have brooked Ira's doing. No wonder Ira had vented his anger with Pop on his sister, especially when she was younger. When Pop was waitering at his Sunday banquets, he had shown Minnie good, real good.

But when Minnie was absent now from the house, a dull cheerlessness took over—except during those times Ira had a job, in the summer, and more rarely, after school; and then a modicum of amiability, even joviality, tempered Pop's manner, relaxed domestic interchange. Otherwise, an air of brooding prevailed. Ira thought he could guess why. But always his surmise was tainted, the clarity of the surmise was sullied.

Sure—Ira studied the candle flames wavering gently a couple of inches above their brass sockets—if the cause of their antagonism were only a matter of Pop's supporting his son these many years through high school and college, when Ira could have been bringing in his earnings instead, helping sustain the household, as the other Jewish youth on 119th Street did, as Minnie was doing. If only it were. Had Minnie succeeded in getting into normal school, miserly though Pop was, Ira was sure Pop would have been willing to contribute to Minnie's support, contribute because Minnie always exerted herself to find part-time work, while Ira was too lacking in initiative, and just plain spunk, to get a job after classes. Mom would have hired out to scrub floors before she would see him give up "his career," as she called it.

Still—still what? The way his mind bobbled a nub of thought. Yes: even if Pop resented supporting his son through college, that would have been comparatively easier to deal with. It would have been a simple case of economics—almost. Or even if Mom's favoring him, coddling him, as Pop said, caused dissension, he, Ira, could have made a show of disapproval, as if he agreed with Pop. All kinds of ways of smoothing things out. But ah, there was one thing you couldn't smooth out. It was the groundswell that he himself roiled up, a secret tension he charged the household with, as if home were some kind of Leyden jar. . . .

Incest, incestuous longings. Jesus Christ, name it for what it was. It didn't matter that Minnie wouldn't give in anymore. She had, once upon a time. He knew it, she did too. She had, right in that cold little bedroom next to the kitchen, with the same blistered kitchen walls, all but capered, and regularly Sunday. You couldn't forget it, that was all. And had come so close to getting it again once or twice. It was the same old goddamn reason: the shock he'd gotten watching that rusty bastard jack off against a tree in Fort Tryon Park. His dark, sullen telepathy ionized the joint. He hated it, he fought it. Lucky there was Stella, fat little piece of ass. Could that be the reason there were no decent conversations in the Stigman household? The kind of homespun discussions everyone else reported as a staple of home life—that he witnessed at Larry's in the years of close friendship—the taking up of a topic of mutual interest and debating about it, differing about it, warmly defending pros and cons, but in a civil way. They discussed ideas—ah, there it was: ideas. Even Minnie developed her own ideas, reached conclusions, on her level. Her ideas didn't interest him, neither did her conclusions, usually, but what did? Nevertheless, he recognized, he had to admit to himself that she could think independently, generate ideas: she could *reason*. He couldn't reciprocate.

With Minnie no longer available, Stella continued to be the kid he pratted down in the glaring cellar in Flushing, from when she was fourteen. But it had been that—sex—that had ruined, rendered turbid, ideological exchange in the household, a monstrous intrusion that had mangled his own intellectual development. What else could it be? Stunted his analytical abilities, judiciousness, appraisals. *Shabbes b'nakht.*

Jesus Christ, what a sinister cyst of guilt that was within the self, denigrating the *yontif,* denigrating everything within reach, exuding ambiguity, anomaly, beyond redemption now. Yeah, but maybe the fault wasn't all his own, maybe a lot of the trouble was with Pop. Not because he was of immigrant birth. Pop didn't seem able to consider an idea, to weigh, to test it against some sort of evidence, to hold it steadily in view. Pop uttered pronouncements instead, *diktats,* commands, expressed likes and dislikes, dismissed, reminisced, yes, told stories, told stories of old times. God, you could wander all over the place looking for the cause, for the blame, like Goosy Gander, all over hell and gone. The blame was with himself, the blame was with Pop, the blame was with Mom too. But how could he ever get free of it? Could he get free of it? Ever? Ever?

That was the crux of the matter. To hell with the blame. Too late to find fault. Get out of it, whatever the goddamn cause. Or causes. But how? That was the worst of it. He was an addict. The minute he saw Stella—just the right moves: an iota of precarious privacy—prickarious privacy . . .

Mom had finished doing the dishes. She put them away in the china closet. Because it was built against the wall opposite the sink, she passed by the table several times.

"Tea I don't care for, but tonight it looks appetizing. I'll have a glass." And addressing Pop: "Chaim? Anything?" Unperturbed by his brusque shrug, as if discounted in advance, she addressed Ira: "A morsel more of *hunik-lekekh?*"

"No thanks, Mom," he said cheerlessly. "Don't you think Minnie ought to be home by now?"

"On Friday night? Another hour." Mom sat down with her glass of tea. "My poor daughter, how she strives, strives—"

Ira could sense rather than see Pop lift his eyes from the newspaper. Mom sucked her tea, steaming hot, her lips squealing in osculation against the rim of the glass. It was like a scene in a Russian play, Ira thought. He averted his face.

"How can you stand it so hot?"

"The tea? I like it when it scalds my gullet." Her lips squealed against the glass again. She laughed guiltily, cut a piece of the dark cake. "How is it you remember nothing of what Minnie does, and she remembers everything you do?"

"Does she? I'm an important brother."

"How?" Pop interjected. "His head's on the roof. How?"

"I don't pay any attention to Minnie," Ira defended himself with asperity. "A lot of times I'm not home on Fridays."

"You *weren't* home on Friday," Mom corrected. "Once indeed that was true. But not now. You don't see your friend Larry very often."

"Well, I do in college," Ira said shortly. Mom deliberated, raised her eyebrows eloquent of resignation.

"To tell you the truth, Friday nights, now that it's almost winter, I'm sure my poor daughter has an ample meal at Mamie's. It's the only time. I'll be happy when the end of her attendance comes this year. I'll forgive her the rest."

"Yeah? What do you mean, Mom?"

"You know how it is," said Mom. "You think Mamie feeds her the same meal the rest of the family eats? Even though Minnie pays her two dollars every week? A bygone day. Mamie gives her eggs, herring in tomato sauce, a bowl of *falsheh-zup*, such things."

Falsheh-zup. Ira's mind wandered to the words themselves: false soup, by which Mom meant meatless soup. How would John Synge have translated the words out of the speech of Aran Islanders? Pseudo-soup.

"Mamie does?"

"Believe me. It's only now, when night falls early, *erev Shabbes* comes early, and Zaida *davens* to an end before dark, they all eat Friday-night supper together. Then she runs off to the college. And Jonas is there too—of course."

"Another pious Jew," Pop commented.

"Well, that's his nature." Mom welcomed Pop's participation in spite of acrimony. "As you're not, he is. Why else would Zaida stay at Mamie's if Jonas weren't observant?"

"*Shoyn tsat tse zahn a mensh.*" Screwing up his face to the utmost, and snuffling as he spoke, Pop caricatured his long-nosed brother-in-law. "Telling me it was time I behaved like a man. *I* behaved like a man. That runt. I spat in his face."

Mom sat perfectly still a moment, and then, animating herself, squealed into her glass.

"She has to kiss the glass every time," Pop disparaged. "Can't you drink a glass of *chai* without a fife?"

"Well, then I won't," Mom conciliated. "I ought to learn to drink tea from a saucer."

"I didn't know Mamie was like that," Ira said, to lead away from the volatile.

"Uh!" Pop voiced his contempt. "A lot you know."

"What's there to say?" Mom shielded her son. "Minnie isn't Mamie's child. It's a boon to Minnie as it is. She doesn't have to fly like mad from one subway to another. Well, what were we saying?" She took a cautious sip of tea. "I have such an ugly quirk: I suck the glass," she apologized. "We were saying—yes—Minnie? No. Ah, yes. To my mind every Jew owes Schwartzbart a debt of gratitude for ridding the world of that monster."

"Well, you already said that." Ira stared at Mom askance. "You said enough about it."

She laughed—culpably, nodded her broad countenance in almost abject willingness to preserve harmony. "What else were we talking about?"

"Nyeh, nyeh, nyeh—*yenta*," Pop accused, then turned to Ira for confirmation. "She's tangled in this Schwartzbart as if he were an angel, a messiah."

"Still, he risked his life for Jews. Another Petlyura will know what awaits him, no? Dead he is, as Ira says, and may he rot too where he lies. But if there came another brute like him, he might think twice before he commits such atrocities against Jews. Is it true or not?"

"A *khlyup* is a *khlyup*." Pop's rimless eyeglasses reflected the candlelight. "If you think that a Roosky *goy* will ever be dissuaded by this example, then you're deceiving yourself. Read and read—to what avail?"

"But they were *khlyups* who gave Czar *Kolky*, that foe of Israel, his just deserts. Every Jew rejoiced."

"Why? Because there were Jews among them," Pop countered. "A Trotsky, a Zinoviev, a Kamenev. I don't even know the names. Jews ran out of the yeshivas to join the Bolsheviks. But now, see for yourself: Trotsky flees. They need him no longer. It won't be the same with the others? Wait, just wait, Leah."

"Now the prophet speaks!" Mom shrugged her shoulders. "But meanwhile they let a Jew live in Russia," said Mom.

"Meanwhile," Pop echoed in rebuttal. "Every letter from a Russian Jew to America begs for help: send a few rubles in God's name. We perish from hunger here. Russian Jews write the *roman* for you and Mrs. Shapiro for a few pennies, just to buy bread."

"Then what do you say is best—for the poor man?"

"Americhka," said Pop. "For the poor or the rich. The *goy* still despises us, but he lets us make a living. He doesn't know about pogroms. A Jonas, like my brother-in-law, a mouse, can be a partner in a restaurant, can work his way up in the world. As my brother Gabe in St. Louis says, one need only work hard and vote Republican, and everyone can prosper here."

"I didn't know elephants were kosher," Ira bantered.

Mom laughed.

"Epikouros," said Pop. "Scoffer."

"Why? I just wanted to know."

"Yeh, why? On the *Epikouros* and on the Zionisten may the same blighted year befall both."

Ira was well aware of Pop's dislike of atheism, especially Ira's, but he couldn't recall Pop's expressing an opinion on Zionism, and such a vehement opinion at that. Ira really felt no interest in Zionism whatever; he felt condescending, actually. Just the least curiosity as to why Pop was so exercised on the subject. He debated with himself whether to challenge Pop in order to find out why he had suddenly taken such a strong stand, then decided not too: for the sake of keeping the Sabbath tranquil.

"This." Pop tapped the lower corner of the newspaper. And to Mom again: "Would you read this, you would read something of importance."

"I read it," said Mom. "That they're trying to redeem Israel."

"That's what you think, these idiots, with Rothschild urging them on. These are *our* idiots. Not Russian Jews who think they'll transform the *mujik* into a noble creature: he'll abide Jews. But Jews of all lands befuddled into returning to Israel, into redeeming Israel, the Land of Israel. Did you ever hear of such a thing?"

"So what is so wrong with Jews building a homeland there?"

"Because without a Messiah, there can be no return of Jews from the dispersion into the Land of Israel. Every rabbi has taught us that. Every Jew knows it. They know it as well as anyone. Still they persist. What they're doing is a disgrace before God and man. A dire fate awaits them, that's a for-sure." Pop said the last words in English.

Ira stood up. So that was it? Lacking one Messiah. Cause for animus and all this diatribe. Ira smirked to himself. Not that he was any more concerned than before. Ludicrous though Pop's insistence on the need for the Messiah's advent to redeem Israel was. That notion of the Messiah—Ira walked over to the china closet under which he had placed his notebook with his blue-bound *Collected Poems of John Milton* on top—that notion of the Messiah was like the notion of infinity, the equivalent of never. "When the messiah comes," Ira smirked to himself again. Mom or Pop or any of the *mishpokha* would say, when the Messiah comes, then this or that or the other obligation or event would be fulfilled or take place—meaning one whose chances were nil. Would it be called a euphemism for never? Or a circumlocution for never.

Anyway, it looked as if the Friday night would come to a peaceful end. The candles were about to go out, guttering in molten wax. Mom seemed to have forgotten her two dollars, or at least gotten over her animosity at having been stalled off. Pop was safely engrossed in his *Der Tag*. All was well with the world—at one flight up in the front of 108 East 119th Street. And Minnie would be home soon. All safe and serene. Watchman, what of the night? Fine, except himself.

What did Milton say? Ira sat down. *License they mean when they cry Liberty.* He turned pages. He'd have to skim, try to read a little faster, maybe skip a little. He preferred not to; he worshiped Milton. That in itself was guarantee of his doing better than his usual dismal level of work in the course. Maybe a B, glory be. He reached the page he had been reading, as Pop slid the back pages of the newspaper to Mom. Homeland in Zion, cloudland in Zion—he deliberately kept his eyes from focusing on the page, so he could pursue the fitful notion in his mind. Jesus, these Jews . . .

But it was strange. The minute he thought about Jews, and realized he was one of them, more or less caught up in the same fate with them, more or less, even though he wanted no part of them, the entire conception dissipated, became a nebula. Who were they, what were they? He couldn't seem to think any further: the thought dissolved, connectives and all. God, here he was again, in the same old predicament. He had no being; the person in his head had no foundation, no perch, no purchase. Same old thing: the rubbled guy—there was no such word: the crumbled guy. Burned, seared, that was it, branded, cauterized—oh, hell. He could say it a hundred, well, a dozen different ways. It always came down to the same thing—and down was right. Here was Minnie coming home any minute now. He didn't have a single solitary chance, either with her or, under the circumstances, with anything. Where Izzy Winchel of Polo Ground days didn't hesitate to contrive any scheme, utter the most barefaced lie, in order to cheat a sports fan out of a little money, as though all compunction were vitiated in the pursuit of the dollar—at the same time as Izzy showed not the least interest in sex, so Ira, overly conscious Ira, seemed to himself almost the reverse. Marked, branded. That was how he thought of himself.

Ruined . . . what a shame. . . .

Plain flat intrinsic state, you could look at it clear-eyed sometimes . . . no self-pity, no pyrotechnics. He would rather have that wicked rapture back than any delight forward. He would rather be mired down in the sordid ecstasy of the past than proceed to the decent sanity of the future. Something like that. Those combinations and modulations of fear and furtiveness, cunning, guilt—an incest cocktail: break the word in half, and you had it. He composed his features, returned his concentrated gaze to Milton—if only he had concentrated so intently in the filthy *cheder* of his youth:

> *But his doom*
> *Reserved him for more wrath; for now the thought*
> *Both of lost happiness and lasting pain*
> *Torments him; round he throws his baleful eyes,*
> *That witnessed huge affliction and dismay*
> *Mixed with obdurate pride and steadfast hate:*

Lost in Satan's throes, Ira continued to read, until he paused a moment, reflecting somberly. He heard Mom ask:

"Are you going to work tomorrow, Chaim?"

And heard Pop reply: "I'll go to the union hall. I'll see what they have to offer. If it's something promising," Pop drawled rabbinically, "I'll work. If not, I'll take *Shabbes* off. I'll be a devout Yiddle like Jonas. I'll rest. Sunday I have a *benket* anyway."

"In Cunyilant?"

"In Rockaway. No tips. Every table has a service charge. You rush your *kishkehs* out, but you make a few dollars."

"A toiler's life, what else," said Mom.

"What else? *Mazel*. One needs *mazel*. Where to find *mazel*? A lucky man can balk the Devil himself."

Mom listened with noncommittal patience. She raised an eyebrow in forbearance, sighed.

"No?" Pop demanded.

"You believe in *mazel*?" Mom asked.

"I just told you I did."

"And what would *mazel* have brought you?" Mom smiled, teasing, knowing. "Something you don't have."

"*Mazel* would have brought me a clever wife, speaking of something I don't have."

"You chose her. She pleased you, no?"

"Well, lost and gone." Pop prolonged uneasy railery. "A colt, don't you know. Later, he gets horse sense."

"Would a clever woman have married you? She would have sought cleverness to match, no? She would have sought shrewdness, judgment, prudence—"

"Aha, here she comes once more."

"Let's not begin that again!" Ira interjected testily. "I've got to do a little studying for an exam. Please. I hardly got started."

"Your father has just eaten a fine *Shabbes* meal on the pittance he doles out to me for my weekly allowance—on which he's still owing, mind you—and he tells me I'm not a clever wife."

"I heard him. He didn't say you weren't clever."

"What else does not being a clever wife mean?"

"You know what he means. He means not clever in business," Ira rejoined impatiently. "You don't have to pick him up on everything he says."

"Who incites these spats?"

"You do." Ira meant to be facetious. His levity was taken amiss. Mom twisted her countenance in wry grimace, and said something in Polish that sounded like *ya bem tvoiyoo motch.*

"Okay. '*Full fathom five my father lies,*'" Ira orated. "Now can I read my book?"

"Go, read your book. A good son you are too."

"You see?" Pop tested a precarious truce. "Immediately she becomes excited. I was at Ella's this afternoon—"

"Oh, that's the business prospects you were appraising."

"*Noo?* I can't go to see your sister?"

"You were so late, I thought you were skulking in some movim pickcheh."

"I was late because I went to Ella's. I may not go there?"

"Go. Go. A good place for business prospects. She condones a pinch or a pat, my sister, with her husband in the insane asylum?"

"Well, what else? She's a mule like you?"

"Oh, for Christ's sake!"

"Do me a favor." Pop wagged his head at Ira. "Spare us your *fahr Crite secks.* It's a Jewish home here. It's Friday night. The candles are still burning."

"Yeah." Ira's chest filled. "I see. I thought they were out."

Strange, how the mind rummaged about for a literary quotation to solace itself with, something noble and universal. *And Troy went up in one high funeral gleam.* Larry had quoted that. Supposing he himself had gone on studying *Khumish* in the *cheder* on 9th Street, could he have said to himself in Hebrew: "Though they forget Thee, yet will not I forget Thee. Behold, I have graven Thee upon the palms of my hands"? Ah, how beautiful that was. He looked down on the open pages of blank verse. Hopeless to read against their everlasting bickering.

"With a wife like Ella," Pop meditated aloud, "I could have thrived. With a wife like Ella, one can get something done. She's lively, quick to see where a dollar can be made. And how deft she is and apt, ah!" Mom's face was turned away, lips curling. "She can jest. She's full of

savor. And she can weigh and deliberate—*yi, yi, yi.* How many blocks—
to the step!—you need to go from the corner of Fifth Avenue and
116th Street, from her house, to the nearest store with thread and rib-
bons and thimbles and things a woman needs to sew. A store like that
on the corner of 116th Street can make a dollar. I venture to say she
would soon learn how to treat a customer in a luncheonette. And ah,
such a welcome as her children give me! 'It's Uncle Hymie! It's Uncle
Hymie!' they shout—as soon as I appear. Even the youngest of the
three prances about me. 'Uncle Hymie, tell us how you drive a horse.
Uncle Hymie, make the noise a horse makes. Uncle Hymie, make a
noise to giddap.' I come into her house, and I skim bliss."

"Well, go live there," Mom invited, her short throat flushing.
"Skim bliss. Who bars your way?"

"Uh! Look at her. The truth chokes her."

"The truth is, Chaim, my sister is careless. She has a husband in
the asylum, she's careless. I don't know it?"

"Uh!" Pop derided. "Find what you seek, but pray let me be. *Bist
mishugeh?*"

"*Ov toit,*" Mom said pointedly. "Mad to death."

"Seek out a suitable tomb then."

Ira sat with locked fingers. Pent, he knew only too well what Mom
was talking about: Ella *was* careless. She wore no drawers. She crossed
her legs often. You could see all the way up to her bush, a great big female bush. He was at her house with Mom, about a few months after
Max was committed, and staring at her cunt gave Ira such a hard-on,
he couldn't help it. He was so close to coming he went into Ella's bathroom, and in three strokes jacked off: in a trice. He hated the recall—
was that Ella's substitute, sublimate? And Pop scrounging like a jackal.
Jesus!

"I'll go crazy myself, if you don't cut that out," Ira complained sullenly. "You said it was Friday. It's Friday night."

"*Noo,* go for a walk." There was a note of pleading in Mom's voice.

"I told you I had a test."

"It's my fault you have a nag like your mother?"

Maybe he ought to leave. Interrupt the course of backbiting. He
had a hunch he was the irritant. He ought to get his coat. Get the hell
out. It was cold outdoors, but what of it? Ten minutes. Less. Minnie

would be home. Ira closed the book on his thumb, opened it again, irresolute. He had to read: page 125—

"Even a wife like Mamie, carbuncles cover her thick hide, still, she loaned Joe all her savings, her whole bankbook, he would have enough to become a partner with your brothers. From a little cap maker, a snuffling namby-pamby, he's become a restaurant owner. I'm condemned to a mate who hoards only for *shmattas*—and a Persian lamb coat."

"Joe is a businessman." Mom refused to budge.

"And I'm not?"

"Joe is circumspect and collected. Are you? No. Joe can reckon. Can you? I don't say it's your fault. Have I ever said it was your fault? It's your trait. You become flustered. When you were a milkman you were always *shutt*." Mom used the English word "short." "*Shutt* and again *shutt* in your receipts. When you were a trolley car conductor you were always *shutt*. I worked with you in the little delicatessen on 116th Street, you became bewildered—"

The little delicatessen on 116th Street, ha, boy—attention found release in lubricity: static flashed off in jagged streaks of recall. Those evenings, alone, with Minnie, wow, at leisure, post–Bar Mitzva, what a charge, what a bolt! If only that damned delicatessen had succeeded. Yeah. He wrung his hands in concealment.

"*I* became bewildered? If I became bewildered, it was because of you!" Pop accused Mom irately. "The woman slices salami like lemon wedges. Just like for tea. Go make a sandwich from that for a customer."

"The customers liked my service better than yours. I didn't become *z'misht* the way you did. I'm not telling you that to bait you." Mom raised a deprecating hand against her breast. "I'm saying that only to show you that you're better off being a simple waiter, working a steady job, living quietly on your earnings, your tips. What does Max, Sadie's husband, do? The brothers wanted to take him in for a partner. He didn't want the headaches. He wanted to work his lunch and supper, and go home. What do the rest of the tenants who live here do, Jew and gentile alike? See, Mr. Beigman on the third floor works in a cleaning and dyeing shop; Lefkowitz on the third floor in the back is a baker. What is Shapiro in the back? An upholsterer. And McIntyre on the top floor, whose wife has only that one fang in her head? In a foundry making stoves. And beside he gives his wife the whole pay envelope—only keeps enough for a bottle of *moshkeh* on a Saturday night. D'Angelo on the second floor works in a barber shop—"

"Away with your stupid prating! I'll be a common *shlepper* like the rest: a noodle porter all my life. I can't sit behind a cash register as well as your brothers, as well as that mealy-mouthed gnome?"

"I'm trying to tell you—"

"You're telling me nothing. Prattle. Ah, if I haven't a clever wife, had I but a little fortune in other things."

"Then go into business with Ella!"

"In a minute. If she had what to contribute, if she didn't have three young children. *Ai.* There's a coffeepot on 26th Street, if I had another thousand dollars I could buy it—like nothing. Give those Greeks two thousand dollars, and I could tell them to take their hats and coats and get out. They're losing their shirts."

"*Oy, gevald.*" Mom snatched at her cheek. "If they're losing their shirts, how can you hope to succeed?"

"It's a coffeepot, don't you understand? It's in a furriers' district. Furriers don't like coffeepots. They like—as if—" he twirled his hand—"half kosher. They're still Jews."

"*Noo?*"

"Ha!" Pop gloried in his vision. "I would take out the round white tables, and put in square wooden tables. I would take out the white tiles from the wall, it shouldn't look like a toilet, and put in nice brown panels. And immediately I would hire away Schildkraut's salad woman for a couple of dollars more a week."

"Why Schildkraut's?" Mom asked apathetically.

"You don't understand anything," Pop rebuked. "It would be a vegetarian restaurant."

"Aha."

"Wouldn't Schildkraut's nose fall when he came to the door, and saw me standing in my vegetarian restaurant across the street."

"Across the street!" Mom cried in dismay. "You mean it's in the same street?"

"The same street. The same street," Pop reiterated triumphantly. "He'll know better next time to fire a man like me. After all I did for him. I opened up the restaurant in the morning. I took in the bags of fresh rolls and bread, and the boxes of milk. I dragged in the crates of vegetables—"

"So what has that to do with it?"

"To get fired?"

"No. To open a restaurant across the street."

"Let him see what he did!"

"But you pulled the chair out from under the headwaiter!"

"He was a right-winger!"

"*Oy,*" Mom mourned. She turned to her son. "Am I not condemned, am I not cursed?"

"Mom, he's just talking," Ira burst in heatedly. "He's just imagining. There's no restaurant."

"No. Because she hoards for a Persian lamb coat!"

"And hoard I will," Mom said defiantly. "I'll pour my skrimping and skimping into his wild schemes? *Ai,* judgment, judgment. He sees one vegetarian restaurant in the street already. And he has to squeeze in with another—why? Out of spite for a boss who sacked him. Isn't that an infant's mind?"

"Say that again and I'll fling something at your head!"

"Fling," Mom challenged. "A novelty."

"There can't be two vegetarian restaurants in one block?" Pop chose to ignore her provocation. "How many times have you seen two jewelers in the same block, two clothing stores, two hardware stores, furniture, florists—even more than two? It's a furriers' district, I told you: furriers and furriers and furriers: of rabbit and of mink, of seal and sable. She babbles on."

"And people will shop from one vegetarian restaurant to the other—the way a buyer shops for clothing, for a diamond ring, for a dining-room set," Mom thrust.

"They won't shop," Pop parried. "If Schildkraut's has sand in the spinach, the next time they'll go elsewhere; they'll come to mine."

"And if you have sand in the spinach?"

"That's why I would hire away his salad woman. She would break in Ella with her wonderful hands. Don't you see?"

"*Oy,* mad to the death," said Mom. "Isn't this a child's mind?"

"Leah, I warn you!"

"Mom, please," Ira pleaded vehemently. "Can't you just let him talk? You're only making things worse all the time. Anh, what's the use." He snapped the book shut.

But Mom seemed obdurate beyond retrieval now, stony, irrevocably desolate. "I'm making things worse. I. Two dollars a whole week he owes me, and if I didn't flay him for it, he'd cheat me. He'd forget. But me, who penny by penny, with tears, scraped together a few hundred dollars toward some comfort in my life, he would wrest away to squander in his lunatic schemes. Oh, my mother, where you lie there in the grave: 'Break it off,' you said. 'Give him back his gift. He's a lunatic.' Everyone in Tysmenicz comes to me with the same story, everyone who knows him: '*Er's a mishugeneh*. Break it off.' Ha, Mamaleh, Mamaleh, that I didn't heed you. But with four younger sisters at my back, how could I? 'No, Mamaleh,' I said. 'My shoulders are broad. Sorrows I can bear, griefs won't break me.'"

"And good wares they foisted on me too!"

"I'm getting the hell out of here!" Ira slammed his book down on the table and sprang to his feet.

"Go, go," Mom invited. "Who's keeping you? Do you still have to hear this story?"

"He won't take your lousy few hundred dollars!" Ira raged. "You're out of your mind!"

"No? I don't know his burnings and his blisterings. He'll burn at me until I offer it, just for relief."

"He won't, I tell you! He can't!"

"Ah, would she come to her senses!" Pop addressed unseen auditors in a transport of fulfillment. "Would she sponsor me with that few hundred. The balance, if the bank didn't loan me, suppliers would advance. And then"—Pop glowed with inner light—"who would sidle up to the restaurant window to peer in and count my customers? *Her* brothers: Moe and Saul, that swindler, and Max and Harry with his long nose. 'Come in,' I would wave from the cash register. 'Come in.' And I would say: 'Why loiter outside? Have a prune tart. Have a coffee.' I can be munificent too. And who would be the first one to brag that her husband had a *kopf* for business like no other? She."

"Mad to the death." Mom sat perfectly still, her palms flat on the figured red cloth of the housedress on her broad thighs; only her head shook, barely, as if trembling—trembling with incredulity. "Isn't this a dreamer? Isn't this a child? What I married." Then suddenly aroused: "Talk till you drop! This time I won't budge. You can't tempt me. Ah." She rubbed her breast in a fierce joy of triumph. "The few hundred are mine."

"Cow!"

"Baby!"

"You goad me?" Pop jumped to his feet. "I warned you!"

"Fling, if you dare. Mad dog!" Mom pushed the table suddenly and stood up. A candle guttered out, smoked.

"Pop!" Ira stood between them. "For Christ's sake, will you quit it! What the hell, are you going crazy?"

"Out of the way! *Shtarkeh! Na!*" He gave Ira a sudden shove.

"I fear you," Mom taunted. "I'm not that same timid, docile slave you brought over from Galitzia."

"No? Let's see." He had turned quite pale. All in one motion he seized Mom's half-empty glass from the table and dashed the tea in her face.

"You filth! You mange!" Mom's voice seemed to drop whole octaves, appallingly, viscerally frenzied. "Vile mannikin!" She wiped drops from her chin that were falling on her florid bosom. "Be torn to shreds."

"You still seek? I'll slap your gross mouth too!" Pop advanced on her.

"And I'll submit?"

Ira threw himself at his father. "That's enough, Pop. Cut it out!"

"Let go!"

"No!"

"I said let go!" Pop stamped his foot.

"No!"

"No?" Pop made a sudden vicious thrust downward toward Ira's crotch—and not a moment too soon Ira pinned Pop's arms to his sides.

"Cut it out, Pop! You do that again—"

They tussled, swayed. Compact, surging with rage, Pop's head in his felt hat butted his son's face, while he tried to bowl him over, yelled curses in Yiddish, and Mom screamed—and then, *from below:* a series of terrifying thumps, like demented gaveling at a mad auction: thump, thump, thump, and unintelligible epithets like shouted bids, undistinguishable babel of opprobrium converging on one distinct word: "Jews!" Thump. Thump. Thump. Pop went slack. And the next instant, as if he were falling away, he tore himself from Ira's hold. Thump. Thump. Thump.

"Ah!" Mom patted her stomach in an exaltation of gloating. "A splendid *goy*! Oh, is that a fine *goy*! Stamp your foot again, Chaim!"

"Leah." Pop retreated. "Leah, enough."

"Why enough? Knock their ceiling down. He'll come up and smash your paltry face. I would rejoice."

"Leah, my jewel."

"Huh. Huh. I'll tell him: there he stands." Her head snapped back, and she pointed at Pop. "*Oy, Raboinish ha loilim*, let him come up!"

"Leah, please," Pop entreated. "Say you tumbled, you tripped, you fell. You knocked a chair over."

"No. Let him know what a cur I have here. Look, I'll show him." She wiped the moisture from her cheek, mocking her husband in what English she had. "Mister Irisher, *azoi* you do vit your vife's gless tea? Look on mein housedress, vie sit's vet. *Ai*, may he buffet you soundly!"

"Mom!" Ira implored hopelessly. "Calm down." And in a sudden fit of wrath: "You were to blame yourself. You didn't have to bring up that goddamn two dollars. Friday, let the goddamn thing go!" He pawed at the air. "Two lousy bucks!"

"*Gey mir in der erd.* It was my money. A whole week he tormented my blood—and now this?" Her chin lowered to the dark stain below the neckline of the housedress. "Lord bless me, that Esau is on the way!"

"Leah, I beg before you. Two dollars is due you. True. True. You're right. Here. Let's not dispute." Pop tugged at his pocketbook, fingered among the banknotes. In the frantic haste he tore the bills out, a third greenback clung to the second.

"*Na, a drittle!*" Irate with himself, he threw all three to the floor. "Here. Peace. Turn him aside. You're my wife, no?"

"Burn to a cinder—for my sake!" The tears starting from her eyes,

Mom stooped and gathered up the scattered dollar bills. "How hideous, my life. *Martira. Martira. L'chaim, na,*" she punned bitterly on Pop's name, and straightening up, the three greenbacks in one hand, she made a fig with the other: "To life indeed."

"Do you hear anyone?" Poised for retreat, Pop shrank against the bedroom door. "Ira, child, tell me."

"Yeah." Ira thought he heard something in the hall. "Yes." Now what? "I hear somebody."

"Maybe it's the virago. She won't devour you," Mom advised her husband—as she herself staunchly confronted the door to the hall. Pop slipped into the dark of the bedroom. Without a knock, the knob turned, the hall door opened—Minnie entered. "Come out, my stalwart," Mom called. "It's your daughter."

Everything took on a different tenor the moment Minnie entered. She dissipated tension. Rosy-cheeked from the cold, breathing quickly with hurrying and climbing of stairs, she looked pretty and animated as she got out of her coat, took off her cloche, shook her reddish bobbed hair.

"You didn't see the downstairsniks?" Pop reappeared from the bedroom. "You didn't see the Irisher on the ground floor, *Tokhterel?*" The very sight of his daughter cheered him.

"No, Papa, I didn't see anybody," was her puzzled answer. "In the hall?" And as Mom took Minnie's coat and hat, saying, "Give me, I'll hang it up," Minnie noticed the stain on Mom's housedress. "Whatsa matter?" she asked in that pacifying tone she so often used with Pop and Mom.

"*Goor nisht,*" said Mom.

"It's the first time nobody asked me what I had to eat at Mamie's."

There were times when Minnie could have been a stranger, as far as Ira was concerned. No connection between the two: the impersonal young woman, with brows knit, reaching for the coat that Mom held, and continued to cling to. "What'd you spill?" Minnie asked.

"Nothing," said Mom. "I had to take the balance of my allowance from him. We became a little vexed, don't you know?"

"Oh, again? So why're you asking me if I saw somebody from downstairs?" She addressed Pop. "You mean the McRoneys?"

"Yeh, we bickered a little here." Pop made light of the matter.

Minnie understood his understatement. "So?"

"They knocked, a once-twice on the ceiling. You don't know Irishers? Right away they get mad."

As he spoke, Mom nodded, in complex, nullifying agreement.

Minnie looked at Ira for elaboration. "Listen," he began brusquely, and then snickered: "They had their regular workout—over two bucks."

"So what's so funny about it?"

"It's not. I didn't say it was, did I?"

"You laughed," she accused. "You didn't have to say."

"Well, what're you gonna do? They squawk over two bucks. You'd think it was two thousand." He leaned back.

"It's not funny, you know. You should feel real sorry," Minnie scolded. "Over a nothing from money. Why didn't you try to keep it from happening—say something to them?" She was scolding him, speaking entirely in English.

"Me? Ho-ho."

"It makes me feel so bad. And over money. Mom, why do you have to do that? It's Friday. There's still a little light from a candle."

"Tell him," Mom said bluntly, pointing at Pop.

"Tell me? A nag of nags—"

"All right, that's enough!" Minnie said sharply.

"Indeed, enough," Mom agreed. "What's doing at Mamie's? Let's better talk of that."

"Oh, do I have news for you!"

"*Azoy?* Wait, wait," Mom said eagerly. "I'll hang your coat and hat. *Noo, zug,*" Mom urged. "What?" She couldn't refrain from a terminal *"Oy, veh!"*

Released from self-consciousness, Pop's eyes became browner and glossier, especially when he listened to Minnie.

"Zaida wasn't there tonight," she said.

"What? My father wasn't there?" Mom exclaimed—between shock and disbelief. "What happened?"

"Nothing. He wasn't there. He's not living there anymore. He's not living at Mamie's." Minnie raised her voice.

"Oh, I swoon!"

"I nearly did too when they told me. When I came in and Zaida wasn't there, I was s-o-o surprised."

"*Oy, gevald!* What for? Why? *Oy!*"

"He's living with Sadie."

"Sadie, you mean Moe's Sadie?" Mom's confusion was utter. "What happened there at Mamie's? What? They told you?"

"Of course they told me—and is Mamie angry! I never saw her so upset—and angry. You know what he did?"

"*Noo?*" Mom demanded peremptorily.

"He sneaked away. He didn't say anything. He just plain sneaked out of the house. He took his clothes, his *siddurs,* his *tvillim*—you know, all those Jewish things—his *thallis.* Even his *yashikish,* his big pillows. And away he went."

"I don't believe it! My father?"

"Well, don't believe it," Minnie retorted. "Your father! Mamie didn't believe it either."

"Who would take him? *Vie zoy?* How could he—"

"Morris took him. He asked Mrs. Schwartz next door to call Moe on Mamie's telephone to come for him—because Mamie was in court with a dispossess. Moe should come right away with the car from his house in Flushing, so Zaida could get to Sadie's before *Shabbes.* Oh, I tell you. Was there a something. Morris scribbled he was taking Zaida to Sadie's. Then he called Mamie on the telephone: the old man is at Sadie's. I'm glad I got there after all the excitement. Oh, was Mamie mad. 'He'll never come back to live here again,' Mamie said."

"*Azoy?*" Mom slumped in her chair.

"The old *kocker,*" Pop jeered. "And Jonas, stunted Jonas, what did he say?"

"You know Joe. *Mir nisht, dir nisht.* If he doesn't want to live here, he doesn't want to live here."

"Ah, khah khah!" Pop reveled. "Sadie will give him a lively time. She's blind as a cadaver. When she begins mixing up the meat utensils, the cutlery and the dishes, with the dairy dishes, *oy,* will he feel a nausea."

"But why did he leave?" Grave and intense in perplexity, Mom sought an answer. "Didn't I go there Sundays, after Baba died, often early in the morning before shopping? I helped Mamie tidy his room, fluff his pillows, change sheets. And kosher. Mamie is faultless. In every shred of food. In every dish, in every spoon. No one could ever be more so. In everything!"

"And the Passover dishes too," Minnie concurred. "Everything wrapped up, separate. And packed up, no *khumitz* shouldn't touch it. Touch it? Shouldn't even come near it. I don't know why," she said abruptly. "Moe said over the telephone that Zaida said his grandchildren were too much for him."

"Oh, the two young hussies," Mom interpreted with rising emphasis. "That's it. The springing and the dancing and the racket of the radio. But then"—she mustered argument to the contrary—"that's nothing new. No, something, something has happened. For my father to bolt away without a word of farewell, without a word of notice. No. Something has deeply disturbed him. Deep. Deep."

"Go," Pop opined, "he's grown fearful of the Portorickies. A Jew with a beard in a neighborhood full of Spanyookies. And the blacks too are already there. Ella whispered to me that Hannah was to be a bridesman at a Portorickie wedding. *Goyish*, Catolickehs. He may have gotten wind of it. He's fleeing. With Sadie he'll be spared that grief. Sadie has only boys, three boys."

"Still, he could have said something," Mom countered. "Ben Zion Farb, my father, was never one afraid to speak his mind."

"No, you're right, Mom. It's something else," Minnie agreed. "But still, he wouldn't say what." She grimaced expressively. "Only he *fumfit* about things going on late at night with his grandchildren. He must have been dreaming. He says Stella is carrying on with somebody—something shameful. She lets somebody in and out after he goes to bed. Can you imagine, sixteen years old, and she's letting a *geliebter* in and out of the house at night?

"What?" Ira cast off listlessness. "What does he mean by that?"

"You ask me?" Minnie shot back. "If Mamie herself doesn't know. Who believes him? She asked Stella, Hannah—they looked at her like she was crazy."

"No. I mean in and out of where?"

"I told you: in and out of the house, that's where." Minnie was close to ridicule. "One night he could swear there was somebody with her. Then he started to think about it, and it kept him awake. He started to think who and how and where and when." She shrugged. "Maybe he told Moe more. Maybe Moe told Mamie more. They didn't tell me." Her manner was fraught with finality; she yawned. "Oh, I had such a hard day today. That new office manager. He's like a nervous string bean. And then the two classes at CCNY. I tell you, Mom."

"Boy, that's a new one, a new complaint about his grandchildren," Ira persisted obliquely.

"Of course it's a new one. He yelled about the radio, he yelled about the jazz bands, the Charleston they did. And of course, the *trombehnyicks* that came into the house. But never this."

"I wonder why?"

"I told you all he said." Minnie spoke through a yawn. "'My grandchildren, my grandchildren. I don't wannna live here.' You wanna know more, go over there yourself. Go to Mamie's. Go to Zaida in Flushing."

"Yeah."

"*Tockin* yeah," Mom echoed her son; and then tutted in dissatisfaction. "Who'll guide me now, if I want to visit him? It's an interminable journey to Flushing, to Sadie and Moe. I'll have to ask Mamie when she goes. Maybe Moe would drive us out there in his car. *Ai*, what to make of it? One grows old." She worried a crumb of *kholleh* on the tablecloth.

"I'll take you next Sunday, Ma, in the subway," Minnie offered.

"Good. Take her," Pop approved—scornfully—in Yinglish. "But *fahr a fahr* sure I'll tell you. Me he won't see. The old leech won't see me, and the blind ignoramus in Flushing won't see me either."

"No need to enlighten us," said Mom. "We're well informed."

"It won't harm you to visit him less frequently too," Pop retaliated. "He'll have less chance to smear me with his dung."

"Chaim," Mom began angrily, caught herself. "You don't have to worry. I'll no longer fluff his pillows on a Sunday morning."

"Good. Let the blind one do it."

Ira contracted within himself. What did it mean? Zaida's sudden departure. His muttering about his grandchildren—Jesus, had the old boy figured out something? What had Minnie said? He couldn't abide . . . what was going on . . . heard Stella . . . carrying on with somebody? Oh, hell, how could he guess? He was a smart old guy, though. All because of that superglorious night, hoisted her pink damp melonions on his tergo hook, whammoh, Israel. Ramp, oh, gramp, oh, gold lions of Judah. Jesus, what a night, what a scare—Now, wait a minute, think, think. Crazy coming back with condoms on Mamie's dollar . . . Jew-dough. No, no, no. Wait a minute. Did Zaida suspect? What if he did? *Wait a minute!* Oh, God!

IX

The fact was the actual event had taken place in the late fall of 1927, had taken place when Ira was in the first semester of his senior year at CCNY. Fact. And he surmised, he had good reason to believe, that if he had aroused Zaida's suspicions by creeping out of the house in his stockinged feet, under cover of Stella's tread, he had confirmed those suspicions in a much more prosaic, a much less melodramatic way: Ira had paid Mamie a visit on the Sunday before, and only Zaida and Stella were home. With only Zaida for chaperon, Ira had been a little too eager to get at Stella. He had paid his ritual, preliminary call on Zaida, and then not to lose the opportunity of having Stella almost without company—without Mamie's presence, or Hannah's—he had been a bit too abrupt in his leave-taking of his grandfather. Oh, Ira remembered well. Because of what happened after Ira had got his piece (as it would happen, only a run-of-the-mill piece). The old man did something he had never done before: he called Ira into his room again—just as Ira was leaving, walking down the hall toward the apartment door. And what had the old man done? Under pretext, Ira was sure, of reminiscing about his early boyhood, he had given Ira a lecture on how one obtained a wife, according to Judaism. Sitting at the keyboard of his word processor over sixty years later, Ira tried to remember his grandfather's version. It wasn't easy: how much sixty years had eroded! But it all seemed to add up to a hint on Zaida's part that he was on to something. It *seemed* a hint—until Minnie brought the tidings of Zaida's departure from Mamie's. Then it no longer seemed a hint; it *was* a hint, and a broad one, in fact, a disclosure of the old man's suspicions about the behavior of his two grandchildren. The

more Ira dwelled on the news Minnie had brought, the more worried he became, the more certain he was that Zaida knew what his two grandchildren
were up to.

Ira could no longer sit still at home, wondering whether Zaida had
told Moe, Moe had told Mamie, whether his sins had caught up with
him—or whether (there was a chance after all that Pop was right) the
old man had left Mamie's for altogether different reasons, reasons
that had nothing to do with Ira's shameful pratting of his sixteen-year-
old kid cousin. But guilt wouldn't down, guilt prevailed over hope.
The old twist in the psyche, the plane-geometry neurosis Ira dubbed
it, chafed within him as the genie of the fable chafed within the vase.
No, he had to find out. Walk over to Mamie's, and find out. Yes—even
if Mamie said nothing, Joe said nothing, the one who would certainly
know and tell him would be Stella; she'd know. He could feel his mind
trapped in disquieting refrain: walk over, find out. Walk over, find out.
Tolle lege, the same as Saint Augustine kept hearing—Saint Augustine:
same one Zaida talked about. Same night. *Tolle lege.* Walk over and find
out. He probably wouldn't sleep tonight if he didn't. Stay awake imagining things. And if he did find out, if it was true that Zaida knew and
had told Moe and Mamie, and Joe knew, well, what? Ira could imagine
that too. No, wait till tomorrow, late Saturday afternoon, Joe's day off
would be over, Joe would be gone. Find out then. Not have to confront
the little guy, Stella's father, as well as Mamie. But then all day Saturday, study for a test, try to skim Milton, knowing his own goose was
cooked, his universal disgrace: Leah Stigman's *ausgestudierteh* college
boy, Leah's preen and pride pratting his dumb little cousin. Stella,
Stella. Why did his star, his *stella,* no longer shine over Mt. Morris
Park? It was getting dark after all. And of course, Mom would learn of
it, Mom, Pop, and now that searching brightness that beamed from
her eyes when she returned from shopping Sunday morning, searching his and Minnie's faces—wow.

Ira got up from the table, went into his cold, dark little bedroom,
and got his overcoat. He would just stroll about, all right? he told himself. He didn't have to go to Mamie's. He'd just try to think. Maybe he

could convince himself there was nothing to the whole thing. Zaida had left Mamie's. He had a right to leave. His four sons contributed toward his keep; he could spend his room-and-board money any-where. Pop was right. The old man objected to the girls, the radio, maybe half-grown swains pestered him. Who knew? Sadie had three boys, no girls. Bet that was it. Bet. But if not, if Zaida didn't say any-thing, well—he could go on all night debating with himself.

For a moment the waning ivory moon above the gloomy gantries of the New York Central trestle seemed poised like a tusk at Ira as he pat-tered down the sandstone steps of the stoop to the sidewalk; boar's tusk aimed at Endymion, he thought, turning left on grubby, cold, dark, deserted 119th Street toward the corner at Park Avenue. Why did he have to think of that, being gored by a waning moon; he didn't like the image at all, the associations—just showed how uneasy he was. The November night air, the *Shabbes* air, nipped at the warmth he had just brought from the kitchen, the little warmth stored under his overcoat. He buttoned the garment all the way up. Single-breasted overcoats didn't retain the heat the way double-breasted coats did, even if they were both made of shoddy wool. He'd know better than to buy a secondhand Chesterfield next time. He had chosen it because Iz was wearing one. It made Iz look slim and ascetic and studious. Well . . . Ira plugged hands into pockets. Across the street, the old Jew-ish couple's shabby little candy store was closed. It was getting late anyway, and it was *Shabbes*. The only store open was Biolov's on the corner of Park Avenue, the resplendent show window featuring an al-most life-sized figure of a fisherman in sou'wester oilskins, facing a green amphora and lugging on his back a huge codfish above the leg-end SCOTT'S EMULSION. Good symbol, the codfish, reminiscent of Shakespeare's gags about the codpiece. His cod, and the moon goring him because of it.

He had told Mom—and the others—he was going for a walk, al-though it was almost nine-thirty. They were surprised. But perhaps that was all he was going to do: walk. Everything was still in suspen-sion—he kept going west toward Madison—and would be until . . . until who the hell knew . . . until he came home again. God, he forgot, until he was keyed up, the slummy—that was all it was: he kept coming back to the same word—the slummy, the dismal streets of East Harlem, as you slanted alone toward the lampposts on Madison. Joe would be there tonight, Jonas. How many times did he have to tell himself that? And—there was something else to take into consideration too, goddamn it—if he called on Mamie tonight, he'd lose his chance to drop in Saturday or Sunday—he couldn't drop in two days in a row. Looked suspicious. Two days. So no piece of ass, no screw—out of the question tonight—not with Joe there. And he'd lose his chance to get a buck from Mamie too, again because Joe was there—and Mamie wouldn't handle money on Friday night. No, no, he was nutty to drop in tonight. He was just plain stupid. But grandchildren, the old man had said: grandchildren. The old boy was in his bedroom studying Talmud—or something. No reason to think he'd got an inkling of what was going on in the front room, even though the radio was turned way down. This goddamn business of getting a piece of tail, getting a lay, a piece of hide, pussy, and all the other goddamn names they had for it, Jesus Christ, drove him nuts, yeah, drove him nuts, especially if he knew it could be had, and he didn't have to resort to ye cousin-handmaiden.

Leo had offered to set him up with his girl's girlfriend. Ira could have embraced and ravished Iola, Edith's former roommate, he had so impressed her with his story in the *Lavender,* and so disappointed her with his manhood. He could even have hoarded Mamie's dollars for a whore now and again. What was a dose compared to this—this? Incest, of Biblical proportions, committed while Zaida, earnest, kosherer than kosher Zaida, pored over Talmud in the back room.

But now—what if Zaida couldn't tolerate the noise, the proto-goyishness, he observed in the girls? Now his excuse, his raison d'être, was in Flushing. Now Mom wouldn't even have to stop at Mamie's anymore to help make Zaida's bed and straighten out his room.

But what the hell was the difference now? Longer or shorter absence. He couldn't get it anyway. No, no, better wait until tomorrow, tomorrow late afternoon. Forget about his fears of Zaida's getting wise—he was a sap to think so. Go there late Saturday, sit next to the fancy new radio, turn it up a little; and Stella would drift over at the right moment, shift the sling of her teddy aside, squat down on his hard-on. But all this was a day away. Christ, he ought to be home, reviewing Milton.

On to Fifth Avenue. He turned. Well, not the first time he'd mashed a grade hunting and haunting a lay. And here he was again, walking briskly downtown . . . just to find out there was nothing to worry about . . . heading downtown. . . .

Boyoboy, hadn't Mom and Pop battled over the two bucks though. He had to laugh, except it was so goddamn awful. Pop scared shitless about the *goy* coming up, and instead who should step in but Minnie. But you know, while they wrestled there, Pop could have gone crazy enough to grab a candlestick from the table and bat his son with it, a sin to touch the candlestick or not. The old days when Pop had a horsewhip and flogged his son with it were gone. For one thing, times had changed and no one carried a horsewhip anymore, and for another, Ira was bigger than his father was. But if Pop had grabbed that candlestick, yeah, what would he have done? Grabbed the other candlestick. Yee-hee-hee! Wouldn't Mom have screeched? His thoughts became impervious to the passing nightscene, or it dissolved. Wouldn't that have made some movie? Ira felt his cheekbones lift in a grin. They fought with everything in the movies: swords, of course: Doug Fairbanks hopping up and over tables, wielding his rapier; daggers too, pistols, rifles, it went without saying, and even whips, and phony medieval knights-at-arms, with maces, Robin Hood with quarterstaves, and fake Roman gladiators with net and trident. But nobody had ever fought with a couple of solid brass candlesticks. Had both candles gone out? 116th Street already. On *Shabbes* you fight with candlesticks? Ha-ha-ha! Reformed out of the nightscene he passed and passed, doorways, lighted store windows of mostly closed stores, autos traveling toward and away with headlights low, pedestrians wearing gloves, bundled-up couples.

Ira felt a sudden twinge of pity as he crossed the trolley car tracks. Poor Mom. Tea dripping down her chin, darkening the neckline of her red housedress. Poor Mom, the way her voice dove down to a distraught bass. He ought to kill that sonofabitch. If he ever busted Pop with a candlestick—they were goddamn heavy, those European ones. Crump: his skull would cave in. Pop goes Pop's pate. Yeah, but no joke.

Cops in the house. *Oy, gevald!* It was all a mistake, officer. It was all an accident. What kind of an accident, Jew-boy? We were playing Loki and the Utgard Giants. I thought he had a mountain between his head and the candlesticks. Yeah? Tell that to the judge. Right now you're under arrest. Homicide. No, patricide. Handcuffs snapped on his wrists. Mom wringing her cheeks, Minnie hanging on to him. Say, maybe, after they let him out, on bail maybe, and Minnie hung around him to comfort him, who knew? Work on her sympathy; he had done it before, and it worked: H-v-v—o-o-h. Woddayasay, Minnie? Tell her how much he needed it. Kill your father to lay his daughter. Wasn't this the meaning of it all? If you knocked her up, you'd be the kid's father and the kid's uncle at the same time, a duncle, with a dad, or a puncle with a pop, or a funcle with a father. And Mom, hey, listen, she'd be a double grandmother, sure, the kid's maternal and paternal Baba. 114th Street.

That sonofabitch went for his balls, didn't he?

Turn backward, turn backward, O time in thy flight—Ira crossed the street, halted in the light of the show window full of electrical fixtures, lamps and lampshades. Turn, turn, Sir Richard Whittington, Lord Mayor of London. Started out with a cat. . . . But what the hell did the old man say when Ira was on the way out? Still with a Trojan on—did he or didn't he have it on? Disgraceful, downright sacrilegious, to sit down with a devout old man, with holy writ, a *siddur,* in front of him, and still be wearing a bag of sticky stuff: semen, Abraham's seed. Onanism, wasn't it? For which you got stoned in the old days. The more he ruminated on it, the daffier life was. Zaida communing with his third-generation offspring, with his fourth-generation seed caught in a condom (he hoped). But who the hell knew the old man was going to stop him? Ira slowly began walking again; he could see the bright drugstore a block and a half ahead. But what the hell had the old guy said? Now think, think. "When I was a child, I thought as a child—" No, no, no. That was Saint Paul: now we see as through a glass eye darkly. No, Zaida had offered Ira snuff . . . not a cigarette this time (because it was Saturday; no smoking?), snuff out of a lacquered black snuffbox, and when Ira declined, Zaida had plied his nostrils with a pinch between thumb and forefinger vibrato. Very good. Go on. "How the Talmud teaches one, how the Talmud prepares the child for adulthood. You would have found out, had you continued faithful to Judaism. How different a college youth you would have been."

That was the code to the cypher, wasn't it? The cryptogram? Or was it? Ira walked ahead, mechanically. He had sat with hat and coat on listening, feigned he was listening, and yet puzzled. Stella had remained discreetly in the front room—or retired to her bedroom. Anyway . . . "What does one understand with the mind of a child?" Zaida said. "I'll tell you from my own experience." Was that a thrust under cloak of reminiscence? Now think: did it or didn't it mean anything? "From my own life experience." His hand in didactic cusp: "When I was eleven, and I first read in *Kedushim*"—was that right? *Kedushim,* whatever that was—"a portion of Talmud: How do you get a wife? How does one acquire a wife?" And Ira with a condom glued fast—it was, wasn't it? "There are three ways of getting a wife." Zaida depressed his little finger as if it were a cash-register key: "One is with *kessef.*"

"Huh?" A few more steps and he'd reach the drugstore.

"*Kessef,* coin, silver. *Seh heist kessef.*"

"Oh, yeh. *Kessef.*" Ira had heard that word before—in Yiddish. "Okay."

"Another is by *shtar.*" By written agreement, by bond. (Twinkle, twinkle, little *shtar*—that was easy to remember.) And the third is by *biyah,*" said Zaida.

"By beer," Ira had chortled nervously.

"By *biyah.* To have intercourse with her. You come upon her, and you have intercourse with her."

"That's simple, Zaida." Ira had maintained his sangfroid with a show of facetiousness: "*Kessef, shtar,* and *biyah.* Anybody can remember those." Holy jumpin' Jesus! How much more did he need to be told? The old boy was driving the spike right through him. That was it, that was it.

And the way he stared at Ira, out of hard, brown, uncompromising eyes. But then maybe it was just because of the cataracts he had in his eyes: "You say to her, 'By this act I have made you my wife.'" (Listening, Ira had forgotten his restiveness.) "What did I understand as a child of eleven: 'By this act'?" Old man with stained vest over paunch speaking, old man in a black yarmulka and with scraggly beard delivering his homily. "But you see how wise the Talmud was to prepare the immature mind for the time when the mature mind would understand?"

"Yeah." How convulsively he had swallowed the saliva in his mouth. "In about a year or so," Ira had jested.

"It could take longer," the old man said seriously. "Who knows how much longer? Each youngster is different. But longer or shorter, before he knew desire, each child knew how God decreed desire should be satisfied: by taking a wife. And how wives were taken."

It's nothing, Ira assured himself, halted again in the light of the French pastry shop, open still, just short of the overhead poolroom on 112th Street, sniffed fragrance. It's nothing with nothing. Look at those brave napoleons and chocolate éclairs. Handsome. If only this wasn't Friday night, he'd blow fifteen cents on a slice of mocha tart for Mom. How she adored it, how little he ever bought her. What a son, what a sonofabitch he was, except calling himself *that* insulted Mom, poor Mom, with the scalding tea dripping down her chin. What did Eliot say, Mr. Tse-tse fly: *I should have been a pair of ragged claws.* You shouldn't have been at all, period—Ira addressed himself as he rounded the closed millinery store on the corner—tell you something—the mind directed itself to the click of pool balls overhead: do you know that "Prufrock" has more in it than *The Waste Land?* Of course. But if you told Edith's highbrow friends that you liked "Prufrock" better than *The Waste Land,* they'd laugh you out of court. What did that mean? Laugh you out of court. Hee-haw. Oh, just judge. A Daniel come to judgment, Jew. 112th Street, trudging west.

Only the little Puerto Rican grocery store was open and illuminated on the other side of the street; every other *gesheft* was dark, *l'kuvet Shabbes.* But the little *tienda,* as he remembered from high school Spanish, was still open, the same one on whose iron step he had fastened together the laces of his shoes. Long ago. Oh boy, what a fuck that had been! What the hell are you gonna do? How are you gonna make love to a nice woman, an intelligent woman, a refined woman?

How're you gonna say: Ah, you're beautiful, you're lovely, exquisite—the way, yes, Larry had sighed about Edith? She was so sweet, so tiny, so fragile. He just wanted to hold her in his arms, protect her. Protect her from what? Protect her from his hard-on. Never mind being lewd about it. Tears of pure worship had come into Larry's eyes. Yeah, as if she were a statue of a goddess: effigy.

Who the hell was it brought the Pallas Athena from Troy, or the Lares and Penates? Well, how the hell were you gonna do that when you didn't feel it? You came at twelve riding Minnie. Wham! So much for Dido and Aeneas. There went your romantic love, keyed into a carnal crevice, plugged into a submerged, unromantic socket, sock it, sock it . . . shorted, that was it. You were no longer capable of romantic love; you were too late. Then how were you gonna use fancy, high-flown poetic diction, when the street words, the slum words of Harlem, already resounded in your ears, and you already had knowledge of what they were? And not only knowledge: the flesh knew, the body and brain knew: tit, knockers, twat, cunt, pussy, and piece of ass, that was what you'd had. Not delicate terms. You couldn't use fancy words. They stood right in your way—balked your hard-on.

Yep—

Once to every man and nation comes
the moment to decide:

Something about choosing the good or evil side. But it hadn't worked out that way for him. The evil side, the line of demarcation, had been Minnie's pink little ass above the bathtub water line. It had been some sensation. Sensation wasn't the word for it. A thousand years couldn't undo its wicked transport.

Apt word, Ira smirked at himself: how buoyantly conveyed. Archimedes never dreamed of that one. Here he was: he had sauntered all that way, yeah, as aimless, as errant as a Western Union messenger boy with a telegram—right to the right address, right to the first of the twin solid blocks of masonry where Mamie lived. Mamie's house was the first, when approached from the east. Ira stood contemplating the empty, lighted tile foyer; he stepped back on the sidewalk and looked up. Oh, the front-room windows a flight up were lit, all right. The family was home. *Once to every man and nation . . . for the good or evil side.* He could walk past, now that he had been here, past the other, the second stone warren, stroll on to the lights of Lenox Avenue. And around to the north again. Plot your course: to 116th East, around the big ice-cream parlor, back to Fifth and the corner theater, and then east to Madison, and uptown this time following the long shiny reins of the trolley tracks—giddap. He entered the foyer: now's the time and now's the hour. See the front o' battle lour—oh, Rabby Burns, *amico fidato*—if only I'd been a Scotsman— and began climbing the stone stairs . . . came to the landing . . . came to the first flight, stood on the wan tiles amid the dark-green-painted apartment house doors, each sticking out the brass tongue of its doorbell in ridicule.

Here goes. Brace for Mamie's—or Joe's—furious Yiddish tirade: *Paskudnyack!* Scoundrel! You dare show your vile face here? *Ferbrent zollste veren! Heraus, fershtinkeneh dreck!* I'll slap you forthwith. I'll spit in your face! Grunk, grunk, grunk. He spun the brass key of the ratchety doorbell.

His grimness waxed with the passage of time, and time seemed unconscionable in duration. Finally, Hannah's voice challenged: "Who?"

"It's Ira." His throat burred.

"Who?"

"Ira!" he called. Damn. Let the blow fall.

"Oh, it's my collegiate cousin." The tongue of the lock slid back; the door swung open. And there, jiggling in her antics, his stripling, saucy, redheaded cousin.

He stared searchingly at her countenance, waited for some sign. There was none. Only an effusive welcome.

"C'mon in. It's cold in the hall. Oh, is my father gonna be surprised."

"Is he home?" He had tumbled into fatuity, the absolute, boundless fatuity of his unfounded fears. He had ruined his chances for the weekend—but hell . . . worth it . . . for the next minute anyway . . . until relief wore off. And then he'd kick himself in the pants.

"Is he home? My father?" Hannah led the way to the farther end of the hallway, brightened by the overlapping of light of front room ahead with that of the kitchen doorway to the side. Traditional Friday-night supper emanations became stronger as he advanced. "My father shouldn't be home on Friday night? On *Shabbes b'nakht?* My father?"

"Of course." Ira passed the open door of Zaida's empty, darkened bedroom.

"You'll be surprised too, you haven't seen him in so long. He shaved off his mustache, did Minnie tell you? He says it makes him look taller. And will he ever be surprised to see you. When was it last? Did you go to Max's wedding? Look who's here," she announced.

"Who is it?" Mamie bulked in the kitchen doorway.

"You'll never guess," Hannah promised.

"It's Ira. *A gitten Shabbes,*" Mamie greeted. She turned her head to inform those in the kitchen. "Indeed a guest for you, Jonas. You haven't seen each other since you've been working so late all the time." And to Ira: "Come in, come in, let Jonas see you. Why so late?"

"I'm sorry." Ira advanced into the kitchen with simpleton apology. "I started to take a walk, and just thought, I'm here, I'll see Joe." He extended his hand in greeting. *"Noo, voos makht a yeet?"* There was nothing, absolutely nothing, to have been alarmed about. What a dope. "How's the *gesheft?*"

"Nisht kosher." Joe stood up from the table. "You're indeed a grown man, avert the evil eye. How long since I've seen you? It must be—God knows."

"I really don't remember." Ira looked down at the face under the brim of Joe's gray felt hat. It was a wholly unprepossessing counte-nance, blue-eyed and long-nosed. Joe was a very little man, scarcely five feet in height, shorter by inches even than Pop. Nor was he the kind of little man that Pop was, strong for his size, close-knit and quick, but trudging in his gait, weak-kneed and deliberate in move-ment. Temperament seemed to conform to outward appearance. He dragged out his words; he was patient in manner; he submitted docilely to interruption. And yet, there was about his lips, his small pointed jaw, something obstinate, canny, of which his very delib-eration was part: one might expect him to ask endless questions, unabashed, about anything he was interested in—unlike Pop—and even then not feel bound to come to a decision, again unlike Pop, so impetuous, trusting in luck. One felt about Joe that it was futile to expect him to show pride or obligation where his interests were concerned.

Ira recalled seeing the apartment years later when Hannah gave him a tour. She supplied Ira with her own shrewd descriptions of her parent's predilections. "Just as my father was short, shorter than your father, he liked everything big. And everywhere they gave you a prize, when you opened up a new bank account, there he would go and open up a new bank account: we had great big clocks, half-naked Venuses with a big round clock in their *pipick*; we had two of them with a clock in their bellies. We had table lamps that he got when he opened a new account; you could get a hernia when you tried to lift them. And the table itself—it was banquet-size. Of course, even when Zaida didn't live with us anymore, he still came to the house for the Passover Seder. So with *our* family, and sometimes with the uncles and aunts—Ella's husband was in the asylum, so she came with the three children; Morris and his wife didn't have any children because she already had a hysterectomy before she was married, so they came—who else? You needed a table as big as a dance floor. When you pulled it out, and put in the spacers, it could seat twenty-four people. That was my father."

"I think Harry's wedding was the last time I saw you," said Joe as he and Ira shook hands.

"I guess so. It's funny, no matter how much time has passed, I still remember you shaving with a straight razor. It was on a Sunday."

"*Azoy. Gotinyoo!* So long ago you remember me? I must have been working on ladies' dresses yet."

"It's funny how some things stick. You were stropping your razor."

"*Azoy? Noo*, come in, come in. Sit down. Sit down. Have a glazel tea," Joe invited. "Let's *shmooze* a little. I never see you."

"He never comes Fridays. We see Minnie, but you only pop in when it pleases you," Hannah accused.

"Well, *Freitig b'nakht*," Ira excused himself. "You know how it is. I came because I heard about Zaida."

"Aha. *Noo*, what do you think?"

"I don't know."

"We know like you know," said Mamie.

"Is that so? No reason?"

"No reason, no reason. He's gone."

"I'll be darned. Where's Stella?"

"She's in the front room reading."

"Oh. It's really a mystery," Ira said in English.

"If he wants to go because we turn the radio up, and we dance the Charleston, so—" Hannah shrugged saucily. "We're girls, what does he expect? So Sadie's got boys. They won't dance the Charleston too? They won't turn on the radio?"

"It's not that alone," Mamie interjected.

"No?" Ira listened intently.

"He dreams they have lovers, *gevald*. They let them into the house at night, let them out. Girls sixteen, fourteen, antics to play."

"What goes on in his head," said Hannah.

"He'll soon talk fetus in their belly," said Joe.

"*Noo*, we all get old. What can you do? Ah, what is there to say? Is your father working?"

"As far as I know."

"What's Minnie doing?" Hannah asked.

"Well, you know what she's doing. Office and night school. She's the one who told us tonight."

"You didn't listen to what I had to say," Mamie intervened. "You didn't listen till I finished."

"Okay. What?" Hannah accorded audience.

"I already know what you're going to say," said Joe.

"*You* know. But Hannah thinks," Mamie stressed with upraised grubby finger, which flowed in gesture toward the front room. "And Stella, indeed: the reason the grandsire left was because of the radio and the Charlesburg, *azoy*—"

"He had dreams," Hannah interrupted.

"So he says," Mamie added. "But the true reason is that we were beginning to bicker about you, about you and Stella. He would not allow good Jewish youth into the house, only you, Ira. And he knew that I was vexed. I told him time and again this was America, and not Galitzia. It didn't help. If his sons work on *Shabbes,* that's their affair. But to encourage—he thinks—that some youth and his granddaughter should embrace each other, seize each other, he would be guilty of sinning before God: fornication, you understand?"

"Oh, *tseegekhappen!*" Hannah scoffed, echoed her mother's Yiddish word.

"Yeh, yeh, *tockin.* He, the patriarch, all the household sins would be upon his head. The coming and going by night, who knows: whether he imagines, whether he feigns?"

"So he isn't here. Don't think we won't invite boys, now."

"Invite, invite, to your heart's content. Why do I have a new radio? As long as they're good Jewish boys. A little *fluden?*" Mamie offered Ira. "I baked such good *fluden* today."

"No, thanks, Mamie. It's late. I just dropped in to get the news to tell Mom. She said something about your traveling out to Flushing together."

"Indeed. We'll have to pursue him now."

"Who is it you don't see here tonight?" Stella proposed a riddle, as she appeared in the doorway, textbook in hand.

"We just told him," Hannah informed her sister scathingly. "What do you think we've been talking about?"

"I know," Ira said to mitigate Hannah's sharpness. "Minnie told me."

"So who do you think is gonna have his room? Guess."

"You?"

"Naturally. She gets everything," said Hannah.

"*Aza mensh.*" Mamie locked gross fingers and deplored. "Whatever I cooked for him, no matter how good it was, he never praised it. He would just nod his head. It passed. *Shoyn—*"

"It was coming to him," Hannah seconded.

"Shah! Don't interrupt your mother," Jonas chided.

Hannah refused to be squelched: "What is it about these European fathers—just because they begot you, like the Bible says, you owe them everything."

"You think he's strict," said Joe. "You should have known my father. We quivered. I had a brother, Leibele. He was eighteen already. It was Yom Kippur, and he was hungry. So he ate something. *Freg nisht.* When he came back to the *shul,* my father said, 'Where have you been? Let me see your tongue.' *Noo, noo.* He gave him with the stick right in front of the synagogue. I can still see Leibele with the blood running from his face. With my father, his word was law. Life and death. Zaida is nothing compared to my father."

"That's because he's here in America," Hannah remarked.

"Well, just the same, I'm not sorry he's gone," Stella said boldly. "Why should I be sorry? If you want to know, I'm glad. Would you want somebody in the house who's always chasing out every fellow that comes in? And good Jewish fellows too. You're the only one he'd let into the house. Everybody else was a *trombehnyick.*"

"Yeah?" Ira scratched an eyebrow.

"Go, who's talking of such things," Mamie rebuked her daughter. "What he wanted I ran to get: the freshest bulkies. I went to the bakery three times a day to bring back fresh bulkies—"

"You ran five times a day," Hannah contradicted.

"*Noo,* five times a day. And those hard egg biscuits I got him for a *nosh* between meals. They had to be just so. If they were too brown, too crisp, he wouldn't eat them. If they were too soft, he wouldn't eat them. All I did for him, and he leaves. What? He flees. All right, he was an embittered man: nothing suited him; he was that kind of a man. But flee without saying a word, I don't understand."

"*Iz nisht* gefilte fish," Joe remarked humorously. "Another kosher home like this he won't find again."

"Yeah, that's what Pop said." Ira watched his uncle cut a slice of *kholleh* into small cubes and pop them into his mouth as if they were bonbons.

"Well." He stood, went for his coat and hat on the washtub surface. Though he had ruled out another visit for the weekend, he had much to be thankful for. He was cleared of all suspicion. That was certain. And besides, when he called at Mamie's again, Zaida would no longer be there: one hazard less when he got Stella alone. Still, why had the old man recited that business about getting a wife, especially that business about coming upon her and having sexual relations with her? Only a week ago, and so pointed in Ira's direction. There was only one person who might know, who could clinch matters. Stella. He had screwed her in the front room only minutes before. Was it possible the old man said something to her after Ira had departed? She was about to leave the kitchen for the front room.

"What are you reading, Stella?" Ira called after her.

"I'm not reading. It's Pitkin shorthand." Her voice trailed from the hall.

"Yeah? I studied Gregg years ago. Is Pitman better?"

"Oh, a lot."

"Well," Ira hesitated. No, he was sure he was out in the clear. Why bother to follow Stella into the front room?

"Well, good night, everybody." He slid into his coat. "Excuse me for coming so late, but you know when Minnie told us—"

"It's nothing, it's nothing," Mamie reassured.

"O-o-h, Papa." Hannah turned to Joe suddenly. "You're gonna let Ira go away without your goodbye thing?"

"Let him be," Mamie interceded. "He has other things on his mind besides that. And on Friday night."

"*Noo*, it won't harm anything," Joe countered, smiling. "The old man isn't here, so I may. Wait, I'll go get it."

"A goodbye thing?" Ira repeated, nonplussed.

"Yeh. Wait, wait. It's in my jacket pocket." Joe left the kitchen for the back bedroom.

"What's he up to?" Ira inquired of Mamie.

"A foolish thing," was her answer.

But Joe seemed to have difficulty finding the object he sought. "Maybe it's in my overcoat," he said. "Where did I—when did I show you?"

"Do you wanna see how Pitman looks, Ira?" Stella called from the front room.

"Sure." Ira was certain she was sending him some kind of signal. Why of course: she wanted to remind him that with Zaida gone, Joe working, and Mamie escorting Mom to Flushing, the house would be virtually empty Sunday. He made for the front room.

"Don't go away," Joe urged.

Mamie kept on the subject of Zaida's departure as Ira tried to insinuate his way into the front room after his prey. "For the children, for me, it's easier. You can see. Would they dare play the new radio tonight? But that has nothing to do with it."

"New radio?" Ira asked in surprise.

"Wait till you see it," said Stella. "He got it at a place on Main Street."

"You fret yourself and fret yourself." Joe savored a *kholleh* cube while comforting his wife. "It's nothing with nothing. He's a pious Jew. Perhaps he was afraid you'd try to dissuade him—"

"But why did he mumble about his grandchildren?"

"Who knows? Go. I'm not stopping you from going. Go in good health. And I wager he won't tell you. He'll give you some other excuse. Faults he has in plenty, but an observant Jew he is. He wouldn't let his own son, Saul, jilt Ida, to whom he had pledged marriage. Why? Because she was an orphan. And Saul had to be led fainting to the canopy. That's how Ben Zion is. Hear me out. If you want to know what my complaint is, it's not his love of fresh bulkies and fresh egg biscuits. At age fifty—you hear, Ira?—when he came to America, what man in his fifties can't work? Hired work didn't suit him. Commerce and trade he couldn't pursue—how? Without a word of English? His brother Nathan was a diamond dealer. That would have suited Ben Zion. But dealing in diamonds you don't learn so easily, and Nathan, brother or not, wasn't willing to teach him—"

"Especially to sell diamonds with little black spots in them to all your relatives," Hannah remarked, and for Ira's benefit, "To all Uncle Nathan's relatives, he sold a diamond with a little, a black spot."

"Shah! He's dead. Wild prattler," Mamie reprimanded. "You know, Uncle Nathan threw himself from the window. He had a cancer."

"I know. Mom told me." Ira's gaze furtively followed Stella as she left the kitchen again.

"It's a great scandal." Mamie lowered her voice. "Zaida was never told."

"So if he leans on all his sons for support," Hannah observed tartly, "how can he be such an *ehrlikh yeet,* when all his sons work on *Shabbes?* Doesn't that sin fall on him too?"

"And he knows it," Stella called from the hall on the way to the front room.

"America is America," Joe yawned, a cruet between thumb and

forefinger. "Everything is a little *traife*. What? I don't take a coffee with milk at night when I'm in the cafeteria? And the cup—it's not washed by the dishwasher with everything else *milkhdik, fleishik*? A piece of steak, like Max, I don't eat. But a piece of fish, yes. Piety is stretched here. It's not Europe, and that's how it is."

"And with Zaida, what you do, you do. What I do, I do," said Mamie.

"And women count for nothing," Hannah added. "It's no use talking. That's how he was brought up. You told me yourself a hundred times," she said to her mother with asperity: "A girl is only good to get married."

"She's a thorn," Mamie smiled.

"I'll save you a trip," said Joe. "Saturday night I go to work, I'll ask Morris: Why? What happened? Morris will tell me sooner than your father will tell you."

"No. I want to see him," Mamie insisted.

"You know what?" Stella's voice preceded her from the front room. She was holding a textbook. "He knows we're not going to get married the way he wants us to get married. Kosher it should be. With a *shotkhin* and pictures. So he doesn't want to stand in the way."

"Go, you're foolish," said Mamie.

"All right, so I'm foolish." Stella held up her book: *Pitman Method Shorthand*. "So why do you take a whole towel along when we go to somebody's wedding, and they say, 'The same should happen to you next year'? Why?" She addressed Ira. "You know I'm sixteen, and I'm supposed to be a *kolleh moit* already, a bride."

"I don't get you."

"Mama is afraid I'm not pure enough for Zaida. He found out maybe some boy was escorting me, and he touched my breast by accident on purpose."

"That's enough," said Mamie. "May it be no worse."

"How did you first find out where he went, if nobody was home?" Ira asked.

"I found out," Stella answered.

"You did?"

"Morris talked to me over the phone. I was the only one home afterward."

"Oh." Ira searched her face. She betrayed nothing: blank. He was stewing over nothing. But then again, she was expert at exhibiting only vacuities. Fortunate too, or he would have been compromised more than once. Still, that last Talmudic comment of Zaida's to his grandson: "By this act." He watched her leave for the front room. Hell, bored to death over nothing. He stood up.

"Ira, are you leaving so soon?" Joe asked.

"Soon? It's almost ten o'clock."

"He's got such big things on his mind. You don't know him, Papa. He's always in a hurry."

And then turning to Ira, she said, "Girl, when it comes to talk, you're a regular geyser."

"You're a geyser. I'm a girl."

"*O-o-y!* Good night."

"You didn't see yet the bargain I made with the radio store for my old one," Joe said, intercepting Ira's retreat. "A piece of furniture you'll never see," said Joe.

"Well, I'll take a quick look."

"When you look once, you'll look longer." Joe led the way to the front room. "Na. You ever saw such piece of furniture?" And a piece of furniture it certainly was, a softly crooning cabinet, massive in size, maple in veneer.

"Hey, that's the biggest I've seen yet," Ira commended.

"Look yet how they painted it," Joe extolled. "He said they got special Chinamen who were the only ones could do it. Look on how that goes, both whole sides. One sticking out the tongue to the other. No? *Dus heist kunst.*"

"Art. I should say," Ira agreed.

"They're genuine."

"Not even Zaida could complain," Stella remarked from the other side of the table.

"What d'ye mean?"

"Does it remind you of any animal or anything?"

"Oh, graven images. Oh, no. What dragons! It's real lacquer."

"I told you," Joe said, gratified. "Turn it up a little. You'll hear." Joe matched act with word. "Stay a minute."

"Oh, yeah." Ira stood rapt in admiration. "What a radio!" With an opportunity like that, he simply had to wait—transfixed with awe—at least another minute. Joe returned to the kitchen.

Ira stepped swiftly to Stella's side, bent over, whispered: "Did Zaida—I mean, did he tell Morris anything about us? Did Morris say anything?"

"Us?" Her smooth face, her shallow blue eyes opened in surprise. "Us, what?" She shook her blond head vigorously—for her.

"Oh. Okay." Disgruntled with himself at final confirmation of the groundlessness of his fears, he was on the point of leaving—then remembered to salvage a little anticipation: "Listen, stay home after they leave Sunday. You hear me?"

"I wanted to ask you something, Ira," she whispered. "Not now. Sunday."

He hesitated. "What? Fast."

"Ira, is it all right if I didn't get my period for four days?"

He had expected the opposite: that she was having her period; he had prepared an answer. Speechless, his lips and scowl formed the question: "What?"

"Is it all right?" Her features were childishly suppliant, lips slackly open in plea.

"No." Her very entreaty sent a surge of savagery through him. "It's not. What the hell's the matter with you? Four days?"

Sound of conversation in the kitchen had subsided. She nodded.

"You're sure?" he whispered into her ear.

"Tomorrow'll be five."

"Holy bejesus," he bit off. "I'll be here Sunday. I'll find out."

She smiled, supplicating.

"Some radio," he said, raising his voice. "You got the best radio in Harlem." He prepared to go. "I'll get my coat." And by dint of teeth and brows alone: "Sunday." He stabbed his forefinger at her. And prepared a face to meet the faces in the kitchen. "Well, *mazel tov*," he said cheerfully. "I'm glad I came. That's some radio. Those red dragons around it. Wow!" He picked up his coat and hat from the covered washtub. "Wait till I tell Mom."

"And don't forget Sunday she should be here. Twelve o' clock."

"Oh, no."

"It cost a good little piece of money, that radio," said Joe. "I'm a *mehvin*, no? Value I recognize right away."

"*Vunderbar!* It's some beauty. Wear it in good health," Ira joked.

"Wear it without Zaida coming out in his underwear, you should say," Hannah appended.

"You're a bright one, all right," Ira approved.

"I should be on the stage, no?"

"Home talent," Stella called from the front room.

"Oh, shut up."

"Well." Ira buttoned up toward leave-taking. "Good night, everybody. Good night, Mamie. I'll tell Mom."

"Wait, I have something else to show you." Diminutive Joe stood up and stretched out his hand. Visible on it, though flesh-colored, a flat round disk was strapped against the palm. "A salissman made a deal with me for a piece of pineapple-cheese pie and a cup of coffee."

"What is it?"

"Shake hands with me, you'll find out."

"It's not gonna squirt water, is it?"

"Nah, nah. Don't be afraid. Give a shake." Ira clasped his uncle's outstretched hand, squeezed mutually. The device in Joe's palm emitted a loud, blatant fart. Involuntarily, Ira drew his hand away—to Joe's beaming chuckle

"It's a real *fortz, nisht?*"

"Couldn't be better."

"If it stank a little, it would be just like my second cousin Meyer, the *shnorrer*. You remember him, Ira?"

"He always looked like he needed a shave."

"*Tockin, tockin,*" Mamie corroborated. "With him such a fart would be a trifle. Nothing to disapprove of."

Hannah giggled. "For once Ira doesn't look like he's got something important on his mind."

X

You dumb sonofabitch, you dumb sonofabitch. Like an animal dragging his trap after him, Ira made through dark 112th Street for the brightly lit store under the streetlamp on the corner of Fifth Avenue. Reaching it, he stopped there, trying to think, could think only of the click of pool balls overhead, sometimes cracking loudly, subdued at others—at the far end of the overhead pool hall, clicking like knitting needles. He moved on, stopped again to watch the big-bosomed woman in white removing the French pastries from show window to refrigerator in the back. It was cold, but he scarcely felt it; nor was he aware of the few passersby, nor throb of low-beam autos rolling along the avenue. Funny only it wasn't funny: the first thing you thought of was to murder them. Clyde, Clyde, lost his hide. Lucky he had already read *An American Tragedy,* so he knew better than to act like Clyde. But he didn't feel that same twist, that same frenzied torsion beyond tolerance, beyond sound return, that had wrenched him so horribly with Minnie, so that even when she told him she was all right he felt he would never wholly recover: the Euclid twist, the fatal snap, the wave of insanity, who would know what he meant? But he had grown wise now, wise guy: blame someone else. What if she didn't? And what if Mamie finds out something from Zaida?

Oh, shit, he groaned, moved on: think, will you, think. . . . Four days overdue. Blastula, gastrula, exponential growth. How big was a fetus four days, tomorrow five days old? Big as a bead? Big as a marble?

Let's see. He didn't know anything about pregnancy. He knew names. That's all he knew about everything: parturition, gestation. Names stuck to him like—yeah, like that goddamn thing is stuck to her. Now, wait a minute. What did Edith say? She tried hot baths. That didn't work. What else? Castor oil. Didn't work. What the hell was the name of that drug? Ergot. Erg is from physics, quantity of work. Ergo, it didn't work. What did Mom do? Picked up Morris with her arms and belly. . . .

He had slowed down to a plod, trying to think, and beginning to feel cold. C'mon, get up a little steam. He quickened gait. Look, Edith turned to you when she needed—when she needed bolstering . . . consoling, yes? This is so shameful, screwing your sixteen-year-old kid cousin. You'd have to tell her everything, if she said: how long? From the time she was only thirteen. And if she asked about anybody else. Who-o-ow. Tell her about Minnie, pratting her when *you* were only twelve yourself; she was only ten. Smash the mask you wear, the pretty gentile mask she'd painted over your twisted Harlem face: pristine innocence; impersonal, nice guy, chaste, noble. Reveal. Reveal. Confess.

Call her up tomorrow—no, wait. Call up Stella first, you dope. What if she says, I'm all right? I'm all right. Oh, boy! But what if not? Then call up Edith, that's all. Call up Edith, and tell her you're in trouble. You're in trouble. You need a favor. Advice. She ain't perfect, right? She double-crossed Larry with Lewlyn. And when you took those walks with her in Woodstock—if you hadn't been so scared because all you'd ever screwed was kids—

At 116th Street, he wheeled east, traveled between the few remaining lighted stores and the accompanying glint of trolley tracks. How will you say it? You impregnated your cousin. You inseminated her. Nah, you donkey, who do you think you are? Milton? Oh, Jesus, Milton he had just barely looked at. If he'd stayed home and read, he wouldn't have known a damn thing about any of this. And maybe Stella would have got over it after a while by herself. All right, you call up Edith, and you ask to come over. All right, so you can't say you think you knocked up your cousin. You had intercourse, all right? Maybe she's pregnant; she hasn't had her period—menstruated, menstruated—four days—it would be five tomorrow. Maybe you don't have to mention Minnie. Why should you? Stella was bad enough. Don't even have to tell Edith when you started. Stella's sixteen now, going on seventeen. That's old enough. So . . . you're waiting for Mamie to come home, and maybe give you a dollar. Edith knows that. So Stella comes over and puts her arms around you. . . .

Just within hearing distance on Park Avenue, and seemingly at eye level ahead, the trestle level above the rise of ground, a New York Central coach glided by, the lighted windows of the train like the luminescence of a deep-sea creature. *Dubito, cogito, ergo sum.* Yeah. Ergo. No fancy Latin is going to talk the kid out of her belly, as Mom would say. Just tell Edith you're stuck, and why.

He turned north again. What the hell happened to that moon?

They must have just gone to bed when he unlocked the kitchen door, switched on the light, and entered—because Mom, Mom spoke to him softly, when he opened the door to the freezing bedroom, and hung up coat and hat on the wall hooks at the foot of his bed. She always fell asleep last, slowly, like himself, while Pop fell asleep at once, slept hard for a few hours, then lightly the rest of the night; and Minnie in her folding cot beside the bed did very much the same.

"Ira?" Mom said.

"Yeah, it's me."

"You won't stay up too late."

"No."

"And turn off the gas stove before you go to bed."

"Okay." He shut the door to the cold, dark bedrooms. No point in holding a long conversation. He'd tell Mom about Mamie's proposed trip to Flushing tomorrow. Time enough. What the hell was the Hebrew word? *Biyah?* Beer, he had wisecracked. By this act . . . of my copulating with you . . .

He pulled out the black looseleaf notebook with the blue-bound copy of Milton's poems on it from the pantry shelf under the china closet, took them to the green-oilcloth-topped kitchen table, and sat down. How the hell could a guy stay as pure as Milton did? Jesus, angelic, and looked it. Traveled all over Italy. Must've been plenty of cash around.

Ira opened the book to where he had left off. Never mind the dreaming. He'd have to skim like hell. And tomorrow, Jesus, yes, he'd have to call Edith—no, Stella first, you boob. Get lost in your book, for Christ's sake. Maybe coffee later. He read, skimmed, held steady on a line, forgot the burden of his troubles in its beauty. Boy, look at that about Satan's shield: *Hung on his shoulders like the moon, whose orb/ Through optic glass the Tuscan artist views* . . . Galileo, Tuscan artist. . . . If you could only have gone up to Galileo, and said: Hey, listen, Gallo, old boy. Instead of wasting your time trying to find out the speed of light from one mountaintop to another, keep your eye on one of those moons of Jupiter. Notice how long it takes before you see it again as the earth moves round the sun.

What a discovery. Trickle. Trickle. Gurgle. Gurgle. Leaky toilet flush valve in the box over the stool. Not a roach in sight. Scan me out that in iambic pentameter. Trickle, trickle, leaky flush—that's a dactyl, hoople-head.

The way Mom picked up Morris, leaning way back like those ivory figurines of Mary holding baby Jesus to conform to the shape of the tusk—ah, the tusk again.

Read, will you? . . . Ira leafed through pages, flattened the text. Man, what that guy knows. What did Mott say? In between studying Hebrew and Chaldean, you were supposed to pick up Italian on the side. Pages passed. The tenement creaked. The blue fringe of gas flame along the bar in the open gas stoved hissed quietly.

Remember Belial's argument. How did Milton say it? *Counseled ignoble ease and peaceful sloth.* Who opposes him? Beelzebub. With what rebuttal? Get at God via Man. Right? *Seduce them to our party, that their God/May prove their foe.* Okay. Belial versus Beelzebub. What time is it? Getting on twelve. A light wind had come up, driveled in colloquy with washlines in the backyard, seeped through the kitchen window, ever so slightly swayed the window shade. How long would he study? How long would his eyes last reading a blind poet? Ira allowed himself the luxury of letting the printed lines swim out of focus.

No, he couldn't ask Mom to lend him money out of what she was saving for a Persian lamb coat. He'd have to tell her what it was for, even if he could find out who did abortions (without asking Edith who did hers).

"*Oy, gevald,*" he could just hear Mom cry out. "How could you bring yourself to do such a thing!" And he: "I could, that's all." She'd forgive him, she'd forgive him even if she knew he used to screw Minnie.

There were some things you couldn't understand: motherhood: she had conceived him, gestated him, just as maybe Stella had conceived by him and was gestating part of him, changing him from son to father. Couldn't you just hear Mom and Mamie haggling over what share of the midwife's bill or doctor's bill each ought to pay? Nah. Better ask Leo. He wouldn't have to say whom he knocked up. Just knocked up a jane.

The irony of it all. A short while ago, Edith had had her uterus scraped, or what the hell ever they do. They go into the cunt somehow: vagina—those fancy goddamn words—with that kind of light on a mirror, parabolic, spherical, with a peephole in it. Open wider. Say a-a-h. Which one of those nimble, little, flagellant, little, spermy, little, protozoan bastards got to her. Christ, he thought he had a bag on; he could have sworn he had a bag on. Next time wear two—if there is a next time. Call him Houdini, if he gets out. You and your stale jokes.

Read, will you. . . . Print swam back into focus, into ken. Okay. Satan is elected: *And through the palpable obscure find out/His uncouth way* . . . Jesus, a guy ought not read this for tests. He ought to just read it and read it and read it. Oh, hell . . . is right. At least to Book III tonight. How many more pages would that be? He moistened his finger, counted: twelve. Well, get going.

> *Meanwhile the Adversary of God and Man,*
> *Satan, with thoughts inflamed of highest design,*
> *Puts on swift wings, and toward the gates of Hell*
> *Explores his solitary flight: sometimes*
> *He scours the right hand coast . . .*

He felt completely alone. With an open book before him. In a green-painted kitchen. Bile green, Mom called it. Green icebox alarm clock on it at twenty to two: 1:40 ante meridian. Box of household matches beside the clock: Big Ben. Everything had connotations: the wrong ones at the wrong time.

Candlesticks yellow on white tablecloth, burned out to little drapes of wax. And outdoors the limitless cave of night like a cold eternity. Big Ben. Oh, Jesus, he'd forgotten. Stella was the one that should have happened to: oh, boy, he'd forgotten altogether. O-o-oh, o-o-oh. His mind was pulled apart. That dumbbell: "Is it all right if you don't get your period in four days?" No, she didn't say that. She said if it's four days late. Boy, what a dumbbell. Tough luck—he didn't know anything about it: tell her to tell Joe, tell Mamie, she was out with a—no, some *goy* caught her in the hallway, or better, a Portorickan. Said he'd choke her unless—They've got enough dough to find a midwife, or someone skilled in the business. Right?

He was thinking old thoughts, rehashing the rehash. And if she accused him, the dummy, never, he when? Oh, that was enough. But you

know, to go over old fantasies again, what do they call it, make a
virtue of necessity—some virtue: if he had to marry her, she'd be his
slave: get him that, and cook him this. And he'd back-scuttle her
every night, maybe day and night and *Shabbes* too. Would it be as
wonderful as that night he'd hoisted her aloft on his stiff petard right
under Mamie's snore? No, that was like the penultimate rocket display with the American flag breaking out in red, white, and blue balls
of flame—better than that: golden lions of Judah rampant on a field
of sapphire. Hey, you know, that was one time cubic phylacteries
turned into spheres, orisons into orgasm.

Shut up. You're in trouble. Read, will you, for Christ Jesus. If you
weren't such a goddamn dope, you'd have been through Book II
long ago. What d'ya got to say for yourself, Lucifer, shorn of glory?

Here we are, here we are: he ought to get a concordance—how
he loved Milton. What gigantic talk. There was nobody like him; not
even Shakespeare could command such ordinance of vowels as Milton, could consign such encyclopedic cohort of learning to his fable.
Boy: *Far less abhorred than these/Vexed Scylla, bathing in the sea that
parts/Calabria from the hoarse Trinacrian shore.* . . . Ah. Ira stopped to
meditate. The guy was a Puritan—unlike Shakespeare—and Ira himself was a Puritan, fouled up and gone astray. He admired Shakespeare, marveled at his inordinate, inexhaustible dramatic, linguistic
prowess, but the artist was ever detached, ever uncommitted, unreel-
ing out of his limitless being myriad characters in myriad situations,
himself seemingly bound to no mystique. That was it. And Milton was
bound. As Ira himself once was, still wanted to be, no longer could
be. Mystique, devotion, sanctity—he was always running up against
them, couldn't rid himself of them. What a cinch—if he could.

He knew what was going to happen. Then skim. But tough thing
to do: to skim that stupendous confrontation. And worse than
that . . . because so close to home. Stupendous and inciting. Would
always be now . . . all incest would: because he knew the inseparable
mingling of the terror and iniquity. That was it: pariah's orgasm at its
highest, the shattering of all taboo, ecstatic reprisal against everything, everybody, yeah, against Pop, even Mom for moving to Harlem,
Zaida for coming here, Jew with the whiskers and his kosher bosher
and *tvillim* and *thallis* among the *goyim.* The whole works. Jesus, if that

time, that Sunday morning way back on 9th Street, when Morris, her own brother, showed Mom his looming blooming bascule, if she hadn't run from the room broom in hand, when he said, "Look what I've got, Leah," but, oh, boy, just sent Ira out, so maybe he could have sneaked back, peeked in. Pop was a *mensheleh*, she taunted her husband when they quarreled, but with Morris—

Come on, quit it—

> *Incensed with indignation, Satan stood*
> *Unterrified, and like a comet burned,*
> *That fires the length of Ophiuchus huge*
> *In the arctic sky . . .*

If that wasn't the mightiest metaphor any poet ever wrote. *Ophiuchus huge.* Jesus, if only he had to make only one telephone call tomorrow, not two. Just one, please: Hello, Stella, you all right? Wouldn't he be happy? What did the other guys in Professor Mott's class think when they read about Satan screwing his own daughter, and fighting his own son, after he knocked her up? What Jewish innocents abroad: only you, you stupid sonofabitch. . . . *Each at the head/Leveled his deadly aim; their fatal hands/No second stroke intend . . .* Keep reading.

Keep breeding. "Blow, bugle; answer, echoes, echo, dying, dying, dying." Nothing much for him to do, except to try and keep on. Spiritless, in the midst of a heavy bronchial infection, he might just as well slavishly follow his typescript. He wasn't capable of much else. Several days in fact had passed since he had last applied himself to his narrative: the bronchitis was one of the reasons for the interruption. Keep breeding. Answer, echoes, dying, dying, dying.

XI

In his dim little bedroom, Sunday morning dawned on sandy eyelids opening on the smudged, slotted wall across the gray airshaft. He listened a second—he scarcely ever could tell time in the dingy little coop. Kitchen door closed, and no sound beyond; so Mom and Pop were gone. And Minnie—still probably dozing—or if awake—who cared? He got out of bed, entered the kitchen. Almost nine-thirty. His volume of Milton and notebook on the table still. Nanh, it was all stupid, all his messages. Mom would have gone to Mamie's anyway to find out the news, and learned of Mamie's intended trip to Flushing. Nine-thirty. Just about the right time to call up Mamie's, get Stella before she gadded off, find out the verdict. He headed for the toilet, came out, began dressing. Let's see. He had a couple of nickels. Otherwise he'd have had to borrow from Minnie—*and* she would have misinterpreted his approach: Waddaye want? Sharp as a buzz saw: Get outa here. Or else waited until Mom came. Ah, the goddamn things he had gotten himself into—you really had to laugh. If you could: old man Chaos last night, giving the Devil his bearings: southeast by east. Ira rubbed his eyes. How the hell? Milton, you ought to have more god-damn sense. That ugly old glob of Sin with the mutts yelping inside her, opening up the gates of Hell that could never be closed again. Got it fixed all tricky. Well, that's theology. Ira dug into his back pocket, found his folded handkerchief. All this guy asks is a break. *Accursed, and in a cursèd hour, he hies.* Oh, bullshit.

Into overcoat, and downstairs, he skipped down stoop, and crossed scuffy old 119th Street to Biolov's drugstore, where he nodded at Joey tending the pharmacy before entering the phone booth, pulled the folding doors to—and then with doubled handkerchief at the ready gave the operator Mamie's number, and as soon as he heard the call go through, carefully ascertaining himself free of witnesses, draped his handkerchief over the mouthpiece. He had seen Bert Lytell do the same in the movies. No reason to think the stratagem wouldn't work. And with that bitter good fortune that so often mocked predicament, his meticulous precautions were unnecessary. It was Stella herself who answered the phone.

"Don't say who it is." Ira removed the handkerchief. "It's me, Ira. Any luck?"

"No."

"No." Chance to tighten lips. "Your mother's still going to Zaida's, right?"

"Leah is here."

"Okay. Never mind. Let me ask the questions."

"Nobody is listening. They're in the front room."

"Doesn't matter. They're going to leave about one o'clock?"

"I think so. Is Minnie going?"

"Shut up, for Christ's sake! I'll be there about two o'clock. At your house. We gotta see what we can do. You understand?" He gesticulated, his voice tightened. "Just say yes."

"All right."

"You'll wait there for me."

"Yes."

"I'll see you later. Two o'clock. I'm—let's see—I'm Esther, you get it?"

"I know what you mean."

"So goodbye, Esther. You say it. Is Hannah there?"

"No. Just Mama and Leah."

"Goodbye."

"Goodbye."

Never in his life had he felt so like a moron as he did when he hung up the receiver. But what was he going to do? He was trapped— and he had to get down to her level. He left the drugstore and recrossed the street, to the stoop of his tenement, and through long murky hall and up flight of stairs.

So Mom was still at Mamie's. She certainly must be expecting he'd be asleep, as in the old days, when she came home with breakfast for him and Minnie. As in the old days. Jesus, what irony: to know Mom was still blocks and blocks away, that he had all the time he needed to tear off a piece, and even if he could, no longer give a damn. The dumb cluck didn't know she might be pregnant, and he did all the worrying. Now try to think, he adjured himself, entering the kitchen.

Minnie waited warily for him to return to the kitchen before entering. Holding her purple bathrobe defensively about her, she skirted him cautiously when he went to the stove to look into the coffeepot, and then she crossed the kitchen to the bathroom.

Mom had made coffee, the blue-enameled coffeepot was on the stove, only the coffee had become lukewarm. He lit the gas flame under it, tried to become interested in the opening of Book III while the coffee heated, couldn't, got up and stood beside the stove, waited until the first bubbles broke the surface, and poured himself a cup, just as Minnie came out of the bathroom.

"Mom isn't back yet?" she asked.

"You see she isn't." He carried his cup to the table. His indifference, or curtness, apparently reassured her.

"No milk? It's outside the window, in the box."

"No."

"Whatsa matter? You're so worried about the exam?"

"No. I'm not worried about the exam." He tested a sip of near-boiling coffee, dipped a spoon into the sugar bowl.

"Mom'll be home right away with some bulkies. Cream cheese. What're you in such a hurry for? You're all dressed up. You can't wait?"

"Never mind—I mean, no." A sudden idea had struck him, and he moderated his tone. "You wanna do me a favor?"

"Like what?"

"Lend me a quarter."

"A quarter? What for? A quarter?"

"Lend me a quarter. Even fifteen cents. All right?"

"Whatsa matter with you? You're so jumpy. You're all upset. Like *auf shpilkis,* Mama says. Like on tacks."

"Well, I am."

Minnie studied him with unyielding gaze a full five seconds, as if trying to pry loose a hint of what was wrong, then gave up with one of her overly furrowed grimaces. "My poor brother. What gets into him. Right away he's in a big panic."

She was getting perilously close to those times when she was the cause, cause of fears that proved groundless.

"Look at you. Fifteen cents is gonna get you out of all the *veitig* you're showing? You can't even say what's the trouble."

He swallowed a mouthful of coffee. He had to keep a tight check on himself. And the effort seemed to carry him further than he had expected: into a subdued kind of reasonableness. "No, I can't. I'm in trouble, that's all."

He put his cup down, clasped his fingers together. "I'm in trouble," he repeated with new grim emphasis. "You know what I mean by trouble."

And now she seemed to grasp his meaning, didn't shrink away, but hollowed her length. She made a tutting sound, turned her face away, not in reproach, but pity.

"My poor brother."

"Yeah, yeah, yeah."

"So what're you gonna do?"

"Lend me fifteen cents, will ya?"

"So with fifteen cents—?"

"That's all I'm asking."

"I knew it. I knew it would happen. That's why I told you I didn't want any more."

"Supposing you got knocked up?" he demanded angrily. "Supposing somebody else knocked you up? One of your *goyish* friends, or that good-looking Cuban guy. I'm not trying to be funny. What would you do?"

He waited a moment for an answer. "All right, tell me. I know fifteen cents isn't going to do it. But I—" He hacked at the air. "Right now I need fifteen cents. So you haven't told me. What would you do? Give me an *eytser,* good counsel."

She hesitated, profoundly serious. "I'd go to a friend, what could I do? Maybe I'd have to keep asking. Maybe one of the married women in the office—"

"And you'd let 'em know?"

"What could I do? I could say it's for a friend. So even if they knew, it's still better than having a baby. Do you want me to ask?"

He waved her away brusquely. "Let me have fifteen cents. I'll take care of it."

"You'll have me more worried than myself." Her eyes glistened as she tilted her head. "I'm glad it isn't me. But oh, God, oh, God! You always get so mixed up in your troubles, Ira. I can't stay out of it. I try to stay out of them. I try to stop it, so you won't get in trouble. I stayed out of it. Now look."

"Jesus Christ, will you stop throwing everything in my face? You know what arguing with you does to me? You're as bad as Mom." His hips lunged from side to side. "Goddamn it!" Ferocity turned desperate. "I wish I was never born!"

"Don't say that!" Minnie pleaded.

"Never born! Dead! Dead as a goddamn mutt by the curb. I had to live in this goddamn 119th Street. Take baths in that goddamn *vonneh!*" He thumbed bitterly in the direction of the bathroom. "The sonofabitch place. Who knows what I'm in for!"

"Please, Ira, you make me so—I could—I don't know what." Her tone nasal with unshed tears, her mien wilting, hand outstretched. "Mom'll be here soon."

"Yeah, I know. So what? What?" He sneered, shook his hand wildly. "Give me the fifteen cents. So I can beat it before—" And reverting to sarcasm again: "C'mon, I don't need—" He couldn't finish. The madness latent in it all.

"I'll give you a quarter."

"Okay. Make it snappy, will ya?" She preceded him to Mom and Pop's bedroom, while he got his coat and hat, and she was in the kitchen again with a quarter in her hand before he had wrestled into his overcoat.

"Here."

"I'll get some dough somewhere. Pay you back."

"You don't—doesn't have to be tomorrow. I wish I was out of this dump." She was again on the verge of tears. "Everything happens here. All kinds of rotten things already. We gotta move, that's all."

"We do?" He turned cruel. "I got all kinds of nice memories from it."

"Oh, stop! Everything is from this lousy Harlem. Even my chance to be a teacher. Who knew when I played hopscotch and I went around the Maypole in Mt. Morris Park it was gonna be like this?"

"Bye-bye." He was out the door. "Boy, I'd like to duck Mom."

"What'll I tell her?" she called after him in the cold hall. "You didn't have breakfast."

"Any damn thing."

Once out in the street again, he turned swiftly east. To go the other way, west, to Park Avenue, was too risky. He'd be almost bound to run into Mom—not that it would make too much difference: he'd have to dream up an explanation, and fend off her distress at his not having breakfast. What the hell would he be running out of the house for on a Sunday morning? Damned if he could think of an excuse. Besides, there was a drugstore on the corner of Lexington and 118th Street. He had bought condoms there several times. Biolov's was just a little too close for comfort. This little pharmacist with the short black mustache didn't know him, except as a customer in the vicinity somewhere. In fact, the slight man's face wreathed in a certain expression when Ira laid down his quarter on the counter, as if expecting the usual request.

"Would you mind changing it?" Ira asked. "I'd like to use the phone."

Change was made wordlessly, and separating out the nickel, pocketing the rest, Ira went into the empty booth. Ten o'clock. Mom way later than usual. But not too early for—temptation an instant surged strongly to make another try at Mamie's—maybe something had happened in the last half hour. He debated a few seconds, while he watched the drugstore owner slip a pale ceramic brick into the humidor of the box of fat Admiration stogies. Oh, hell, don't be a sap. He pressed the nickel home. Five days. He'd be just wasting money. The coin clinked down into the holding receptacle, the operator made her stereotyped inquiry, and he gave her Edith's Greenwich Village exchange. He heard the repeated short hum of the busy signal, and in a few seconds, he heard, "Sorry, the line's busy," and the jitney jingled down. Well, at least that meant she was home. Meant he had another minute or two to think about his decision. He opened the folding door. Yeah. Well, who else? Two o'clock he'd said he'd be there. Five hours nearly. An hour to travel downtown, well, maybe less, another uptown. An hour with Edith—oh, plenty of time. Three hours from five hours. You know if they were pregnant, you could screw 'em to your heart's content. And without a Trojan on. Save money. Yeah—if they were pregnant. Five days. He pressed the nickel into its aperture, heard the ringing signal this time, pulled the folding door to.

She must have just finished her last conversation, and be still sitting within reaching distance of the phone, for she had lifted the receiver from the hook and was answering even before the first ring ended. "Hello, Edith. It's Ira," he said.

"Heaven's sakes, lad, where have you been?"

"Oh, exams and things."

"Are you all right?"

"Yeah, well, that's why I'm calling."

"Anything serious? I hope your family isn't in trouble."

"No. They're all right."

"You're not leaving home?"

"Oh, no, no. Wonder if I could come over for a few minutes?"

"Why, of course. You know you're always welcome."

"Thanks. How have you been?"

"Oh, much better than for a long time. You sound serious. It isn't your father again? It isn't Larry, I hope."

"Oh, no. Look, I'm only a couple of blocks from the subway. I—it's better if I come over and tell you."

"Do, please. You really have me concerned."

"I won't be in anybody's way? It's not too early?"

"Heavens, no. At ten-thirty? You won't be in my way at all. You should see the dull batch of student themes I've been grading. Ira, I very much want to see you."

"I should be there in a half hour or so—no, three-quarters of an hour."

"Please come right along. Ira, you know if there's anything I can do, please let me help."

"Yeah. Thanks. Somebody's here for the phone." Raptor. Hawk's eyes, brilliantined approach. Middle-aged dame dolled up. Rouged, perfumed muskily, she brushed by to stuff herself into the booth he'd vacated. Off to a party, somebody's engagement, peroxided tresses like Morris's Ida, that phony tramp Pop had procured. Reminded him of the one Leo stuffed it into, wanted to fix him up with. So what? Been a goddamn sight better than the ones—the one he stuffed it into. No, not because no periods, no condoms. No, but to be a man: so you put a pillow on her puss, if she's as fat a *yenta* as Leo jokes, so long as you get a piece o' hump. Be a man, that's the main thing. Not knock up a sixteen-year-old, and have to tell Edith. Jesus Christ, this lousy Harlem.

He sallied out of the store and headed for the 116th Street station, and as he neared the kiosk thought he heard a train pulling in. Never make it. He'd have to change the dime. An express roared by as he came away from the change booth. Well, he hadn't missed anything. He pressed his jitney into the turnstile slot, paced on the platform a few minutes, looking down the dark tunnel for telltale headlights. White orbs of a local appeared at length, lurching toward the station. Locals always gave the impression of being so damned self-important, cocky, brash, what the hell. . . .

XII

His eyes briefly assuaged by the sight of the dull wintry-brown leaves still clinging to shrubbery in the little triangular park across Seventh Avenue, he cleared the last subway step of the kiosk at Christopher Street. After the jaundiced ambience of subway train and platform, the sky seemed a cleaner blue. The southern sun, though low on the jagged horizon, still radiated meridian warmth as he proceeded south. As if reluctant to leave their cozy folds, a few fleecy clouds drifted up out of the deep, irregular gaps in rooftops of miscellaneous buildings downtown. Reluctant too, his heavy legs alternated between trudging and need. He'd have to make it to Mamie's by two o'clock, to a waiting Stella there, waiting for advice, guidance, help, who knew what, waiting for something he could tell her to do. Jesus. At least there would be time, as Mr. Eliot said. There would be time to find out what to do—or where to have it done—and get back to Stella. Thank God he wouldn't have to shuttle at Times Square. West Side to East Side, the way Minnie went to CCNY from her office. Jesus Christ, the disgrace. But could he wait any longer? Five days. That was his portion in life: disgrace . . . disgrace. Swiped a filigreed fountain pen, overreached, was caught, and how stupidly caught, confessed. Nah, he had found it, he could have said, as he had told himself a thousand times. Was he going to go through that all over again? It had meant expulsion, and expulsion had meant he eventually met Larry . . . and eventually left him behind, and on to Edith grown so fond, so warm, admiring—of *him*, Jesus, trustful, eager, her utter confidant, kind, generous, dainty woman. Okay, you were meant to kick over the apple cart . . . and you're about to. Sing a song of sixpence, a pocket full of *merde*. Seventh Avenue traffic on Sunday, mostly checkered taxicabs with blue smoking tailpipes. And birds, turds, surds, and words. What the hell is a surd: a square-root sign . . . any irrational root. That's you, an irrational root, absurd. You've been maimed, all right? You stood on the flat diving rock on the shore of the Hudson River, and you said there was a meaning, and you would find an answer. But why does it always have to be on your own hide? Answer. What do you mean by answer? Almost a glimpse at times: like Thoreau's hound and horse, and hawk was it? Buildings were squat and jammed together, and now and then buildings reared high into the blue; some were loft buildings, some were warehouses, and some of yellow brick, and some of red. It was not really just an answer he was looking for. Something more. Hmph. What the hell was it Iz went around quoting from Rimbaud? *J'ai fait la magique étude que nul n'élude.* But Rimbaud didn't say what he found. Meanwhile, as Larry sang, he burned a hole in his only pair of trousers—

Look how serene Barrow Street is, how retiring Commerce Street next. Coign within the great city, recess within the everlasting clamor, within the havoc of the heart. Young trees rise from the sidewalk, bare of leaves now, and prettier for being so, in a way, appropriate to the day and the season: slender branches caressing bare sky . . . opposite them the remodeled townhouses, haphazard and habitable, ah, so many shades of weathered masonry you never could imagine, soft and umber with age, set with dormer windows and topped with attic slopes—oh, Attic shape. This was that world he dreamt was elsewhere, like Coriolanus, when he stood as a kid on a certain Harlem street corner on the West Side, beatified, euphoric. But you've screwed it up now. And in deed. What do the barkers in Coney Island yell to get you to fork up a quarter to pitch a couple of baseballs at a hole in the wall? Sock it in, and get a baby doll. How true. Gone is the enclave in turmoil for you, forever.

The owner of the little service station at the foot of Morton Street, muscular, limber Italian, sloshed water from a garden watering can with sprinkler removed on a small puddle of gasoline on the asphalt next to the pump stands, looked up at Ira as he passed. Curious, how recognitions became implicit, without need to reside in specific acquaintance. Morton Street—Ira rounded it—felt as if it were here the Village tapered off. The dwellings were mostly remodeled, reclaimed from townhouse and tenement, De Lux, as the To Let signs read; still two decidedly slummy tenements remained side by side across the street from where Edith had moved this fall, slummy tenements still occupied by Italians, whilom immigrants, of Pop's and Mom's steerage-vintage, matrons in widow's weeds, and others on the twin stoops, still accompanying their native speech with twirly gesture of hub and spoke of digits. Joe lived there too. Ferret-eyed, anarchist janitor of Edith's house, he believed in finishing off the richa bosses with a banga-banga, and brought Edith the bootleg gin for her cocktail parties. Ah, respite: meandering reverie as crisis drew near, like the last meal of the condemned.

The street curved slightly in the middle, but passing the bight, 61 Morton came into view, and spying the stoop, Ira quickened gait—grimly and scared. Eager to cross the Styx, like one of the damned souls in the *Inferno*. Fear turned into desire—wasn't that what Dante said? Odd, he should suddenly recall that short Italian footnote at the bottom of the page: *Come augel a la sua richiamo*. He didn't need old Charon, the ferryman, to smack him with an oar. He pressed the doorbell, bucked the door open at the peevish buzzer's insistence, entered the foyer, and mounted the carpeted stairs. As usual, Edith had come out of the apartment and was awaiting him above at the banister.

"You're like a ministering angel up there." He kept his eyes down on the carpet under his feet as he climbed.

"That's very sweet of you," she said—and paused, then met him with outstretched hand and a smile, when he reached the floor level where she stood. "Also a little alarming. Come in, Ira."

"Thanks." He preceded her with embarrassed shamble into the apartment.

"Whatever is the matter? I've been cudgeling my wits trying to guess what's wrong. I know something very much is."

"Yes." He removed his coat with the slowness of despond.

"What is it, lad?" More comfort and solicitude could not have been compressed into such faint compass of smile.

"That's new." He gazed admiringly at the short jet-black silk kimono she was wearing. "Is it Japanese?"

"Oh, yes, it's a great extravagance. And black shows the dust so. I'm afraid I've splurged."

"Yeah?"

"You can see why." She half-turned.

"Wow." His eyes dazzled at the gold-embroidered sunburst that covered the entire back of the garment.

"It gives me the illusion of warmth. Actually, silk *is* warm."

He headed uncertainly for a wicker armchair, and sat down at her invitation, traced the course of the interwoven wicker, while she seated herself opposite him on the new black-velvet-covered couch. Black kimono, black couch cover, taupe silk stockings over trim calves projecting at right angles, ending in tiny black pumps. How often had he and Edith sat that way, her large brown eyes solemn and solicitous. His right sideburn itched; he scratched it. Poetry books in a bookcase against one wall, her desk between backyard windows on the other. And on the desk, her masssive Underwood typewriter rising from a welter of blue examination booklets. She turned a pensive face from him to the oval mirror above the bookcase, and back.

"I'll tell you what's on my mind in a minute," he said.

She smiled, winning and meek in her tenderness: "Whenever you're ready. That mess you see on the other side of my Underwood is only a few of the many candidates for the *Urban Almanac*."

"Your anthology?"

"Yes. The trouble is that good poems by good poets are expensive. And the less royalties the publishers have to pay, the more profit they make. And friends and colleagues who fancy themselves poets, and will

let you publish their poems for the privilege, aren't worth publishing—
John Vernon, for example, imagines himself a second Walt Whitman,
and of course he isn't. But I'll have to include at least one of his poems,
as a matter of policy, and they're all so long-winded. And of course
there's Harriet Monroe, and oh Lord have mercy, what makes her
think her long catalogs of things are poems. They're excruciating. But
she's Harriet Monroe, editor of *Poetry* magazine. And I've got to include poets who are really passé, Sandburg and Bynner. Oh, I've just
been scrambling around, doing the best I can on a very limited budget.
Very limited. I had to be quite strenuous with Dr. Watt to convince him
that an anthology of modern poetry has to have a fair sampling of Eliot
and Stevens and Pound and Williams. Cummings too. They know the
name Edna St. Vincent Millay, and that's about all. Again, I don't think
she's indicative of the modern trend any longer—I've decided to leave
out Amy Lowell altogether, and spend a little more on Elinor Wylie."

"Yeah?"

"Fortunately I've been able to include fairly good poems by relative unknowns who are good poets at very little cost. Roberta Holloway
and Taggard. Greenhood. I'm afraid it's a hodgepodge, and a profit-
making scheme on the part of Dr. Watt and the publishers at the expense of the students in the modern poetry courses, but I've agreed to
do it." She paused, waited a few seconds, and when he said nothing,
smiled archly, to help allay his tension. "Oh, yes, I'm including a poem
by Marcia. It's what you'd expect of her, a clever little sermon."

"I didn't know she wrote poetry."

"She doesn't." She raised her eyes to the oval mirror.

"You mean you're being altruistic?"

"Oh, no."

"You're not being altruistic?"

"Definitely not."

"I see. I wish I could hide in your class, so I could learn something."

"You already know more than I could teach you."

"I mean about poetry. Modern poetry. . . . Well." He frowned.
What was the use of stalling any longer? He was only wasting time, his,
hers being considerate of him. "I . . ." His lips clamped closed.

"Ira, dear, you're so obviously troubled," she pleaded.

"Yeah. I'm troubled, all right. I don't know what I'd do if you didn't like to hear trouble." He tried to mitigate bluntness by a humorous glance, failed. "You're so interested in other people's troubles."

"I suppose I am. It's my way of keeping in contact with other human beings and avoiding getting wrapped up in myself. It's not everyone's troubles I'm interested in. Only certain people, interesting people. People like Ira Stigman."

"You know I've always put you on a pedestal."

"Oh, pooh. You've seen me in every state of disarray, and some not very pretty ones. I've never hesitated to tell you about my distress, and I don't think you ought to hesitate to tell me about yours. Believe me, I'm more interested in helping you at the moment than being on a pedestal. But I can't—unless you tell me what's wrong." Her brown eyes never wavered from his, and as direct as her look was her tone of voice. "What is making you so unhappy? What is it?"

"Well . . ." Pleats went the long way on a dress, up and down; so those must be ruffles on her tan skirt, folds that went the other way.

"I've turned to you on dozens of occasions," she said.

"Yes." Leaning sideways was like token toppling. "You've heard me talk about my Aunt Mamie."

"Is she the obese one?"

"Obese is right. She can't cross her legs. Looks like a balloon. I've told you about her."

"She gives you a dollar from time to time, you've said."

"Good-hearted, yeah." Before him black kimono swam into black velvet couch cover, above them a ringed face circled. "She has a daughter named Stella. I've been having sexual relations with her."

Interval of quiet, the quiet of comprehension; her eyes averted in momentary comprehension. What she knew, she would never unknow. "You never mentioned her, to my knowledge, Ira. Stella?"

"Yeah. My aunt's oldest daughter—older daughter." He felt the need for grammatical rigor, as if it were a support. "She has two daughters." He knew that behind the solemn face listening so intently all the correct anticipations had been formed. "I've been having sex with her off and on I don't know how long."

"How old is she?"

"All of sixteen."

Edith concealed surprise, only sighed very slightly.

"Anyway, I guess she's pregnant."

"Why? Why do you say that?"

"She hasn't had her period—she hasn't menstruated in five days— I mean she's five days overdue." The wicker creaked as he tossed himself wrathfully.

"For pity's sake, child, five days overdue in a sixteen-year-old is nothing unusual. You can't expect the established rhythm of a mature woman in a sixteen-year-old."

"No? Not even five days?"

"Oh, they may skip even longer than that, an entire period. Has she been subject to any kind of stress, or emotional upset?"

"Not that I know of. She's kind of—kind of—well, I don't know. On the outside, what would you say? Slow."

"She's probably not pregnant at all. She's not overworking?"

"She goes to business school."

"Of course, there are blockages; something may go wrong with the organism. Only a doctor could tell."

"So she may not be pregnant at all."

"I wouldn't be the least surprised if she isn't."

"Well, I feel better—and I feel worse." He pushed his glasses back up. "What if it goes on seven days, eight days, nine days?"

"She'd better see a doctor. Any practitioner can tell by what's called a dilation whether she's pregnant or not. That's how I found out I was." Her very normalcy of tone, her matter-of-factness, sent her statement skimming out of plausibility: See a doctor! "Why don't you bring her here?" Edith suggested. "I'll take her to see Dr. Trower. He's not an abortionist. He's just a general practitioner, but—"

"Oh, no!" Ira groaned. "Oh, no!"

"Why, Ira? I don't understand."

"Bring her here!"

"Why not?"

"Oh, God! She's a tub."

"Don't be a goose, Ira," Edith rebuked sharply. "She's an adolescent. What did you think I would expect an adolescent girl to look like? Heavens. She's going through an entire physiological change."

"Oh, Jesus, wait till you see her."

"Ira!"

"Yeah. What a dumb tub."

"Will you please be practical?"

"Yeah."

"And exercise a little common sense?"

"I thought there was something she could take. I thought maybe you had something left over you could give me. Some drug. I thought you said something about ergo—"

"Ergot."

"How?"

Edith spelled the word out. And then added: "It can only be had by a doctor's prescription, and it may be too dangerous for an adolescent in any case. I don't know. I'm not a doctor."

"So what can she do? What's safe? All right, tell me. What did you try? Did you go to a doctor right away? My mother—" he began, interrupted himself: "What?"

"There are two things she can safely do, pregnant or not. They didn't work for me—neither did the ergot. But they may for her."

"Yeah, what? I gotta get back there by two o'clock."

"Oh, is she waiting to hear?"

"Yeah. It's my best chance to tell her."

"She can try very hot baths. As hot as she can stand them. And a strong cathartic: castor oil. As I say, nothing helped me. The embryo must have been attached to me like iron."

"Hot baths. Castor oil," he repeated with doleful earnestness.

"And if nothing works—and as I say, you're unduly worried, I don't believe she's pregnant—bring her here after a few more days. A few more days won't matter one way or the other—if she *is* pregnant."

"Like when? When should I bring her?"

"I'm free all afternoon Friday. I can make an appointment with the girl in my doctor's office the day before. Of course, I can cancel it if she's menstruating by then."

"Friday." The only thing that kept him from wringing his hands was counting his fingers. "Today is Sunday. Monday, Tuesday, Wednesday, Thursday, Friday. Ten days."

"But even then only a doctor's examination can tell whether

she's pregnant or not. Are you the only one having sex relations with her?"

"I don't know. I guess so . . . I never asked . . . I just hung around till I got a chance."

A silence as she contemplated him. He could feel an unspent sigh lodge deep in his gut.

"Ira, may I ask how long it's been going on?"

"Since she was fourteen. Since I was a sophomore at CCNY."

"Almost as long as I've known you."

"That's right."

She shook her head the slightest bit. "I thought you were completely attached to your mother. I thought you were completely withdrawn into yourself, shy and unawakened. I suppose I can't be blamed for misjudging you. I'm not blaming you. I'm just surprised that I did. You never spoke about girls. You spoke mostly about your mother. Your sister occasionally. And of course, there you were, such a close friend of Larry's."

"Yeah. You can see why." Her dainty fingertips played among themselves; her level brown eyes invited an explanation. "Why I never mentioned girls."

She shook her head—in sympathy. "Child, don't punish yourself so. You are what you are, and it's your extreme sensitivity that's to blame, if anything. Besides, I'm sure that kind of thing is very, very common. Sexual experiences begin much earlier than people realize, or pretend they do. The few times one hears or reads about it—between cousins and even closer relations—incest—"

"Yeah?"

"They're probably no more than tips of the iceberg. Your aunt never suspected?"

"I told you. She thought I came there for the dollar she gave me. Makes it treacherous, doesn't it?" His voice thickened, and he hemmed to clear it, smirked: "I wanted to play a decent part—where you were concerned—you know?"

"You poor lamb. What time do you think you could get her here Friday? Where is she? She's not employed yet?"

"No. That business school that faces Union Square Park, that's where she goes. I don't know the name. Near 14th Street."

"And what time can you get her here?"

"Any time you say. If it's an emergency."

"About two—that is, assuming she hasn't menstruated by then."

"Will I ever call you to tell you!"

"I'd better make the appointment for two-thirty. I take it she won't have any trouble getting out of the business school?"

"Oh, no—I'm sure of it. It's a private school. Secretarial, that kind of thing."

"Near 14th? You can get her here by taxi in a few minutes then. What is her name again?"

"Stella . . . *kubella.*"

"What?"

"It's Yiddish. Cybel."

"Is that her name?"

"No. Cow."

"Oh, Ira, please!"

"That's how I feel. Dumb, dumb satyr, Minotaur."

Edith slid off the couch and came toward him, even before he'd gotten to his feet. "Ira, I want you to know I don't think any less of you for what you've told me than I did before. You may think I do, but I don't. You're caught in the grip of nature's most powerful drive—we all are, and we're going to satisfy it somehow, men and women—in spite of religion and society, and everything else. It's unfortunate she's so young, but she may simply be more mature sexually than most girls her age. There's no clear line. It just happens she's your cousin. What if she were someone unrelated to you? You would still need help if she's pregnant, and I can only repeat, as young a girl as that probably isn't. I just hope you don't become so panic-stricken and frightened by guilt and God knows what that you let this thing ruin your life. Do you understand what I'm trying to tell you? Don't go to pieces. Don't let this thing do that to you."

"No."

"Ira—" She waited for him to stand up. "You're very dear to me. You know that. If necessary I'll do everything possible to prevent any disaster. Will you trust me?"

"That's why I came here."

"And I'm glad you did. You'll keep in touch with me?"

"All right."

"Over the next few days. I'm home evenings. Phone or come over."

He began getting into his coat. "It's just that I—you know. I'm a—" He swayed for lack of adequate words. "No good, that's all."

"Oh, fiddlesticks! Would you have been a better person not to have tried to take care of it, to have run away from it all? You've had the courage to take the responsibility for the whole thing—which in some ways is more than Lewlyn did."

"I don't know." He hung his head. "I—I better go tell her."

She pushed his chin up with dainty finger. "You're not to go to pieces and you're to keep in touch with me."

"I won't go to pieces, you know why? It isn't as bad as it might be."

She regarded him curiously. He felt as if he were switching all he had in mind to another track. "It isn't as bad as it might be because of you."

"I'm happy you feel that way, my dear. And I *will* take care of everything possible at this end."

"Thanks, Edith."

"And please stop being so downcast."

"It's hard not to. My type of guy."

"And wait a minute—before you go."

"Oh, no. Edith!"

"Oh, yes. God knows all this might have been avoided if you had some money."

"I *did* have some money. I thought I was playing it safe—that's what gets my goat. I can't remember."

"Even with Lucerol or a pessary one can't always be sure either. Not that—" she extracted the expected greenback from her purse while she spoke—"in the circumstances you could possibly use them. Please take this with you. It's for carfare, phone calls. Anything. Taxi, if you need it."

"Thanks. If one could only say—you know." He rubbed the folded five-dollar bill against itself. "There's nothing. It would take words made out of bronze."

"Don't try. But do keep in touch with me." She patted the back of his hand. "And do keep up your courage."

XIII

Drab and disconsolate, the stairs he climbed, informed with his own state of mind—and dim too, dingy, dim, with the landing between ground and first flight starved for light by the even taller tenement to the east. It had always been such a pleasant revelation when he was a youngster to climb up a flight or two, and especially to the top floor, where the window at the landing rang with daylight. But that was long ago, fifth grade long ago. First-landing window, ten-thousand-fold familiar, gave on a narrow slot of adjacent tenement, backyard and fence, drab scene to be climbed . . . upward to the obscure first flight, of a house that seemed quieter than usual, because of the cold, traced with fewer sounds and odors. First flight, "first floor," where the dumbwaiter, now retired, was nailed shut. . . .

There were three flats per floor. The one on the left, Mrs. Shapiro's, was *tsevorfen*, scattered, the two on the right, separated by a gloomy hallway, were railroad flats. Mrs. Shapiro's flat was "in the back," all her rooms looked out on the backyard; the railroad flats were in the front: each had a front room with two windows overlooking the street, and the long, obscure hallway between railroad flats borrowed a little illumination from the frosted glass of the front-room doors at the very end of the hallway. They were permanently locked. No one ever used them—except that one time at Ira's wintry Bar Mitzva, when his parents' bed was dismantled and taken through the front-room door to be stored out of the way. Still, if the family had a boarder, and the Stigmans had had one once, a young woman, during the Great War, so long ago and so briefly, Ira remembered only that she, like Minnie, had red hair, if the boarder was given the front room, she (or he) could go to the hall toilet without having to disturb the family.

During evening hours, unless it was very late and everyone had gone to bed, Ira could always tell whether anyone was home or not, by merely glancing up at the paint-spattered transom over the door: whether friendly light shone through. But not during daylight hours: speckled glass was all that met the eye, and only voices in the kitchen told him it was occupied. Automatically, Ira reached into his pocket for the key, realized that he hadn't transferred Edith's five-dollar bill to his wallet; the banknote lay together with what was left of the quarter Minnie had loaned him. Better get the bill safely stored away now, or reaching in and out like that, he would lose it. Goddamn him and his lousy predicaments, his sordid little crises that swelled up like monstrous balloons and preempted the sane, the lissome world. Minnie's delay of a couple of days had produced terror, twisted him out of shape forever; and now that dumb bunny Stella . . . immune to his pleas, his begging: all she would agree to was a hot bath—she liked hot baths anyway. But castor oil? Ira, castor oil! What are you talking about! Hannah and two or three of her girlfriends had been there too, so his importuning and haranguing had to be done in whispers, to no avail against her vapid optimism. If she didn't have her period by Friday, she'd go with him to his professor-lady. That was as much as she would concede, the *klutz,* too silly-sanguine to know the danger she was in—screw her—Ira tried the doorknob before inserting the key— somebody else gave her the big belly: Zeus, the Juice, the golden rain, Zeus, the Bull, the Gander, no, the Holy Goose. The door opened.

Alone, the Yiddish newspaper spread open wide in front of him on the green oilcloth of the kitchen table, Pop sat reading, *Der Vorwärts.* He was still wearing his vest, though he had removed the starched collar from his shirt, leaving only the brass stud protruding through the open neckband. Cigarette smoke was in the air, and Pop was smoking, evidently one of the Lucky Strikes from the several midget packs of cigarettes strewn on the table, revealed when Pop shifted the newspaper, complimentary little open packages of Lucky Strikes he must have salvaged from the banquet where he had been an "extra" this afternoon. He had a round-lipped way of smoking, unaggressively sipping smoke, with mouth softly shaped into an oval around the tip of the cigarette.

"Hi, Pop."

"Hi, hi. *Noo?*" Pop lifted brown eyes behind their gold-rimmed glasses, in habitual acknowledgment of Ira's presence: due and without affection. How differently they lighted up when Minnie appeared; they beamed. But with Ira they appraised.

And this time, apparently, they were none too pleased by what they saw, for Pop looked away more quickly than usual. Was it his imagination baiting him? Ira wondered as he removed hat and coat; he had a sense of being furtively scrutinized. Still, what could Pop guess about the fix his son was in?

He returned from the bedroom to the kitchen again—and to the tension he always felt when alone with Pop. The days had long passed when he needed Mom's protection against his father, her amelioration of their antagonism. Still . . . if there wasn't the old fear, there was the same lack of affinity, and still the same need for token concealment of their estrangement. So what? He was twenty-one years old, and bigger than the little guy. And there was Edith. . . . There, that made him feel a little more secure, almost patronizing—like a shield against Madame Curie's radioactive speck of guilt: "Well, how did the banquet go, Pop?"

Pop went through his elaborate evolution of deprecation. "May it please them that kind of death," he said. "A fruit cup, a half chicken with vegetables, a devil's food cake and coffee. Nothing fancy. One plate, *und shoyn.* No stairs."

"Yeah?"

"May it never be worse."

"Well."

"I shared three tables with an Irishman. They say Yidlekh. Were the Jewish waiters half the man he was. Strong. And with his laugh. They make the jop a nothing. Shoulders. He could have served *me* on his tray. 'Hey, Charley,' he called me. 'Hey, Charley.'"

"Oh, yeah?" Ira grinned appreciatively.

"*Mazel, mazel.*" Pop's amiability increased, catalyzed by his son's. "Sometimes one has a little luck. Even I."

"Yeah?" Ira encouraged.

"With a *yeet* I would have rushed my *kishkehs* out. With him it was easy. Seven and a half dollars apiece. And then the Irish police lieutenant slipped us another five dollars between us—a countryman, you know? Would a Yiddle have told me? A *goy* is a *goy.* If he hadn't such a hatred against Jews, we could live."

"Yeah."

"After, I stayed."

"What do you mean?"

"They give you another dollar and a half if you stay after the banquet and fill up the ketchup and the vinegar bottles. And the salt and pepper and the sugar bowls."

"I see."

"Would God, next week it should be the same," Pop prayed. "Do you want a cigarette?"

"I'm not crazy about Luckies. You?"

"He who wanted picked them up. To every diner they gave a package. So . . . they were on the tables." Pop paused. It was as though he were waiting before testing Ira with the gesture. "You want, take. You don't, *iz nisht.*"

"Oh, no, thanks, Pop!" Ira was hearty in acceptance. "I gotta try one." He shook out the single cigarette left in the mini-package, struck a match, and lit up. "Not bad." He puffed. Could he safely cut off the old boy without offense? He still had three books of *Paradise Lost* to skim through. "I wonder where's Mom, where's Minnie?"

"Indeed, where's Minnie?" Pop rejoined. "Mom will be there at the *alter kocker*'s until Mamie, the clever, decides it's time to leave. And God alone knows when that will be. Let's both—you know what?"

"No."

"We'll both have the *kugel* and sour cream she left. And a cup coffee, and a piece of that poppy-seed bread, yes?"

"Oh, sure. Good idea, Pop. That sounds swell." And after that, what a fine transition to an end of currying cordiality, spinning a web of friendship across the void. Grab his Milton and shut up.

"Yeh? All right." Pop locked palm in palm. "I had such a good-luck day, come with me to the movies."

"What?"

"And when she comes home, there won't be anybody here. Well, Min," Pop conceded. "Let her wonder."

"Mom, you mean?"

"Who else?"

"Yeah, but I've gotta do some studying."

"Uh!" As abrupt as his exclamation was the change in Pop's mien.

"But I do."

"I already know."

"I have a test tomorrow. I'd like to get a decent grade. It really counts."

"Yeh, yeh, yeh. Do you know who's playing in the Jewel Theater on Fifth Avenue? Duffy?"

"Duffy?" Ira repeated, puzzled.

"Tomorrow he won't be there."

"Who's Duffy?"

"You don't know? You saw him yourself, you said, in the last picture: Duff and dynamite."

"Duff and dynamite?" Ira strained at memory. "I didn't—you don't mean—you mean Chaplin?"

"Duffy, yeh. You want to go?" Pop reverted to customary brusqueness. "Don't do me no favors. You want to go, or you don't want to go? *Iz nisht.* I'll save a dollar."

"But that isn't the idea—" Ridiculous: his own confusions, Pop's confoundings. Everything a welter of predicament, compassion, and irresolution. "No, I know you're doing me a favor, Pop—I mean—I love Chaplin."

"*Noo?*"

"I told you I have to study. There's a test coming up."

"Yeh, yeh, yeh. And all day? I come home. You're not here. Now you have to study."

"But Pop," Ira pleaded. "You never asked me before." It was beyond belief, Pop's being so—importunate, demanding, in his generosity. Beyond belief. Unique. "I'd go. You know that."

"I know. I know already from long ago. Everything you see through her eyes. She made you herself. And then she says, see what you are. I know. I know." He mashed his cigarette in the dish. "Let it be that way. I'll go alone. I need no companion. Only Minnie understands a little bit, a little bit." He stood up, locked both ends of the neckband in the collar button, then went into the bedroom.

What the hell was he talking about? As if he didn't have troubles enough, his head churned listening to Pop. Ira went irresolutely to the shelf under the china closet, where he had left his copy of Milton's poems this morning. Maybe he was all wrong about the reason he thought Pop was scrutinizing him when he came in. See things through Mom's eyes. Was the old guy going off his pulley? He didn't seem that way. And Charlie Chaplin: Dough and Dynamite. Christ Almighty. Dark and hostile, his old self, Pop reentered the kitchen. He had his hat and overcoat on, was dressed to leave.

"You're not going to eat?" Ira asked noncommittally, only too aware how quickly roles had been restored.

"I'm obliged to her." Pop flapped his hand in customary dismissal. "As she is, so are you. If there's no pity, nothing helps. As she made my life—and you made my life—then I'm the sinful one."

Ira listened in silence. No use answering something he couldn't make sense of.

"Tell her I'll be back I don't know when."

"Enjoy yourself, Pop."

His father barely nodded. The cold gloom of the hallway pried into the kitchen through the open door, which Pop closed again behind him.

They must have had a hell of a battle this morning, after he left to go to Edith's. That was all the feasible conjecture Ira could reach. Minnie wouldn't know what it was about either, since she had left when he had. He let the pages riffle through his fingers. The tight book had a way of returning to its own equilibrium, unless borne down upon and held open, and he had neglected to do so, talking to Pop. Did you ever hear of Pop offering to take you to a movie? What was wrong? Ira asked himself sarcastically. That cheapskate, what the hell had gotten into him? And that stuff about sinning. Pity. And Duffy. Remembering, Ira snorted: Duff and dynamite. Jesus, if that wasn't—boy, pitiful. . . .

The flipping pages stopped—or he stopped them, deliberately, though he had already perused the one that attracted his attention—the all too relevant lines of verse mocking his state. No wonder people sorted—was that the right word? Told their fortunes by opening to someplace in the Bible:

> *Pensive here I sat*
> *Alone, but long I sat not, till my womb,*
> *Pregnant by thee, and now excessive grown*
> *Prodigious motion felt and rueful throes.*

Damn right. He slapped the pages over. Book X, Book X. That was where he had left off: Full of sticky theology that old man Mott would be sure to ask about, pose questions requiring essay-type answers—at which he stunk. Well, he'd have to resign himself to losing credits—hell, skip it. Adam couldn't figure it out either:

> *O Conscience, into what abyss of fears*
> *And horrors hast thou driven me; out of which*
> *I find no way, from deep to deeper plunged!*

The tread in the hall was light—Ira listened, his ears straining to the light tread: he heard the door opposite open, and a youngster's voice: One of Mrs. Gruberg's kids. . . .

Ever since he was twelve, he thought to himself. No wonder he was a virtuoso at dissembling. Even fooled Edith. What would have happened if Minnie hadn't refused, if she had yielded every time, like Stella? Oh, they'd have found out, Pop, Mom, by now. Boy, what a racket. Worse than the silver-filigreed fountain pen. Then what? A whipping like nothing ever before. But would it cure him? What happened in families where it happened? If the guy was grown up, as he was now, and was caught—out, bum! Out, crumb, out of the house, yuh miserable punk! "Aw, I was just givin' her a fuck," he'd say, if they were *goyim*, the way the Irish say in the street, I was just fuckin' around. And make a gag out of it: "What about you, Pop? She's better'n Mom, ain't she?" And Ira had always thought as a kid "yuh motherfucker" was just a fanciful insult, like "Aw, yer father's hairy balls!" Boy, though, a father fucking his daughter, like Satan fucking Sin, that must be wonderful—see what Milton had done to him, see what he was? Ira bowed his head—impenitently. But if they were Jews: *Oy, gevald, Peigern zollst deh! Paskudnyack!* Be torn into shreds—he could just see Zaida's whiskers opening like a maw to hurl curses at the abomination. He'd rend his garments. And worse: raise his walking stick. But if it happened now, now that he was twenty-one, it would be just as he would have been with Pop the other night, Friday. Frig you, Pop. Maybe bust him one and run. Oh, nuts. Read, will you? Book X. You're not in enough of a mess with Stella already. Ho, Jesus, what if he had gone back to Edith, and told her he had knocked up his sister too. You knocked up your cousin. You knocked up your sister. You busted your old man. Could you sleep on the floor till you found a job? Boyoboy, and she thought you were an innocent: unawakened, was that what she said? If she knew when you were awakened. And how. Boyoboy, what paralysis that was, that awakening, after Moe went off to war: in the springtime, the only pretty ringtime: *erev Pesach* of 1918—

Her color heightened by cold and exertion, Mom swept the kitchen with her brown eyes as she entered, bringing a merciful end to wakeful nightmares. "He's not here?" She removed her black turban hat, shook her speckled gray hair. "Was he home?" She freed herself of her dark coat.

"Yeah. He was here. He went to a movie."

"Wandered off." She nodded—with undue, unpleasant emphasis, features creased in unspoken grudge. "Wandered off." She opened the bedroom door, muttered something in Polish: "Let him go hang. May I never see him again." Coat over arm, she was about to enter the bedroom.

"Whatsa matter?"

"May he be slain."

"Why? He even wanted to take me along," Ira probed.

"*Azoy?* My fine husband, he'll be tender as a mulberry, may he moulder." Her voice was vengeful, even for Mom.

"What did he do this time?"

"May they do him under." She refused to answer his direct question. Instead, she stepped into the bedroom.

What was up now? Ira wondered. What the hell was up? Oh, nuts. He had too much on his mind to be concerned. Finish up Book X, Book XI, Book XII, call Stella on the phone tomorrow. If he could only get a break—this once. He ought to look at his ed texts. Oh, balls.

Mom returned, shut the kitchen door to the cold bedroom."Have you had anything to eat?"

"No."

"I left *kugel* and sour cream. He didn't eat either?"

"No."

"He's the affronted one, my mannikin. I'll warm up the *kugel*."

"What the hell's the matter now?" Ira demanded irritably. "He gave you your allowance Friday."

"Go! Why deliberate on the carrion? Let him rot." She opened the kitchen window, brought out a pan, a bowl. "I'll warm it right away." She busied herself with frying pan and gas stove. "I'll cut some bread. I have some farmer cheese."

"All right. All right. What I want to know is, what did you find out at Zaida's? I mean at Sadie's. What was the whole to-do about? It wasn't about Pop, that I'm sure of."

"Only that I lack."

"Well, the way you're talking, anybody would think—"

"It was nothing with nothing."

"No? Please, no chicory in the coffee, Mom."

"I know, I know."

"What do you mean, nothing with nothing?"

"To me, to Mamie, it would have been nothing with nothing. To him, he's a *koyn*, a priest—ekh, who can follow it all. An old man, he imagines—don't you know? He swears he once heard Stella and a lover—anh, weeks ago. At the door, you hear?"

"Yes?"

"The radio music fills him with terror. That we know already. And the neighborhood grows more and more Portorickie. The girls grow friendlier and friendlier with them. And then blacks too moving in. Ask not. He imagines, God knows." Mom laughed in short pained resignation. "A disgrace, a bastard, and a dark one."

"Is that all?"

"Preys on his mind, ever since that night he swears he heard—and wouldn't the dire year befall: on his way home from the synagogue Friday morning—and you know how much it pleases him to be a Jew with a beard among Portorickies and blacks?—his fortune it is on his way home from the synagogue he comes to the corner of 112th Street near Fifth Avenue—and there, in an empty lot, where a house has been torn down, in the rubble stands a policeman—and while bystanders gather and watch and as Zaida goes by, he sees the policeman take out a newborn infant from a paper grocery bag—dead. Now," Mom nodded in imitation of Zaida's admission, "he confesses it was illusion. But then, when he saw the dead infant: Stella's features, Stella's light hair—*noo, noo*. You needn't ask."

"What bullshit."

"Go debate with a panic-stricken old man, and one eye half blind. He fled. In an instant he makes up his mind—he's defiled if he stays at Mamie's. *Heraus* from Mamie's. *Heraus erev Shabbes*. The neighbor calls up Morris: Bring the *meshinkeh* at once. He fares forth."

"Well, I'll be—"

"And now, do you think he's content?" Mom set plate and cutlery in front of Ira. "A bygone day."

"He's never content."

"This time he may have reason. Sadie, with all her thick eyeglasses, is also half blind. And blind as he is, he says he thought he saw her once about to confuse a meat with a dairy dish—so he whispered to us."

"Yeah? Tough. Somebody told me that would happen. Joe, I think."

"It's as I told you. The *kugel* is good?"

"Oh, your *kugel* is always good."

She laughed at his mock-serious tone: his mother, all love and devotion—love and devotion out of her ever-receding world. She set a white saucer and coffee cup on the table. "Take more sour cream. I have yeast cake. And jelly too that I made out of plums."

"Yeah? I don't see you eating anything."

"I ate enough for the whole day at Sadie's. Mamie brought pickled herring, creamed herring. Two jars. Borsht, a jar. And *verenekehs*—like all the Farbs. Afterward she was sorry."

"What do you mean? "

"She wanted to punish him for leaving the way he did—to remind him." Mom placed white saucer and cup in front of Ira. "But then, when she saw how unhappy he was, she got no satisfaction. You understand?"

"What else is bothering Zaida besides food?"

"The children."

"Why the children? They're boys, three of them." Ira snickered. "The oldster won't have to fret about bastards in a paper bag."

"No, no, it's my brother Saul's imp comes over and eggs the others on. They tied a cord across the door, and screamed and goaded him, until he ran after them. And half blind as he is, don't you think he stretched out his full length?"

"Jesus, an old guy like that?" Ira watched Mom pour coffee out of the small enamel pan.

"I said to him, 'Father, if you can't live here, then together with you as a boarder, we could find a better place than 119th Street—near a synagogue. And I swear to you I would keep a kosher home.' He knows I would keep my word."

"That's all we need, a kosher home."

"Go, he wouldn't live here. He loves Chaim'l like the Angel of Death. And with reason." She cut a slice of yeast cake. "My paragon would soon be grinding his teeth and stamping his feet. Who doesn't know my Chaim'l? But even I didn't know him until this morning." She placed the freshly cut slice in front of Ira.

"What?" He looked up at her face—a kind of implacable disdain graven on it. What was she dramatizing now? Or concealing? They had seemed as amiable as they ever were, when he and Minnie had said goodbye to them this morning. "What the hell's the matter now?"

"You have your own woes." She refused to clarify. "I can see it in your face: your examinations, your penniless existence. A youth without a groat."

"That's nothing." He was about to cheer her with mention of Edith's gift of five dollars, but stopped himself in time. He'd only have to think up some phony explanation—or defend himself of the charge of cadger.

"The old man took off his yarmulka, and bowed to me."

"What?"

"Zaida." Mom sat down with her cup of coffee.

"Zaida?"

"When I gave him my word I would keep a kosher home for him. 'I abused you when you were young,' he said. 'I didn't know how noble you were, Leah. Forgive me.'"

"Zaida did? That haughty Yid? Jesus."

Her full lips smacked the coffee mug. "What was there to say after so many years? That his righteousness helped him as much as my nobility helped me? A little more jelly? The cake is so dry."

"No, it's not bad, Mom. Thanks." Were those his two profiles he saw staring at each other in his mind? Or just any two profiles that wore eyeglasses? They could never become a single face that way, he allowed himself to ruminate: if you slid one past the other, they still stared in opposite directions, like Janus. No good. You had to have a third dimension for their views to coincide—

"Shtudier, shtudier," Mom interposed.

"Oh, yeah." Only to him was Milton so easy, a diversion from the drama of his own home. He applied himself to the italicized rubric of Book XI: "The Son of God presents to his Father the Prayers of our first Parents now repenting, and intercedes for them. God accepts. . . ." What the hell, Satan had had a point when he disputed back then with Abdiel. Jesus was asking God to forgive Adam, and the whole damn thing had started because God had anointed Jesus to reign as coequal. Satan wasn't to blame if he objected to the dichotomy. So did Jews. *Shmai Yisroel, adonoi elohenu adonoi ekhud!* Every Jew knew that: it was the Credo: God is one. Lefty Louie, the gangster, when he sat in the electric chair, yelled it out loud. Otherwise, what? A split divinity. A split infinity. Object, and you're on the side of Satan; even if the whole thing is sheer figment, you're on the side of Satan. So he, Ira Stigman, was on the side of Satan. That was why he had to call up Stella tomorrow afternoon, after the exam, and find out if she had had her period—boy, what an emancipation proclamation that would be. Maybe he ought to pray to Jesus Christ. Cross himself thrice and pray to Christ—

"Shtudierst?" Mom asked.

"No, I was just thinking about the exam tomorrow."

"Zoll dir Got helfen."

"Yeah." If he had knocked her up, so what the hell was the difference if Divinity were unity or twinity or trinity? He would have had to marry her, if it happened in Arkansas: they would have had shotguns for a *khuppa.* Read, will you: God accepts them, but declares that they must no longer abide in Paradise; sends Michael with a Band of Cherubim to dispossess them. . . . With a dispossess notice, like Mamie with a Portorickie . . . in court . . . the day Zaida beat it to Flushing . . . boy, like that old, old, old, old gag in the vaudeville show: Who was dat lady I seen you wit' in dat sidewalk café? Dat was no sidewalk café. Dat was my foinicher.

Why the two pages of notes had been lying on his right-hand typing table all this time—literally all these weeks—and to just what use he had intended to put them, Ira could no longer recall—nor even when he had typed them. Sometime in the late sixties, he guessed, judging by the discolored border of the yellow second sheets. But here they were, Hannah's recollections: he ought to use them or dispose of them. If he was ever to use them, this would be an appropriate time: when he was writing about the jam he had been in with Stella. The notes seemed to alter his interpretation of his sexual conduct, not entirely, but enough to be significant—by injecting a curious element of external and deliberate influence in his behavior. At the same time as the notes mitigated his acute self-reproach, by appearing to shift the blame slightly, they also tended to diminish the importance he assigned to his guile; they made him feel chagrined—almost: less culpable, but more foolish—as if he had gone to great lengths to reach a goal that was practically at hand—kinked himself into farcical postures to achieve a simple gesture. Typical of him, absence of acumen about the other person's motives. Not that it was entirely true—Ira meditated—but as a quip, one might say that the notes on the yellow sheets adulterated the construction he placed on his adultery, except that technically speaking, it wasn't adultery, but fornication with a minor.

Ira recalled taking deep breath before posing the question to his cousin Hannah: "What did you girls do for pastime in the twenties, when you lived in Harlem?"

"Oh, we went looking for boys, like other girls did. Or we went to the Y to dance. It was fifty cents admission." Inflection of Bronx or Brooklyn virtually marinated matronly—and widowed—Hannah's drawl. "Or we took long walks through Central Park. And always we talked about the boys. What would it be like? What was sex like? Why did we get so excited when a boy took our arm to cross the street, and by accident on purpose touched our breast? And sometimes, kissing, we could feel he was getting an erection.

We were excited. Still, we pushed him away. My mother had a different view of sex than most mothers."

"Yes?"

"She was terribly afraid of the mental results of a girl not having sex." Hannah tapped her temple. "She believed that if a girl didn't have sex by twenty at the latest, she would be a mental case."

"By twenty. At the latest?" Ira queried.

"In Galitzia, with the *shotkhins,* they married so early they didn't have to worry. But here—a girl had to have sex before she was twenty."

"That's interesting," Ira said meditatively—and then with a start: "Mamie believed that?"

"Oh, Mama as much as told me if I wasn't married by nineteen I should go to the Catskills to a summer resort and get laid. Naturally a nice boy, and be careful."

"I'll be damned." Ira gazed at his cousin intently. "That's illuminating."

"Isn't it? She really had a phobia. And with Stella—"

"Mamie didn't have to worry about that," Ira scoffed.

"No. But about marriage. Stella was having such a good time, she didn't care about marriage—" Grief suddenly intruded: "My poor sister. So soon."

"Yes." Ira sympathized. "One question more: How would you characterize Stella during those years?"

"Those years and now. She was shallow. Stella is a shallow person. Intellectually she's sluggish. Not so much now as she was then. My poor sister," Hannah mourned. "I should see her walking again."

XIV

Sense of impending tragedy—Ira was carried along with the swarm of fellow students into the lecture hall—impending tragedy, with only Edith to intercede, with only Edith to relieve the strain. For him, only him, the midterm exam served as respite from agony. He climbed up the steep stairs of the lecture hall. Relieve it and compound it. He found his assigned seat among the curved tiers of chairs. Relieve it and compound it: the immigrant boy's ultimate terror. He envisaged himself leading the tubby sixteen-year-old through Morton Street, and up the two flights of carpeted steps to Edith's urbane, genteel (or was it gentile?) apartment: "Edith, this is Stella." Oh, Jesus, oh, Jesus. His eyes roved unseeingly about the auditorium, unseeing, uncaring, registering faces he knew, just as his ears registered familiar noise of hinged chairs lowered, hinged side desks opened. Monitors checked off the attendance against the cardboard seating plan. Goateed Seymour was one of them, the only undergraduate in all of CCNY to sport a beard—probably because Professor Mott wore one, and Seymour was often seen carrying Professor Mott's briefcase to Amsterdam Avenue, where he hailed a cruising taxi for the elderly scholar.

The bell rang the beginning of the period hour, just as Professor Mott entered, followed by a student carrying a stack of blue examination booklets. The usual white examination question papers were not in evidence; were they in the booklets? They were being distributed by the monitors. Suddenly there was a loud guffaw. And shaken out of his unhappy reverie, Ira saw that the old professor had fallen on the steps leading up from the floor to the lecture platform where his desk was. Seymour leaped forward to help him, and one or two others jumped from their seats to lend assistance. With an irritated shake of the head, Professor Mott waved them away, climbed up the last two steps, and placed his briefcase on the desk. He sat down behind it; then, bending over, he inconspicuously rubbed his shin.

"Professor Mott." Seymour drew himself up resolutely. "I wish to apologize for the rude behavior of my classmates." Professor Mott nodded his silky white head in terse acknowledgment and opened his briefcase. Through the tic about his left eye, Seymour scowled up at his unchastened classmates. He strode to the lecture-hall door and shut it, and still glaring up in reprimand, came back and sat down in his seat in the first row.

"In the interest of all concerned," Professor Mott kept surreptitiously rubbing his shin, "I've decided to vary the form of the midterm examination. There will be no written questions." He drew out a leather-bound volume of Milton's works. "I shall review briefly some of the chief arguments thus far, and then ask you to answer to the best of your ability a single question. First I shall present a brief summary of the course of events, and at the end, pose the question. Is that clear? You'll have a half hour to answer. I have deliberately limited the time." Professor Mott waited until the murmuring in the lecture hall died down, indicating the class had recovered from its surprise. "You recall that Satan, having rallied his ruined cohorts, volunteers to explore a certain happy seat—in the words of Beelzebub—of some new race called Man. By discovering it, he hopes thereby to frustrate the designs of the Almighty. Frustration of God's designs has now become the consuming purpose of the denizens of Hell, the former imperial powers of Heaven. It is interesting to note, by the way, that while their chief has gone on his mission, his confederates pass the time variously, according to mood and temperament, some violently, some in melancholy, singing to the acccompaniment of harps—fallen angels, it appears, also have access to harps. Much of this part is drawn from paganism, much is reminiscent of Homer, of the activities of ancient Greece, including, if you remember, the holding of Olympic Games—again attesting to Milton's vast erudition. At any rate, after a long, arduous flight, Satan finally reaches the gates of Hell. Nothing better exemplifies Milton's absolutely sublime powers of poetic rhetoric than the dramatic confrontation that takes place between these personifications of the triad of foremost evils in the world: Satan, Death, and Sin— Yes?" Professor Mott raised his silky white poll questioningly. "Please be brief."

"Professor Mott." Sol P, stubby and carrot-topped, lowered his hand and arose to his feet—knocking his large loose-leaf notebook from the armrest and sending it flopping loudly to the floor. "If God in His heaven was all-seeing, all-knowing, om—er—omni—"

"Omnivorous," Yarman, who sat just below, heckled in a whisper.

"Omnipotent," Sol shook off Yarman's insidious prompting, "why did he allow all this to happen?"

"Of course, you could ask that question from the very outset. Why did He allow Satan—Lucifer—to incite mutiny in Heaven? This is the very problem that has bedeviled Christianity from the beginning. I use the word 'bedeviled' advisedly." Professor Mott's mild blue eyes brightened in appreciation of his jest.

"But Professor, doesn't that imply God's complicity in Satan's actions?"

Low groans could be heard. Someone hissed, "*Shmuck*, sit down."
Yarman turned completely around and muttered *sotto*-ventrilo-
quistically between rigid lips: "It wasn't enough he fell flat on his
whiskers today. You gotta add to his *shmertz*?" Sol tossed his red head
defiantly.

"I'm sorry. I can't go into that, for the very simple reason that the
pros and cons of the answer to that question make up the answers to
the question I intend to assign." Professor Mott looked down at his
leather-bound volume, then raised his head in snowy afterthought.
"Of course, you understand that the theological debate on the subject
still goes on, and is far beyond the scope of this course. Your question
concerns the compatibility or incompatibility of predestination and
free will, and the role played by grace. Churches have been split by dis-
putes over these doctrines. Innumerable theses have been written on
them. *Paradise Lost* may be classed as the most sublime of these, and
now at the end of the poem, I hope you'll have derived some notion of
the doctrines themselves, quite apart from Milton's interpretation of
them."

Sol sat down, then crouched to retrieve his loose-leaf notebook;
but it had been kicked from neighbor to neighbor, and into the aisle.
"Bastards," he hissed, and when no one heeded his urgent gestures to
return his possession, he stood up again and stepped on foot after foot
in his journey to recover it.

"Dumb cluck. Bullshit artist," they baited him under their breath.
"Ouch! Rivington Street shyster." Through it all, and for the next ten
minutes afterward, Professor Mott in level tones summarized the
twelve books, dwelling now and then on some special point. "There is
probably nothing so poignant in all of Milton," Professor Mott turned
pages, "as his invocation to Light at the beginning of Book III. And
here his invocation has added relevancy because the poet has escaped,
as he says, the Stygian Pool. Nevertheless, being blind, he has only the
light of his imagination to irradiate his mind. He beholds Jehovah sitting on his throne, who Himself spies Satan flying toward the newly
created Eden. Here we have the assertion of Divine Justice, and the
role of the Son of God offering Himself as a ransom. . . ."

No, he wouldn't call Stella today. It would be smarter if he called
her tomorrow, Tuesday: the seventh day, lucky seventh. If not, he was a

goner. Be no use hoping anymore. Call Edith to make an appointment for Wednesday. And meet Stella in front of the business school on 14th Street. Take a cab. Right? Oh, Jesus. Come seven, come eleven. Seven, Tuesday, eight, Wednesday, or was it nine? He was beginning to forget. Hang on one more day: Tuesday.

"No doubt it hasn't escaped your notice," Professor Mott commented as he looked up at the tiers of students, "that in Book VI, during the gigantic battle between the forces of good and evil, the account of which the Angel Raphael reports to Adam, it is the forces of evil who introduce artillery. It is the invention of Satan himself." Professor Mott locked a delicate hand on his white beard as he sought the appropriate quotation. "Yes. An infernal device, naturally." He read from the open page: "'Shall yield us, pregnant with infernal flame, which into Hollow Engines, long and round thick rammed—'" Ira smirked drearily. "Parenthetically, the innovation was already censured even before Milton by Shakespeare, who speaks of firearms as a coward's way of felling many a tall lad. Still, not even these engines of destruction are of any avail before the infinite power with which God has clothed His Son. Satan and his cohorts are cast down into Hell. And Raphael, having told Adam all this, warns him to beware of Satan's designs." Professor Mott pointed a pink finger at the ceiling: "'Listen not to his temptations,'" he recited from memory. "'Warn thy weaker. Thy weaker—'"

Professor Mott drew out his watch. "I'm going to have to stop here. You have a little more than a half hour left. Please try to write as legibly and as concisely as you can, and with pen and ink. Name or describe at least six events in *Paradise Lost* which will prove to be the most crucial to Man's future existence. And why. Please don't forget to write your name and seat number on the front of the blue book." Professor Mott bent sideways, and with decorous mien reached down behind his desk—manifestly toward his shin. "Yes, I'll repeat the question," he answered the tacit inquiry of a few raised hands. Six events.

Ira unscrewed his fountain-pen cap. All about him fountain pens already scratching. Hell, there was only one event, the one that had occurred to him last night: the creation of a coequal only son, later to be incarnated as Jesus H. Christ. What in hell did He need Him for? Ira recalled somewhere, sometime reading that the Son had been coeternal with the Father. That made more sense than appointing a straw boss late in the game before whom to genuflect twice, or something to that effect.

He'd better get it down on paper, and fast. Quit dawdling. He applied gold penpoint to paper. And giving the key to Hellgate to Sin. Let's go. What the hell did God expect the old broad to do? Keep her word? Christ, and then the door wouldn't close afterward. Was that an event? No. The holy disposes, oh, yeah. But giving the key way before was already two: she opened the gate. Then there was Pride. Why the hell did Lucifer get a dose of Pride, anyway? Didn't the Almighty know what that would cause? Was that an event? Pride, pride, pride—and then that burning in the mind that made old Nick giddy, old Nick sick. Was he himself familiar with that one: Jesus Christ, his thoughts reverted, madness, geometry planes, will you cut it out? Whew. Damn near added that one. Wouldn't old man Mott's snowy locks stand right up on end when he read adolescent rosebuds opening before the suppliant? Gather ye rosebuds while ye may. Oh, no, sap: the apple, the apple. A key event. Let's see, what was he supposed to do? He was supposed to call Stella—tomorrow, tomorrow, not today. Tomorrow and tomorrow steps in this petty pace—so the guy started screwing his own daughter. Hey, there was an event: an archangel screwing—Jesus, what bullshit. So get it down on paper. How? Copulating. No. Coitus, no. Too impolite. Venery. Intercourse. How the hell did Milton say it? Took a fancy to her. No. Such favor found. Event, come on. He impregnated her with Satanic semen vile. Write something—Ira's suppressed snicker brought a sidelong look from his neighbor. So she bore him an heir: Death—who immediately raped his own mother. Some heir. Hey, wait a minute: that's an event. Is that four? So if Sin is Satan's daughter, and Death is Satan's son, they're brother and sister. There you go: father and daughter, son and mother, brother and sister.

What a bunch. But that's not an event, you halfwit. Get away from it and forage, will you: the defeat of Satan by the Son of God. Artillery. That was an event. Mott gave the class that one on a platter just now. That was five, or was it? What the hell did the rest of these Jews think? They didn't think about screwing their sisters, or knocking up their cousins, did they? He was living the real thing and they only thought it was a course, that was all. If there was a hell, where you'd be. Where would they all be? They're Jews.

Oh, wait a minute, wait a minute, before the bell rang: Jesus offered Himself as a sacrifice to redeem man for having sinned against God Almighty. And what a selfish prig He was, offering himself as a sacrifice for no one. But that was an event. Damn right. He said six, a half-dozen.

What else? Ira squinted at his scrawl on the lined pages, looked away. Below him, hoary and tranquil, Professor Mott sat with fingers clasped on his already fastened briefcase, old scholar musing on . . . what? Musing on getting ready to leave. Did he believe that stuff? He couldn't; how could any intelligent, learned man believe it? And yet, you never knew with these *goyim*. Poppycock, Edith would have said. Still, what pleasure Ira's love of Milton's wonderful, orotund lines gave her— The gong sounded. Period's end.

"Please stop writing," Professor Mott directed. "Deposit your blue books on the desk as you go out. Mr. K, would you mind collecting them, please."

"Certainly not, Professor."

Seymour eagerly jumped up amid the bustle and scrape and clatter of the class in motion— One more event for good measure: Ira scribbled frantically: Chaos gives Satan directions to Eden.

XV

Ira joined the throng of classmates flocking noisily toward the stairs. There was a good chance Larry would be in the '28 alcove. Both had free periods next. Time and change, time and change, never ending, never resting. However much they seemed to shift and dance, the two variables were like the solid earth, whose motion the pendulum, with the feather at its end, marked in the sand the spin of the sphere. The two variables, the only constants, carved into the instable sand, and left nothing untouched. Once, in another time, he would have looked forward eagerly to meeting Larry, meeting him, exchanging the latest, the latest Jewish joke or the latest about Edith or—or just the opportunity to shoot the breeze. But that seemed ages ago . . . like so much else, like so much else. Besides, Larry had made so many new friends since transferring to CCNY, especially Iven H, blond, husky, and outstanding physics major, who seemed as unworldly as Larry was worldly. They had taken to hobnobbing together—for which Ira was thankful, since their friendship relieved him of the responsibility to provide vitality to an intimacy no longer viable. He descended to the dingy ground floor of the alcoves. Perhaps he ought to duck out of the building, just as he was, trot the short distance to the library, skulk— never mind the overcoat in the locker—he had too damned much on his mind for trivialities, for glossing over crisis. But then what would happen? Anxiety would grab hold, and he'd be in the phone booth trying to reach Stella—but that wasn't the plan. He could only allow himself one or two more tries at the most, with that Bert Lytell trick of masking speech with handkerchief over the phone. No, he'd better head for the alcove. Iven might be there, or Iz S, with news about a new play at the Provincetown Theater—and a possible bit part for Larry, now interested in the stage, having abandoned poetry, sculpture, and all other creative outlets Edith might indulge. His latest stage, Ira smirked. Trouble with Iz was he was so damn studious; he might be in the library himself—and Iven in a physics lab.

And so it appeared. Unaccompanied, Larry was sitting at the end of the mahogany bench of the '28 alcove, poring over a text. The guy might be boning up for midterms too, it occurred to Ira. Why hadn't he thought of that? Let him be, and slip into the unappetizing lunchroom until time for his ed class. Instead he allowed himself to stand at the entrance to the alcove, until Larry spied him.

"Ira. Hey."

"Larry. Wotcha got? Midterm next?"

"No. Lewlyn—Dr. Craddock," Larry corrected himself, "said the finals would be enough."

"Yeah?"

"Sit down."

Ira slipped into the well-polished space between Larry and Yerman, who had already gotten there.

"I just came from Mott's little midterm," Ira informed his colleagues.

"Do you know why he bothers?" Yerman, slight of build, but with a plump, impassive face, had the reputation of having read everything, and retaining it—phenomenally.

Ira shrugged. "What're you gonna do with *goyish* religion and Jewish students?"

"Why? What was the test?" Larry asked.

Ira mugged. "Why we got driven outta the Garden of Yeeden."

Larry smiled. His mustache was now fully rounded out, black and thick, contrasting with his dappled skin. "You didn't have to read Milton to find that out. I could have told you."

"No." Yerman remained staunchly serious. "You don't have to trivialize the course, just because it involves Christian theology. Mott ought to emphasize the difference in the Puritan construction of religious doctrine—and practice too—as against the upper class, the Cavalier Anglican. You don't get any idea of what a radical Milton was."

"You mean Satan wouldn't give Sin the business?" Ira jibed at Yerman's lecture.

"Oh, come on. That's not what I'm talking about. It was the sixteenth century, not ours. And there was a helluva split going on at the time. How many in the class realize that Milton was speaking for the same Puritans who came over here on the *Mayflower*? They were radicals. They were the Reds of their day."

"We didn't know because we took a later boat," said Larry.

"Ah, go on. Even if the course dealt with the contrast between the prevailing knowledge of the cosmos in Milton's time and what it was in feudal times, we'd get more out of it."

"Oh, boy," Larry interjected.

"There'd be a little life to the course, instead of Professor Mott just sitting up there reading and commenting. As if we couldn't read for ourselves."

"All right, tell Seymour to suggest it." Ira leaned heavily on the facetious. "Sure, I know Milton mentioned artillery. And Milton must have looked through Galileo's telescope too. So?"

"So the globe wouldn't be hanging from Heaven by a gold cord—"

"Okay. Okay. So where's Paradise?" Ira questioned.

"It's done lost, I heard," said Larry.

"There's more truth in that than you suspect. Even John Donne had to acknowledge that the round earth had imaginary corners. Milton's cosmos lacks all unity—just compare it to Dante's."

"Okay. I believe you. Here comes Sol." Evidently fresh from the lunchroom, Sol pried morsel from teeth by dint of tongue and toothpick. "Hey, Sol, when did Paradise get lost?" Ira asked.

"Who wants to know?"

"Yerman."

"Yerman shouldn't know? He's covering up."

"You're a Philistine. What's the use of talking to you?" Yarman commented on Sol and Ira's exchange.

"It comes in handy to be a Philistine," said Sol."What's wrong with being a Philistine? So I don't read the *Dial,* and I don't read Mencken. But the whole country is Philistines. Do they read the *Dial,* do they read *The American Mercury?* No. They read the tabloids. They make a living. They dance the Charleston, listen to soaps on the radio. And they'll support cool Cal Coolidge, because he stands for prosperity. And prosperity is what I want. Look at the stock market. It's way up in the sky, and going higher. The best people are playing the market. You think I'm gonna fight prosperity? Only a *mishugeneh* aesthete, like Yerman here, would do that. That's not what I'm going to college for. I wanna be up there with the other Philistines. You know, we're gonna read *Samson Agonistes* next week. Did you take Hebrew? Did you go to *cheder?* You were Bar Mitzva, no?" Sol addressed Yerman.

Yerman merely shifted disdainfully in his seat.

"You remember Samson saying, '*Tammus nafshi im plishtim?*' You know what it means?"

"No, I don't, wise guy." Yerman was satiric.

"So you do know what it means. That's you aesthetes. You're gonna wreck prosperity—if you could. Why did your father come here from the *shtetl?* For the same reason my father came. To come to the *goldeneh medina.* So it's a *goldeneh medina.* Fine! Why should I complain?"

"It's mercenary, crass, banal, and materialistic." Yerman listed.

"So take advantage of it."

"Sell more trusses on Delancey Street."

"Listen, that's *ad hominem!*" Sol accused. "Because my father happens to be in the orthopedic supply business— You owe me an apology. You know that?"

"Here, *makher*, take my seat." Yerman stood up.

"I don't want your seat." Redheaded Sol followed Yerman out of the alcove. "What's wrong with selling trusses on Delancey Street?"

"Don't get excited," Yerman replied.

"Who's excited?" They moved out of earshot.

"Is that what your Milton midterm did to you?" Larry asked.

"No. The questions were really a snap, too. But when Sol and Yerman get together, you better duck: the bullshit flies at high velocity."

"Does Sol's father really own a truss shop on Delancey Street?" Larry asked.

"Yeah, trusses, artificial limbs. Braces," Ira replied.

"Nothing wrong with it."

"No, but you know how they bait Sol. He gets so excited. The old man has already put his two older brothers through law school."

A moment of silence ensued as Larry relit his calabash. "I've just been made a job offer," he said.

"Just? A job offer?" Ira asked. "No kidding."

"By Chapman."

"The head of the ed department?"

"Yeah."

"You mean it? Are you that good in your ed courses?"

"I just sling the bull."

"There must be more than that. You've got some kind of knack."

"I don't know." Larry let a billow of fragrant smoke mushroom before his open lips, and reclaimed it before it escaped. "He seemed to think I was unusually qualified to go into ed. He practically offered me a tutorship if I'd go on and get a master's."

"He did?" How much of that same attractiveness Larry still had, surface attractiveness in countenance and bearing, in subdued richness of clothes, in uninflected, articulate speech. He was heavier now than the lyric youth who had bewitched Ira in high school, entranced Edith in her freshman class, beguiled John Vernon in the Arts Club— to the point where the two virtually competed. Larry was heavier, and with his thick mustache looked much more masculine, but still as winning as ever—on the surface. No wonder Professor Chapman was taken with him. "What'd you say?"

"I said I'd think about it. I'd rather get out into the world, to tell the truth. Sixteen years in school is enough."

"Is that what you told him?"

"Not quite. I hinted at it. But he was keen." Larry leaned back and let out another cone of pipe smoke. "He came right back and asked why was I getting a minor in ed if I didn't intend to teach. I might as well be doing it in a college."

"Teaching, you mean?"

"Yes. I admitted I did want to make sure I'd have something to fall back on, like teaching—I didn't say just in case the stage didn't work out—or"—Larry twitched his head slightly—"selling housedresses for Irv, and eventual partnership doesn't work out either. Anyway, I'd like to go out into the world for a while. He said he understood. Anytime I changed my mind to let him know."

"It's a wonderful break," Ira said with enthusiasm.

"Have you seen Iz in the last couple of days?" Larry wondered.

"Just to wave. Why? The e.e. cummings play is still running."

"He told me last time the Provincetown may be putting on a Pinsky play next. Jimmy White has been talking about it. He's strong on experimentation."

"Pinsky? What did I ever read by Pinsky?" Ira questioned.

"There are quite a few bit parts in it, Iz's sister says. So I may get a chance to play one."

"That would be great."

"Wouldn't it?"

"Do you get anything for it?" For once, Ira thought monetarily.

"I doubt if it's very much. A few bucks. But—" Larry left the rest pending a moment—classmates at the alcove study table were closing their notebooks and getting ready to go. "What I get isn't important right now. It's the experience I'm after. I've had some on the borscht circuit, but it isn't the same thing. This would be legitimate theater, serious theater."

"I get the idea. I can't remember—" Ira wrinkled brow to convey perplexity. "Seems to me I read a Pinsky play—in translation, of course—when I was going through a play-reading phase. What's the title?"

"I don't know the title. Iz will probably tell me in a day or two—if they decide to put it on."

"Then what d'you do?"

"Hoof over pronto and ask White for a tryout."

"I ketch." Ira nodded.

"Listen, why don't you come over to the house? Say, in a few days. It'll be Thanxy. We'll both have some time off. We can *shmooze*. What say?"

"I really don't know, Larry."

"Why?"

"I don't know what I'll be doing."

"Look." Larry's big hands adjusted his jacket. "I'm sure you know all about what's happened between Edith and me."

"Yeah." Ira looked straight ahead—to the wall above the wainscotting on the other side of the alcove. Wasn't it strange to be talking about Edith here in CCNY, in the '28 alcove? Talking about an NYU English professor and a dead romance here in the '28 alcove? A dead romance, while your mind was on a live embryo in your cousin's gut, or wherever it was: womb, tomb, uterus. Would such a combination of circumstances ever happen again, anything like that to two guys seated on the rich, smooth, pants-smoothed, mahogany-dark benches of CCNY? Or of Oxford? Or of Cambridge? Or of Heidelberg with its students' ritual scars—the Sorbonne? Oh, Jesus, what was history? Shadows impinging on shadows impinging, darker and darker and darker. God, what had already happened in one short span. And was happening. Or was it just to him? "Yeah," Ira answered, reluctant to engage in the subject any further than he had to. "She told me."

"That's what I wanted to talk to you about. After all, we knew each other before Edith came into the picture, right? In DeWitt Clinton. When we were both freshmen, and I was a predental student. We knew each other. We palled around together. There's no reason why all that should end just because I don't see Edith." Larry's toes lifted at the same time as his hands on his thighs turned palm upward. "So that's over, but not our friendship, you know what I mean?"

"Yeah." Ira could feel a certain hardening within himself—or about himself—a kind of crust forming, a sullen obduracy that beat back appeals to former friendship. Boy, that was queer, and cruel, and ungrateful. But what was he going to do? At a time like this? He couldn't take Larry into his confidence. First of all, he didn't need Larry, in fact, didn't want his intimacy. Larry would be a clog now. Ira stared at shifting patterns of guilt and obligation merging into each other before his eyes. He was in trouble, and the only thing he wanted to talk about was that, and he couldn't talk about it to Larry. Edith was the only one he could talk with about the nasty fix he had gotten himself into, because only Edith could get him out of it. What was he going to do? Say that he had knocked up his sixteen-year-old cousin? He might as well say that before that, he once fucked his sister. He could have divulged his secrets to Larry long ago. But he hadn't. Now Ira could give a lecture, no, a term paper, on the adventures of incest—something dirty like that—like his freshman plumber's helper theme: got him a D, and publication in *The Lavender*. But bullshit, bullshit. That wasn't what Larry wanted to talk about. "What's there to talk about?"

"A lot. For one thing, what you'll be doing. I'm out of the picture, okay, but I'm still your friend. I'd like to talk about things. I don't see any reason for a barrier between us, just because of Edith. We've got lots in common—the same things as before."

"Well, we don't."

"Why not?" Larry remained calm.

Ira felt himself retreat before the pleading in Larry's gentle brown eyes. "Trouble is, I'm all frigged up."

"What about?"

"That's just it. The things that happened between you and Edith you could talk about—most of the time. I mean, when the affair was going on with Edith, when you were in love and so on. But I can't."

"I don't understand. Who's stopping you?"

"Nobody. But I'm the center now. That's what you're interested in—I'm not flattering myself," Ira added glumly. "The whole thing has shifted. And on top of that, I'm all screwed up by all kinds of things I can't talk about. I won't. I wish I could, but I won't. It's a—" He shrugged, shook his head.

"All right. I don't intend to pry into your personal life," Larry persisted reasonably. "I just don't see the objection to talking about what your plans are. What Edith thinks of them."

"I don't know what they are myself." Ira's rejoinder was curt.

Again Larry tried to contain disagreement within amity. "Listen, I know Edith is crazy about you. She's crazy about you in a way she never was about me. And I think I know why too. It's the kind of a person you are. It's the same thing I found in you when we met by accident, absolutely by accident, in high school, in old man Pickens's class. What is it? I don't know how you get it, how you got it—when I visited your home there in Harlem—I mean—I'll be honest with you—I couldn't understand how anybody brought up in that place, in that slum," Larry nodded for emphasis, "*could be so sensitive*—listen, all I'm saying is I want for us to keep in touch."

"Okay. We'll talk about it later. I think the period is about up."

"But Ira, come for dinner this Thanxy? We'll have all the fixings. And special cranberry relish only my sister Sophie has the recipe. You'll love it."

"I'm not sure."

Larry was quick to allow latitude. "All right, you got another Thanxy dinner?"

"No."

"We'll see each other tomorrow. We've got till Wednesday. You can tell me the day before. If not Thursday, then Friday, Saturday, Sunday."

It was like a reenactment of an event in the past: that first time Ira had been invited by Larry to have supper at his home, and Ira had declined, deliberately, intuitively, not to appear overeager. Almost four full years ago, at the foot of the stairs of the Eighth Avenue El at 59th Street, amid the battering din and under the autumn shadow. But how different now—no, how different-seeming now. He was still a *shlepper,* still a pauper, but some kind of self-awareness had come into play, awareness of distinction, arrogance stemming from what he was, the awful, unique things he had done, suffered—who the hell knew. It wasn't because he was smart or had become smarter than Larry— Gee. "I don't wanna make you feel bad. I don't think I can make it," Ira said.

"What?"

"I mean don't count on it." And in answer to Larry's questioning look, "I'm sure I'm gonna be tied up this weekend." He frowned, as much to convey his preoccupation as to discourage further exploration of the topic. "Maybe I'll try."

"What about we bum around a day together? Wilma is married. We've got room. Any night you want to stay over, my mother is adjustable. She loved having Iven stay with us."

"Yeah? Hey, there goes the bell. I'll see."

They both stood up.

"Which way you going?" Ira asked.

"Sociology."

"Oh, that's right." Ira kept his tone neutral.

"I registered for it before my relations with Edith broke up."

"I know. You told me."

"Or else I wouldn't. But it's all right. I don't care anymore." And Larry added: "He's a good lecturer." And appended: "He's a nice guy. I don't hold it against him."

"No. What life is like."

They joined the students beginning to swarm through the dim midway dividing the two sections of class alcoves.

"You know, Edith had an abortion." It was the first time Larry had mentioned the fact.

"Yeah, I do."

"Joke was on the subject of birth control last time. In his last lecture."

"Yeah? Boyoboy."

"You could see he had to be discreet," Larry said as they climbed the stairs to the administration floor. "The examples he gave were from English and Continental practice. We knew where he stood just the same."

"Yeh? I think I remember Edith saying that the church gave him a grant to study that and juvenile delinquency in England. Jesus, that's a combination."

"What do you mean?" Larry paused momentarily on the next flight.

"Nothing special. Juvenile delinquency, birth control. He goes to England to study that while his wife, Marcia, is out in Samoa someplace studying adolescents and their sexuality. 1925 they set out. In the fall. And they both fall out of love. Coincidence, huh?"

"I see what you mean. We waited in a tent in your uncle's place. And I got a telegram. Which way?"

"I got an ed class."

"Tell me one thing." Larry held Ira's arm lightly. "Does she still see him—Lewlyn?"

"No, that's over and done with."

"I thought so, the way he acts in class."

"See you later."

"Try to make it over Thanxy."

"Okay."

XVI

Manhattan Street was the name of the street along which he had hobbled for his abbreviated afternoon constitutional walks when M was still alive. Manhattan Avenue, of all the ironies, was also the name of the street on which a tall woven-wire fence enclosed one side of a slovenly mobile home court. The very trees of the court, he allowed himself to imagine, recoiled in affront at the clamorous squalor below them—or shrank away, as if maternally protecting their newly budding branches from the noisy mess perpetrated by the humans on the ground beneath. While high in azure overhead, above the court, above the troubled trees, the cranes flew warbling by, like petals of aureate rose against the blue, the cranes flew warbling balm. Old hat (Ira gazed unseeing at the black connectors of his word processor plugged into the long aluminum box of the electric strip), old hat, this contrasting of natural loveliness with man-made unsightliness and tumult. *E come i gru van cantando lor lai*—Dante had written that line some six, almost seven centuries ago. Like cranes singing in formation, so flew the damned to their eternal torment: *e come i gru van* . . . To the east, the snow on the Sandias was radiant as a cloud resting there, the Sandias where the labs for atomic research were situated. What can you do? Resignation was a comfort at his age.

He wondered where his musings would have led him if he hadn't stopped for a cup of Zinger tea, where, and how far. And wondering, he had gotten up to take an Awake, a caffeine tablet against his drowsiness. And on his way to the bathroom door he had stubbed his toe against the caster of the table, which was usually at his back. And were it not for the little shelf on top of the table, with its IBM manual on it, he very likely would have fallen. "You'll break your goddamn leg," he swore at himself. He was sure that would be his end—like old Bernard Shaw breaking his hip, at age ninety or so, and saying it would be a miracle if he recovered from this one. He ought to have a cane nearby, Ira told himself, to steady himself that first second or two after getting up. He ought not get around without a cane, but canes were a damned nuisance. And when he returned, after taking the tablet, he thought he ought to begin the paragraph with: Ira tapped the tab key cautiously. But didn't. It would clog the paragraph's opening, make it too busy, as they said. Seated again, he tried to recall the thought a moment after he had sworn at himself.

Not that he had more than the foggiest notion of where to resume his narrative (nothing new there), but as usual, the compulsion to clear away the debris of existence before resuming his narrative took precedence. Life was full of chaotic fragments, discreet, in the mathematical sense, disparate, often dull and banal, but often fiercely engrossing, disparate but often desperate. And as often unexpected and unforeseen.

Unable to face his narrative again, pick up where he had left off, lacking the resolve, he had gone back to bed after breakfast, slept another hour; and even then, he stalled fifteen minutes, during which he located with indelible pencil the spot on his lower denture that was irritating his gum—then with the aid of a small metal burr in his electric drill he gouged out a hollow in the hard plastic of the denture that he hoped would relieve the pressure, the point of chafing on the gum. You goofiest of all scriveners, he told himself: always you opt for last things first. . . .

XVII

He had called Mamie's home Tuesday, according to the schedule he had set himself, called from the college phone booth, but got no answer, although he continued stubbornly ringing until the operator told him that the party didn't answer—and sent his jitney clinking down the coin-return chute. Classes over, he left campus, took the trolley home, and at 125th Street entered the waiting room of the New York Central station, and carefully arranging two layers of his handkerchief over the mouthpiece, he called again. This time Hannah answered. And between evasions of self-identification and message, he was told Stella was at the library, and wouldn't be home until later. She was at the library—Ira frowned speculatively. He knew the public library at 115th Street, just as he knew every library in Harlem, had frequented every one of them during boyhood in search of new fairy tales and legends and myths. He was on 125th and Park Avenue, ten blocks to go to 115th, and a half-dozen long blocks west. Well, nothing unusual about that.

He was already on his way, envisaging finding her in an ideal place to talk, to learn how lucky he was. The smirk of wicked conniving he felt on his face reminded him of Death's ghoulish grin in *Paradise Lost* when he heard of the multitude of souls that would be his to devour once Satan exited Hell. "I had not thought Death had undone so many," said Eliot in *The Waste Land,* quoting Dante. Only trouble was there was no place in the library—hell, her monthlies wouldn't bother him. He strode on, trying to imagine some coign, retreat, where he could lead her, as once he had led her down to the glary basement of Max's new home on the occasion of the infant's *bris.* Jesus, there wasn't a single place in Harlem—except the Park, Central Park. Why of course. If she was okay, why of course. There would be light enough—and dark enough: around the lake, up the paved path above the granite outcrop, among the grove of trees where he had wandered (with Psyche my soul), and sipped of that rill—ugh—when Baba and Zaida came to America. How could he be such a dope to drink that water of Central Park's rocks and rills? That was the place to lay her.

Against a tree, in the shade, in the glade, it wasn't too cold—if only she had had her monthlies—he strode doggedly to the inner beat: had her monthlies, had her monthlies.

The American flag hung above the entrance. How standard the exterior of public libraries, always a gray wall in which large windows were set, and how standard the interior, the checkout counter, the shelves, oak tables under incandescents. Where? He sidled past the counter, looked avidly about. That table. No. Not there. Aisles of bookcases? No. He made careful search. Nothing doing. No sign of her. So maybe that was her way of tricking Mamie, her ruse to get out of the house and meet a guy. He hadn't encountered her on his way there, that was sure. Nuts. He was wrong. If she was having her period . . . No, there were too many factors to contend with, yes, no, maybe. She had probably left while he was on the way, and she would be home now.

Should he call again? The first drugstore. And once more he gave the operator Mamie's number, and once more Hannah answered. No, Stella wasn't home. "Who is this?" Hannah's voice had more than curiosity in it, as though she were striving to identify something familiar. Another minute of talking, and she'd probably recognize his voice— even through the muffle over the mouthpiece. It was only in the theater they could carry on that charade indefinitely. That meant he hardly dared telephone again.

"Tell her it's a friend. When's her school over t'morrer?" he tried to growl with gritty, hardly intelligible voice.

"Stella's business school? Like always. Three o'clock. Who's this?"

Ira immediately hung up the receiver.

What a fiasco! Glowering, he left the drugstore, his hopes shriveling. Hell, this was probably her seventh, eighth, no, seventh day without menstruating. What was he dreaming of? He was out of luck. Might as well face the truth, meet her in front of the business school Wednesday, brace himself for the ignominy of taking her to Edith's— of exhibiting her before Edith! Oh, Jesus, that simpering wad o' lascivious lard. *Oy.* One glance at her and Edith would be appalled at the fake he was.

That evening Minnie was absent at supper, a calm supper, at long last. She was attending evening class at CCNY, but she came home so promptly afterward, Ira couldn't help but think she did so out of solic-itude for him. Confirmed—he was sure he was right by the anxious way she eyed him, so obviously expressed was her concern that he could have snarled at her, except he knew doing so would be com-pletely baffling to Pop and Mom—or worse, excite their curiosity, their surmise, maybe questions. He managed to keep his scowl averted and his mouth shut. All he could see was a hopelessly intricate skein, an untidy web within a small household, like those sooty webs the spi-ders tended in the crannies across the air shaft, to which every soiled strand and particle adhered, a web composed of every grubby thread of his soiled worries. Not until Mom and Pop went to bed did Minnie, lingering, get a chance to ask, to whisper the question he had been try-ing to evade:

"It's still the same?"

"Yeah." He felt himself squirm.

"My poor brother."

Her sympathy he dismissed with a brusque flap of his hand. But she was not stopped by the gesture. "You need any money?" she per-sisted.

"I told you. I got somebody to help me."

"So then you don't have to worry so much if you got somebody to help you." She had a way of frowning her compassion so that lines formed on her brow, and dark wreaths on her cheek, that threw her countenance into shadow. "If you got that professor to help you, what more can you want? Don't worry so much," Minnie entreated. "If you—I mean she—she wants to spend the money, and she knows where to go, you can't do any more. Another few days, Ira," she stressed, and came over to whisper her encouragement in lower breath. "You'll be all right."

Wednesday morning, lived through somehow, lived through on a plateau of numb anxiety that couldn't go any higher. Morning passed in a monotonous pall of crisis. A stuporous early class in economics. He saw Larry for a second day in a row, Larry genial, only the least aware of how irritating to Ira his coaxing had been the previous day. Larry's every new entreaty to Ira, "Spend Thanxy," "Spend the night," seemed to grate, to plane the edge, to near Ira closer to fissure. Every little extra thing seemed too much. Who the hell cared about Thanxy? He finally snapped at Larry: "Why don'tcha invite Iven, for Christ's sake?"

Larry hadn't taken offense, merely laughed. "Okay, let's have Iven over too."

Ira had made no reply, sullenly engrossed in his fingernails.

"I can see you've got things on your mind," Larry said earnestly. "Maybe I can help."

"Yeah." Was it to ease the strain that he allowed all sorts of obscene images to dwell in his mind?—Larry backscuttling Stella, laying Minnie for good measure, for auld lang syne. He was heavier-hung than Ira. What a picture. Especially with Stella, younger, more salacious. And Ira the bystander, extracting the erotic. Would he have to pull off when they came, or would he come just watching? His mind was steeped in foulness, pickled in it. "I should have been a pair of ragged claws," he quoted.

Larry thought the quote amusing. "All right, I'll meet you for the subway ride. Okay?"

"I got an appointment."

"When?"

"About three." He never could think fast enough to lie, lie in a way that left no openings.

"Oh, that'll leave you plenty o' time."

"I was going to cut ed, anyway."

"What is it, next period? What for?"

"Yeah," Ira said hopelessly. "It'll only mean a trip to the dean."

"So why cut it?"

"Oh, nuts. No reason. Just want to stew by myself for a while."

"Listen, if you go to class, we get out the same time. We can shmooze on the way," Larry urged. His handsome face became sober. "Maybe a few minutes' really serious talk would help."

"It'd help you."

"Why not you?"

"I'm frigged. That's what my appointment's about." Larry arrested his sigh of frustration, regarded Ira with his gentle brown eyes, almost pleading for enlightenment, that failed of forthcoming—an answer literally stillborn, the trope darted through Ira's mind.

"Well, you have your reasons," Larry conceded the minor defeat after a pause. "Okay, we take the train together?"

"Okay."

"May take your mind off things. That sometimes helps."

"Yeah. *Vie a toiten bankehs.*"

Intrigued as always when a new Yiddish expression came within his ken: "*A toiten bankehs?*" Larry queried.

"Yeah. It means cupping a corpse, cupping a cadaver. You know how much good that would do."

"Oh, yes."

"Abyssinia." Ira invoked their old parting logo.

"Abyssinia."

Ever the peregrine lout, lackluster, purposeless, wayward, roaming from car to car, left the doors open between them—to skate and slam with every lurch of the train. Cold, drear tunnel draft swooped in, swirled the dust and pounced on newspaper scraps, Hershey penny chocolates and Tootsie Roll candy wrappers on the floor, flapped the pages of tabloids in the hands of seated, swaying readers. The short, husky Italian in flannel shirt and raveling gray sweater under nondescript mackinaw fixed his brown hat tighter on his head against the gale; and with tabloid gripped in one fist, stood up, grabbed the brass door latch, exposing the longshoreman's cargo hook in his belt, and banged the door shut, permanently. "Punk!" He scowled through the glass of the door after the departed vagrant, and then sat down again.

Across the aisle two teenage girls studied Larry, trailed rapt gaze away to chatter to each other behind the covers of raised loose-leaf black notebooks, stole glances at Larry again, who remained oblivious. It was early afternoon, Wednesday afternoon.

The train slanted up the grade from 137th Street, where Larry and Ira had gotten on, as usual, as was their custom—an almost four-year custom by now—slanted up the grade from the tunnel to the cold elevation of the 125th Street station. With its outdoor view, anomalous for a subway. But somewhere, in his geology class last summer—Iven would know—the land had dipped here because of a terrestrial fault, or been gouged out by a glacier—there was even an obsolescent, beat-up escalator under the station to lift passengers aloft. Years ago, how bemused he had stood, East Side kid from 9th Street reconnoitering along 125th.

Out of the windows of the train, the solid, fused apartment houses each lowered their roofs a jog as the train climbed, and at street intersections, offered brief panels of the slaty Hudson and the wintry bluffs of the Palisades across the river. The subway car doors opened. A few passengers boarded, among them a Salvation Army couple in uniform. In rushed cold air with them. The doors slid closed. And now the train slanted downward again past concrete parapet to reenter the stuffy, snug tunnel.

"All right, we get off at 96th?" Larry asked. "I have to change there anyway."

Ira was loath to mesh with the imminent encounter he had sensed was coming from the minute Larry proposed riding downtown with him. But there was no evading it: it had to be faced sooner or later. "You're gonna pass your own station? 110th?" As if reminding Larry would bring a change of mind.

"I know. We'll both have to change. When you change for the Lenox Avenue to Harlem, I'll grab the Broadway local."

I'm in a double bind now, Ecclesias. I've got to use essentially the same episode, now on the same file, in two places, to serve two purposes.

—I know it.

What do you advise? Do you have any advice to offer?

—No. Nothing plausible. Indeed, it's impossible to do what you intend to do. At least I don't ever recall the narrative use of substantially the same episode in two different time frames.

I can't either. So do what?

—Do what you may do.

What? Do what you may, and wisdom is early to despair—if I quote Gerard Manley Hopkins with any fidelity.

—You may, as far as I can tell, but you can't quote your way out of difficulties. You could, of course, rewrite to suit, or shall I say, rewrite clear of your temporal contradictions. Two meetings, two encounters, more or less devoted to the same subject on the same subway train, on the same station? *Creo cano.* I don't think so.

Then what alternative do I have? I've already interrupted, greatly interfered with, the course of the narrative. So be it. I'm too advanced in years—

—Oh, I've heard all that before. That plea grows tiresome.

I'm sorry. Nonetheless, 'tis so.

—Fact is that Larry is eager to take this occasion to make his pitch to retain some remnant of his former intimacy with Ira. And Ira is far too worried about his responsibility in Stella's pregnancy to care about discussing such matters with Larry, at this point, too preoccupied with this, as well as the obligation preying on his mind, excessively, as usual, of escorting Stella into Edith's presence. The coming confrontation, or whatever to call it in this case, the full revelation of his disgrace, almost sickens him. . . . Well, why make any more bones about it. We know what faces him. Do the best you can.

The best I can will be a fiasco. . . . Nonetheless. I thank you. . . .

Ira refrained from answering, and Larry appeared nonchalant all at once. Larry appeared to have discovered another fleck of color in the large turquoise gem of the Navajo ring bestowed on him so seemingly long ago. He turned it pensively, appreciatively, on his long pale finger, unconstrained, oblivious of the girls across the way, candid in the boldness of their admiration as Ira was surreptitious in his admiration of their boldness: *shiksas.* Cute. Pert. Staring blue-eyed, the intensity of their interest forcing their knuckles to press whitely on girlish, weak clenched hands. Little wonder they stared. Despite his thick black mustache, his added weight, Larry still looked like Ganymede, a little older, Ganymede a few years after being snatched up to Olympus to wait on the gods, chief butler now, chief steward: Greek nose, winged eyebrows, milky skin—and dressed like a prince: his ample gray camel's-hair topcoat, tweed trousers showing below, his woven, woolen burnt-umber necktie, his finely tooled brogans. Nothing needed adornment with Larry. Nothing needed superfluous gloss; everything was rich, everything spoke of good taste and fine rearing. Clothes, features, deportment, person. Only his full lips, his big hands, deviated from some ideal, his big hands, his longer-than-average arms, fused Michelangelo's *David* to classic Greek.

Raising his voice against the din in the tunnel, Larry leaned toward Ira: "All your midterm tests finished?"

"Narbhill had the flu. So we had public speaking the last minute. Pain in the ass. You have him too, don't you?"

"That's why I'm here today. Had to come in for only a couple of classes."

"How did you make out?"

"In public speaking? I didn't tell you. Oh, Narbhill beamed approval when I finished. I gave him Alfred Noyes's old chestnut 'Highwayman.'"

"Wow. All o' that?" Ira feigned amazement.

"I still had it more than half memorized from last year. Did I put on the dog? 'Impeccable diction,' he said."

"Yeah? Well."

Larry chuckled, and then again, amused by his own amusement. "You should have heard Sol. The guy was a scream. He set out to deliver Kipling's 'Recessional': 'God of our fathers, known of old,' and all that lofty, imperialist invocation, but he didn't know it, let alone have it memorized pat—'What's the next word, please, Professor Narbhill?' 'Beneath . . .' 'Oh, yes. Thank you. "Beneath whose awful hand we hold—" What's the next word, please?' He had old Narbhill practically reciting it for him." Larry lifted his head in renewal of mirth. Ira joined him—noting how Larry had won soulful smiles from the two girls over as well. Who could resist his charm and mimicry?

"What was your selection?" Larry asked.

"I still got a wrong *t*—a Jewish *t*, I guess. But it was content of my selections that got the old boy's thumbs down. No room for expressiveness, quotha. Expressiveness with a capital X."

"Why?"

"I chose Eliot's 'Phlebas the Phoenician,' and Masefield's 'Cargoes,' and Walter de la Mare's 'Lady of the West Country.' And what else? Anyway, the old coot disapproved so of my absence of expressiveness, you know what he did? As a demonstration of the kind of thing he expected from me, from all and sundry in fact, he brought out the text for the course, and did he ever rant away on Shylock's speech before the Duke. You know it: 'To bait fish withal. If 'twill feed nothing else 'twill feed my revenge—' I thought he'd blow a gasket."

"That classifies more as acting rather than public speaking," Larry objected.

"Yeah. Histrionics. Well, he was going to show me how cramped my expressiveness was, my eloquence. So that, together with my flat-footed recitation, makes a D for the midterm."

"Really? Does that mean you're on the way to losing another eighth of a credit?"

"Don't I pile them up? I have to take a summer course anyway."

The last enameled 110 of Larry's station whisked by. The two gave up trying to outyell the roar of the train, rode awhile in silence. At 103rd, the two girls got off, peeled off, with a last longing glance at Larry—who still never noticed. Instead, before the train began moving again, he turned impulsively toward Ira: "You know, that's where we came in."

"Huh?"

"Elocution. Elocution 7, sitting next to each other. We had to double up in the same seat."

"Oh, that? I was a big galoot. That big galoot in the second row, fourth seat, or what the hell ever it was, stand up! You know, I'll never forget that: *you* stood up."

"I really thought he meant me. He was looking right at me. He did have rather close-set eyes."

"Old man Pickens. We used to call his sister Slim Pickens."

"Just one period in class together," said Larry. "Can you imagine? Just because her ship was delayed a couple of days getting into New York."

"I've thought about it a hundred times."

"So have I. Do you think we would ever have met otherwise?"

"Hard to say—in a high school as big as DeWitt Clinton. I have me doots." When pressed for reminiscence, mugging was easiest for Ira.

"I would have finished my predent by now. What am I saying: a year ago. Finished a year of anatomy, cutting up stiffs. Begun to do some real dentistry."

"Yeah?"

"Can you hear me?"

"Yeah, sure."

"Did I ever get thrown off course."

"You?"

"You feel that way too?"

"Way, way off."

"For you it's different."

"What? Oh. Why?"

"Well, you know why." They were both silent. The next stop was 96th Street, so no use wasting breath when the big moment was only a minute or two away. What would it be about, if it were a big moment? What form would it take? His own feelings about what lay ahead were uneasy, fateful and yet formless. Not a horrible crisis, a ghastly turning point, like being kicked out of Stuyvesant—or waiting for Stella to hear the news—or telling Edith about it. Or Jesus, how many were there? That sick, harrowing feeling of maybe confessing to Edith about Minnie. No. But some kind of big moment just the same. Momentous in its way—even if not a cataclysmic upheaval. Decisive, that was the word. Not everything had to be a tornado, a blast of recriminations. Momentous confrontation. Certainly. But why not dealt with calmly, or as calmly as possible. The imperceptible, the rift within the lute, had begun long ago. Larry beside him was probably thinking the same thing. What did he want, what did he hope for? He was bound to ask about Edith. Bound to have something to do with Edith—Edith and Ira.

Try to figure out, try to get ready for the coming colloquy. What did Larry mean? For you it's different. Of course it was different. The 96th Street station was next. He would soon find out—definitely.

He saw Larry prepare for alighting from the train, grip the handles of his handsome stippled briefcase, the very opposite of the workaday walrus-hide briefcase Mamie had presented her nephew—that had been stolen from him. Everything reminded him of something else. Was it because of his uneasiness? He followed Larry's lead, gripped the peeling handles of his cowhide briefcase. They both stood up, with others getting off, clung to the enameled hangers to steady themselves from the thrust of the train's deceleration as it pulled alongside the local platform.

"Well, we'll get a chance to talk now," Larry said.

"Right."

Misgivings seemed to pile on misgivings. And after he and Larry had come to grips, and *that* was settled, if it was settled, Ossa on Pelion would follow, waiting outside the business school to take Stella to meet Edith. Owoo.

The train lurched to a stop. A local train, an early hour, exit was uncontested. With a scattering of fellow passengers, the two stepped across the gap between train and platform, to encounter a scattering waiting to step the other way—into the train—across the gap that always seemed to ask a question.

"I've got an appointment at about four o'clock with Jim Light," said Larry.

"Who?"

"Jim Light. He's the director of the new Pinsky play they're putting on at the Provincetown."

"Good luck."

"Thanks. It shouldn't be hard getting a bit part."

They traversed the short tunnel under the tracks of the express-train island overhead, climbed up the stairs to the uptown local side. Once there, Larry looked about smartly for the station bench, located it, the massive oak bench, next to an O'Sullivan Heel poster, in front of the penny Hershey bar vending machine that was wedged between the riveted flanges of a smudged subway pillar. At the other end of the bench sat an old guy in a greasy-looking coat, peeling an orange in a paper bag. His fingers were stiff, fingers evidently tacky with orange juice; he kept wriggling them to separate them.

"Helluva place to *shmooze*." Larry led the way to the other end. "We could go back to the apartment—"

"No, no." Ira realized he was too peremptory. On guard, he warned himself as he sat down: Watch it.

"You know why I wanted to talk to you?"

"I can sorta guess."

"It's the same thing we started to talk about in the alcove the other day."

"I might as well tell you quite a lot else has happened since then."

"Yes?"

"Larry, I've got to tell you that Edith asked me to help her on her new anthology of modern poetry." As always Ira could only tell Larry half of any given truth. Edith's trust in him offered a future, out of Harlem. Ira had just begun to see his machinations, his spells, begin to come to fruition. And, as always, he couldn't share his plots with his friend.

"I'm not surprised. I heard about that too."

"Okay. And now you have something—" Ira began, gave up before the clash of an incoming uptown express train, immediately augmented to overpowering din by a downtown express pounding in on the parallel track—deafening. "Helluva place is right." Even shouting, he barely made himself heard.

"Let's wait a minute," Larry said, raising his voice. A cheerful couple with a youngster in tow sat down between them and the orange-eater; a lively kid, but fixed into quiescence by the sight of the old man peeling the orange. The trains came to a halt; the thunder of metal subsided. "I've always thought it would happen, you and Edith." Larry resumed. "I knew she was humoring me, long before she told me that Lewlyn was engaged to the woman in England. I knew she would turn to you."

"All right. So it's all sorta predictable on both sides."

"Now it is. I didn't foresee that I would be a rung in your ladder. Did you?"

"Sure. I had designs on Edith from the beginning." Ira's candor shocked him.

"Oh, come on."

"Fact."

Larry sat with one large hand in the other, watching the two express trains rumble apart. They seemed to stretch an elastic transparency between them. Then he turned to Ira: "I don't believe it."

"You said 'rung,' didn't you. We could go on indefinitely. I'm not going to. Because it'll get to be damn painful. I know you've got some kind of trouble with your heart—"

"Oh, to hell with that! Just a transient thing: a small clot. I lost consciousness for all of five seconds."

"Edith was damned concerned."

"She's always ready to magnify any disorder: a cough becomes TB."

"Okay. Okay. Is that what you wanted to complain to me about, your being a rung in my ladder? Let's have it."

"No, I wasn't going to complain at all."

"Then what?"

"We were friends, weren't we? You were my friend, weren't you? Clichés about bosom companions aside, that's what we were. And that's what remains precious to me, more than I can tell you."

"Yes?" Ira could feel himself congealing defensively.

"Look, what I'm trying to tell you is this—"

The family trio sitting beside them got to their feet, the young mother holding firmly to the child's lifted hand, as the Broadway local pulled in. The old man carefully separated orange segments. Larry kept on speaking: "When I went to bed at night, I would think of things I would tell you tomorrow—storing them up, from my reading, Irving's latest salesman's gags. Do you remember the winter you stayed overnight in my room, so we could see the eclipse the next morning on the roof—when we were still in DeWitt Clinton—everything had twice the meaning when we did things together."

"Yes? I felt that way too. All right." Just what would he have to brace himself against? The outlines were becoming more defined.

"That night in that dusty old tent in your uncle's summer hotel when your uncle brought that telegram from Edith, you were with me—we were together. When we shook the crowd after the soirée in her St. Mark's Place apartment. And there was the cottage in Woodstock."

"Yeah. And we visited her apartment in the Village together." Ira wondered whether the crease of irony in his cheek would betray him. It didn't.

"That's what I mean."

"So? Okay."

"I'm making a kind of appeal. You were on my side from the beginning. Because you've become Edith's confidant—I guess that is what you'd call it, right—doesn't destroy for me what you were. I just don't want you to cut me out of your life. I want to feel that I continue to share in it."

"Oh."

Larry made a peculiar motion, with rigid white fingers directed toward his heart. "You can't let it all die."

"And how do you intend to keep it alive?"

"By keeping our friendship alive: sharing your impressions about what you're doing—if you're writing—mostly what you're thinking, feeling. And—anything else."

"I don't know, Larry. I'm not that generous, I guess."

"No?"

"It's the way I'm built. I don't feel that kind of allegiance." The more liquid the brown eyes looking into his, the more appealing the features, the more ruthless Ira had to be in Stygian caves forlorn, in subway caves forlorn. "I'm sorry, Larry, the best thing we can do is cut loose from each other. I'm going my own way." Boy, that was brusque. Boy, that was cruel.

Larry's breath snagged in his throat. He snuffed up tears. He would have run for cover, sought hiding place—Ira felt—if he could. The last ties were breaking. And there were others due to break, Ira reflected gloomily: he had to announce changes at home, renounce home—and Mom, say to her: or ever the silver cord be loosed, Mom, or the beaker be shattered in the chemistry lab, the threads be stripped off the screw, the battery shot, the what else is ruined? The straw kelly bashed in at the end of summer.

"I'm thinking of leaving my long home on 119th Street, leaving Mom. Part of the time anyway," Ira said aloud. Give the guy a decent interval, a chance to recover. Ira let a minute go by. The old gaffer at the other end still had a couple of orange segments left. Jumpin' Jesus, the guy must be toothless to take so long. He probably was, masticating nose to chin. He probably had nothing else to do: orange peel in a bag, and licking the cleft between stuck, stiff fingers, while subway trains came and went, came and went, local and express: Bronx Park

and Van Cortlandt, and Lenox Avenue, plunging into the tunnel at
the end of the platform, an incandescent-stippled murk in which track
and train disappeared at random. And the guy was young once; once
the guy was young.

A pale, middle-aged man sat down, his hair the smoky hue of
once-blond hair faded. And pouting with thought, he opened his
newspaper: Polish. *Hobo Canobo* was the name the top of the paper
seemed to spell out, almost like Hobo Canoe, Hoboken. But of course
it wasn't: in Cyrillic, half the time the alphabet was written backward.
Polish was in Cyrillic, wasn't it? Larry reached down, retrieved his
briefcase. His full lips were scrolled in, features set into a determined
equanimity.

"Ready?" he asked.

"Sure." They stood up, paid their ritual respects at the edge of
platform, leaning over to see what was coming. The guy was all right,
wasn't he? Leaning over that way? After the way he'd pointed to his
heart.

"I think the next one's mine," said Larry.

"Oh, did I miss the local?"

"If I'm not mistaken," Larry answered.

Suppress everything, Ira counseled himself: suppress everything.
Anything you say is out of place. But Jesus, what a—academic, yeah,
academic temptation to pitch it all away: destiny, destiny. Bullshit.
Recover the old hobnob: come back to Aaron, Mavourneen,
Mavourneen. Say to him: Listen, pal, doesn't she give it up to anybody?
Boy, that was vulgar: gutter smut. What the hell. Come back to each
other the way they did after they parted with Edith at Woodstock. Not
to jeopardize her job at the university. Not to be seen in the same train
with a couple of freshman. Took different routes home, and skulked
in the shadowy midship of the ferry boat when it grew dark . . . to hide
the ten-day growth of beard on their chin-chops. Was that ever hilarious: Larry rid of the strain of courting an older woman, Ira rid of the
strain of good conduct, the two youths howled with mirth. Do it in reverse: your turn now. Never. Never. Never.

"That's a Lenox Avenue train coming in." Larry took another
quick look down the track. "I must not have seen your local."

"White and green headlight. I guess you did," Ira confirmed. "It's mine. I'll see you in the alcove." And as the train ranged into the station: "Where you going?"

"I'm going to tear over to the express side. I think I hear one. Abyssinia."

Larry broke into a quick trot toward the downstairs exit. He was right about the train. And apparently in time. The Broadway express charged into the station a few seconds after the Harlem local had arrived, and the local kept waiting, until the magisterial express pulled out. And then the local, which Ira had boarded, left, gathered speed rapidly—and insolently overtook its ponderous rival . . . sped by the last cars . . . until almost abreast of the first—and there was Larry on his express, on the opposite seat of an opposite train, his eyes raised perusing subway ads, oblivious of Ira traveling parallel at the same speed. And so for a few seconds, and only a few, they traveled within view of each other, as if they were still pals, still cronies, once again.

PART TWO

I

Seemly oddly mundane, squeezed between the two narrow stylish office buildings, with ornamentation and lofty balcony and fluted col-
umn embedded in their facades—and dwarfed by their height as
well—the three-story building that housed the Union Square Business
School had the appearance of a chalk box—a chalk box with windows,
with the wall painted blue. A flight up, Ira could see intermittent rows
of typewriters in sunken typewriter tables at which girls sat, busily tran-
scribing from steno manuals beside them. A flight above, a woman
with a yellow pencil in her hair and a book in her hand walked to the
window, glanced out, and moved away, her lips moving as if she were
dictating to a class. Earmarks, repugnant earmarks of the business
school. Ira rested his briefcase on the low stone wall surrounding
Union Square Park across the street: the only thing not in view was the
bookkeeping class, that damned farrago of debits and credits, and accounts receivable and payable. Hadn't old man Shullivan back in junior high gone wild with him over his inability to determine when one
debited and when one credited? Makeshift junior high school, and
the blue veins crinkled on Mr. Shullivan's temples: shtand up, shit
down. She was in there somewhere. She had to be. He had such lousy
luck. All that had to happen now was for Stella to skip school today.
That would cap everything. Ah, no. There went the chime.

  He turned his head to look up at the pyramidal belfry atop the

Consolidated Edison Building off 14th Street, just as a matching chime, playing Haydn, like an echo, sounded from a similar pinnacle uptown, the Metropolitan Life Tower, or whose? Quarter past one, the ponderous iron hands read. Forty-five minutes to go. He didn't need to have cut his ed class, but hell, he was too nervous. As it was, the damned combination lock on his locker when he went to get his coat and hat had proved refractory, always did when he became keyed up, keyed up, pun. He'd have gone wild if he had only a few minutes to spare. Better this way with lots of time to collect his wits. Such as they were, damn horse's ass, what was he doing here? Waiting on a little tub he'd screwed and knocked up. Jesus, can you imagine that? In a frumpy, blue-balls little building across the street where the wheeled traffic and pedestrians flowed and flowed. Din, din. Honk, honk. Dong, dong, from here to the 14th Street trolleys. People and wheels. Shuffle and squeal. Glitter and gleam of windshield and hubcap. And sickly sweet blue gasoline fume, and next to him, the hot dog cart, under whose umbrella the proprietor sat reading, redolence wafted— of the *kishkelikh*, Mom called them. He saw himself for a moment as if formed and forged by a million, billion impacts of his surroundings. Jesus Christ, and go break the worthy eidolon of self you presented to someone who admired you, was fond of you, oh, oh, a wax face such as he had seen in a movie once, wax features that someone bashed with his fist, fractured and fell off, revealing the gruesome horror of hideous nothingness. . . . So, you, trailing into Edith's apartment the little kewpie doll you pratted, the wax mask dropping off you: Edith, this is Stella. And like one who came breathless out of the sea, said Dante, you look back at the storm-tossed waves of what's to happen. You gotta harden yourself, that's all. God! Orestes, meet Oedipus. This is all I have to say to thee, and no word more forever. Ay, ay, Jocasta. Boy.

Turmoil, turmoil. Uptown, downtown, on the avenue, on the street, fretting, fretting, everything . . . shoppers and window shoppers and vehicles, movement everywhere, to the right, to the left, in Union Square Park behind him, where voices squabbled, and he could distinctly hear words spoken in foreign accent, Russian Jewish, "de right-vingers . . . Piss-voik . . . Ladies gomments . . . Mittings fom de union." And now someone taunting—Ira turned to look. "Hey, Mistah Faschis-

tah," someone from a group seated on a bench mocked a man hurrying by. "Vere you ronning?" Unrest, Jesus. There must have been a
more quiet time, once. That narrow, white building, which overlooked
the business school, must have been built in a quieter time, difficult as
it was to imagine, a more leisurely time that could afford dispensations
like that single coy marble balcony high up on about the twelfth or fif-
teenth story, the arched windows, and the overhanging eaves like mor-
tarboards with dovetails in them. A quieter time—what was it
like?—and what would he have been like? He wouldn't be waiting
here to make amends, mortified at having to take the little klutz he
was screwing to Edith to get him out of a scrape. The spectacle he was
going to make of himself! Oh, nuts, better than having no one to take
her to. He felt his restlessness within himself mount. Get moving.
Goddamn it, this was the last time he'd go to Mamie's.

   Should he walk all the way around Union Square? No, no, it made
him uneasy to lose sight of that damned doorway. Even though he had
plenty of time—how much?—almost twenty minutes. But that was all
he had to do was miss her. As far as the bandstand at the north end of
the park, say hello to Mr. Abe Lincoln, honest Abe, standing under the
bare trees in his crumpled bronze clothes on his pedestal, and looking
downtown. A few steps more—all he would allow himself—around the
corner where the cars were parked on 16th, "Socialism is inevitable"
was scrawled in large letters in back of the bandstand shell at the end
of the park—and somebody had crossed out "Socialism" and written
"Communism" above it. Far enough; Ira turned back.

   Damn. He seemed to need more air. Like those pitchers—Pen-
nock, Sad Sam Jones—he had seen coming on the mound when he
hustled soda pop in the Polo Grounds and Yankee Stadium. They
hadn't pitched a ball and were already short of breath. Excitement,
yeah. C'mon, ye goddamn little twat. He rammed his hand in his overcoat pocket, groping for pipe, changed briefcase to his other hand
and rummaged, found the briar. But he didn't feel like smoking, just
clenching the stem between his teeth was enough. Keep an eye out.
Don't forget, for Christ's sake. He passed abreast of the school doorway, on his way downtown. Some guys would be cool about it. How
many times did he have to tell himself that? What d'ye mean, cruel
about it? "Oh, shit, I didn't say cruel," he protested aloud. Oh, nuts,

calm down, ye cold-wet-under-armpits coward. Nuts to you. What comfort there was in the thought that some guys could be cool about it. Go on, act the part: be cool about it. What relief. Jesus, he'd gone over that role too, but still, what respite.

If only he were different. So he knocked her up. So what? Oh, to have the gall to say to Mamie: "Look, your daughter and I, *vir hutzikh tsegekhapt*, ye know?" Funny goddamn Yiddish expression: it's natcherel. We grappled. No, not quite. Hooked into each other. That's closer. Clasped. Got fouled in each other. You weren't on the lookout, Mamie, you were loafing on the job, Mamie. It's partly your fault. Heh. Heh. Joke's on you we fouled into each other. You gotta foot the bill, Mamie. Fooled ya. Or she has a kid. Allee samee me. It's your baby. Heh. Heh. You want me to marry her? Sure, plunk down ten G. I'll *yentz* her day and night, and get a Ph.D. Pah. But just to finish the thought, what a father he'd make. What the hell would it be like to be a father? Goo-goo, ga-a-ga-a, da-da. Hail Columbia, happy land, baby shit in Pap's hand—Hey, what time was it? Ten minutes to three.

He had reached George Washington in bronze at the other end of the square—and facing south too, dauntlessly fronting the clangor of 14th Street. Why did both presidents face south? Ira prompted himself to worry, worry rather than wonder. Why south, and not each other? Because Washington, D.C., lay in that direction? Was that the reason? Like Moslems facing Mecca? No, that couldn't be it. At Washington Square, the marble statues of Washington looked north. Oh, balls. When the hell would they start coming out of that school? LINDY WINS MEDAL, one of the headlines on the corner newstand read. All engrossed with himself, Ira drew closer: AL SMITH FOR CHANGE IN VOLSTEAD . . . NO. AGAIN NO SAYS COOLIDGE.

"Paper, Mister?" the wind-blown, blocky newstand owner suggested pointedly. "Woddaya read?"

But stung, Ira blurted out an offended "No!"

"A'right."

There was no mistaking the meaning of the way he jingled the coins in the little apron around the blue pea jacket in which he was stuffed. Nor the jerk of his stubbly jowls. The man did not tolerate loiterers.

Bastard. Ira backed away. Giving him the bum's rush. Fuck you, he wanted to say: fuck you and your papers. God, everything got under his nerves; anything could throw him into a fury. Jesus, that was all he had to do: get into a battle with a barrel for ears. Hell. He looked anxiously at the business-school door. Empty. Damn. Christ. When?

"Atta boy, Garrity, lessee ye nail him dis time." The newstand owner might have been talking to himself, so barely tinged was his gruff voice with sour approval. He couched wrist in weathered hand expectantly.

Across busy 14th Street, on the thronged, bustling sidewalk on the other side, a black street vendor, with display case closed and light folding stand clutched, was running pursued by a cop, was at the curb when Ira looked, and only out of reach of the young, speedy bluecoat because of intervening pedestrians, who delayed him a split second, while the other, lithe and nimble—and reckless—sped into the street, dodged among cars, and, dropping trinkets from his display case, distanced himself. For a moment, the cop aimed his club to throw, thought better of it, and instead shook his head with a loser's good grace, flushed, watching his quarry escape.

"He'll git him," said the newstand owner with hoarse confidence. "Black bastard, he's been comin' down here peddlin' dat shit every day."

"Yeah?" At least amity was restored.

"Look at it. Dere's a car goin' over it. See? Fuckin' brass lockets, an' phony lavalieres wit' glass in em."

"Yeah?" LINDY WINS MEDAL. AL SMITH FOR CHANGE IN VOLSTEAD. NO. AGAIN NO. COOLIDGE. "De bastard's got more noive den brains. He ain' de on'y one. Ye see more 'n' more o' dem boogies on Fawteent Street every day."

"No!"

"Betcher ass ye do!"

"Oh, Jesus!" Ira exclaimed, turned to look at the business-school door. Students were coming out. "Oh, hell." He broke into a run.

II

He could have batted her with his briefcase, he was so furious with her dawdling down the steps, seemingly the last one out of the school. And he had been almost on the point of running up into the accounting classroom, Mr. McLaughlin's class, where the first students out said she was. Goddamn her, he raged when she recognized him—with her simpering, sappy surprise at the top of the stair. Jesus, somewhere else, he'd have let loose all the obscenities he knew, as she descended the wide steps, fat knock knees in fawny silk stockings under spongy green coat, chewing gum, her pleased and complacent shallow blue eyes shining behind silver-framed eyeglasses on pork nose, her gold curly hair compressed by black cloche. Book in hand, banister in hand. God, the temptation to upbraid her, insult her—if possible! *Could* she be insulted, the dumb bunny?

"What're you doin' up there, layin' for the guy?" Ira could barely contain the nervous impatience of his tone, just short of savage. "For Christ's sake, ye know I called Hannah. I couldn't get you." Still inside the building, he brought his voice within testy limits.

"I was with my accounting teacher, Mr. McLaughlin, going over the test I flunked."

"Yeah. All right. But I'm waiting. I hinted—" Ira jerked his arm emphatically.

"So what's the hurry?" Insipidly nonchalant, she was actually cheerful.

"What's the hurry?" He glared at her. "What's the hurry! I come all the way downtown. I wait." Again, he fought himself to lower his voice. Irate, watched her plant her foot on the ground floor. "Don't you know we're supposed to go to a doctor? I'm gonna take you to that— that lady I told you about."

"With the castor oil?"

"No, for Christ's sake!" He snapped. He gripped her arm. Dawdling little bitch, was she ever going to move? He led her through the building door and into the street. "I don't— That's the reason we're going. Let's get a move on. We don't know. We gotta find out."

"I know."

"All right, then let's get going." Ira all but tugged the green-cloth-covered arm toward 14th Street. "I'll get a cab."

"But I told you I know."

"Waddaye mean, you know?" He felt absolutely vicious. Lucky they were in a crowd.

"I don't need it."

"What de ye mean, you don't need it? Don't need what?" Other pedestrians alongside, no matter: he was shouting.

"I don't need a doctor."

"Why? Don't tell me you're not going to go?"

"I don't have to go."

A tiny inkling was beginning to make headway. "You don't have to go?" His voice that began as bluster subsided ludicrously: dopy Doppler effect. "What d'ye mean?"

"I told you, you worry too much, Ira."

"All right." He frowned warily. "So I worry too much. Who do you think I worry for?"

"For yourself. If I was somebody you didn't know, if I was pregnant, you wouldn't worry." Her voice held an uncommon note of firmness. "I worried about you, and you weren't pregnant."

"What the hell are you talking about? What do you mean, 'if I was pregnant'? What am I here for?"

"What I said: because you only worry about yourself."

"Wait a minute. Are you all right?"

"Of course I'm all right."

"You had your period?" He arrested both their progress, an abrupt embolus in the flow of the throng; a woman's face turned in passing, her rouged cupid-bow lips affixing a fiery stigma on air. "You did? You're not kidding? You did?" He drew her after himself out of the current of passersby against the plate-glass embankment of a store window. "I wanna know. Tell me."

"Tell you? I told you. You think so much about yourself you don't even hear."

"Never mind that. Tell me!"

"I did."

"You're not pregnant?"

"You want me to be?"

"O-oh! O-oh! O-oh!" He could have whooped, he could have capered for joy, cubits high. Fourteenth Street ahead, gray mass of building, slash of blue sky, solid street and park trees and highway, and everything in it became supple as a tapestry, undulated. "Oh, that's wonderful! You're really not?"

She simpered, again her old self, compliant, eager to please. "All right, enjoy yourself."

"Am I? This is like a dream. A-ah! You're wonderful." His hand on her arm checked her from moving away. "Look inside the window a minute."

"It's Barron's." She peered through the glass. "I told Minnie about it Friday. They're having a sale of fall dresses. She wants me to come with her tomorrow, Thanksgiving. They're giving twenty percent off. You know, Ira, your sister is small around the bust? She's nearly like me."

"Yeah?" Beatitude of reprieve was what he felt, so exultant, ferocious in its exultance—how could the plate glass in which he saw himself reflected show only a stupid smirk on a face wearing round shell-framed eyeglasses under a gray felt hat? Jesus Christ, Jesus H. Christ, his visage should be transfigured, radiant. Just a dumb dope listening to a kid cousin blabbling. Jesus, he ought to sprout wings with joy. Instead he was already looking sideways down at the short round figure in green beside him: little pork-nose Stella in a black cloche. He had never been out in public with her before. Why the hell didn't he meet her all the time in front of her school—or whenever he had a chance? Yeah? Where would they go? Smooth, juvenile, fair face, vapid, blond. Ever ready, like a flashlight, but where would they go? Jesus, wasn't he a goddamn goat? A minute ago, damn near shitting in his pants with dread, now ready to go. And here they were. Alone, alone in a mob.

"What d'ye see?" he asked.

"That navy dress there with the tassels, that would be just right for Minnie—I mean the color. Be just right for winter in the office. And like Mama would say, it's a *goor nisht* money: eighteen dollars."

"Yeah? I don't know anything about ladies' clothes. I don't even look— Boy, do I feel good. Ah-h." His bespectacled open-mouthed face in the plate glass looked moronic. "Fur-trimmed coats for thirty-nine fifty," he read the price tag on the mannikin.

"That's what I mean. You know how much Saks Fifth Avenue gets for them? Twice as much."

"Really?" He nudged her into the stream of pedestrians. "Boy, I could give you a big fat feel I'm so happy." He patted the waist of her green coat. "Don't you feel wonderful too?"

"Not why you feel wonderful. I got a collegiate boyfriend. Somebody in my class should see me. Wouldn't they look. But they left already. Mr. McLaughlin should see I had a date." She glanced over her shoulder.

"Mr. McLaughlin wouldn't bother me," Ira bantered. "Max, Moe, Harry. Or somebody like that; one of our uncles. What they'd think."

"You're like Zaida when he lived with us: worry, worry, worry. Now I know where you get it from."

"I'm not worrying now." Ira caressed the green coat sleeve.

"Hey, that's nice," she tittered. He kneed her thigh in stride. "Oh, boy."

At the corner of 14th the two stopped, close to the curb, but to one side of the crossing; the young, placid face beside him—protoplasm came in all shapes and sizes, but none better than the little piece beside him—for what he wanted—as if he mirrored within the distorted, sordid mirror of himself the turmoil all about him, the noise, the traffic become predatory, the crouching storefronts. He was ravening again—like a guy who quit a habit and then caved in, became twice as addicted. He had to fuck her. Where? Jesus, the nuttiest goddamn notions: Ask Edith; she was broad-minded; he was broad-minded—could he have her apartment. Everything had turned out all right: Please: five minutes, he who a half hour ago was ready to crawl with mortification. Oh, God—

"You going to see that professor-lady?" Stella asked.

"Yeah. But I was thinking. Wait a minute. Give me a minute."

Stella surmised his drift of motive. "I can't go anyplace, Ira. I have to be home. You know Mama. Ten minutes late, and there's a big *geshrei.*"

"We don't need a half hour."

"Where? I can't."

"I'm trying to think. Someplace. Damn!" An interval passed, desperate interval, while he wracked his brains, while crowds passed, wheels turned and a million million things changed position, and the clock on the Edison tower struck the quarter hour. "What time you supposed to be home?"

"You know. About four o'clock. Same time as Hannah comes home from Julia Richmond."

"Oh, Jesus!" Ira stared about—at illimitable motion and commotion—and then at the placid pleading, appealing, girlish smiling a trace, blue-eyed, fair countenance—himself and that rusty pederast, but different. "What a goddamn world!"

"We could go into a telephone booth," Stella ventured.

"A what?" Ira was startled.

"Down in the subway."

"And then what?"

"Hold a newspaper in front of the glass like."

"Hold a newspaper?"

"I could go around the world. Underneath."

"Christ's sake, when'd you learn that?" She reddened, but kept mum. "I just got an idea. C'mon!"

"Where? Where, I said?"

"No, I've got a better idea. Let's go." And when she balked, his voice sharpened. "I said, let's go."

"But I can't. I gotta be home. I told you."

"Tell Mamie it's a goddamn Thanksgiving party. A party, a little party after school everybody stayed for. Why not?"

Overborne, she was fearful, whined, yet submitted to his lead. "Where you gonna take me?"

"You'll be a few minutes late, that's all. We can be real quick. I'm not going to take you a mile away. I know you have to be home."

They stopped only briefly at the impacted, milling intersection of 14th and Broadway. The same young cop Ira had seen before now stood in midstreet, unkinking anarchy with beckoning hand and whistle. He pointed to his feet in strict signal to the left-turn driver. "Ira, where are you going?" Stella pleaded. "Oh, will I get it from Mama."

"No. It's right here."

"Where?"

"The same street. The other side." Her gaze ranged along the low drab row of buildings. "Read the name," Ira encouraged.

"You mean that theater?"

"Fox's. Right."

"So what d'you wanna go in there for?"

"I worked there."

"Yeah, but you gotta pay to get in now, don't you?"

"Damn sight better than a telephone booth. C'mon, you'll see," he encouraged. "It'll be in and out, in and out. Maybe you won't even be ten minutes late."

She let the elbow he was holding relax permissively. "Oh, in there?"

"Smart, huh? Let's cross here."

"I never was in Fox's."

"It's a good place. Used to be. It's got a great balcony."

"Oh."

"All right? Boy, am I dying. Hey, maybe I'll let you. I never tried it. You still got your period?" He squeezed her arm, masterfully amorous, steering her toward the run-down theater marquee. "A-ah. You still—?"

"What?"

"Got your period?"

"No. I finished."

"What?!"

"I finished this morning already."

"You did!" He all but came to a halt. "How could you?"

"I began Sunday, that's why, right after you called. Isn't that funny? Nearly right after I just hung up."

"Holy crow! I suffered all those days, thinking you— And I made arrangements. Jesus, I haven't even told her. And boy." He screwed up his face, clawed at his brow. "I spilled the beans. All about—me. Jesus, I didn't have to. If I'd only known— Why couldn't you have stayed home that goddamn afternoon? Roxy, shmoxy." The words poured out of him rife with contempt.

"You're not the only one." She turned on him resentfully. "It's what I keep telling you, Ira. Only you count. Just like Zaida."

"Just like—now, listen—" He nipped off his truculence. Jesus

Christ, he'd lose her if he didn't. "All right," he appeased. "All I'm saying is you could have given me a break. You could have let me know. Somehow. Oof, Jesus. Have I got luck."

"What d'you think I did? I tried to tell you." Stella lifted her face in bland challenge.

"What d'you mean? What did you do?"

"And I got myself in trouble, too."

"When?"

"You know how much I love your neighborhood, with all the Irish and the Italians. They're worse than the Portorickies. Even your hallway. That long, dark—o-o-h. Don't tell me I wasn't afraid."

"Is that what you mean? What were you doing in my neighborhood? My house? You mean 108 East 119th Street?"

"Yes, I mean 108 East 119th," she repeated. "Your house. Where else?" And she suddenly added: "Let's go back."

"Oh, no, no!" Ira truckled. "There's the theater. Where was I? Me?"

"You weren't home."

"I wasn't?"

"No."

"I wasn't!"

"You talk about me? Why shouldn't I go to the Roxy afterward? I'm gonna wait? You'll find out later."

"Oh, that was Sunday morning! Oh, Jesus Christ Almighty! I would go get advice I didn't need. Oh, Jesus!" he wailed. "Talk about Romeo and Juliet."

"Who?"

"Oh, you know, Romeo and Juliet. Christ." His voice slowed under freight of utter disgust. "Oh—" And then suddenly spurred on: "So how'd you get in trouble? Some mick follow you in the hall, or what?"

"No. And don't think there wasn't somebody on the stoop."

"Then what? So what happened?" Again, her mum, obdurate mien met his question. How could she be so blue-eyed, blank, and recalcitrant: sappy enigmatic. "Okay. Forget it, none of my business," he slurred. "Let's go."

"But not to watch anything? No flick?"

"No, no. I told you. Listen, the subway gets jammed." He gesticu-lated. "It's a holiday tomorrow. Things like that can happen."

"So you tell Mama." There was a new note of defiance in her tone.

"C'mon, kid, you forgot something in school." He patted her butt. "Hey, Mr. McLaughlin—he wanted to show you something," Ira teased provocatively. "Is he good-looking? Married? I bet you're teacher's pet." She refused the lure.

"Ask me no questions, I'll tell you no lies."

"Right. Lucky guy. Okay. Here we go. In another ten minutes we'll be walkin' the other way."

"You make me feel I'm doing you a favor, Ira, because I worried you so much."

"Oh, no," he patronized. "It's Thanxy, it's Thanxy. Let's celebrate. Turkey-lurkey. Goosey-loosey." He winked. "And here's Foxy-loxy. Foxy-loxy with cream cheese on a bagel."

Rewarded with a token simper, he got out his wallet, approached the ticket booth. There. He had gotten around her again. But she baf-fled him just the same, baffled him, once she made up her mind she wouldn't talk, wouldn't let on; fooled him because so unexpected: sud-denly her flaccid mask became impenetrable. What kind of trouble did she mean? Well, just as he had his tricks of artful dodging, she had too: like that round-the-world stuff. What d'you know about that? Mr. McLaughlin's big mick uncircumcised cock with her heavily rouged lips around it. She was getting way ahead of him, the little cunt. A head was right. Jesus, the way street words had ruined him. What if she takes it into her head to make money, now? Lucky she had no inkling of what he could do in Fox's, no, what he could think of doing in Fox's. Boy, wild— He laid a dollar in front of the half-moon opening at the bottom of the glass cage shielding the woman cashier: "Two in the mezzanine."

"Admission's the same as the orchestra till six o'clock." Spoken crisply from behind the glass cubicle. Glimpse of regular, chiseled fea-tures no longer young, heavily made up, in eyeglasses, too.

"Oh, I didn't notice. Okay. Two." Flat brass mechanism crackled under the woman's fingers. The tickets sprouted magically from the metal, were tendered through the opening, along with the change.

His briefcase under the crook of his arm, Ira scooped up tickets and coins. He still had comfortable surplus from Edith's fiver. Could anything plait together the mat of irony that got him here because of Mamie's dollar that he was going to replicate with a Trojan bought out of Edith's fiver: out of Mamie's kitchen to Fox's smoking balcony. He had an odd image of primitive, of African statuary—the plum-and-striped-uniformed swarthy ticket taker returned the stubs—the grotesque faces they maybe thought were beautiful. Try to map, to match, the different cultures, Edith called them, and smart-ass Marcia—with Stella hesitantly in his lee, Ira made for the balcony. Their thoughts must have converged within the dingy plaster of the spiral-walled staircase.

"Isn't she waiting for you, Ira, that lady we were going to?"

"Yeah. I shoulda called her. She made an appointment—for you."

"So?"

Ira climbed a couple of steps, turned. "She'll know." Stella's shallow blue eyes glistened up at him. These females really had their own rivalries. Or whatever you call it: their own fortes, circean premiums, something like that, niches for bitches—Jesus, the dirty valences of terms.

"What do you get out of all of this?" he asked, two steps before the balcony top.

"Wouldn't you like to know?"

"Yeah."

"You'd be surprised." In the last dull street light of the small window of the staircase, her lips barely swelled out, her short throat barely inflated. Boy, that was a new one, all right. From the gray light of the staircase they stepped into the stale perfume of piano musical gloom of the first balcony. Disoriented a few seconds, they groped through tenebrae, through movie-house night pegged to the red exit lights, under the cigarette smoke meandering in the beam high above them that fell on the screen. The usher's flashlight moved toward them.

"Right here, Stella." Ira anticipated the usher's approach, led her to the very last row, behind barrier and curtain, at the top of the balcony.

"Here?"

"Yeah. Last row." She understood: he meant the first two seats on the aisle—the last aisle, with the heavy protective curtain behind them. Just in front of the curtain, she stood poised a moment uncertainly. And Ira after her: "You want help with your coat?"

"No. Should I take it off?"

"A minute. It'd be easier." Ira set down his briefcase, doffed his Chesterfield. They both sat down, coats over their knees. Her pudgy face emerging out of the beam-lightened gloom looked contented, reassured, spreading her short legs to invite the course of his ardor. With his hand on her thigh, working up, they watched the screen: a few minutes of hot petting, fingering her parted muff under her green coat, till her legs stretched rigid. With graven, expectant face, her eyes followed the hand he guided to the hard-on sprung like a pale spar from his open fly. President Coolidge—grave-faced, austere countenance, the embodiment of Puritan rectitude—shook hands with Gene Tunney on the newsreel. Below the scanty audience, men scattered here and there on the balcony, here and there puffing on a cigar or cigarette.

"You want me to?"

"Go ahead." He spoke before he even looked, and only when she lowered her curved blond lock under cloche-covered head did he turn his head away from the screen to peer athwart. Was everything all right? She was just bending down under cover of his coat. Oh, was that it? That was what it was like? She pressed hard against the hand on her pussy. That was his part, to cooperate, as she bent almost double, latent, unguessed, limber little fatso.

"Oh," he breathed silently—could see her eyes were closed tightly shut, always open unseeing when she straddled him before, but shut now: swoggled, the word arose spontaneously—"O-o-h," his turn this time: "O-o-h, Stella." Hornswoggled—inner ecstasy hers, hermetic, supreme, too deep for utterance—

Light from the opened balcony door darted into the gloom of the balcony. She neither saw it nor heard the quiet sound of hinge. Her eyes popped open as he lifted her face away, covered receding stalk under coat—but before? Or not before? The three spindly, springy black youths reached the top of the balcony stairs. Oh, Jesus, they were inspecting Ira and Stella with glistening white eyeballs. And then furtively, knowingly, one another. Oh, God. Ira sat upright.

Stella too now realized what had happened. She recovered resignation first: "Should we go?"

Between fear and fury, Ira sat immobilized. "Sonofabitch luck." Yeah. They had bounced down to the lowest tier of seats, just before the brass railing, and the tallest looked up. Then dark faces leaned together. They talked as Ira squirmed about. Where the hell was that usher? If he could hear them jabber, everybody else could. He heard a soft tread behind him, saw a flashlight beam on and off. About time.

"Get your coat. Wait a minute, my briefcase." He saw Stella get ready, just as the uniformed usher, flashlight like a baton, began descending the aisle.

"Listen," Ira whispered, "do what I say."

"What? What're you gonna do?"

"Never mind. You ready? When I tell you, follow me." Ira could see she was dismayed. He shook his hands at her more in menace than reassurance. Fuck her. Fuck them. "Get ready to get up." His mind seemed in uproar. He didn't give a damn. Guardedly, he turned his head to peer over his shoulder: was everything still the same? The white, rubber-covered chain still stretched across the steps to the second balcony? Jesus, it was. And so was the white NO ENTRANCE sign still hanging from the chain—he had ducked under it a hundred times on his way to and from the projectionist's booth on top of the stark third balcony, where the chairs had no cushions. Jesus, everything *looked* the same. But it would take nerve, boy, it . . . would . . . take . . . nerve. But he wasn't going to lose it—goddamn her, them. Red Grange carried the ball, shaking tacklers, running like a phantom through the broken field. Maybe give it up. Open his fly again, hold her twat, and jack off—and go. Play it safe. Mamie was waiting. He was about to reopen the top button of his fly. Nah. Jimmy Walker was doing the honors with visiting dignitary; not Mussolini, was it?

Unaware of the usher's flashlight descending, the three black youths below seemed to have shaken off theater protocol, buoyant in their mirth, unfazed by fellow patrons—and again they looked up, but this time saw the beam approaching. "It's nearly now," Ira warned.

"Where do you wanna go?" She turned plaintive, puerile face.

"Follow me. Another sec."

"What?"

"Shut up." Between this and his next word, he caught a flash of rosy Irish face, so reminiscent of that Irish serving girl who with her husky amorous escort descending the sloping path through woods had saved him from his rusty predator long ago. They had saved him, saved him in Fort Tryon Park. Jesus, he spurned the prompting. Save her? Little cocksucker. What the hell, did she think he wasn't going to get his piece of ass?

"Now! C'mon, c'mon!" And even as he had once docilely complied, she did too, in his power: out into the aisle, and then quickly, while he lifted the heavy muffled links of chain, she ducked, to be prodded under, faltering or not, and up the first dusty carpeted steps. Crouching, he followed.

As down below, the usher's subdued and subduing voice rose after them: "Hey, you, where d'yuh think you are?"

"Yeah, man," was uttered with risible abandon. "We just come in, yeah. Sittin' down."

"Well, take it easy. There's others in here . . ." But he got away from them that time. Just beat the gleam of the eyeball?

"Go ahead." He shepherded her up the dust-laden carpeted stairs. And climbed quickly after her—to his backward glance, the movie on the screen of the first balcony disappearing below the tallest black youth, before the second balcony hove into view, utterly deserted, dark and private. They had made it. He pressed her plump, round rump under palm exultantly. "Oh, boy!"

"Ira, here?"

"No, wait a minute." First harbingers of rekindled furor fired every sense, every second, transformed into accessories rank on rank of dim, empty, raised seats sloping to the antic screen below where spare, sparsely smiling Lindbergh received a medal to silent applause, translated into increased volume of piano accompaniment—private roost above the world, cozy terrain of gloom under shaft of projected cinema, staked out by a couple of red exit lights. Just one little step more, and it couldn't be beat for utterly seamless, pulsating solitude—almost like the kitchen green walls—

"In here." He opened the door to the merest glimmer of a flush toilet stool.

"O-oh, it's so dark, Ira."

"Waddaye want? Light? Git in." He shut the door after her. Tomb darkness encased them: mummy-yummies. He felt for the light switch. "Okay, honey bun." Through dusty bulb, the snapped-on weak, spongy light bound them together in exquisite depravity. "Boy, everything!"

"It's for ladies." Her chalky blue eyes behind eyeglasses, so tractable, regarded self in the smudged square mirror above the lavatory, and him beside her, she regarded him. Her amorphous, juvenile countenance below his stubble-shadowed features met his relentless brown eyes behind glasses, she timidly basking in his leer. She didn't need to be told; she responded to the mere movement of his head, as if his ferocity, compressed by close quarters, was permeating her with his desire, his will, chalky-eyed. And as her bosom began to heave, she set down her *Elements of Bookkeeping* in the dusty enamel bowl, her green coat over it, and bowed, tugging up skirt, down panties—

"Ah—h!" Maniac bliss at the sight, dropped briefcase on covered toilet bowl, coat in rumpled heap on top. And oh, boy, what bulbs of ass. He unbuttoned fly, "Oh, boy, this is better. Way better." Sight of her fed the greed of eyes, sight of her whetted, as did feel of her, the greed of hands insatiable of contour. And oh, boy, that face of his, though bespectacled silly, transcendentally gloated in the dusty mirror: carnal guerdon, wow. Little pig, little sow, let me in. The dumb little punk in pleated blue up, dappled ass-rise above cloud of lacy drawers, as she clutched the caked lavatory rim with pudgy hands, thrall to abuse, ecstatic for defilement, obeisant before ravaging, his chattel, chattel to destroy. No wonder guys beat up on 'em, gave 'em the works, left 'em for dead—Jesus, the terrible ultimate mutilate spawned by a whole week's fear and humiliation bloating consummation, damn her, oh, to plug and throttle in blot of bestial woe-betide—boy, it was a shame to ram it into her, and get it over in a few seconds— And then was heard . . . what the hell?—footsteps in no uncertain sound and number. And oh, Jesus, a scared and shrinking pause, two faces staring open-mouthed with alarm at a cobweb trapdoor, while automatic nerveless hands restored garments, picked up briefcase, bookkeeping manual.

"Sh-h!" But his panicky warning failed to avert the footsteps: too late to turn the light off, door-crack light, boxed into light, immovable as a picture in a frame, gripped in concrete, yet breathing—oh, Jesus

Christ, the usher! No, the tread was multiple: usher and manager. Bluff it out, plead it out, whine it out. Already on his trembling lips abject imploring, Please, mister, please. Extenuate. He had worked here was why. Never again—grovel, as he did in Stuyvesant. Maybe the guy would be Jewish.

The door opened—to Stella's short startled "O-o-h!" The three young Negroes seemed to pull the light toward them as they swung the door wide open. Like a net, like a seine, they pulled the light toward them. And happy with their catch, pale eyeballs, polished brown skin, grew lustrous with pleasure. They seemed quite young. And even spindlier in the light, like reeds, but already at least Ira's height, or taller. Elastic, brown striplings, fourteen years old, fifteen, who knew? None had a coat, but under an array of motley, raveled sweaters wore sweatshirts, gaudy summer sport shirts. One sported a striped knit cap, a second something resembling a beret, the third a sawtooth-brimmed and incised-diamond-crowned gray felt.

"Hey, man," the tallest greeted with flip of wrist and lilt of shoulder, his voice just above a whisper. "We come up t'see how you doin'."

"You doin' all right." The shortest might be the oldest. He had a small scar across his upper lip. His brown face gleamed amiably; his white-nailed hand lingered on his crotch. "We see you an' her duck the man. We knew y'all gonna finish it."

"Ri-ight," commended the third, his gaze lingering appreciatively on Stella. "How 'bout dat? She friend o' yo?"

Were they serious? Was he in danger? What course to follow? Demeanor what? Tough-bluff. Sheepish, sharing-prank. Options ripped through the mind; his eyes riveted on three brown, flippant faces; he strove to plumb intentions, adjust actions—all in gnarled seconds. Mostly, it was their conspiratorial, their knowing leering he feared, their feral implications that bound together. Penned in here, cornered, he could let out a yell, an outcry: Stella would follow suit. Then what?

He let instinct take control. "All right, fellers." He moderated a resolute front with concession of foible. "We just tried to duck away— you're right." He tried not to move precipitously toward termination. "You know how it is." He made to edge Stella toward the open door. "Let's go, Stella."

But none of the youth showed the least sign of accommodation, no one made room for him. "You ain't gone break up de party like dat, man?" the tallest objected. "What about us?"

Time to fence—for all he was worth: "You already have."

"Aw, no, man, we jes' join it."

"You just spoiled it." His chuckle was staple, nonrecriminatory. "Let's quit kiddin', fellers." He appealed to reason. "Waddaye say?" He again leaned in the direction of passage, which they again blocked.

"Say? Nothin' t'say, man," the short youth said. "She blow you, she blow us."

"You get outta the way." A frightened Stella pushed at Ira's shoulder, her voice rising. "Get outta the way. We wanna go."

"Better get outta the way before the usher hears you," Ira advised.

"We don' want no trouble, Stella. Dat yo name?" The third youth—nearest the door—pulled it to behind him. All five locked in: ladies' slate-partitioned toilet, dusty lavatory with rust ring.

"What're you lockin' us up for?" Stella's voice rose in panic. "Open that door!"

"We jes' want some fun, Stelly."

"Right. Jes' a little fun," two voices blended. "Ev'body like a little fun. Don't you like a little fun, Stella. A little fun neveh hurt nobody."

"Sho thing, Stella, bebeh. You do us like yo do him."

"C'mon, fellers," Ira pleaded, his ineffectiveness a lead weight within him. "I tell you, you're gonna get in trouble."

"I'll scream." Stella drove to the fore of opposition. "You let us go!"

"Aw, Stella, bebeh, don' go gittin' yose'f all excited." The tallest youth's brown finger was curved around its own pale inner pad, hooked like a setting about something metallic, a Gem safety razor blade. "You tell her, man, we ain' gone hurt her." Stella shrank back. "Look, man, we don' like messin' aroun'." A bright blade appeared, clicked open out of the pearl-handled knife, pale in the brown hand of the shorter youth.

Ira contracted to nothingness. "Waddaye want? I got three bucks."

"We don' wantcher money, man. We wan' a little fun."

"Nobody lookin' t'cutcha up. We all have a little fun."

"We all stay here, an' everyone gone take a turn in de ladies' booth."

"Yah." So apropos, persuasive, the shortest youth.

All three brown faces beamed. "Rotten niggers!" Stella screamed—and threw herself forward with flailing fist and manual. "Help! Lemme go!"

"Help!" Ira shouted, surged in tandem. "Goddamn you bastards! Git away from us!"

They gave ground. The door cracked open, flew around, and out they burst into gloom.

"Poleese!" Stella screamed, fleeing toward the stairs. "Help! Poleese!"

"Here! No! This way! Stella!" Ira plunged through the obscurity of the balcony, the movie foaming on the screen below. He hurled himself at the brass bar of the fire-escape door under the red exit light. He flung it open on daylight, with Stella behind him. Were they following? They were—and they weren't. They lagged. Bluff hadn't worked, or something like that. Past the edge of daylight, with Stella pressing bodily beside him, out on the fire escape the two charged. Ira led the way down: iron steps under skipping feet, and Stella keeping pace with hand sliding along black iron guardrail, as though gripping a pike, and bookkeeping manual raised like a shield, rushing frantically down by his side. As he ran free, he was surprised at her speed, the reckless patter of her feet in women's shoes flickering from step to step to the first-balcony level.

"It's closed. It's locked. The doors."

She stopped, perceived the dead end of fire escape, was about to hammer on the metal door.

"Ira, where you going?" she screamed after him.

"Don't be afraid. Watch." He felt—what?—a stirring of respect, camaraderie, never felt before. "I'll show you." He took hold of her arm, pressed it in encouragement. "Come on. Just walk out after me." He led the way forward to the end of the cantilever staircase that jutted like a peninsula into empty space over the street, a gangway to nowhere—

"It's moving!"

"I know. I did this already." He felt solicitous: libido metamorphosed by stress: poor kid.

"Oh, it goes right to the sidewalk."

"That's the whole idea. We'll be down in a second." Across the street, windows in the warehouse wall rose above them as they descended—descended in the open air to the level of wooden packing crates beside doorways gathering afternoon shadow. Hardly anyone below paid any attention to them; the few pedestrians on 13th Street had their backs to them. Only the driver of a sedan spared a hasty stare, and was gone. Doors creaked open above them as he steadied her the last few feet of the sinking trammel. The blue-uniformed fireman about to enter the squat brick firehouse a few buildings east regarded them askance, as if tricksters inciting his reproach.

"Just easy. That's it. Walk off." Ira tightened his grip of her arm. "Now!" And they stepped onto the sidewalk.

A quick glance upward in the direction of the freed cantilever floating up again: "Hey, fellers. Downstairs, fellers. You ain't suppose to be up there. That's against the law." The usher in plum uniform hanging partway out of the fire-exit door, with neck twisted and face skyward calling to three black visages above like a cluster of coconuts suddenly cracking open from grave witness, while higher still on the third balcony the projectionist in undershirt gaped down, at a loss. "Hey, what're you doin', wise guys?" he directed censure downward. "Yous can get locked up fer dat."

The avenue, the avenue at last, the higher airs—he helped her with her coat, as she juggled her purse, plunged arms into his, as he juggled his briefcase, while all the time the two hurried toward the thronged avenue at the corner that meant safety, meant deliverance. Once there, they lost themselves among window shoppers and strollers and the hurrying, dodging ambitious individuals, holiday-homeward-bound, weaving with purpose. In seconds he and Stella were anonymous, in seconds blending with the crowd, liberated, noncommittal among the crowd walking briskly toward 14th Street.

Ira puffed with relief. "Wow!" She was breathless too, giggled, busy trying to rub grime from her hand—and still constrained to whisper. "Mama's right, ye know, Ira. It's just like what she keeps saying. That's all the *shvartze* and the Portorickies think about. But I've never had a razor and a knife at me before. Was I scared."

"Same here."

"All I could think of was if Mama knew where I was—o-oh, what could have happened."

"I know. And I took you up there." He tried to make amends. "How the hell was I going to know one of those sonsofbitches saw me?"

"So where was the usher?"

"Yeah, where? Maybe they didged up the way we did. I don't know."

"A *babbeh* waked up for us, like Mama says in Jewish."

"Yeah. That scream you let out helped too."

"Was I scared. You think they all had a razor blade, a knife?"

"I don't know. I don't even know if they really meant it. When you called 'em niggers, I thought, oh, we're lost."

"I just couldn't help it. And you know what, Ira? Now I wanna cry."

"I don't blame you. Go ahead. Want my handkerchief? You got one?"

"In my coat pocket." She sniffled, plied the handkerchief while she leaned against him, walking. "First I laugh and then I cry."

"It's okay, Stella, it's okay. We're outta the woods." He stroked her back soothingly.

"I told you," she said without rancor, "let's go into a telephone booth." She suddenly laughed, wiped tears from her cheeks.

"I should have listened. I'll never try that again." What kind of new tenderness seemed to flow from the cloth of her coat, from the soft girlish shoulders beneath the coat through his hand, to his arm, his mind. Jesus, he had felt that only once before about her: when he had come so prodigiously the night he humped her, with Mamie snoring spasmodically nearby. He had kissed her that time—tenderly. No wonder the kid wanted to cry, after what he had put her through just now. No wonder. "You all right now?"

"Yeah. I'm all right."

"I'm sorry."

"It'll be over soon. It's even over now." Her bland cheeks wreathed, though she blinked, and her voice was still wrung. "It's over now. How fast everything becomes then. When I look at Mama, or Tanta Leah, your mother, or the other *tantas*, I keep thinking they must have all grown up just waiting for a *khusin*, you know what I mean? Even Hannah. Is Minnie like that, too?"

"I don't know."

"You're her brother."

"Yeah, but you know how it is. She has her secrets."

"Like I have mine. Do I look all right?" She tilted her face. "Tell me honest. It was so dirty, everything up there. I can use where I cried in my handkerchief to wipe my face." She was amused.

"No, no, you look fine. Say, you look all right," he complimented. "You look all right." She was really rather pretty, with her blond hair peeping out of the black cloche, short throat, fresh, fair skin of round cheeks heightened in color now, blue eyes, shallow, yes, behind glasses, and short girlish lips parted, plump, no, "adolescent" was the right word, adolescent phase, and kind of cute. He had never thought of her that way—just something to bend to his will, really bend, simpering pudding-compliant, implicitly at his disposal—his tubby, juvenile Trilby—and why? He surmised why: a collegian he, and schoolgirl she: not mettlesome like Hannah, but ungifted, held in low esteem at home, a cinch, a drippy cinch for the picking—or the pricking. Cynical? Sure.

He had previously honed his perfidy on Minnie. Consider the mitigating circumstance: he tolerated Stella's drivel—long enough to achieve his ends. But never had he been tender, except for that momentary impulse—and maybe even then he was bestowing a token remuneration for supreme consummation. Till now. And now? So that's what he wanted—his mouth watered at the new perception of himself, the perverse evolution of desire. Skew of screw—that's what tenderness meant to him before something impressionable, half-formed, pathetic, susceptible, ductile, fawning: extension of the evening they sat opposite each other on the love seat at the *bris* in Flushing, extension of the initiation, when he first stuck his tongue into her mouth, seduced her, reduced her to trail him in a trance down the steps of the glary cellar.

Now Edith knew all about him too. Christ, he wasn't worth living. "Let's get you down the subway. You won't be too late."

"I'll tell Mama what you told me. We had a party before the holiday. You going to go uptown too?"

"Not right away. I'm going to walk—no," he contradicted himself, annoyed. "I've got to call up that lady. Jesus, what she must be think-ing." He felt stunned, disoriented.

"You're not going there?"

"I better just call."

"Why?"

"Guess."

"You should be happy. She should be happy. She made a doctor's appointment. If she made a doctor's appointment—"

"She must have canceled that long ago," Ira interrupted irritably. "Say, what would you have done if I had to take you there? What would you have told Mamie? It might have taken a long time—longer than this."

"I couldn't—I wouldn't go. Only on Saturday. I could say I was going for a walk on 116th Street."

"Oh, hell."

"Why?"

"Nothing. Nothing."

"Maybe if you told me you were gonna be here for that, I could have told Mama about a party—I don't know," she said with unusual animation. "Look, Ira, I'm a girl, and I'm already over it. All right, razor blades, knives, those guys, they scared me. But you—I don't mean you didn't get scared too. But now, you should be happy. We got away. And look at the trouble you saved. You thought I was pregnant. And I'm not. You thought you would have to take me to that lady. And she would take me to the doctor—"

"I know! I know! All right."

He looked straight ahead, determined to encourage her forward movement through the crowd, then, dissatisfied with progress, steered her along Broadway.

"How did you remember that toilet up there from all those years?" she asked curiously.

"Will I ever forget it?"

"They must not have cleaned it for a—was it clean when you worked there?"

"No, it never was clean. It was already closed, that whole gallery, I mean. I just took a chance. Oh, what the hell," he added snappishly.

She suddenly laughed. For a moment Ira thought she was laughing at his discomfiture. But no. Talking as always before she finished laughing, her words tumbled off pointless mirth.

"That projectionist looking down, will I ever forget him?"

"Did you see him?"

"Did I see him? In his sagging undershirt. If he didn't look funny. But you know, Ira, it really is funny. You wouldn't believe it."

"What?"

"I had a boyfriend who was studying to be a projectionist. I thought of him. If he was looking down."

"Oh." How cheerless was spoiled lust. Her lips moved like larva—oh, Jesus, just get to the subway through the crowd.

"When I was fourteen, he worked in a projection booth. And Ira, you were fourteen, and you worked in a projection booth, too."

"Yeah, I know."

"When I was fourteen, he wanted to marry me." Her dumb correspondences.

"Yeah?" He could feel his face crimp with fretfulness. If he had even gotten a piece of tail out of all this. Christ, nothing. "Fourteen? Who was fourteen? I mean, was he fourteen?" He felt as idiotic as she was—just as irascible as he had felt when he waited for her to come out of the business school. Mopey lout, he deserved what he got. "What're you talking about?"

"I said I was fourteen. He wasn't fourteen. He was already twenty-one. But he wanted to marry me. He hounded me. Gerald: Let's go out and have an ice cream sundae. Let's go to a dance. Nearly every evening he came to the house. But he wasn't my type."

"No?"

"He was short and fat, and already a little bald. Mama liked him, and Pap said it would be all right. Next year I'll be going on eighteen."

"Yeah?"

"But I kept telling Gerald, That's all. I don't wanna see you no more. I don't care if Mama likes you—"

"Was that it?"

"Of course. I'm the one who has to marry him. And did Mama cry at the next wedding: two pillowcases. She was going to have an old-maid daughter on her hands. Can you imagine, at fourteen, no less."

"No."

"Who is your type, Ira? Is that lady your type?"

"I don't know who my type is."

"Mine is the married-man type. The tall, blond type. They're not Jewish, but they're married anyway, so it doesn't matter. You I can tell, but if Mama ever knew." Stella giggled.

Engulfed—enthronged (the word coined itself)—amid the home-going crowd, the air of holiday about them, swarming out of Klein's on 14th and meshing with those from the smaller stores, he and Stella turned west toward the subway kiosk across Broadway. The first chill encroached on the last wedges of sunlight in the park, first chill seeping through the growing shadows. It had begun to empty the benches in the park, gave briskness to the stride of those crossing, and even seemed to increase the agitation of arguing groups, those pitted against each other, with shaking fist and stabbing finger. As undaunted as ever, Washington on his bronze steed on concrete pedestal contemplated turmoil and incessant noise. It made Ira wonder how much difference he himself made, how much, how little, even if he bellowed at the top of his lungs. It would be like going aboard an ocean liner, infinitesimally, imperceptibly lowering her hull in the water—like the time he delivered steamer baskets as a boy, like the time he accompanied Edith—Edith, yes, she must be waiting, wondering. Well, what excuse? In the eddy flowing around Orange Drink Nedick's at the corner of University, in the aura of grilled hot dogs, he eased pants at the crotch. And the horror of it all. He was worse than even Joe, the bum, in Fort Tryon Park, who had pulled on his *petzel* while Ira, all of eight, recoiled in fear. He was worse than Pop, too, smashing Mom a glancing whack and little Ira, too. How the sins, the *shande*, had come full circle, and all of this in the eddy by the Nedick's stand at University and Broadway, a hundred blocks from Harlem, but one thing was sure, though: maybe one guy couldn't add a perceptible increment to tumult, but a lot together could. That bunch—those two bunches—shouting at each other certainly added distinct stridor. What the hell were they all about?

"You know something funny?" Stella asked.

"No, what?"

"We made a big circle—from my school over there, through the theater, and back again."

"Oh, yeah." His wry voice ended by inhaling a squelched sigh. "What d'ye do? Take the shuttle?"

"I have to." She led the way across the sidewalk to the kiosk. "I have to, but you don't. You can go on the Lexington."

"I know, but I'd better make my call first."

"You can make it downstairs."

"You mean the phone booths in the subway?"

"There's three, four. Those big wooden ones—when you go from the IRT to the BMT."

"I'm not sure," he hedged. "Okay. Let's go," he said hastily. "Jesus, I'm late. Later than you're going to be." They both flowed down the steps with the cataract of commuters heading home. "Show me the booths, will you?"

"Around the platform. This way. I'll wait for you."

"You don't have to." His voice sharpened.

"We both gotta ride to 42nd. A minute more."

"Holy Jesus!"

"Why? You're not gonna tell her what happened?"

"Oh, no! Get in here. It's too goddamn noisy. Or do you wanna stay out?" She was already in the way of the folding door, giggled as he dropped the nickel into the aperture.

"You know," she whispered as he waited for the operator, "I wanted to meet her, but I didn't wanna meet her. You know what I mean?"

"Sh!"

"Number please." Oh, Christ, in the interval, preparing for apology. In the phone booth—that she had recommended. Oh, man, oh, man, the jibes of those boys still echoing. He felt as though he were losing his mind—heard the simulated ring of the phone, hoped Edith wasn't home. Whee-ooh, he whistled, windily audible, while Stella watched him. In a minute there is time, said Eliot. And Larry this afternoon. No, Jesus, she wasn't home. Oh, Jesus, the teetering. He wedged his briefcase on the shelf in the angle of phone box and wall—

"You know, I forgot my steno book up there," Stella whispered, waited a second. "She's not home?"

"I don't know. A coupla more rings."

"The operator'll tell you."

Jesus, he was crazy enough he was ready to tell Edith it was all right. He was going to marry the little cunt. He couldn't say "cunt." No, she wasn't pregnant; he was just crazy: *Mishugeh auf toit,* Mom would say. There she was pressed against him. Go ahead, give her a feel. Go home with her. He could just see himself escorting Stella through 112th Street, her native heath, and Mamie coming out of the neighboring apartment house, and simply transported with delight at the vision of Stella on Ira's arm, and Ira suddenly a prospective *khusin* for her daughter. And then he could have all the latest she had learned right here in a phone booth. A slave. If that wasn't crazy, if he wasn't crazy. Two poles, he ought to have two poles. Yeah. His insufferable, imperious need, and hazy, imperious bidding of the future. If only it were one or the other, not jeering at himself as he jauntily advanced to greet his putative, rapturous mother-in-law. Oh, you're off your pulley. So what? All right, Mamie, start furnishing that empty apartment. He reached down for the neighborhood of Stella's muff, to her simper—

"Hello. Sorry, I was—"

"Edith."

"For pity's sake, lad, where on earth have you been?"

Muff, pneumatic muff, Eliot echo. "I don't know where I've been. I don't think I could tell you." He leered cruelly at Stella. "Everything's all right. I shoulda called you. What about that doctor?"

"Oh, I've taken care of that. I waited till the last minute. What on earth—"

"I got sidetracked. I'm sorry."

"Is the girl all right? You sure?"

"Yeah, that's what threw me. You were right."

"You sound very strange just the same. Are you all right?"

"Yeah. I'm sorry I bothered you— Hell!"

"Where are you?"

"Fourteenth Street subway station."

"Please, will you listen to me?"

"What?"

"I want to see you. As soon as possible. Ira, please."

"Yeah."

"I'm serious. Will you take the first taxi you can, and come here? I'm very worried. Ira, do you have enough money? I'll wait in front of the house."

"No."

"You will."

"Yes."

"As soon as you can. Promise."

"Eftsoons his hand dropped he."

"What? You're mumbling so."

"I'll tell you."

"I'll be waiting for you."

"All right. I'm going upstairs. Give me a minute."

"You be sure?"

"Yes. Sure. Goodbye." He hung up.

"You going there? To that lady?" Stella asked.

"You heard me." He shoved the folding doors open. "Fresh air. Go home, will you, Stella?"

She opened her purse. "Wait a minute. Which way?" He got a nickel out, strode. "That's the BMT—Ira!"

"Oh, the other one."

"Don't you know yet?" Her acne stood out in surprise. "I can pay the carfare."

"I know it. Come on." He led the way to the IRT turnstiles, dropped a nickel in the slot. Her green coat pressed the revolving petal, banging admission.

"Bye-bye," she smiled, juvenile, vapid. "Bye." Utterly lost within himself, he climbed the stair, sole, single-file counter to the throngs descending. And up into the street, auto-exhaust-laden autumn air, slant sun artificially bright on the facades of tall east buildings, on the clock in the Edison tower—half past four—feigning light on the limp lusterless top leaves of trees in the park. A cab? He wheeled about, searching, gaze sweeping the corner, where the vendor had been. A Checker cab, but occupied. Maybe more as far as the Union Square Secretarial—raggle-taggle, coming out of the park, the women in both groups were wearing babushkas, the men caps; the larger group seemed to be hounding the smaller one; and the smaller though pursued was uncowed: they hurled back defiances at their adversaries, taunts in heavily accented English: "Splitters! Wreckers! Stalinist gengsters! Vot did Abramovitz tell us, hah?" A truly stentorian voice bawled out, "Lenin hugged him ven he vas dere. He came beck, and he said, 'Clara, it's not for us.' No?" Cab? Oh, hell, at this hour. There went another—with a fare—"Not for you, reformist, scissor-bills vot de Vobblies call you. Sqvealers!"

"Wreckers!"

"Recketeers!"

"Go to hell!"

Hell was right. Where the hell was a taxi? He had worried her enough—"Singk, singk, everybody!" A very short woman in the pursuing group, as stocky as she was tall, broke into song, and her cohorts soon followed, inundating those ahead with scorn; above the counter chant of "Bendits! Moscow Bendits! Stalinite tools!" rose the derisive song: "Oh, de cluck-meckers union is no-good union, it's a right-ving union by de boss. De stinkin' ga'ment meckers un de doity labor woeckers give de voikers a doity double cross. Oh, de Kahns, de Hillquvits, un de Thomases, dey give de voikers all false promises. Dey pritch sotsialism, but dey prektice fatzism in de toid kepitalist pahty by de boss!"

"Hey, taxi, taxi!" Ira waved frantically. "Hey! Right here!"

PART THREE

As if he had been traveling for hours on end, Ira got out of the cab in a stupor, told the hackie to keep the change from the dollar he handed over, dazedly aware that the tip came to more than the fare, and walked unsteadily through the cold blanching of day's end to Edith's house door. He pressed the nacreous bell button below her name, leaned inward at the buzzer, laboriously entered the carpeted hallway. Reverberations of streets through which he had just been, of acts, Stella at a drinking fountain, knife blades, faces in subways, moving hordes on station platforms, places and grimaces, all seemed to have gotten into his nerves, seethed in his blood—stairs settled like a fire escape as he climbed—along with voices and cries, a reeling farrago of his libido, his lunacy, almost palpably filling the softly lit hallway, like a half-delirious transition to the new surroundings, new atmosphere of Edith's apartment. Adjust—with heaving chest, recognize the scent of lemon oil at the nostrils at the same time as the rich gleam of piano and piano stool told him the cleaning woman must have been here today. Adjust, try to sequester the topsy-turvy memories that he had no time to dwell on, no time to abate.

His gaze held by the gold sunburst on her kimono, Ira followed Edith into the apartment. A profound breathlessness heaved within him as he entered, a breathlessness that seemed much greater than that due to physical exertion—of climbing up two flights of stairs—but like a panting of the spirit trying to recover from all that had assailed it. Dully, and always conscious of his lack of grace, as if his shambling were a safeguard against too much being expected of him, he shed his coat and hat, dropped them on a chair, his briefcase between, and stood swaying to his own pulse, looking about the apartment as if he weren't familiar with the decor, the location of chairs, the gray Navajo rugs scattered about, the black maw of the fireplace under the sheen of marble mantelpiece, desk and manila files, bulldog bulk of typewriter, bookcases, telephone. He found his favorite wicker armchair, sank noisily into it. He felt utterly jaded; his tongue seemed twice as thick as normal, and he kept wanting to double it under his palate. He wished he could have refused her unyielding request that he come to her apartment. Still, it was almost a compensation for compliance, to sit there so blissfully relaxed, only a shade away from slumping, waiting for her to arrange herself on the black velvet couch, yellow pencil, blue NYU exam booklets beside her: Professor Edith Welles of the NYU English Department, dusky in the light of the end-table lamp, large-eyed, petite, shadow-brown hair in a bun at the back of her head, and pretty calves and ankles protuding.

"Did you take a taxi?" she demanded severely.

"Yeh."

"You look completely done in." She regarded him so intently and for so many seconds he felt like lolling his head. "You scared me out of a week's growth," she said. "I didn't know what to imagine. Not hearing from you all afternoon."

"I should have called up. I know."

"Where on earth were you, child? You knew we had a doctor's appointment."

"Yeh. I was hoping you'd cancel it."

"There wasn't much else I could do—when nobody appeared after four."

"I'm sorry. It's been awful. Some afternoon. I mean it." He slapped the wicker seat. "It's been all my own doing, too."

"It's about what I expected when a girl is as young as she is." Edith apparently misunderstood his reference. "I should think you'd be much relieved at the way things turned out."

"I am. I am. I was." He debated revelations. "What gets me is that she claims she tried to get in touch with me. She went to my house and all that. I was here Sunday, wasn't I? I tried to think back when she told me."

"Yes. I'm sure you were here Sunday. Does it matter?"

"No, but it would have saved everybody a lot of trouble: me a lot of dumb worrying. And you making doctor's appointments and having to cancel 'em." Ira looked off obliquely, paused for breath. "I guess the worst of it is my having to confess the louse I am."

She shook her head, so characteristically: not disapproving, but with sober, sympathetic disagreement. "You were only confessing to the need that's part and parcel of being human, of any species of life, I imagine. Marcia knows that better than all of us. We all satisfy it—in different ways, but we do satisfy it."

"Yeh? I satisfied it."

"Is there any reason why you shouldn't? There isn't. There are puritanical ones. You're shy. You're inhibited. But you needn't feel that what happened is so very sordid, what you've done is so very sordid. If you but knew how really sordid—" Edith groped for words a moment, laughed. "You have no idea. Most children experiment at an early age."

"Yeh."

It was no use. He was what he was, and he couldn't tell her what he was—or only as much as he had, and that was too much, and maybe now that he had, it would be best if he stayed away, let the friendship taper off. Let her words slide over him until he could leave politely. He was expert in attitudes of listening. And he was just tired enough so that he was afraid he might let go altogether, if he allowed himself to become too engaged, if he fueled her interest with rejoinders. She spoke of the practices of respectable businessmen, churchgoers, affluent and married and influential, ways that were truly sordid, with young children and prostitutes—married uncles and young nieces, and all the time maintaining a sanctimonious exterior. Those people were really despicable, because they were hypocrites, and she loathed hypocrites.

But as far as Ira was concerned, his sex relations with his cousin Stella were almost inevitable, because he was extremely sensitive and, unlike Larry, shy and unworldly, and unlike Larry, poverty-stricken and deprived. It was just too bad that he felt so guilty in the matter of sexual intercourse with his cousin. Sexual behavior sprang out of the mores of a culture; so did the attitudes people developed about sex. Because there was no genuine sex education, no sex education in the schools—"Heavens, no! The churches would be horrified, the Watch and Ward societies would be up in arms!"—attitudes about sex with few exceptions were determined by ingrained and often fallacious notions about sex, by sheer ignorance, by social custom and taboo, by religious and puritanical nonsense about sin and punishment—

"Yeah, that's the way I am," Ira agreed. "It's inbred. When I read about Satan and Sin—" he hesitated for fear Edith might draw a parallel—"in Milton, the whole thing hit home despite myself. I don't believe it, but what if you're brought up that way? It's bad."

"Poor lad, I wish I'd known. But of course you—I'm bound by Victorian decorums too. No use crying over spilt milk. Ira, it's bred in all of us, that sex is wicked—for some even in marriage," she consoled. "I know I once thought so. I was deeply affected—influenced by my mother's Christian Science priggishness. I've told you about it. My sister still feels that same way. I'm sure that may have been one of the reasons—I don't know—of her divorce. It would be the last thing she'd talk about. But sooner or later we learn to escape from that kind of domination—it's really nothing but superstition. You yourself have already thrown off much of it, haven't you?"

"Yeah. It's different throwing it off when you know what you're doing."

She smiled comfortingly. "I'm sure it is." Her eyes strayed to the mirror above the fireplace at Ira's back. "That very thing you were so concerned about: Stella's menstruating. When I lived with Sam H in Berkeley, who I suppose had been brought up in much more Orthodox fashion than you were, he told me that Jews considered menstruating women unclean, practically untouchable for a whole week—they had to undergo a ritual bath afterward—he used some word—"

"*Mikveh.*"

"Ah, that was it. *Mikveh,* you say?"

"Yes."

"*Mikveh,*" she repeated. "What does it mean? Bath?"

"Swimming pool," Ira said gruffly.

She laughed—always relishing his dumb sallies. "I think if I had agreed to submit to all that folderol I might be Sam H's wife today."

"Yes?"

"Sam told me bluntly he couldn't conceive of marrying anyone who wasn't Jewish. That's when I left. But you see, it's the same thing. It was perfectly all right to live with one."

Ira sighed quietly. The way she had of deflating dogma and bugaboos, the way she quelled fears and guilts, as if bleaching them out of sight with her objectivity, he recognized had a kind of dual effect on him: she reduced the onus of his wickedness, eliminated much of the sense of heinousness, quenched the shimmer of guilt, stealth, risk that informed, that magnified his furor.

"And you must remember," Edith was saying, "your cousin Stella is no child."

"Yeah, not now. But then, then—when she was only fourteen."

"Even at fourteen. Young people, girls especially, mature at quite different ages—no matter what the law has to say in the matter. It's only a rule of thumb. I still hadn't been sexually awakened in my twenties. It took Wasserman to do that."

"Yes."

"I'm sure I told you."

"Yes. In Woodstock. With Larry."

"Speaking of an utter waste of time!" Her tone of voice and the movement of her head were full of severity. "How could I have been such a ninny?"

The cat perched on top of the stone wall; the cat leaping down to the ground, brushing against her leg under the filigreed white table—the hysterical scream. Prophetic intuition, smarter than the intellect.

"Well."

There wasn't much to say: regret: vain synapse between fingernails.

She resumed the didactic. "The thing I wanted you to realize, what you have already surmised from Marcia, was that in other times and places, other cultures, Stella would be considered nubile, marriageable. You needn't feel as if you had committed a grave offense. You needn't feel you were vicious. You're not."

"No."

"It's a lesson. Fortunately not as costly as it might have been. The whole point is, don't go into these things without a contraceptive of some kind."

"I did. I thought I did," Ira defended himself, too spent for vehemence. "I thought the—the thing didn't work—when she was late, that's all." He felt as though they had entered a stage of repetition, of pointlessness. Why had she insisted on his coming to her apartment anyway? He was most ungracious when it came to expressing gratitude. He didn't know how. It irked, it pained him.

"Would you like some coffee? Or tea?"

He pondered, was about to decline. "All right, coffee," he conceded. "If it's not too much trouble. Mind if I go to the bathroom?"

"Oh, no. Go ahead. I'll make some coffee meanwhile." He got up from the chair, as she slid off the couch—garter-belt ends winked—

He stopped in the doorway that led to both bathroom and kitchenette. "You were talking about Larry—"

"Yes?" She walked toward him, petite, tender smile glistening from points of olive skin. Her presence, her nearness, gave him pause. He would have wished to ponder with all his strength the contrast: Stella, the Jewish kid with blond hair under cloche, girlish, at best bland, subservient. And Edith, brunette and dainty and knowing and womanly—and a world apart. He could crook his finger at the one, and would shrivel at the other's tenderness—

"Yes?" Edith repeated.

"Oh, I got thrown off."

"So I've noticed. That's what makes you so interesting, your withdrawals. And a little maddening. What's it all about this time?"

"What a day. It starts off with a midterm quiz on Milton. Anyway, I had a long, long confer—I don't know what you call it—with Larry in the subway. Was that today? Boy, it seems like yesterday."

"Yes?"

"He wanted to hang on to our friendship. It didn't matter that his love affair with you was over. He said we were friends before that."

"There doesn't seem to be much reason it shouldn't continue, if you were interested."

"That was it. I told him I wasn't. Poor guy. I guess I hurt his feelings."

She had busied herself in the cubicle of a kitchenette, filled the electric coffee urn. "It's sometimes impossible not to. Lewlyn trampled on mine—and in not a very honorable way."

"Yeah. Anyway, I said no. I said something about going my own way. I really don't know what I meant. Just another way of saying no."

"I can understand, Ira. Your ways have separated. Just as mine and Larry's have—if ever they were very close and not an illusion. It can very well be that once, given time, this pseudo-romance begins to fade, we may become good friends again in a different way. If Larry matures."

The perking of the electric coffee urn became audible, like a prompter to an actor.

"I gotta go," Ira said.

"Do." Edith smiled. He went into the bathroom, familiar bathroom, but more in order than usual, towels, tissues, washcloth, because of the late ministrations of the cleaning woman. Boy, you take your cock out to urinate, you think a thousand thoughts. Did anybody ever ask a woman whether urinating had the same effect? It couldn't, could it? And he wanted to explain so much, but he buttoned his fly.

"Gee." Aroma of coffee met his nostrils as he came out. "What I wanted to say, and I suppose he felt, I owed him such a debt of gratitude. I mean Larry."

"Did you think of what he owed you? You provided him with a view of another world he never would have had otherwise. He was always repeating the things you said. These things are never completely one-sided, you know that, Ira. In this case not even remotely. Toast?" Edith asked.

"No," he began. "Yes. I love toast, but I can eat just bread. You still have raisin bread?"

"It happens that I do. And butter? You sure you don't want me to toast it? It'll only take a minute."

"Yeah." He adopted a dour front. "But that's enough. My grandfather always said that anybody who had bread and butter to eat shouldn't look for more."

"Did he?"

"Especially raisin bread. Of course, he ate everything else, the old tyrant."

"I know you don't take sugar or cream."

"Well, this time I want everything. Zuleika Dobson got hungry with deep emotion. So this guy Larry has been smashed, like a kid's paper boat in a curbside brook, you know what I mean? You know, when he asked me to share in my life, and he envisaged, he made all kinds of offers—I don't remember, because my mind was on Stella, pregnant, all that—he spoke of our different backgrounds, lives together; we could write about it—collaborate, yeah, the thing that kept coming back to my mind—I don't know whether I ought to tell you. Oh, thanks. That's toast."

"Be careful of the raisins."

"Hot, you mean? Yeah, they are. I wonder why?" He gobbled.

"You think you're good for another slice or two?"

"Yeah. Thanks, I mean. If it isn't too much trouble."

"Oh, no. You were saying?"

"I kept thinking of sitting here—I mean in that basement room—reading T. S. Eliot, while you two—well, you spooned." She turned from the frustum of the toaster over the gas to look at him, stood quietly gazing.

"Yes?"

"I thought, boy, I'd never share that with you."

"Is that what you thought of?'

"I mean even through all my troubles, it kept coming back." He smiled apologetically. "I got my nerve, haven't I?"

She shook her head. "You are beyond all doubt the strangest, most unusual person I've ever met. And I've met many, young and old."

"It wasn't because I wanted to be."

"I don't think you could." She removed the slice, quickly, with dainty finger. Bearing the plate of toast, she crossed the room so gravely Ira was sure he had said something wrong. He shouldn't have told her what he thought. The giddiness of the day had slackened everything.

"Thanks. It's good." He took the plate from her. "I still haven't thanked you enough for all the trouble you took, and all the rest I put you through."

"It really wasn't very much trouble. Mostly I was concerned about you. Especially not hearing from you all afternoon, as I said."

"Yeah. I was inconsiderate."

"She might have come here in any case."

"Oh, no, what was the point?"

Balancing her coffee cup, trim, petite, in her brown dress under the open black Japanese kimono, she went back to the couch, sat athwart. "I might have cared to meet her."

"That's exactly what I didn't want to happen."

"But why?"

"I told you."

"And I explained to you before that I didn't expect to see anyone but an adolescent girl—not a mature beauty, nothing of the sort—with very little charm of person, and no sophistication. You already described her to some extent."

'I know. And that's what you would have seen, only more so."

"Oh, fiddlesticks, Ira! Honestly. Oh, I'm sorry. I forgot all about napkins. I'll get you one." She slid off the couch again, more carefully this time. What a pretty figure she had, so feminine, neat, and yet so modest, as if she were bred to deprecate it—something like that: the way she cantered her horse that golden September afternoon in Woodstock, so adeptly, so modestly. And now, a glance at the mirror was all that betrayed awareness, and yet, judging by the angle of her gaze, it was directed at her face. It was her face she cared about. Well, why not? Odd irrelevant wisp of speculation: exchange Stella's. She was outside the realm of permissible comparison, in a forbidden world—

"Thanks." Ira took the napkin, and as he watched Edith sit down: "In my house, we don't have napkins. Only, my father brings home a napkin sometimes from a restaurant, you know? We got two butter knives from the Waldorf Astoria. We're not kosher, you see? So—well," he snickered wearily, took a large bite: "Yum!" He chomped: "Gr-r-r." He sipped, grunted: "Ah."

He felt an insane impulse to abandon all pretense to seemly behavior, to alienate her entirely, to do any number of idiotic, uncouth things, pick his nose, dig at his ears, scratch his rump, hoist his scrotum. He wasn't sure why. To fend off what he sensed coming. Or like an insolent tyke, to punish her for having learned what he was, and to build new barriers against her finding out more. Samsonish, Parsifallic, ho-ho, he was weary. He would have paraded any kind of immature caprice, except that he knew she wouldn't be in the least deceived, in the least fazed. He'd only prove himself all the more a futile ass. Besides . . . he had a little pride left, a little stoicism, the recalcitrance of disgrace, maybe, the obduracy of frailty. Or a smidgeon of maturity that dictated that he endure his own failings—and she knew only half the story. So: preserve a scrap of rectitude.

"Did you part friends?" Coffee cup in hand, Edith sat on the edge of the bed, crossed her knees modestly—she was always modest. "My, you eat so fast."

"I am what's called in the old country a *fresser.*"

"A what?"

"A glutton. You must have noticed."

"I think you're plain famished—heavens, how can you drink your coffee so hot?"

"I learned that with my mother's milk. She loves to scald her gullet. I guess it's kind of fitting."

"Would you like some more?"

"Yes, I would, thanks."

She brought the coffee urn over: it had a slender waist and a high arching spout. And as she poured: "I presume you were so late talking the whole thing over."

"Oh, no."

"You're not on good terms."

"I guess so. That's not what I meant." Ira squirmed, scratched, gobbled. "I saw her off on the subway. Is that what you mean?"

"More or less. I'm sure you remember how my pregnancy ended anything I had to do with Lewlyn. That was the last straw: when he showed what a baby he was. Trying to shift the responsibility to Larry or Zvi, as if I didn't keep track of that sort of thing, or were trying to trap him into marrying me. And bringing Marcia into the picture, turning to that bully for support."

"I'll tell you one thing, Edith, I understand the guy, now I've been through the same—the same crisis. I've been a baby too. And I turned to you for support. And thank God for your generosity too." He wasn't sure why he brought the matter up in that form: to steer her away from further questions, and spare him further revelations. He tried to keep his voice level, free of provocation, but with a hint of challenge he hoped might deflect her curiosity. He failed.

"Rubbish," she said. "You've not been a baby at all."

"No?"

"You're as different from Lewlyn as day is from night."

"I am? I must be the night."

"You're only beginning to learn who you are. And sooner or later you will. I've overtaken everyone I know: Hamb, I know I've told you about Shmuel Hamberg, Lewlyn, Zvi, and with Larry there never was any question. In fact, all those who've wanted to dear me and darling me. But I already know I'll never overtake you. You'll always be ahead of me, young as you are."

"Yeah? It's flattering." He scarcely paused to masticate a mouthful. "But you know something, I think that's because you're kind to people, you sympathize with people—me. I might as well tell you: I don't. I can't seem to separate anything from the ulterior. What can I do with them? What they say? What can I use it for?"

"That's the artist," she said solemnly. "Without that kind of self-centeredness you couldn't be one. I lack it. I can't keep from helping people, from responding to their needs: to my parents' needs. My father, whose health is ruined. My divorced ninny of a sister, because of her child. Lewlyn was a good example. Perhaps if I didn't, and could devote myself to writing poetry, I might be a better poet. But I've always placed other people's needs ahead of mine."

"And that's so important?"

"I worship the artist, as you know. It's the only religion I have, Ira."

"All right." Ira gulped the last of his coffee. He sensed that she wasn't being strictly logical, was too lenient in his behalf, couldn't be swayed by anything he said. Answering to the point, but the edge had been taken off his appetite. He smeared the paper napkin across his mouth. "Boy, that was good. All I can say is I'm glad I'm out of it. I never would have lived through it without you."

She didn't seem to realize—or chose to ignore—the finality of his tone of voice and his forward-leaning movement. She seemed intent on keeping him there. "You spoke just now of the similarity between yourself and Lewlyn. But consider the differences in your ages, child. Here was a grown man, and a married one too, a former priest seem-

ingly able to dispense comfort to others and all that folderol, acting
like a child, turning for comfort to the wife who discarded him, turning to a woman ten years older than he is to reassemble him."

"Yeah."

"You're not going to leave?" she asked.

"Huh?"

"You haven't told me anything."

"What'll I tell you? I'm afraid to tell you—no." He suddenly felt
himself swept by a contrary urge: a last resort, a last defense. "All right.
When she told me she was okay—after she came out of the business
school, and told me she was all through—with her menstrual period."
The words tumbled out. "She said she tried to get the news to me—I
already told you." He gesticulated. "What the hell. Anyway, old Priapus
busted forth. I tried to take her to a place for intercourse."

"I might have known it."

"Yeah. Well? So now what's there to say?"

"You're very dear to me, Ira. There's everything to say."

"That's the trouble. I'll be a lot less dearer in a minute—I mean if
I talk." He met her profoundly compassionate, large-eyed gaze, her
hands lying quietly in her lap. "I took her to Fox's movie house on
14th—where I worked lugging film. The place has three balconies. It
musta been a garlic opera house once. I took her to the middle balcony—that's an empty one—into the ladies' toilet. And Jesus, three
Negroes came up there after us. They wanted a piece of her, and one
of them had a safety razor, another one a knife."

"Heavens, Ira!"

"Yeah. So I didn't get my lay—of the last minstrel." He sat bowed
over, unable to face her.

"Gracious, child, your life was in danger. You were in serious danger." No word of Stella, her danger too.

He couldn't speak for a few seconds. "I guess she gets the credit—
Stella—she gave me a shove. I gave them a shove. The door—" He gesticulated, scowled. "The catch went, and so did we—out to the fire
escape."

"Gracious!"

"I shouldn't tell you." He squeezed the wicker arms of the chair;

they creaked. "Boy, I feel like I'm ripping it all outta myself. Jesus, was I scared. I'm scared now." He could feel tears smarting at his eyes. "Jesus, down that fire escape. We could have broken our necks—mine and hers. No, but the worst thing is I felt like, I felt like murder."

"Of whom? You mean the Negroes? That's understandable."

"No, her. In that toilet. For a second, you know. It wasn't the first time either. I'm crazy. She's like mush." He blinked. "It wakens everything evil in me. You know, those black guys may have saved her life."

"I don't believe it."

"No? Everything starts to scintillate. I want. I'm greedy. I want to destroy the bold—much, much more than my sister, Minnie. I might as well tell you that too. I had my first orgasm with her when I was twelve. All right?"

"How old was Minnie?"

"About a year and a half younger. I told you you'd like me a lot less before I was done. I was kicked out of high school for stealing—fountain pens." He began sighing uncontrollably.

"No, don't!" She had been shaking her head, and now stood up from the edge of the couch and was crossing the room. He tried to fend her off. But silently, in utter gravity, she would not be denied. She slid past the card table, pushed his shoulders back to make room for herself on his knees, and sat down. Firm, trim buttocks palpable through bone, from thigh to thigh. He felt no desire, only need. He put his arm around her trim waist, and wept. She bent over and kissed him with small, delicate lips.

"I'm filthy after where I've been," he said. "I'm filthy anyway. You shouldn't do that."

"I'm simply not going to let you mislead me another time." As she spoke, she undid a button of his shirt, undid it with determination. "Poor lamb. You should have told me all this a long time ago. Did you think I'd be shocked?" She slipped a cool tiny hand into the opening she had made; her palm glided along the bare skin of his chest. "You seemed quite without interest in sex, as I said before. I took that to mean you hadn't been awakened—since I hadn't either until late. I told you how my German-born husband and I threw books at each other because he demanded his rights as husband. It's only later that men seem to develop an overriding interest in sex. Do you still have sex relations with your sister?"

"No, she won't let me anymore." He tried to conceal errant stir of desire from Edith on his knees by leaning sideways to drag out his handkerchief.

"And doesn't your Aunt Molly—"

"Mamie."

"—guess why you come to her home?"

"She thinks I come for the dollar she gives me: indigent scholar. I imagine so. Ironic, isn't it? I get a buck for a—I'm sorry. I—"

"Were you going to use the word 'fuck'?" He felt the blood rush to his head—with a suddenness that made him feel faint. Those dainty lips to form that word! The very sound of it in her voice rendered him speechless. And yet she looked so calm, unruffled, ladylike. His arm slackened about her waist. She must have guessed why, but how impassive she was, drawing his arms about her again.

"I've told you. I've outgrown everyone I met. One at a time. I left them completely in the past, and done with. But you're something I'll never part with. You're something that's—that's mine. It doesn't matter what you think of yourself. You're outside of me and beyond, and at the same time you're mine. I'm not going to let you go to waste, do you understand?"

"I don't think so. I'm not sure."

"It was you I thought of when I had the abortion, not Lewlyn, but you. It was you I wanted near me. And thank heaven something drew you here at just the right moment." She regarded him with unswerving brown eyes in dusky countenance.

"Yeah, but what am I supposed to feel?"

She laughed—merrily for her. "Whatever you do feel."

"But it's not the way Larry felt. I remember."

"Larry felt something altogether romantic and ephemeral. He'd tell me he loved me, maybe two dozen times each time he saw me. Gratifying for a while, of course, to a woman just turned thirty. But only for a very short while. And then a bore and constricting besides. You let me be myself. That's what I treasure about you. There's no false idealism to hem me in."

"Maybe I don't know any better." She laughed again, and they were silent: the woman on his knees, as if it were the most natural thing in the world—and inconceivable at the same time. She was an assistant professor of English literature, and he was—what?—a lout, a *shlemiel*, laying his sister, until he spoiled it—he hadn't told Edith half the Jesus Christ Almighty awful details. But could there be anything further than Larry, than Lewlyn, than anybody? And yet here she was. Two things twisted about in his mind simultaneously, without his knowing which to give preference to: the sense of a stage, a new stage entered upon: a leap, a transformation, her lover—impossible—and yet here she sat contentedly on his knees, like the consummation of some kind of mopey plan he had willed—and so he had, he had. It was like that aureate promise to the kid on a street corner in Harlem long ago. And yet, here he was alone with a woman, all alone, private, in her big studio apartment, without dread, without furtiveness, like a friend, despite her sitting on his knees, her petite body close to his, and yielding—what was the word, what was the word? Normal. "Hmph!"

"What is it, precious?"

"You want me to be honest with you?"

"Of course, darling."

"I feel like a friend."

She smiled down at him indulgently: "We've been friends much too long, more's the pity. I wish we had been more than friends long ago. And we will be."

"Yeh?"

"Won't we?"

"You won't get mad?" He waited for tacit permission. "With Stella I told you most of the time I felt like a criminal. In that insecticide-perfume balcony, I told you, I could go out of my mind. That was bad enough. But when I was with Minnie—everything started to dazzle, the walls, the green-painted walls, when she said yes. The calendar on the wall, the furniture—" He gesticulated. "They lilted. So what am I going to do?"

"You're going to stay here tonight."

"I am? I told you. I'm filthy."

"Oh, no you're not. It's nothing water won't take off. Would you like a shower?"

"Yeah. But inside?"

The smile on her lips was small and tender, her brown eyes large and grave—and steady, her whole expression sober and reflective. "I'm not going to say, darling, that the kind of thing you've suffered won't have its lasting effect. I'm not an analyst either. And perhaps you ought to see one to help you get over the worst of the effects—"

"Oh, no!"

"I thought not. I'm not inclined that way either, apart from the expense. They may help some. I'm not at all sure they help the artist. For all I know they may neutralize rather than help. And you're so obviously the artist. But to return to the wounds, the neuroses, you'll have to live with them, if you can. Do you think you can?"

"I have so far."

"You know that I've suffered some rather bad wounds myself in childhood. I'm sure I've told you about the violent quarrels between my father, with his heavy drinking, and my weeping Christian Science mother, protesting, weeping—it could all be heard through the house. You can imagine the effect on a child. I seem to have suffered more than either my brother or sister. At least as far as I could tell. I was so sensitive too, Ira. I saw my mother growing more and more unhappy. I actually could tell when a new wrinkle appeared on her face." Edith pointed to her own. "I suppose my antipathy to sex, my frigidity until well into my twenties, may have been the result of that. It took Wasserman to break through that—practically rape—to awaken me. I told Lewlyn about it. So of course Marcia knows it. She was amused by it all, Lewlyn reported back, skeptical: I could so easily have screamed. Well." Edith clasped her small hands even closer; she looked off into reminiscence with a kind of fixed disconsolateness. "You had your sister, you had your cousin. I discovered orgasm with one of those hand electric massaging things."

"Yeah?"

"I've never told anyone else."

"I don't know. Here I am: East Side. Harlem. New York. And you come from way out in Silver City. What do I mean to say? I don't know. How can you get so—well, you know: dark. I thought only slums, you know, breed that. Way out west it would be all different."

"It isn't. It may be much worse." Her tiny hand traveled over his chest. "Strange, unhappy lad. Let's put as much of that behind us as we can."

"All right. How should I begin? As Eliot says."

"You already have, dark eyes. Now, you go shower. You prefer that to a bath, don't you?"

"Oh, yeah. I need to shave too."

"I have a lady's safety razor. Will that do?"

"Oh, sure—I'm pretty sure: it's a Gem, I bet."

"I think so. It's on the top shelf in the medicine cabinet." She stood up from his lap, began smoothing her brown skirt under the sunburst on the black kimono, viewed herself in profile in the mirror over the mantelpiece. "Do you want me to show you?"

"No, no. I know what it looks like. Three guys in Fox's theater in a vision I once saw."

"The razor? Heavens, child, are you still thinking of that?"

"Yeah. Trauma, I guess you call it. It's unbelievable, you know." He waved his hand in front of him. "That. This. You." He rubbed the day's stubble on his chin.

"Please promise you'll never do that again."

"Never, never. Something dumber next time. On the other hand, look at the boon they brought me."

Something about what he said or the way he said it seemed to affect her. She sat down on the edge of the couch and watched him with intent gazelle eyes, so intent, so candid in her tenderness, she immobilized him; he stood uncertain and embarrassed. Nobody should show feelings as deeply as that. . . . What a hold it had on him. Like Mom. The embryo Edith lost, the abortion she had: good and bad: he had a berth, he heard himself pun. What was bad about it? The intensity. And you couldn't shake her the way you could Mom, cavalier. She was your equal, and better than your equal: native stock, the Ascendancy, John Synge called it.

"What're you thinking about?" he asked, as gently as he could. "Maybe I should just wash my hands and go home?"

"Oh, no. I want you to have dinner with me, as soon as you've showered—if you don't mind tearoom food."

"Tearoom food? I should cavil at tearoom food?"

"And your mother? What will you do about her? Your parents. You have no phone."

"Min would answer—she'd go down to the drugstore. But they'll die of fright. I've been away before." He was sure she had something more important in mind.

"Do you think you could love me?"

"I don't know."

"You're the most unromantic person I have ever had anything to do with. I often worry that you remind me of my father, but then you don't drink." Her smile seemed unable to contend with her seriousness. "But at least you're honest. Do you think you could learn to love me?"

"I don't know what it is! Edith—I—I'm ashamed of myself. You know what I am. I began at twelve. That's all I could think of, that one thing: there was no love."

"You never had a crush of any kind, on any girl?"

"Once, I think, for a little while. She wore her long underwear under her black stockings. She became an usherette in a movie house later on—looked like she was drumming up trade. Her older brother was shot and killed by a cop when he was running away from a crap game he'd just held up. The younger brother fell through an awning of a German meat and sausage store on Third Avenue I used to stand in front of and drool. I guess he was trying to swipe something. I don't know why I tell you all this. That's the nearest I came to love. I guess I was already doing things to my sister. So I can't tell you. Why should I love you?"

"Because I've begun to love you." Edith stopped shaking her head. "More than a little. More than I can tell you. I know it sounds trite. I want to be loved—and by you."

"Yeah, but everything with me is ulterior. I told you."

"That's only because you've seen me so often in other men's arms."

"You think so? Maybe. I like you, you know—that's kind of stupid. I worship you. I think you're wonderful. What should I say?"

"Nothing. I think you should go take your shower."

"You sure?" Could anything be more prosaic—could anything seem more portentous.

"I'm quite sure. I'm beginning to feel a few hunger pangs. But are you sure?"

"Of what?" He looked at her in surprise. "I told you what I am. You're taking all the risks."

"But I haven't told you what I am: I can't stand being tied down. It was what Lewlyn knew, though I suppose I could if I were married. I've had affairs."

"I know."

"I think very little of the body, Ira, do you understand what I mean?" She smoothed a fold in the black velvet couch cover. "Other than something to be taken care of, be kept in as good physical condition as possible—and mine isn't very good—very robust—I have no great regard for it." She paused to note whether he was following her. "I have no great sense of sanctity about, exaggerated holiness about. . . ." Again she paused—for emphasis: "But I do have a great curiosity about men. Do I need to be reassured continually that I have some physical attraction for them? I'm sure I do, even though I know I haven't that kind of sexuality that some women have—Louise Bogan, for example. But it's mainly my curiosity, Ira. It's almost compulsive. And I know no way of knowing them better, my dear—not in bed."

"No?" It seemed the opposite of what he expected her to conclude with; he frowned, probing for a channel in perplexity.

"No. Bed is something to get out of the way. Sex is something to get over with. It's their minds I want to get at. It's their minds I find stimulating. It's their minds that will sometimes set a poem going through my head. When that happens I feel as if I've put my body to some use, something really worthwhile."

"Oh."

"Can you stand that? I've known men who can. No. Only Zvi can. But he's in California. Can you? Because crazy as I am about you—and it must be evident I am—I'll only hurt you badly, worse than you are already. Please be honest."

"Sure. I don't own you." Ira chuckled wearily. "I haven't even begun." More was on his mind: contraries: a certain kind of relief from obligation: she had been others', hadn't been his, wasn't yet, but precarious possession too: others more. . . . More mind: snug haven gone glimmering.

"Then let's go have dinner. You won't mind doing the honors?"

"What do you mean?"

"I'll give you enough to pay the check before we go in."

"Oh, yeh, yeh." He began taking his jacket off. "You mind if I leave everything here in a heap? Shirt, shoes, socks."

"You can leave your trousers here too. I really think we ought to have a cocktail to celebrate."

"The pants I'll take with me," he said. "Boy it feels good standing on a Navajo rug."

"You have such beautiful feet."

"Yeh?"

"You'll find an extra facecloth and towel inside," Edith said.

"You know, in my house they never use them."

"I think you told me. What afternoons do you have off from college?"

"From classes? I have Wednesdays, I have Fridays."

"Fridays would suit me."

"Why?" He paused in the bathroom doorway.

"We ought to go to Wanamaker's."

"Huh?"

"I have a charge account there. You ought to have a bathrobe. Do you have one?"

"No."

"A jacket. Something attractive that fits you. A shirt or two. At least one pair of decent trousers. The men are all wearing tweeds."

"Yeah?"

"You might bring a change of underwear. There's room in the bottom drawer of the chest."

"There's words running through my head, a kind of rhythm."

"That's the way my poems always begin, with a rhythm first. That's always a sign I'm incubating a poem."

"Yeh?"

"Now run along, Ira."

"I'll try to make it snappy. Tara. Tarara. The urchins are writing their names on the torrid sidewalks of the East Side of New York—with watermelon rinds, with watermelon rinds."

The last thing he saw as he entered into the bathroom was not so much a smile on her face as a brief variant of her habitual gravity. Large-eyed—she leaned over on the couch to reach a yellow pencil.

II

It was as if everything had risen up to impede him in the last week or fortnight, ever since Easter Sunday. Ira turned the wire-bound pages of his small green plastic-covered log, pages on which his scrawl had become well-nigh illegible, almost out of control. He was no longer able to enter more than the merest tags of things, and then with the aid of his word processor to elaborate his reflections further.

He studied his notes, scribbling jotted down on May 4, 1987, Yom Ha'atzmaut, Israel's Independence Day, when M, shielded M, was still alive. He had decided on Easter Sunday, 4-19-'87, as a suitable time to begin an account of his tribulations—or to convert his scrawled mnemonics into a semblance of prose: overcast A.M. Cooler. On my walk along Manhattan Avenue yesterday afternoon (and he still wrote in first person then), all the foliage on all the trees in the messy mobile home court across the street—and they are blessed with many trees—say enviously—every trailer with a full-grown tree over it, cottonwoods, aspen, elm (which have doggedly survived the inroads of the pestilential beetle), are all quite laden with fresh verdure. Each is a green burgeoning parasol—often shading some of the most slovenly yards in creation—an arboreal parasol over abandoned bedsprings, doghouses, warped plywood kitchen chairs, and auto parts—as if by the design of a slob virtuoso. The woodbine with its five-six fingers is already spreading its green quilt over the six-foot-high woven-wire fence of the square, well-built white-painted adobe house on the corner of Marble Avenue. The place is well-kept and spacious, has a guest house, a two-car garage, and occupies a large corner lot, and yet during the five years we have lived here, it has changed hands at least four times—and is presently advertised for sale. Why? Is it because of the proximity of the "mobiloon" courts, as I call them, ours and our seedy neighbors'? I don't know.

In our own court next door, in front of toothless, garrulous, ultra-God-fearing, widowed Mrs. Hurst's trailer, and also diagonally across the pavement, at stocky, muscular, health-spa-frequenting Mr. Nolsten's place, rows of tulips stand guard like gaudy pickets. Incredibly, this is my eighty-first spring, I reflect—with rampant solipsism: 81. Nine 9's. In answer to a request from the *Jewish Publication Society* for a better Xerox copy of a memoir I published some years ago in *Midstream*, I hunted through the cartons where my writings are packed helter-skelter—as usual. I found the Zionist magazine with the article in it, but I also found something else which intrigued me greatly. I had forgotten I owned it: it was the restaurant workers' union house organ, the *Hotel and Club Voice,* and in it a published account of an interview in April 1966. Pop was born twenty-eight years before me, in 1878; he was eighty-three when interviewed: eighty-three, and still occasionally waiting at table. He is categorized as a Roll Call waiter: "I make three lunches a week," he is quoted as saying. "I can't stop working."

It was because of the "runaway" best-seller status that my novel had achieved a little more than a year before the interview that Pop had been sought out for this signal honor. "Are you the father of Ira Stigman?" Pop reported his patrons everywhere asking. "Are you the father of the man who wrote the best-seller?" (How had Pop replied to those who asked whether his insensate rage as portrayed by his author son had been exaggerated?) The magazine was already packed away in its carton, and in too awkward a place for an old arthritic to get at conveniently. Pop had said something to the effect that he was a little stern, but not like the book. He had been "a little sore" at first, at his son's portrayal of his father, but he figured that was fiction. (Still, I recall Mom telling me that Pop remarked after he first perused the book: "I'm sorry I beat him so much.") Of Mom he said, "She would give her neck for him." Meaning me. And how much she loved to have me kiss her brow. Curious: M prompts me to an identical show of endearment.

Most of the interview could be characterized as typically Pop: a matrix of confusions, confabulations, inventions, contradictions. He had me Bar Mitzva'd on the Lower East Side instead of in East Harlem. Some of it, his errors of omission and commission, might have been due to advanced age and failing memory, but the bulk of it was due to his incurable evasions, his

inability to face himself, or simply to admit the truth. It was the trait that
drove Mom crazy, literally—she had to be committed—his ineffable glosses
on his own erratic, impetuous, infantile behavior, glosses that presented him
as a *feiner mensh,* generous, cogent, steady—all the things he wasn't, poor
guy. Infant—Mom baited him with the word, and it was the word that infu-
riated him most, because it struck nearest home: infant. And when he was
forced to face his own senselessness, face his own puerile self-deceptions,
beyond all equivocating, beyond all denial, he either struck out at the one
who had the temerity to show him his error—or he wept. Pop wept. Poor
unfortunate. What a martyr he made of his wife. The juvenile who pleaded
with his father to apprentice him to a fiddler, so that he could play in a
kletchmer at weddings and merry-makings, that he might contribute to jol-
lity, to joy. What a difference that might have made in the man, all the difference in the world.

But . . . but the thing that attracted me most, the feature I pored over
the longest time, although I must have seen it many, many times years and
years ago, was Pop in a photo, a vintage 1913 photo, leaning against one of
the fills or shafts of his milk wagon, a milk wagon painted dark. (It was a dark
shade of brown—as well as a seven-year-old remembers it seventy-four years
later.) Beside Pop stood one who Pop had told me was the inspector, a man
even shorter than Pop, although stocky—Pop was slight, but wiry. The former wore the street clothes of the time, high, starched collar, tie, overcoat,
and fedora hat, as befitted a company inspector. Pop wore his milkman's
pea jacket and visored cap. On the side of the wagon were printed the
words that I still remember. I had already learned them at age seven, not
only learned to read them, but to chant them: Sheffield Farms, Slawson
Decker Company. And the horse, Billy—the centerpiece, the most charis-
matic creature in the picture—a big brown horse whom I saw urinate blood
the first day Pop drove him, when I accompanied Pop in the milk wagon:
Billy was just at that moment looking around and facing the camera, his ears
pricked up, his long, equine visage contemplative and uncomprehending.
Gentle beast. The caption under the photo, in Pop's handwriting, read: "My
horse Billy."

Pop told me once that he tried to organize his fellow milk wagon drivers
when he worked for a company named Levi Dairy—and was fired for his
union activities. And he described a restaurateur "shooing" him out of his
restaurant with a table napkin for attempting to organize the waiters there.

Poor feckless man. Undoubtedly he was telling the truth when he told me of his "union man" activities. But as my son Jess cannily observed: "Pop meant well, but his judgment was atrocious." Ditto his son. . . .

Of late, my work has been delayed by severe hindrances and obstacles, trolls on the bridge. In addition to some mental confusion, I have been quite unsteady. Especially, so it seemed to me, after first taking massive doses of cortisone just prescribed for me. Before I knew it, I had three times come close to falling. Once I saved myself by grabbing the handle on the freezer compartment in the kitchen, another time landing on the bathroom stool, a third time against the wall, scraping the skin off my elbow. Allowing myself even two or three degrees variance from the vertical when I stand or walk, I now realize, is a precarious deviation. I perambulate with a cane, and I would use two canes if it weren't such an infernal nuisance, didn't hamper me in my other movements—not to mention rendering me more tottering and conspicuous than I already am.

Such is the condition of the aged writer, or this one: no different from other individuals of his species, except that in this case he has still to tackle seventy-five or a hundred pages of narrative before he can lay claim to having completed a second draft. Not a completed piece of work (is there such?), but a second draft. How long will it take? How long will he live? Two unknowns, and in all likelihood, two inequalities, of benefit only one way and not the other, and guaranteeing nothing in any event: simply sine qua non. You are not required to finish, ran the Talmud dictum; neither may you desist from your task while you can do it. I would very much like to finish; I would very much like to complete a third draft. Perhaps it is because I seek to consummate my wish that I live. How strange that I should still strive to accomplish the task, even though the proceeds of all this travail are posthumous. How strange, in a word, is man, to whom almost everything finally becomes marginal—while still hale and in possession of all his faculties—except (probably a delusion) the Promethean catalytic exercising of his consciousness. In a universe of a billion trillion stars is there another like him? I'm inclined to doubt it. Man is matchless, man is peerless. (Far be it from me to lay claim to that revelation.) And yet, most peoples are unable so far to live in more than nominal peace with their neighbors. And some with virtually none: I think of Israel.

In the meantime my beloved M has received a phone call from Rosemary in Los Alamos, erstwhile secret city of the atom bomb. A vivacious woman in her mid-thirties, Rosemary teaches piano there, and lives with her husband, a nuclear physicist employed in the Los Alamos complex—a most melancholy-looking man who repudiates any imputation of melancholy, disavows it completely. Would M accept a commission to compose a suitable piece of music to celebrate the fiftieth anniversary of the Fuller Lodge in Los Alamos, Rosemary asked. The answer was: Yes. Before she went off to fetch Marie, our dear and trusted cleaning woman, M had already left word with me to answer in the affirmative, in case Rosemary called. I relayed the message to her, to Rosemary's great satisfaction. M has chosen a selection from Peggy Bond Church's story about life in Los Alamos, before, during, and after the installation of the plant for creating the atomic bomb, and its successful detonation in the desert afterward. The name of the book is *The House at Otowi Bridge,* and it recounts many of the experiences of Edith Warner, who lived in the neighborhood more than twenty years, opened a tearoom next to the Rio Grande, a tearoom which was accessible to the research scientists at Los Alamos. In the course of time, though at first she had no inkling of what the project was about, she became acquainted with many of the foremost nuclear scientists of the period: Oppenheimer, Bohr, Fermi, Teller—who rode down the hill in their jeep to partake of her ragout and her famous chocolate cake. M now had to wait to receive permission from the author's heirs and the publishers of the book to use the selection, incorporate it into her composition. No hitch was expected from that quarter; permission was assured; it was a mere formality.

So—considering the magnitude of the occasion, its importance as a musical event, M's success in measuring up to the challenge would establish her fame as a composer nationwide. An artist she had already demonstrated she was—with her setting to the poem "Babi Yar," and even more impressively, her Unaccompanied Cello Sonata. And now this in the offing, due by September, by my wife—I knew she would do an outstanding, perhaps a superlative piece of work, my wife, at age seventy-nine, an artist, once a student of Boulanger, to be reckoned with in her own right, an admirable, a noted musician—how strange to wrest away my own ego, try to anyway, render homage to that modest, unassuming, devoted woman, grown in stature in old age. The prospect fills me with a sweet serene joy. How much did I have a hand in that growth? How much did my own groping tenacity affect her development, spur it by example? I didn't know, I felt it did, and then discounted my intuition as another example of my supreme egotism.

III

Sense of foreboding? And why not? Through all those scruffy streets of this his childhood and youth in slummy East Harlem. What gave them that character? You—suppose you were a writer, as Edith said you were meant to be, and would become—how would you describe that quality that made them scruffy, slummy? What? The neglect? They weren't too dirty. The "white wing" street cleaners with brush and barrel—wheelbarrel—did their job every morning. Mostly wops, they didn't do a bad job either, rounding up trash and scraps of garbage of all sorts with their characteristic shove-and-pause of the coarse-bristled push broom. Horseshit, in less than two decades, had practically disappeared from the asphalt, replaced by the automobile, both boon and bane; so cleaning up that was no longer a chore. No, it wasn't an impression of uncleanliness, of the presence of noisome litter, that gave the slum its hopeless, joyless look. But rather that everything seemed worn, spiritless, the houses, the housefronts, the stoops, all weather-worn and stained, as if the very masonry became impregnated to some degree by the treadmill of existence within. Ah, that gave them that quality, the streets he wouldn't be going through much longer—not with that regularity, that monotony, of day in, day out, to and from the Lenox and 116th subway station, or to and from 112th near Fifth for a piece of ass: Fifth for a filched piece of ass. Fifth Avenue, Filched Avenue—oh, Ira, don't drift now: What gave them that forlorn, frowsy look? Monotony. Stagnation. Meanness. What do you mean by meanness? he asked himself. Just utilitarian, run-down, and nothing else to redeem it: like a subway station, like the 96th Street and Broadway transfer station, a place where you had to wait, longer or shorter, depending on your luck, before you could get the hell out of there, out of Harlem, to get somewhere else, somewhere you wanted to go. So you didn't give a goddamn about the place itself—that wasn't part of your life, except of necessity, a bustling, perfunctory channel, a subway turnstile, a stepping-stone to somewhere else. So the slum streets exuded grubbiness; that was it. Everybody wanted to get out. He did also. Oh, Jesus, yes. And he was—already he was halfway out . . . and

Mom too was talking about moving to the Bronx after he graduated from CCNY, so why the foreboding?

He ought to be blithe. He ought to cheer. Halfway out of these goddamn streets, and the nine different, sad ways home from the Lenox Avenue subway, sad and autumnal, sad Friday after Thanksgiving, Thanxy, Larry said, with the sun south like a kid's hoop tipped over behind downtown buildings. Approaching the equinox. No, no, the solstice, the winter solstice, when Minnie's boss let her go home way early for the *erev Shabbes*. Was her boss ever religious? Almost as bad as Zaida. Get home before sundown, start cleaning up, bathing, primping, fluffing out the waves in tresses, all in order to prepare to pay homage to the Sabbath Queen. Minnie got both ends and the middle out that way: Thanxy on Thursday, and *erev Shabbes* on Friday, and Saturday and Sunday off too—wow.

But—what? Yes. He was about to sever from existence here, breaking away from nearly fourteen years of it. He had formed part of his milieu while he lived here, grew up here; he had formed part of it, and he was formed by it. Look at yourself: all you've become, and all you wish you ne'er had become, can't obliterate and can't give up. . . . Cut it out. You've got Edith. Yeah, all right, all right. But he was made; that was the point. He was formed, set in the mold, made. And now he had to break up what he was. Or try to. In Edith's apartment, on Morton Street in the Village, the answer was yes. He could. Coming home, into 108 East 119th Street, on the first-floor front, he'd bet the answer was no. On 118th Street, right here, this minute, between Madison Avenue and Park, still walking home in the cold-empty dreary street, the answer was maybe.

He ought to have been happy—Edith had tucked him inside her, and had laughed when he got a hard-on, and said, "Wait for me, lover." Lover, he! Larry was the one the word fitted. He had been damn harsh with Larry, cruel, the way he cut his friend off. Cut him off from sharing in his life. But what the hell was he going to do? He didn't know how to be politic, or civil, never did. He hadn't been raised that way. He and his superstitions: that was another gift from Pop. Put your underwear on backward or inside out, uhuh! That was bad luck. If you've forgotten something, and come back into the house to get it—uhuh! You might as well not go, give up your mission, you're going in vain. Praise something, admire something too warmly, uhuh! A *gitoik*, you've blighted it with the Evil Eye. How do you pry that out of yourself? *O saisons, O châteaux*—was that Iz's quote from Rimbaud?—*Quelle âme est sans défauts?*

Oh, Park Avenue under the steel viaduct of the Grand Central, oh, shabby tenements, what've you got to say? Or what was he trying to tell himself? Himself—he had to laugh—he wasn't a self; he was a manifold, he was a clump of chumps, he was like a swarm of interacting creatures about to leave the old . . . the old warren. That was it. He was about to leave home, break with his surroundings, break away from Mom. How many times did he have to say that: apprehensive because of it. No matter if the new was better than the old, no matter if he was to live with Edith, part of the time, for a while, and permanently afterward. He had figured it out: change, change, that made one forbode. Okay. Okay. "Home art gone, and ta'en thy wages." Okay, okay—he heard a Grand Central train approaching overhead, a muted rumble, saluting his a-home-again stumble. "Yet once more, O ye laurels, and once more ye myrtles brown." Okay. Okay. "O fare thee well"—that was a good one from Hausman—"for ill fare I." No, that would fit Larry, not him. But after all, what had he said to the guy? Nothing so bad, only the way he said it.

You turned the corner around Jake's six-story pile, ugly six-story pile of Jake's house, bricks brown as coffee grounds. Fitting landlord Jake was too, like a steer, poor fat Mamie's counterpart, though she was no longer landlady. After Jake's house came the three-story dwelling next, where the Italian barber once had his shop and his spiral red-white pole in front, and Leo D and his widowed mother had once lived on the first floor—oh, boy, that pasta, after they moved—his reward—and the awful bellyache, wow! And the terrible hike to Edith's in bed with Lewlyn, her olive-skinned body naked under dark bathrobe coming to the door laughing guiltily felicitous . . . from opening the calipers of her thighs around Lewlyn, now closing them around his. Wasn't that strange? And what made the difference? Time. Time and change. You couldn't compress it all: Larry get off, Lewlyn get on, Lewlyn get off, Ira mount her, Ira get in. Gang fuck stretched over months and years. . . . Jesus, the things that came to mind: gang fuck, whorehouse, geologic eons: what would the past year be, compared to the billions of Precambrian years he was walking on? The metamorphic mica schist, the gneiss. Not even yesterday. Not even five minutes ago. Human time and change. Who would know as he knew that beside Jake's brown fortress had once been the escape doors of a movie house on Park Avenue, a movie house that failed: metal-sheathed escape exits where in the summer you put your head against the other kid's ass to make a train of horses, while the opposing side jumped up on your back, yelling as they landed, "Johnny on the pony, one, two, three!" and tried to break down the train. What crude games these micks brought over from Ireland. Or their grandfathers did. . . . 108 East 119th Street.

IV

Mrs. Shapiro was in the kitchen with Mom when Ira entered, dumpy, shapeless Mrs. Shapiro. She lived "in the back" on the same floor, in the five *tsevorfeneh* rooms, because she didn't object to looking out at backyards and wash poles the way Mom did, and she had been living in the house almost as long as the Stigman family. Despite her illiteracy, Mrs. Shapiro managed to keep abreast of the latest news, usually of Jewish interest, thanks to Mom, who read the paper to her neighbor almost every day, when both had a little free time. And of course she read her as well the latest installment of the *roman,* the serial that appeared daily in *Der Tag.* Mrs. Shapiro was in better circumstances now than when Ira was a kid. She had taken in boarders then, and one of them Ira still remembered: a tall, lanky guy, a men's garment presser by trade, a Mr. Zolichef, who openly offered Mom, in Mrs. Shapiro's kitchen—and in Ira's presence—five dollars for letting him gratify his sexual cravings on her person. How the hell it was said in Yiddish, Ira no longer remembered, but intercourse with her was the gist of it—and so crude, the two women burst into laughter. And of course, Ira would remember exactly that. Mrs. Shapiro no longer took in boarders, no longer had to, because her three children, Meyer and Joe and

Sophie, were all working and contributing to the household. Meyer was a bookkeeper, and Joe worked in Biolov's drugstore—still worked in Biolov's drugstore, where he had taken the job after Ira quit in resentment at being docked for the five dollars he lost, or that was stolen from him. Sophie was a file clerk. Long ago, Ira, as he did with every little girl he had a chance to, tried to induce her to "play bad" with him, without success.

So life was easier for Mrs. Shapiro now, for which Mom was very happy, goodhearted Mom, because before the children began to earn and contribute to the household—and had become old enough to insist that their mother get some of their earnings—her husband, Abe, squat, bald, pompous ladies' garment worker, had allowed her a pittance, even less than Mom's, on which to run the household. And Mrs. Shapiro, in order to make both ends meet, as soon as the children were off to school, left the house to work as a domestic—of the most menial kind, scouring floors, cleaning windows and woodwork, boiling and scrubbing clothes on corrugated washboards. Mom had previously thought—and so she had informed the rest of the family—that Mrs. Shapiro was a *shnorrerkeh*, a moocher, a spurious mendicant, who frequented Jewish philanthropic and charitable institutions for which she could beg or solicit, because Mrs. Shapiro frequently returned home with all manner of bundles and packages in her black oilcloth shopping bag, sometimes clothing, obviously castoffs according to Mom, or household articles, or half loaves of bread, staples, *matzahs* when in season, leftover *kugel*, leftovers in jars. Quiet and meek, the poor woman seemed to accept the unspeakable stinginess of her husband, his contemptuous—and contemptible—treatment of her as her fate: she had brought no whit of dowry to her marriage, came of a large family of a *bali gooleh*, a stage driver, was homely and illiterate. No wonder the bastard, her husband, lorded it over her, lorded it over her unconscionably. It was only by accident—from the caterer of a wedding Mom attended—that she learned that Mrs. Shapiro did domestic work for the caterer's wife, and the things she brought home were discards and leftovers, meted out to her by her employer. She worked. She was not the illegitimate recipient of Jewish charity. She toiled to eke out the miserable pittance her husband thought fit to dole out for

her household needs. Compared to Abe, Pop was a model of munifi-
cence. So there were worse than Pop, Ira reflected: worse in that respect, like Mr. Shapiro, the skinflint, miserly Yid. But how was he
toward his kids—and they toward him? They were fond of him, and he
of them. Ah, there was the difference. Figure that out.

Much as he despised Mr. Shapiro, Ira felt a genuine affection for
Mrs. Shapiro. Her humility, her resignation, moved him; she aroused
his sympathy, all the stronger because she didn't seem to feel sorrow
for herself about her condition, even to the extent that Ira felt for her.
Her deprivation, her squat dumpiness, her flabby homeliness, even
her illiteracy she accepted so meekly it made pity cry out within him.
But then, he was a nut. He felt things beyond all bounds; he felt his
own notions of them, not what they really were.

Still, he owed Mrs. Shapiro a debt. Perhaps he owed her his life.
That was no mere notion. She had intervened years and years ago to
halt one of Pop's atrocious, demented thrashings, administered at the
time Ira was wrongfully accused of knocking down Mrs. True's little
boy. Accompanied by a bunch of kids from the street, Mrs. True, pretty
young Irish matron who lived on the top floor, had come into the
house and immediately slapped Ira's face for knocking her kid down
to the sidewalk—which he hadn't. Patty True was the smallest of the
crowd of kids trailing Ira and chanting "Fat, fat, the water rat." And
when Ira turned in feigned threat of pursuit, they fled, and knocked
Patty on his face, bruising his cheek and bloodying his nose. Pop had
gone mad. He had trampled on Ira, picked him up by the ears, and
thrown him down, picked him up again, groveling and shrieking,
from the floor. Even Mrs. True had been taken aback. There was no
telling what would have happened to him if Mrs. Shapiro hadn't interposed herself between them. Undaunted by Pop's insensate rage,
his snarling menace, she demanded in Yiddish: "Are you going to
slay your own son on the word of a *goya?*" How staunchly she stood
there, unflinching, obdurate—stood there a whole minute while Ira
howled—blocking Pop from administering any more of his maniac
punishment—until Mom, hearing her son's bewildered, hectic and
belligerent cries, flung a furious "Vot you vant?" at Mrs. True that sent
her and her retinue of Irish gamins packing. And then she turned the

full brunt of her wrath on Pop, cursed him so fiercely for an insane murderer, so fiercely, fervently, her hyperboles of execration seemed on the verge of materializing until Pop retreated to the front room.

"Hello, Mrs. Shapiro, *vus makht ihr?*" Ira said in passing as he set briefcase down on green oilcloth of the round table.

"*Mein kaddish'l iz duh,*" Mom beamed. What joy she got out of the mere sight of him, what maternal bliss—

Even Mrs. Shapiro smiled slowly, admiringly. He was a collitch boy, soon to graduate, an *ausgestudierteh mensh.* He had reason for pride; still, his heart felt sunken within him, and he didn't know why. Oh, maybe he did: the brusque spurning of Larry, of a friend who had meant so much, his pending separation from Mom, and from all this snug, sheltered life. *Oh, fare thee well, for ill fare I.*

He doffed hat and coat, went into the frigid, dismal little bedroom behind the kitchen door—the crypt, Mom called it, one of the *kvoorim.* Or did the word mean tombs? Apt translation, for here he was about to die. He laid his coat down across the bed—he could have hung it up on the antlers of the old clothes tree, but he would be leaving soon. So there it was across the bed—where Minnie had been across the bed, athwart but nevermore. Oh, no. If only he noted as attentively other people's lives—couldn't, though, obsessed with his own. Only on the East Side, 9th Street and Avenue D, he had been part of everything. Same old story. Why the hell didn't Mr. Dickson in English Composition 1, Mr. Kieley in English 2, ask him: submit something else, a story, a sketch, an impression, that could go in the *Lavender,* like that Sacco-Vanzetti episode in the car barn that summer—socko!—given him a purpose—Ah, don't blame them. It was himself: his mind always on Minnie, or on simpering, adolescent Stella to straddle him by the radio. He ought to be glad Edith had broken him at last into making love, as she called it, to an intelligent, full-grown woman. But he wasn't happy, not right now. *Moishe Kapoyer.* Mr. Topsy-turvy, he dreaded happiness. He was breaking with what he was with little hope of any remaking into anything else; little hope of remaking, and with too much expected of him—by himself above all: that was it, that was the worst of it. He was inadequate to the task. He reentered the warmth of the kitchen.

Mrs. Shapiro was standing up, one hand on the doorknob, ready to leave.

"You don't have to run away because I'm here, Mrs. Shapiro." Atrophied neighborliness was like a dead weight, self-conscious and Sisyphean.

"I have to do a little more shopping. It will soon be time to begin preparing for the *Shabbes*," Mrs. Shapiro replied.

"So? It's only about what?" Ira directed a pro forma look at the Big Ben on the icebox lid. "Not even three o'clock."

"It's almost winter, it's November, Ira," said Mrs. Shapiro. "It grows dark early. Don't you know? Everything must be done earlier. The Sabbath meal prepared earlier; the candles must be blessed earlier."

"Yeah, but everybody comes home the same time anyway."

"Today's world. What can you do? I keep to the way I was brought up. I prepare and I wait. I have followed the Commandments of our great Rabbi of Rabbis, Moses. I pay tribute to him in my thoughts on Friday night, and he repays me with peace." She smiled her slow, remote smile. "Show me money, show me gems more valuable. True?"

"I guess so."

"Let others do as they see fit. For me, *erev Shabbes* cannot be tampered with."

"Oh, yes."

"Indeed, so says my father also," Mom concurred. "A devout Jew, he lives off the earnings of four sons who work Friday night, Saturday all day. Only not on the high holy days. Still he makes no complaint that they break the Sabbath. Let them do as they see fit, he says also. But how else can he live unless they work on the Sabbath? How many bosses are there like Minnie's observant to the letter?"

Mrs. Shapiro nodded. "Well, I must go." Her face, so flabby, double-chinned, and pale, paid open tribute to Ira, the educated man. "May God further your work in the collitch."

"Thanks. I need it."

"Do you still believe in God? Tell me."

"I? I wouldn't want to hurt your feelings, Mrs. Shapiro."

"Then I have my answer. And why don't you believe?"

Ira chuckled mirthlessly.

"Go. At fourteen," Mom intervened, "his father accused him of being an *Epikouros*. He declared there was no God."

"*Azoy?* At fourteen? I was fourteen once. I have children who were fourteen once. I and they, and of course Abe, all believe. How did you learn God didn't exist?"

He recalled the disks of pigmentation on her pale cheeks as she stood, squat and obdurate, between himself and Pop's fury: the homely, homely Jewess, despised even by that unspeakable pisspot of a husband, she saved his life, for all he knew—Jesus, the labyrinthian implications he no longer wanted to think about. "I don't know, Mrs. Shapiro," Ira said abruptly. "It didn't make sense to believe in God."

"And I don't know what to believe. I half believe, half not. But go through the motions I must. I can't help myself. Would to God I got the comfort out of it you get. You see: I don't believe and I call on Him in whom I don't believe. It's a form of madness."

Mom laughed her apologetic, contralto laugh. "Then you're half an *Epikouros*."

"Indeed. Perhaps more than half." Mrs. Shapiro rested her puffy hand on the white ceramic doorknob. "To me, He doesn't make sense either."

"What? What do you mean, Mrs. Shapiro? How can He not make sense for you?" Minor surprise, minor perplexity, oscillated fleetingly within Ira's mind. Was she serious, twitting him, or what?

"You'll forgive me: I don't know. That is for the educated."

"Oh." Ira relaxed. He was about to chuckle.

"When one speaks of sense, of wisdom, then for the educated, the *Epikouros,* it must spring from here, no?" She touched the thin, graying hair of her temple.

"I suppose so." This time Ira did chuckle. "And for you?"

"Only when I go to buy something, if it's worth the money, if I can get it for less, from the seller or somewhere else."

"Yes?"

"But of God I can't think. He doesn't spring from the same place, because as you know, I'm an illiterate woman. He has no place, so He makes no sense."

"Oh, boy."

"But on Friday nights, *erev Shabbes,* He seems to alight here." She spread a hand over her heavy breasts. "Here where the tears flow from."

"I see."

Here where the tears flow from. How bitter the taste of his own lips, and how fitfully they matched together again. He exhaled breath in a gust.

"*Noo,* Mrs. Stigman." Mrs. Shapiro turned the doorknob. "You'll read me the rest of the *roman* tomorrow?"

"Of course."

"*Ihr zolt hub'n a gitten Shabbes.*"

"*A sheinem dank. Ihr aukh.*" House keys clinking, Mrs. Shapiro padded out from kitchen into hall.

"She's smart," Ira acknowledged.

"Indeed, she retains more from my reading to her about political matters than I do myself. She retains more and construes better."

"Yeah?" He sat down in his favorite chair.

"Are you going to become a guest?" Mom said, after a pause.

"You didn't worry about me?"

"One night. I'm used to that."

"I'm afraid I'm really going to become a guest, Mom."

"Yes? When?"

"Beginning now."

"*Azoy?*" She moved her forearms across the strawberry-and-white sheaves printed on her housedress, until her elbows locked against her abdomen. "Are you staying here tonight?"

"No, I'm staying at Edith's apartment."

"*Azoy.* And for how long?"

"That's what I came to tell you. I don't know."

Edith had asked him to bring some of his belongings to the apartment. Now that he was her lover, she saw no reason why he shouldn't stay overnight more often. She would rather he did, she said: she missed his company. And that way too, staying with her often, he would avoid, avoid as much as possible, a recurrence of the ugly situation at home. Ugly situation, she called it. There was his father to consider, Edith emphasized: the always latent violence between them.

"Have you got a carton in the house?" Ira asked.

"For what?" And then she nodded. "I can empty one. It has summer curtains in it. A large one I don't have."

"I don't need a large one. I'm only taking a few things: some socks, my BVDs, a couple of ties, a couple of shirts—what else? My new pair of pants. A few books. I gotta carry my briefcase in the other hand."

"And the heavy underwear, Ira? It'll soon be December, you know. How about a sweater?"

"Maybe the one without sleeves."

Mom sighed. "I'll go empty the carton." She went into the other part of the house. Even though the kitchen door was shut, he could hear the familiar thump and slither of cardboard. She was probably emptying the contents of the carton on her bed. . . .

Foreboding. . . . What the hell was the matter with him? Foreboding and cuckoo combinations of disparate quotes: Woe is me, my mother, that I was ever born to set it right. Foreboding of long journeys: "Oh, who is this one has done this deed?"

Mom brought the carton into the kitchen: medium-sized, sturdy, all four flaps intact. "It's a handsome one," she said. "Joey Shapiro brought it to me from the drugstore."

"Let's see if I can get my arm around it." Ira stood up. He rested the carton on his hip. "Just about."

"And while you're collecting your belongings, I'll make a little snack."

"Don't bother. I'm going to have supper with her tonight—dinner, they call it."

"A little snack won't mar your appetite. I have smoked whitefish."

"Please, Mom."

"A little Muenster cheese and a bagel. My son, my only son, how can it harm you?"

"Okay, okay."

"And a little *jabah*." She always punned bilingually on the English word "java," making it sound like the word for frog in Yiddish.

The cardboard of the carton was cold to the touch when he picked it up—as cold as his dreary little bedroom when he entered it—his single bed with the coat across it. Maybe Minnie would sleep in it now—nevermore to return.

Couldn't help his thoughts, though, his goddamn swoon of fantasy. He began packing the carton from the drawers in the mirror-surmounted bureau in the front room. Socks, oh, two pair—you could always wash them. BVDs, a couple. All right? One pair of gray flannel pants? Joke: how many pair of gray flannel pants you got? And two laundered shirts pinned to cardboard. Oh, where has the chinky Chinaman gone who gave you litchi nuts on the East Side? Hey, you know? It's you you're forsaking, you who took the litchi nuts. Well, bless my soul . . . No neckties with gravy spots. Jesus, no room for old cardigan either. Hey. Look up there, will you?—on the wallpapered wall: Zaida, Baba, Mom's parents, wearing earlocks he, and wig she, with what horror watching their young crazy grandson about to go live with a *shiksa*. *Oy, vey iz mir!* Well, not so bad, Zaida, Baba: Which is better? A little dump of a Harlem habitat with everyone crammed into the kitchen, or a cozy little corner of a Greenwich Village apartment under lemony lampshade on a card table? Or lusting after your sister or tearing off a paltry piece of your kid cousin—that, or being a *shiksa*'s lover. A petite Ph.D.'s pet, a petite *shiksa*'s lover-lad—such a sweet sound. Now, there's one for you. Propound me that: untutored sister or ungifted kid cousin—or refined *shiksa*? There's one for Solomon, for *Shloimeh ha Mailackh*. Gotcha there. . . . Look out the north window, through the lace curtains, at the red-brick six-story, sick (sic) story dump, where Mrs. Green in her dingy white shift used to lean on her mop handle—mop handle in hand, mind you—framed in the first-floor window. Goodbye. Not bad, huh? And farewell, a long farewell to the little Dresden wolf and sheep and the shepherdess on the mantelpiece. Oh, fare thee well. And you too, dirty old lime-daubed bricks across the airshaft. Jesus, how you used to peal out, when that wasn't a coat got laid across the bed. Like morning stars when they sang together. Comin' through.

Carton under arm, he returned to the kitchen, relegating the cold behind the closed door. Strong aroma of Mom's primitively brewed *jabah, jabah* coffee wafted through the room. On the table, two, no less, bagels, gold slab of whitefish, thick, inelegantly sliced Muenster cheese, big wedge of butter right out of the tub, were set out in hopes of filial seduction.

"What do you think I'm going to be able to eat tonight, Mom? If I eat this?" Ira tried to keep his voice gentle.

"*Seh goor nisht, goor nisht.*"

"Some *goor nisht*." Well, no point in making an issue of it with Mom, poor Mom. Don't argue about it; just try to exercise a little restraint. He went to the drawers under the china closet, got out a couple of ed texts, and his copy of Milton, and put them in the carton on top of his clothes. Then he sat down at the table.

Holding the chipped blue enamel coffeepot in the scorched pot holder, Mom poured coffee into the white mug. "Have you everything you need?"

"I think so, Mom."

"Handkerchiefs too?"

"Oh, yeh. I nearly forgot 'em." He reached for a bagel.

"Take. Eat. Don't skimp."

"When did I ever?"

"I have to entreat you to eat now. You're my guest."

"I'll be home again. I told you."

Mom sat down opposite him. If he hadn't long ago become accustomed—become inured—to the mournful, deep-eyed fixity with which she regarded him, he would hardly have been able to eat.

"I might have sliced an onion for you, except that I know where you are going."

"Thanks."

"And what does she say about your frayed underwear?"

"Aw, Mom! What does she say about my frayed underwear?"

She laughed her light, humble, extenuating laugh. "Undoubtedly, she can buy you better."

"I won't sleep in my underwear anymore. She bought me pajamas."

"*Azoy?*"

"At Wanamaker's, this morning." Ira chomped away. "She bought me a bathrobe too. A woolen one. A red one. She said it made me look like a Turkish sultan when I tried it on—he's a king."

"Will I ever have the bliss of seeing you in it?"

"I don't know, Mom. She would like to meet you."

"And I her. *Noo?* When?"

He delayed before answering, sought noncommittal evasion. "Well, it's up to her."

"Are you ashamed?"

"Of you?"

"Of your crude mother?"

"No." Ira shook his head, not convincingly, but in predicament. "What will Pop say?"

"He'll grieve."

"What? What for?"

"Friends you're not."

"That's right. I thought he'd be glad to get rid of me."

"On good terms you will never be," Mom continued. "And a burden you've been; don't think you haven't. But he's an odd, peculiar creature. Follow him I can't. Would I could understend him. You're his son. His son, and for all the ill will between you, when he knows you're going away from us, leaving us for a strange world, with its strange ways he can't follow—well, God forbid, as if you were to die. Or as we left Austria for America. He'll grieve."

"Yeah? That's news. You sure it's not you?"

"No. It's your father. A stupid man he isn't. Shrewd, no. Not at all. But for some things, yes. Some things he discerns, he has pity for, he has feeling—who knows him? Only the bleak year."

"So what would he want?" Ira stopped eating, could feel himself become grim and contrary.

"He hoped when you graduated, we would all move to the Bronx—in a handsome apartment near the Concourse—Minnie is working—someplace where she could entertain a caller. A caller; he doesn't have to be a suitor. Lately, something has come to pass: he has the manner of a swain. So she whispered. He's been accepted for training in the fire department. Now he's a temporary policeman in a new reservoir they're building. Of course, nothing is decided. I'm not even supposed to speak of it."

"No. So what did he have in mind for me?"

"With you a schoolteacher, in a larger place to live, in a better one, of course, for you an extra bedroom. That was what he counted on. You would live with us."

"In the Bronx?"

"Indeed."

"Minnie would have a bedroom, I would have a bedroom. We'd be like Larry and his family."

"*Noo,* about time. Would it harm us to live together until one of you married?" Mom asked rhetorically. "Bedrooms with doors. Genteel. Upstanding. A fine bathroom with a tile floor."

"Yes?" Ira looked about the green walls, his gaze coming to rest on the clock: the hour was approaching four. "When was all this going to happen?"

"When you become half a schoolteacher."

"Half a schoolteacher?"

"It's a saying we Jews have. After you graduated from college. More coffee?"

"No, no. Thanks." Ira tempered impatience. "I've got to be going."

"She doesn't make an early *Shabbes,* your *dama?*" Mom jested.

"Neither early nor late. No."

"*Noo,* if it's time to go," Mom concluded obligingly. "Your friend Larry didn't leave a good home to go live with an old *shiksa—*"

"The hell she is! She's not old!" Ira snapped.

"I only told you what he said. Old or not old, you're leaving us, no?" She indicated the carton. "And just when home might be *shayn,* nice, good." She mixed English with Yiddish.

"I'll be back. I told you I'll be back. Where do you think I'm going? I'm only going downtown!"

"But strange it is. Can you say it isn't? Where will you stay, when she has her own visitors, collegios, professorim, who knows?"

"I may have to disappear for a few hours. What else? She's talking about moving across the street to a bigger apartment, maybe with an extra little room. I'll come back here. Don't worry."

"Not here. To the Bronx—with God's help—if only for Minnie's sake."

"Okay. Then to the Bronx."

"And what if she taunts you with that good word: Jew?"

"Aw, come on, Mom! For Chrissake!"

"She loves you so much?" And at Ira's silence. "*Noo*, why not, why not indeed? Handsome and young and full of beguiling fancies. There grows another Maxim Gorky, said our first boarder on 9th Street: Feldman. You enchanted him with your tales, even as a child. 'Mrs. Stigman, there grows another Maxim Gorky.' Well, what can you do? Do you remember Feldman?"

"Yeah, and I'm gonna leave in about ten minutes."

"Then you do remember him?"

"A short fellow, wasn't he? With curly hair. He used to stand on the stoop in 9th Street in the summer and watch us kids whirl punks against the mosquitoes. Punks are those long thin sticks that give off a smell. That's how I remember him."

"He was a very gentle, refined man."

"That's good. Mom, I love talking to you, but—" Ira stood up and began interlocking the flaps of the carton. "Let's get some string."

Mom stood up also—slowly. "Don't you want to say goodbye to him?"

"Huh?" Ira rested hands on carton. "Pop?"

"He'll be home soon. And he'll be home promptly."

"Oh, you mean Friday, and all that? No, what for? Let's have the string. Tell me where you keep it. I'll get it."

"I'll get it." She went to the sink, pulled the little polka-dot curtain back under the dark recess of the sink, to disclose the wooden box where she kept household items. "It's not because of Friday." She stooped down, rummaged in the box, before she brought out a ball of sorted, knotted twine. "It's not because of Friday he'll be home so promptly. When was he ever so pious as that?"

"We're getting all mixed up," Ira said irritably. "I didn't mean what for, when I said it. I meant stay around to say goodbye. I'm not going a thousand miles. I told you that." He beckoned for the string impatiently. "I don't want to get into a big quarrel with him."

"I understand." She handed him the knot-fringed ball. "It's stout enough?"

"I'll go around each way a few times." He was beginning to feel uneasy: there it was again: something impending. He rolled the carton from side to side, binding it. Get out as soon as he could.

"Do you love her?" Mom asked.

"Boy, what a question. I guess so."

"Sinful mother that I am, I seek to live in my son's life. How did you make known your passion?"

"I didn't. I wept. I think I said once when we were in bed that I wanted to be reborn."

"Why?"

"I didn't like what I'd become. Is that enough?"

"My own son."

"Well." He strained at the knot. "I'm going to need a knife."

"I'll fetch it." She plodded to the cutlery drawer, next to the one in which he kept his texts and notebooks, brought out the heavy carving knife that Pop had sharpened and resharpened so often against the rim of the cast-iron sink, until the stained blade had become concave in the center. "Do you want it now?" She offered him the worn handle.

"No, I better go around once or twice more. Some of this string— just put it down."

She laid the knife on the table. "*Ai*, my ears have begun to roar."

"Your catarrh bothering you again? It's clear outside, Mom. It's cold, but it's clear."

"I can tell a day before when the weather changes. But it's not always the weather. Woe can also wreak havoc. Ira, the roaring gets stronger."

"I'm sorry." Ira let the string go slack. "What do you want me to do, Mom? I can't stay here. I absolutely can't stay. And I'm not going to," he added vehemently.

"But an educated man you are. You've studied such things. I can speak to you now."

"Speak to me about what?" From slack to motionless, the string, and motionless the silly ball festooned with knots. He set the carton down on the table. "What are you talking about, Mom?"

"Stella was here last Sunday."

As though he were deprived of independent speech, Ira kept looking at the carton. "*Stella* was here," he repeated.

"You left early."

"I left early."

"You remember?"

"Oh, sure. I went sleepwalking that morning."

"Ira, I'm serious."

"So am I. Go ahead."

"I left soon after you did—minutes. He was packing up his little satchel to go to that Catolisher benket in Cunyilant."

"Yeah? *I had not thought death had undone so many.*"

"What? I don't understand such deep English."

"Don't mind me."

"I buy roach powder always from the same old Jew who has a small niche of a store on Park Avenue, smaller than even Zaida had in Veljish. And he reads the Talmud too, just like Zaida. And he sells other such items. Cleaning fluid. Camphor balls. Candles. Bon Ami for the windows. He gives me a few pennies off—he does it of his own accord. 'You never haggle with me,' he says. 'You're a fine woman.'"

"Yes, my mother."

"I had already gone—what?—three blocks: to the top of the 116th Street hill—when—*Gotinyoo!*—I remembered: the keys! I didn't have the keys to the house. How would I get in?"

"Where was Minnie?"

"She went to her friend to have her hair primped. Oh, where one's mind strays sometimes! It's unbelievable!" Mom became visibly incensed at herself. "To set out on an errand with one's brain underground!"

"Oh, yeah."

"I hurried. I ran. I flew. *Got sei dank,* from 116th Street the way is downhill. I hastened and I sped. I rushed—to 119th Street at last, with might and main. And to the house. And up the stairs. Breathless. I burst into the kitchen—" Her lips closed, her broad countenance slackened with despondency, became forbidding in its quietus: "Isn't he standing there with his member in his hand, fondling her?"

"Her?"

"Stella. Who else?" Mom said.

"Yeah?" Heartbeat flagged. "Pop?"

"'Why did you come back?' He ground his teeth at me—with such wrath, with such fury. As if *I* were the culprit. 'Why did you come back?'"

Ira nodded, in the very depth of loss, loss of self, a very rubble of being. "He didn't have much else to say."

"But such fury! At me!"

"And now you have to tell me."

"So you'll know what kind of a father you have."

"Goddamn it, I know what kind of a father I have!"

"Then you'll know what you're leaving me with."

"You've got Minnie, goddamn it." Ira struck the carton. It leaped away from him, pulling the ball of string out of his hand. The nubby sphere rolled no farther than his feet. He kicked it in a sudden onset of rage. "What do you want me to do? Stay? Christ's sake, you'll be worse off if I stay. I'll kill someone!"

"I'm afraid he'll kill me." She moved the knife toward him along the green oilcloth of the table.

"Kill you!" Ira jeered. "Kill you! You're dead already, for Christ's sake. You've been martyred. I'll kill that sonofabitch." He grabbed the knife. "You gave me just the right thing. He'll be home right away. I've had dreams of picking this thing up, again and again, and it always stuck to the table. Here it is. Free! Loose."

"*Oy veh, oy veh.*" Mom kept nodding as if in prayer, *davening.* "Alas and woe is me. Ira, child." She clasped her hands. "I spoke. Forget I spoke. Spare me! Spare me! Child, I beg you! Only this I lack! I beg you. A foolish thing I spoke. Ira, Ira. On my knees!" She made to seize the hand that held the knife.

"Go away! What the hell did you tell me for? I should've freed you from this bastard ten years ago—when all the other kids went to work. It's been in my mind all these years. I had to go to high school, I had to go to college. Because of you. What do you want me to do? Pay off the debt?"

"No, no, no! It's my fault—"

"You said it's your fault—more than you know!"

"Forgive, forgive. Out of my anguish I had to tell you. Come, child. Remember this, this Professora, this Yeeda named. You're going to another woman, another life." She stooped, snatched up the ball of twine from the floor. "Child, let's tie up your carton and be gone. Let's not delay."

"Anh, what the hell's the use?" Ira threw the knife down on the table, took the ball of twine from her hands. "I'm through, Mom. I'm finished here. Do you understand? Don't get me—" He gesticulated with gyrating hands. "Don't get me tied up again. I can't bear any more."

"I understend. I understend. I can live with him. I've lived with him all these years. I'll last till the end. I have Minnie. Go your way. It's tight enough now, no? The string."

"Yeah." He found a clear length of string, free of knots, viciously yanked motley strands tight, pulled the knot he made as hard as he could. "You hold that here. Right here. Give me the knife. I'll cut it. There. I'll make a couple more knots."

"Now you can go. I'll get your hat and coat."

"Oh, don't worry. Nothing's going to happen."

"You swear? You won't say anything?"

"Oh, no."

"This week he's been tender as a mulberry. This week I got my allowance on time. He said he wouldn't fill the salt cellars and the pepper cellars and the ketchup bottles today. He'll dispense with the extra dollar. He talked about coming home early to take me to a cinema show."

"Today? On Friday?"

Mom nodded her head in a peculiarly negative way: "What? He used to slip in by himself on Friday night. Honorable Jew. I am not acquainted with his wiles? It's some actress he wants to see: Pola Negri, who reminds him, he says, of Hannah."

"Oh, yeah." Ira paused at the bedroom door. "Pola Negri. I passed her pictures there in front of the theater on 116th Street."

"Pola Negri. Such a name: Pola Negri."

He went into the cold bedroom, put on his hat, picked up his overcoat athwart the bed, slid an arm into a sleeve as he came out into the kitchen. "How's your catarrh?"

"It's to be tolerated. And tolerate it I must. It's quieted."

"That's good. Well, I better beat it, Mom." He wriggled into his coat. "Say goodbye to Pop and to Minnie."

"I'll have to leave her word."

"What do you mean?"

"We may be gone before she comes home."

"Oh, yeah." Ira hefted the carton reflectively. "That's right."

"The great sire will have to write her a message: to wait a little while for supper. The gefilte fish is in the window box. She can light the stove under the soup again if she wants to. I told her about his—" Mom's fingers waved in ironic festoon—"his magnanimity. She was glad. Naturally."

"You didn't tell her about anything else?"

"Only you I would tell." Rotating turbines. The empty house. Bleak kitchen. Wintry ambience of humid glistening blistery green walls. The brain needed a circuit breaker. Edith was like a shunt to a new life, but the old was still there, intact, accessible, with all the ferocious allure of the forbidden—Satan's dilemma in Milton—the forbidden that augured ruinous foreboding, but still— Ira affected dawdling, set down the carton on the table. "What did Stella say when you came in?"

"You're not going?"

"I can spare another minute. I'm not wrought up. Honest. Calm down."

"Truth?"

"Truth."

"And if he were to come in the door this minute?"

"I told you." Ira shrugged emphatically. "It's passed. I'm outta this dump, this life, if you call it that, this craziness. I'm outta your *tsuris,*" he capped sentiment with false toughness in Yiddish. "I don't care if he comes home. 'So long, Pop,'" Ira projected facetious farewell.

"I'm glad. I was afraid for a while. He's not worth your ire. The whole thing. It's Chaim'l, *noo?*"

"Yeah. Chaim'l is right. So what did she say?"

"What could she say? She turned red as the clout she was wearing."

"The what? She was wearing a clout, you say?"

"That too." Mom pressed her lips sideways in revulsion. "Shameless she, and shameless he."

"Yeah. I don't blame you, Mom."

"Well. Nothing. But what fiend possessed her to come here?" Mom contracted in a fresh spasm of indignation. "She knows I have nothing in common with her. She's flavorless. She's insipid. The silly nonsense she talks about—she prattles. I can scarce abide her. And to come here to our neighborhood, to 119th Street. She fears it. But here she is. Why?"

Ira shook his head. "Got me, Mom," he said in English. He lifted his briefcase. "Sorry, Mom. They say in English: Parting is such sweet sorrow."

"Indeed, so it is. At least you'll be in better hands. When will you come home?"

"Soon as I can."

"And your career you won't abandon? College you won't abandon?"

"No, no. Listen, Mom, you asked me before, and I told you. I can't stay there all the time. Part of the summer she goes west and rents the apartment. So I'll have to come back here. And she's getting that book together that I told you about. An anthology it's called. She'll be busy. Maybe I can help, but I'm not sure. Anyway, I don't know where I'll stay a lot of the time. You haven't lost me yet."

"No? *Zolst gehen gesint.* Give me a kiss."

"G'bye, Mom." Ira laid briefcase on carton to embrace her. He clasped her bulky, thick body in his arms, kissed her surprisingly soft cheeks, kissed her brow, as she had always wanted him to do since childhood. His throat tightened.

"God protect you," she said.

"I hope so." He transferred the heavy carton from table to washtub, so that he could the more conveniently take hold of it when he opened the door. He opened the door, hooked fingers into the carton strings, and was about to lift his burden from the white-oilcloth-covered washtub when he heard out of the hallway chill, out of the dim corridor, the light step, saw the slight figure, saw the glint of eyeglasses. His hand on the crossed cords of the carton opened. He stood with briefcase dangling from his arm.

"Hi ye, Pop." Uttering his usual preliminary puff, the unsmiling little man came into the kitchen.

Unfriendly—offended—he looked first at Mom, then at Ira, and then at the carton on the washtub. "*Noo*, you've driven him off," he said. "You weren't content until you drove him off."

"I? I drove him off?" Mom countered. "Are you mad? He's going of his own accord. Tell him, Ira."

But Pop interjected before Ira could speak: "You take me for a fool? I don't understand that you already told him last night? And now he flees for good." He pointed at the carton.

"Go. You're demented."

"I can't recognize it?" He pointed up at Ira's face.

"Listen, Pop—"

"Listen, Pop," Pop mocked. "*Noo?*" he challenged. "It was such an abominable thing? And even so, a wife will tell a son about it. This isn't an abominable thing?"

"Nobody said it was," Ira palliated.

"Aha!"

"So I told him!" Mom flung defiantly at her husband. "Do I need to be ashamed, or you?"

"You see how her head works? Does she need to be ashamed, or I? Not that she shouldn't be ashamed to tell her son, to besmirch his father. That's nothing. Only to show how blameless she is. Why did you have to tell?" Pop confronted his wife. And then to Ira: "She enlightened you greatly with this? What have you to say?"

"Leave the boy alone," Mom warned.

"Listen, Pop, will you listen? As far as what happened, it's none of my damn business, all right? I'm not leaving home because of anything you did—about that—all right? I'm leaving because I'm going to live with somebody else. I'm going to live with a woman. Okay? In Greenwich Village. You've heard me talk about her: Edith, yes? I'm going to live with her. Part of the time. It has nothing to do with you at all. It's practically my only hope. That's why I'm going."

"There you have the truth," said Mom.

Pop, his suspicious, dog-brown eyes staring behind spectacles, searched Ira's countenance with rare fixity. "Your only hope?"

"Yes."

"To go live with an old *shiksa?*"

"I won't go into that—that's my affair."

"And my affair?"

"That's yours."

"It's so heinous?"

"I won't go into that. It's yours."

"But she had to splash you with it. What have you to say? Tell."

"Leave him alone!" Mom intervened.

"I demand to know."

"As far as I'm concerned, Pop, all you did was, well—" Ira shrugged, denigrated. "It was just human, all right? Can I go now?"

"Tell her." Pop pointed to his wife. "A man is left alone with a toy. What she's doing here I don't know. But a comely little toy she is. So what terrible thing has he done? *Noo?* He played with her. A pretty young plaything yields to a man's caresses. He toys with her, and such a little toy. Does he merit the gibbet for that? I have such a dear and loving wife that I'm not tempted, tell me? Such a doting wife—"

"Gey mir in der erd," Mom cut in stonily.

"Uh! That answer she has ready."

"All right, let's cut it out. Please." Ira looked toward the door.

"And how many times need I hear about her brother's prowess? She knows about her brother's prowess. How?"

"Indeed. Moe would have suited me."

"You see?"

"Mom, cut it out!" Ira snapped. "Let's forget it! Jeez, I've got no argument, Pop. It's one of those things. Please! As far as I'm concerned, I may be as much to blame as anybody."

"How are you to blame?" Mom demanded.

"Maybe everybody is, and nobody is." Ira wished to Christ he hadn't lingered. He could have been gone and out of it. "Mom said you wanted to take her to a movie: Pola Negri. Why don'tcha both go. Make up for this damn foolishness. Come back in time for *Shabbes*— a little later. What d'ye say, Mom? Please!" She remained obdurately silent, contemptuous. "Please, you're always complaining he doesn't take you with him to see a movie," Ira beseeched. "It's soon Friday eve."

"And if you don't agree to go soon, the matinee prices will be over," Pop pleaded.

"Please, Mom. Go this once, will you."

"My spendthrift," Mom said scornfully. "My prodigal."

"Cut it out, I said!" Ira raised his voice. "Will you go? I'm going. I'm going to leave you."

"I have a choice," said Mom. "My liberal sport. I'll go put on another garment." She made for the bedroom.

"*Makh shnell,*" Pop ordered. "This will be a Friday."

"Only because it's Pola Negri. Your kind of sad actress."

"Write Minnie a message. She can eat, or wait."

"I'll write, I'll write. Go. Hurry with your *shmattas.*" Mom disappeared into the bedroom. "Till she moves," said Pop. He pulled a stub of pencil out of his pocket. "You have a scrap of paper?"

"Yeah." Ira tore a sheet of loose-leaf out of his small notebook.

"Okay." Still in hat and coat, Pop sat down at the table and began scribbling a note.

"So long, Pop." Ira hooked his fingers in the strings of the carton.

"So long, so long," Pop replied curtly.

"I already said goodbye to Mom." Ira opened the door.

"Well, let her get dressed."

"Say goodbye for me to Minnie."

"Goodbye, goodbye." Pop scarcely looked up.

Corridor debouched into hall, hall led downstairs. Stairs thirteen years long, to ground floor, and ground floor to stone stoop, and stoop to sidewalk in front of 108 East 119th Street. All familiar, the expected number of kids and people for a cold day between the forsaken tenement facades. Dark veil of the Third Avenue El beyond Lexington to the east, and the gray Grand Central overpass—the Cut—at the west corner. A few cars parked against the curb, and fewer passing; a cat darting across the street; an elderly matron lifting heavy blue shawl to mouth, as she led a wizened poodle out of the cluttered midblock grocery. He walked west, crossed shadowy Park Avenue under the trestle. The strings cut off circulation, made his fingers cold. He wedged the carton under his arm, continued on toward Madison Avenue, westward along the abject block between graystone P.S. 103, stout oak doors locked, and cutout paper pumpkins and turkeys in the windows, cutout Pilgrims in high hats, and carrying blunderbusses. They came to America to be free. He was free. He was going to live with Edith, with a *shiksa*, and nobody to stop him. He was Edith's lover now. That was what she called him: "Wait for me, lover." That wasn't what he would have called it with his cock inside her.

He'd have to try and relearn everything—like a veneer on everything he was. With an old *shiksa*, as Pop jeered, the old bastard. Ira couldn't have done that in Galitzia. But neither could Pop have taken Mom to a movie to see Pola Negri at this time on Friday in Galitzia either, under the stern gaze of the old boy wearing his *peyot*, his sidelocks in the portrait in the front room. It was Chaos. Old man Chaos who showed Satan the way out.

He was tormented for good. Ira shook his head. The fact that he could think of Minnie and Stella en route to Edith, and think of her the way he did, showed he wasn't free, Pilgrims or no Pilgrims. He was still a prisoner: quiescent flame was banked in the mind: ever ready to awake at a puff of air, ever hopeful it would kindle a ruby jewel under thatch. See how his mind ran. He was lucky, that was all.

He was protean, he was capable of anything, he wasn't sure of anything. Only that he was lucky that he had a goal that kept him walking west to Lenox Avenue, to the West Side subway station at 116th Street. Oh, it was just luck, just luck—stop.

And he did halt in midstride. Supposing he was sure beyond a doubt, the way he was always a hundred percent sure about Stella, that if there was the slimmest chance, she'd let him prat her some way some where. Would he go back? Turn, turn, Sir Richard Washington. Would he? Oh, Jesus, he couldn't get over the cravings. He couldn't get over it. He could only get away from it; that was all.

And what the hell was the matter with him, anyway? He had Edith, now—that was the difference. She had opened up for him—oh, cut out the smut at long last—a vibrant, new vision, vision of liberation, of independence, vision consummating the aureate promise he had experienced one summer afternoon on a busy West Harlem avenue. She kindled pride, self-esteem. She had faith, she said, in his literary potential. He had to develop more, but she was sure he would get there in his time.

And Fifth Avenue opened before him. Another long block to Lenox? Or should he turn now and take the three short blocks to 116th? Either course would get him to the subway.

He cut south, avoiding the monotonous facade of the 119th Street tenements, preferring the holiday smells of the clangorous avenue before him. Turn back? God no. He could only get away, that was all. He switched the parcel from right to left, the only evidence of Harlem past lying in that motley carton. Ira peeled down steps of subway station. As luck would have it, the express shrieked to a halt. Ira boarded the train, his cold fingers still aching, and strait was the route, and strait the rails—the IRT swerved, squealing on the tracks of the long curve westward as it repaired downtown and the hell out of Harlem.

EDITOR'S AFTERWORD

I spoke with Henry Roth for the last time on Monday, the ninth of October, 1995. Having been unable to reach him at his home, a ramshackle former funeral parlor that he had purchased after the death of his wife, Muriel, I surmised that he might be in the hospital. I checked an ever-expanding list of Albuquerque hospital numbers that I kept in my address book, and was able to track him down that evening, shortly after I had come home from work. Despite the frailty of his condition and the excruciating severity of his pain, he sounded even jolly, his voice lilting and upbeat. Handed the receiver by a nurse, he was pleased to hear from me, his editor, his occasional analyst, but mostly, his friend of nearly four years.

Since I had first become acquainted with him back in December of 1992, just after Roslyn Targ, his devoted agent of over thirty years, had sold me the first volume of *Mercy of a Rude Stream*, I had become inured to his expressions of gloom—his lugubrious moods that would descend on him for a day or two, sometimes even a month. Some of these depressive seizures were so intense that he would exclaim dramatically that he wished to die (*"apothonein theilo,"* he'd write in Greek), and that he would kill himself as soon as he turned ninety and had a big party.

But this night of October 9 was not like so many of those other nights. Gone was the gauze of melancholia, the "dark sullen telepathy" that had so often encumbered him, preventing him from continuing with the monumental task of writing, editing, and constantly revising the four books that form this quartet, which he had called *Mercy of a Rude Stream,* borrowing a phrase from Shakespeare's *Henry VIII.* That Monday night, he was genuinely pleased that I, together with his assistant and final literary muse, Felicia Steele (the last of three women who had enabled him to create literature throughout his life), had made so much progress completing the editing of *From Bondage* and *Requiem for Harlem,* the third and the final volume of the *Mercy* series, respectively. Even as his limbs and his bowels had failed him with increasing regularity throughout 1994 and 1995, he had worked compulsively to complete the arduous task of shaping and rewriting over 5,000 pages of text, which comprised the four volumes, a large portion of which had already been hailed by numerous American reviewers as a "landmark of the American literary century," in the words of the critic David Mehegan. Even when Steele was no longer able to work with Henry, since she herself had gone off to graduate school in English at the University of Texas, he had engaged another young University of New Mexico undergraduate, Eleana Zamora, and the two of them had worked on the various revisions that were required in the final editing and restructuring of the last two volumes.

That October evening, Henry politely asked me how my own father, his senior by a mere seven months, and physically in no better shape, was doing, as if the two old men were competitively engaged in a race to see which one would meet his maker first. Not wanting to alarm Henry with dire medical reports from California, I lied, of course, and said that my dad was holding his own, and Roth replied, "Carry on the good work, my friend," as if he were a literature professor from one of his 1920s screwball plots. Four days later, on Friday, October 13, Henry was gone. He had died just after sundown, having made the Sabbath in the very nick of time, and to mix Hebrew and Greek images, as he was wont to do, just after Helias in his horse-drawn chariot had raced by Albuquerque on his nightly run.

Felicia, in touch with Henry's two sons, Hugh and Jeremy, left the news of Henry's passing both on my telephone machine at home and in the office, messages that I picked up in California soon after my plane had landed. My father was in worse condition than I had imagined—his head drooped so low, his consciousness so dim that the doctor advised the next afternoon that we not feed him intravenously. I sat that afternoon in the kitchen of my parents' apartment, at work at the table, numbed, grief-stricken, with the manuscript pages of *Mercy* spread out willy-nilly before me, struggling with the editing of a particularly salacious description of sex between the fictional cousins Ira and Stella. Yet as stunned as I was about Henry's death, I took great comfort in knowing that Roth, at least for me, had not died; in fact, the very pages before me represented his very tree of life, and what better way to show my love than to do just as Henry had commanded, "Carry on, . . . my friend."

I am sure that I was concentrating so mightily on Henry's prose because I wished to distract myself from my own father's predicament—Dr. Reed's pronouncement of gloom, and the knowledge that Henry's departure was a harbinger of my own father's imminent death. And as the doctor was packing his bag, my father suddenly struggled to lift his head—he even bolted—and like the stirring of a shroud, acknowledged my presence, speaking his first words in over two days. Casting his gaze on the messy sheaf of papers, my father suddenly uttered, with his thick, barely comprehensible German accent, the questioning words, "Henry Rot, Henry Rot?", "*rot*" being the German pronunciation of Roth, as in the color red, although Henry of all people was not unaware of the pun.

"Doctor Reed, did you hear that, he knows what I am working on, he said 'Henry Roth,'" I exclaimed. The doctor was as stunned as I was; so was my mother, and although this was the only phrase my dad uttered that weekend, the doctor immediately called for an IV bag and an infusion of fluids, and arguably, because of Henry Roth, my father lived another sixteen days.

I felt that autumn that I had lost two giants, both men atavistic in wholly different ways. Having had the privilege of working with Henry, I can unequivocally state that my perception of the world has been remarkably altered. In fact, I can no longer walk the streets of Manhattan without feeling a far greater empathy for the poor. It is as if I had discovered a new Dostoevsky, and at the end of our stultifyingly narcissistic twentieth century at that. Despite our gap in age, I felt that Roth was writing about *my* city of New York in the 1990s, even though

Henry's stories detailed a far more technologically primitive world of a greenhorn generation long since vanished. Roth was perhaps the last voice of an era, yet his description in *Requiem for Harlem* of crosstown traffic on 14th Street—"shuffle and squeal. Glitter and gleam of windshield and hubcap"—save for the eloquence of his language, could easily pass for a street scene in 1997, so constant is the farrago of whirling images that New York manages faithfully to project. The immigrant Jews and Italians who were, of course, so hated in Roth's youth have long since entered the mainstream, made complacent by the prosperity that education and middle classdom bring, yet the privations described endow us with a vision of poverty so compassionate and transcendent that we can never forget that there are millions of people in New York City alone who remain destitute. I as a reader have learned that behind the grimace of every street sweeper, behind the fretful countenance of every hot dog vendor, there exists a fellow journeyman, whose plaintive gaze or feral eyes bespeak a magnificent drama that remains untold. In listening to the story of a Pakistani taxi driver talking about his children at school in Queens, I am confronted by an immense pride and beauty, mine for the listening. Manhattan, despite the passage of seventy years, despite the incursion of television, graffiti, new racial tensions, and E-mail, has not changed at all—and the Rothian immigrant world of the 1920s remains as immanent today as it was when David Schearl, the young protagonist of *Call It Sleep*, was but a small boy on the Lower East Side.

There are, of course, numerous critics and countless readers who still continue to hold on to the notion that *Call It Sleep* is indeed the only masterpiece that Henry Roth ever wrote. As the first two volumes of the *Mercy* series came off press, most reviewers felt compelled to compare these new works to a book published in 1934 when its author was a mere twenty-eight years old, as if a man in his late eighties was simply expected to pick up writing in the exact manner as he had done as an unexamined young man. The notion was absurd, and this wretched form of comparison would be enough to dissuade any blocked writer, like J. D. Salinger, Harper Lee, or the late Ralph Ellison, from even contemplating a new work late in life. Yet Roth possessed in many ways an elephantine hide, and when he happened to glance at a review or two (most he never even looked at), he merely

shrugged, and said, "Baah, she just didn't get the book," and that was
that. His mission was manifest—it was ordained that he carry on his
novels, as if writing were the only force that was keeping him alive, and
a hostile review did not deter Roth in the slightest. It would often
amaze interviewers who came to his home in the early 1990s to listen
to the old man describe his one novel "from childhood." He would tell
not a few visitors that he had disavowed the first book—that it was a
boy's work no longer worth reading, a book that had been inspired
under the spell of his erstwhile mentor and now necromancer James
Joyce—and that he cared no longer to discuss it or its themes.

Call It Sleep was simply a book that had died when another man by
the name of Henry had perished decades ago. Didn't they have something else to ask, he questioned the parade of interrogators? When
asked why he was writing the *Mercy* series, he prided himself in telling
people that it was simply "for the dough," and that this newly found in-
come was required to pay for his nurses, doctors, and the cornucopia
of medications that rested on the kitchen table.

It was only after Roth's death, and with the publication of the third
volume, *From Bondage,* that over a dozen critics and reviewers hailed
the third book as a masterpiece in its own right, not a novel that had to
be reviewed in the context of a distant literary antecedent. As *Call It
Sleep* is arguably one of the finest American novels that has ever depicted childhood, so too can the four volumes of *Mercy of a Rude Stream*
now be viewed not only as a necessary complement to the prior work,
but as a unified body of literature that stands on its own. No less a
scholar and critic than Mario Materassi, who for many years was Roth's
closest friend and soulmate, and who deserves singular credit for
transforming Roth into a writer of such huge international stature, has
written that "*Call It Sleep* can be read as a vehicle through which, soon
after breaking away from his family and his tradition, young Roth used
some of the fragments of his childhood to shore up the ruins of what
he already felt was a disconnected self. Forty-five years later, Roth em-
barked on another attempt to bring some retrospective order to his
life's confusion: *Mercy of a Rude Stream,* which he has long called a 'con-
tinuum,' can be read as a final, monumental effort on the part of the
elderly author to come to terms with the pattern of rupture and dis-
continuity that has marked his life." My own personal feeling is that

there are few works in this decade, much less in this century, that have come like *Mercy* to reflect as acutely the internal dislocation of the intellectual and the society at large.

Just when we think we know what Roth as a writer is up to, what course he has charted for his journey home, he twists and turns, and changes his mind, and with each new volume, we must constantly reassess our agile narrator as his epic proceeds. As Materassi has commented in his insightful essay, "Shifting Urbanscape: Roth's 'Private' New York," Roth "has never been interested in any story other than the anguished one of a man who, throughout his life, has contradicted each of his previously held positions and beliefs." A superb holder of secrets, Roth as a novelist does not even alert his readers (there is a one-line hint in the first volume, however) that Ira Stigman has a fictional sister until one-third of the way through the second volume, *A Diving Rock on the Hudson*. The revelation must be a surprise.

I once asked Henry if his wife Muriel, with whom he shared a compact one-bedroom trailer home, had ever read any of the early drafts of *Mercy*. "She never asked, and I never offered to show her," he told me, as if it were completely natural for a writer's wife not even to get one glimpse of the thousands of pages that lay on each side of the computer whom he chose to call Ecclesias. Although I cannot think of a human being who was more honest with me than Henry, Roth's varying accounts of his life's story, as Materassi has suggested, did shift frequently over time. For example, after having told reporters for decades that it was his Communist experience, and the resulting disillusionment, that prevented him from writing again, Roth suggested in the last few years of his life that his sexual preoccupations and obsessions lay more at the root of his unwillingness to continue writing for more than forty years. Yet on other occasions, he maintained that the block was caused by his early break with Judaism and his family's departure in 1914 from the hermetic, *shtetl*-like world of New York's Lower East Side.

Like their creator, these modern books effortlessly mutate in tone and sensibility, and while the arc is unerringly tragic, the seismic waves registered throughout are unpredictable, and deliberately so. While *A*

Diving Rock on the Hudson is purposefully scandalous and confessional in its often Augustinian tone, *From Bondage,* despite the brilliant sexual tension of the last third of the book (Roth called the Ira-Stella-Zaida section a "novella" in its own right), is largely redemptive, as if Roth were indeed seeking deliverance in this penultimate work. Yet the final volume, *Requiem for Harlem,* contains a sexual wantonness and "depravity," a word favored by Roth, that seems surprising for a man of eighty-nine laboring to finish the epic of his life. As his close friend and literary executor, Larry Fox, once explained to me, "Henry could not die false. He was a truth seeker, and only when he could review the truth about himself could he become free. In fact, he remained alive to unburden himself so that he could die free and perhaps free all of us. Once Muriel died, Henry could finally tell the truth, and then it was only between him and his Maker."

Roth would have been the first person to note that nothing in any of his books was gratuitous, so why would he so deliberately debase his alter ego Ira? Few people like seeing their idol so compromised or disgraced; no one indeed wants to see his revered novelist revealed to be a predator, an agent of incest, and victimizer himself. So why then did Roth in his eighties become so emotionally patulous, or why did he begin to flirt with Nabokovian flights of fancy, choosing to make Ira as sexually compulsive and loathsome as possible? Having known Henry quite well, I would refute anyone's contention that this octogenarian's "need" to eroticize his life was merely a way to jolly himself as his body disintegrated. This quite conscious decision to debase himself—to make his "rude stream" as repellent as possible—as he depicted "the last onerous lap" of his life, was meant, I suspect, to bring about a spiritual salvation in the only way that he knew how. In any given interview or even in the text of this work, Roth, however, would have been the first to negate any such redemptive refuge. Listen to his own words: "What a sinister cyst of guilt that was within the self, denigrating the *yontif,* denigrating everything within reach, exuding ambiguity, anomaly, beyond redemption now." And so, *Requiem for Harlem* is a work fraught with often unimaginable family cruelty, the young man emerging from his adolescent chrysalis the very tyrant his father Chaim was. Indeed, we revisit more so than in any previous volume the unprecedented violence of *Call It Sleep.* At last, the abuse that the young boy witnessed so viscerally when his father beat his mother gets replayed here with equal ferocity—the cup of scalding tea hurled in Leah's face, for example, or the horrific way in which Chaim torments his wife after she has caught *him* flagrantly fondling their lustful niece. It must be *her* fault after all, so Leah is led to believe.

No wonder that Roth's mother unknowingly "had indoctrinated him into tragedy, given him a penchant for it, the tragic outlook," for her path toward depression and episodic madness seemed destined, given her docile and even masochistic nature. And while the mother so lovingly depicted in this final volume becomes a "wavering demi-agnostic" and questions the existence of *Adonoi,* so too did Roth throughout his life simultaneously embrace and reject the notion of a forgiving God. Yet while Roth no doubt inherited his depressive gloom and his religious ambivalence from his mother, he learned far too ably at his father's knee as well. The brilliant boy, once David Schearl, now Ira Stigman, absorbed from his father a relentless pattern of violence and verbal imprecation that mixed often explosively with his mother's maternal kindness. The boy, as precocious as he was, learned at a very tender age, whether from his father or through a pederast named "Moe," that the star was no longer shining over Mt. Morris Park (*stella, stella,* it was getting so dark after all). And familial incest, many psychiatrists have maintained, comes twinned with family violence, and the fictional relationship between Ira and his sister Minnie and cousin Stella must have had some basis in the models provided in various ways by both of Ira/Henry's parents.

Yet despite Roth's constant claims that redemption, particularly at the end of our materialistically excessive century, was no longer viable, I contend that he was transfixed in his declining years by the possibility of mercy, perhaps not for himself, but rather for his wife Muriel, for both of his sons, for Eda Lou Walton whom he had abandoned in the late 1930s, and, in fact, for us all. If we could as readers still like, empathize, or even pray for Ira, even after all that he had perpetrated, then there might be mercy even for us. And so the old man pecked away furiously, keenly aware that his days were diminishing, the stream of urine dripping from his leg not even deterring him as the story reached its terrifying dénouement. And "for a moment the waning ivory moon above the gloomy gantries of the New York Central trestle seemed poised like a tusk at Ira as he pattered down the sandstone steps of the stoop to the sidewalk; boar's tusk aimed at Endymion, he thought, turning left on grubby, cold, dark, deserted 119th Street toward the corner at Park Avenue." Entranced by the drama of the narrative, age seemed almost miraculously to disappear, and once again life had suddenly achieved a unity; this unity, despite a persistent theme of alienation, being perhaps the crowning literary achievement. And as many readers have no doubt noticed, the dialogue with Ecclesias, the philosophical chatter between the old man and his computer, actually recedes in *Requiem for Harlem,* for the old man is once again in his prime, not distracted by physical decrepitude, this work being the last gasp of existence before the proverbial jig was up.

While Roth commented numerous times before his death that *Mercy of a Rude Stream* comprised six volumes, his publisher, along with Felicia Steele, Larry Fox, and Roslyn Targ, have all agreed that the work would best be served by appearing as four. In fact, Roth did write six separate books, the first four which he called "Batch One," and the last two, which he simply labeled "Batch Two" of *Mercy* for lack of a better title. The truth is that these first four volumes, now completely edited and herewith published, possess a stylistic and thematic unity which are quite distinct from the other two books. The first volume opens with Ira's move to Harlem, while Volume IV concludes with Ira's decision to flee Harlem into Edith's overprotective arms. Likewise, all four volumes take place over a sustained period of thirteen years, from 1914 through the end of 1927. Written in two voices and two type styles (Roth was adamant from the beginning that the Ecclesias passages were essential to the thematic wholeness of the works), the books are linked by a chronologically coherent and unified style.

On the other hand, the two books (no decision has been made whether to bring them out as one book or two volumes as yet) that Roth called "Batch Two" do not contain an Ecclesias narrator, and jump the reader by over a decade to the end of the 1930s, and tell the story of his breakup with Edith Welles and the love affair with the young composer named M, who would soon become his wife. The final revisions that Roth was able to undertake both in 1994 and in

1995 were of *From Bondage* and *Requiem for Harlem,* so that the story that unfolds in "Batch Two" was written in the late 1980s and was revised with Felicia Steele in 1990 and 1991.

"'You are not required to finish' ran the *Talmud* dictum" notes Roth in this final volume of *Mercy,* and perhaps the same thing can be said of this opus, as if "the past coalesced into a kind of opaque introspection that marked the end." As Edith Welles in the story quelled Ira Stigman's "fears and guilts, as if bleaching them out of sight with her objectivity," so the same can be said of Roth pecking away at his beloved keyboard at the end of his life. "She [Edith] reduced the onus of his wickedness, eliminated much of the sense of heinousness, quenched the shimmer of guilt, stealth, risk that informed, that magnified his form," and so do these books, their completion being a deliverance from the vile self-loathing that had consumed Roth for almost all of his life.

"Strange, unhappy lad. Let's put as much of that behind us as we can," his mentor and lover—the woman of "brown eyes very large in the sallowness of pallid olive skin"—tells Ira, and *Mercy of a Rude Stream,* as fine a portrait of the artist in old age as we may ever see, achieves in virtuosic fashion just that what first Edith and later the senescent genius Henry Roth set out to do.

—Robert Weil
September 1997

GLOSSARY OF YIDDISH AND HEBREW WORDS AND PHRASES

Note: Some spellings reflect Galitzianer pronunciations and may seem unfamiliar to speakers of "standard" Yiddish. Some words are mixtures of Yiddish and English.

a gitten Shabbes   a good Sabbath
alles   everything
alter kocker   old man; (der.) old shit
a shvartz yur auf is   it is a black year
auf shpilkis   on pins and needles
ausgestudierteh   studious
aza mensh   such a man
azoy   right; is that so
babbeh   grandmother
bali gooleh   stage driver
Barukh atah adonoi elohenu melekh ha oylum   Praised are you, Eternal our God, Sovereign of the Universe
benket   banquet
bensht lekht   to recite benedictions over lit candles on Sabbath eve and holidays
bist mishugeh?   are you crazy?
biyah   sexual intercourse
bris   the ritual of circumcision
chai   tea
cheder   Hebrew school for boys of pre–Bar Mitzva age

chibeggeh   nonsense word meaning chattering
dama   woman
davens   prayers; **davening**   praying
diktats   dictates, commands
Dummkopf   idiot
dus heist kunst   that's called skill
ehrlikh yeet   honest Jew
Epikouros   Epicurean; loosely, hedonist, atheist
Eretz Yisroel   the land of Israel
erev Pesach   evening of the Passover
erev Shabbes   Sabbath eve
er's a mishugeneh   he's a crazy person
ess   eat
eytser   piece of advice
falsheh-zup   false (i.e. meatless) soup
fleishik   foods prepared with meat
fluden   pastry
fortz   fart
freg nisht   don't worry
Freitig b'nakht   Friday night
fresser   glutton
fumfit   speaks
geldt   money
geliebter   beloved
gesheft   store
geshrei   screaming, to-do
gey mir in der erd   go to hell; drop dead
gitoik   the evil eye
glazel   glass; **glazel**   tea
goldeneh medina   golden country
goor nisht   nothing
Gotinyoo   our God
Got sei dank   God be thanked
goy   gentile (noun); **goya**   female gentile; **goyim**   gentiles; **goyish**   of
   the gentiles (adj.)
heraus   out; **heraus, fershtinkineh dreck!**   out, stinking dirt!
hivnuh   contract
hullupchehs   stuffed cabbage
hunik-lekekh   honey cake
ihr zolt hub'n a gitten Shabbes   you have a good Sabbath
iz nisht   it is nothing
jabah   frog
Kaddish   Hebrew prayer for the dead

Kedushim   wedding
kessef   money
khlyup   to strike a blow
kholleh   Sabbath bread
khukhim   wise person
Khumish   the study of Hebrew
khumitz   matzah crumbs scattered before the Passover
khuppa   wedding canopy
khusin   groom
kishkehs, kishkelah, kishkelikh   stuffed pastries; (coll.) genitalia, in-
    nards
kletchmer   string band that traditionally plays at weddings
knubl   garlic
kocker   shit (person)
kolleh moit   girl old enough to be a bride
kopf   head
koyn   Hebrew priest
kubella   cow
kugel   pudding
kvoorim   tombs
l'kuvet Shabbes   in honor of the Sabbath
landsfrau   landlady
l'chaim   to life
makher   businessman, big shot
makh shnell   make haste
martira   martyr
matzah   unleavened bread
mazel   luck; **mazel tov!**   congratulations!
mehvin   maven
mein kaddish'l iz duh   my child is here; (lit.) the one who will say **Kad-
    dish** is here
mensh   man (indicates dependable, mature person); **mensheleh**   little
    man
meshinkeh   machine
mikveh   ritual bath
milkhdik   foods prepared with dairy products
mir nisht, dir nisht   nothing to me, nothing to you
mishpokha   relatives
mishugeneh   crazy; **mishugeh auf toit**   crazy as a loon
Moishe Kapoyer   a person who does everything wrong or in reverse
mujik   Russian peasant
na, a drittle   okay, a third
nisht b'mutchkeh   it's not much

nisht kosher   not kosher; not right
noo   well
nosh   snack
nudnick   nagger, nuisance
ov toit   completely
oy, gevald   cry of alarm, concern, or amazement
oy, veh   oh, woe; **oy, veh iz mir**   oh, woe is me
parakutskie   low-life
paskudnyack   scoundrel; an odious person
peigern zollst deh   he should drop dead
petzel   penis
peyot   earlocks worn by devout Orthodox male Jews
pipick   navel
Raboinish ha loilim   (Hebrew) God in Heaven, Master of the Universe
roman   serial romance, novel
riebahsel   grater
Seder   Passover service
seh goor nisht   it's nothing
seh heist kessef   it's called money
Shabbes b'nakht   evening of Sabbath
Shabbes   Sabbath
shande   shame
shayn   nice, good
shiksa   gentile girl, usually a servant
shlemiel   an ill-fated person; a bungler
shlepper   laborer
Shloimeh, ha Mailackh   Solomon the king
Shmai Yisroel, adonoi elohenu adonoi ekhud   Hear, O Israel: Adonai is
    our God, Adonai is One (Deuteronomy 6:4), the Jewish creed
shmaltz   fat; **shmaltzy**   fatty
shmatta   rag
shmooze   chat
shmertz   pain
shmuck   jerk; (lit.) penis
shnorrer, shnorrerkeh   beggar, moocher
shotkhin   matchmaker
shoyn   already
shoyn tsat tse zahn a mensh   already that is a man
shtar   written agreement
shtarkeh   strong
shtetl   traditional Eastern European Jewish community
shtudier   study; **shtudierst**   are you studying
shul   synagogue

shvakh ill
shvartze black
siddur prayer book
Talmud Rabbinical commentaries on the Torah
tanta aunt
thallis prayer shawl
tockin indeed
tokhterel daughter
traife nonkosher
trombehnyick ne'er-do-well
tseegekhappen fornication
tsevorfen, tsevorfeneh scattered
tsuris worries
tsvei'n dreizig thirty-two
tvillim phylacteries
uhmein seluh Amen, so be it
und and
veitig sorrow
verenekehs fried pastry made of rounds of dough filled with jelly, fruit,
    or meat
verfallen lost
vie a toiten bankehs cupping a cadaver
vie zoy how come?
vir hutzikh tsegekhapt we grappled
vonneh bath
voos makht a yeet? you've become a Jew?
vunderbar wonderful
vus makht ihr? how are you?
yeet Jew
yenta shrewish or gossipy woman
Yidlekh little Jew
yontif holiday
zindle child
z'misht confused
zoll dir Got helfen may God help you
zolst gehen gesint may you go in health
zug speak

ABOUT THE AUTHOR

Henry Roth, who died on October 13, 1995, in Albuquerque, New Mexico, at the age of eighty-nine, had one of the most extraordinary careers of any American novelist who lived in the twentieth century.

He was born in the village of Tysmenitz, in the then Austro-Hungarian province of Galitzia, in 1906. Although his parents never agreed on the exact date of his arrival in the United States, it is most likely that he landed at Ellis Island and began his life in New York in 1909. He briefly lived in Brooklyn, and then on the Lower East Side, in the slums where his classic novel *Call It Sleep* is set. In 1914, the family moved to Harlem, first to the Jewish section on 114th Street east of Park Avenue; but because the three rooms there were "in the back" and the isolation reminded his mother of the sleepy hamlet of Veljish where she grew up, she became depressed, and the family moved to non-Jewish 119th Street. Roth lived there until 1927, when, as a senior at City College of New York, he moved in with Eda Lou Walton, a poet and New York University instructor. With Walton's support, he began *Call It Sleep* in about 1930. He completed the novel in the spring of 1934, and it was published in December 1934, to mixed reviews. He contracted for a second novel with the editor Maxwell Perkins, of Scribner's, and the first section of it appeared as a work in progress. But Roth's growing ideological frustration and personal confusion created a profound writer's block, which lasted until 1979, when he began the earliest drafts of *Mercy of a Rude Stream.*

In 1938, during an unproductive sojourn at the artists' colony Yaddo in Saratoga Springs, New York, Roth met Muriel Parker, a pianist and composer. They fell in love; Roth severed his relationship with Walton, moved out of her apartment on Morton Street, and married Parker in 1939, much to the disapproval of her family. With the onset of the war, Roth became a tool and gauge maker. The couple moved first to Boston with their two young sons, Jeremy and Hugh, and then in 1946 to Maine. There Roth worked as a woodsman, a schoolteacher, a psychiatric attendant in the state mental hospital, a waterfowl farmer, and a Latin and math tutor.

With the paperback reprinting of *Call It Sleep* in 1964, the block slowly began to break. In 1968, after Muriel's retirement from the Maine state school system, the couple moved to Albuquerque, New Mexico. They had become acquainted with the environs during Roth's stay at the D. H. Lawrence ranch outside of Taos, where Roth was writer-in-residence. Muriel began composing music again, mostly for individual instruments, for which she received ample recognition. After Muriel's death in 1990, Roth occupied himself with revising the final volumes of the monumental *Mercy of a Rude Stream.* The first volume was published in 1994 by St. Martin's Press and in paperback by Picador in 1995 under the title *A Star Shines over Mt. Morris Park,* and the second volume, called *A Diving Rock on the Hudson,* appeared from St. Martin's Press in 1995 with the paperback from Picador following a year later.

The third volume, *From Bondage,* which appeared in hardcover in 1996 and in paperback from Picador in 1997, was the first volume of the four *Mercy* books to appear posthumously. *Requiem for Harlem,* being the fourth and final volume of *Mercy of a Rude Stream,* concludes the cycle, which began in 1914 with the Stigman family's arrival in Jewish-Irish Harlem and ends with Ira's decision to leave the ancestral family tenement and move in with Edith Welles on the night before Thanksgiving in 1927. Roth was able to revise both the third and fourth volumes in 1994 and 1995 shortly before his death.

Both Roth and his publisher had tentatively scheduled six volumes of *Mercy of a Rude Stream,* and Roth had labeled volumes V and VI as

"Batch Two" of the *Mercy* project. Completed in the late 1980s and revised with his literary assistant, Felicia Steele, in 1990 and 1991, these two volumes—in manuscript form divided into five separate "sections" totaling 1,457 manuscript pages—contrast markedly in tone, structure, and sensibility from the first four volumes, and Roth called them "Batch Two" at the time for lack of a better title. Set in the late 1930s, the events occur over ten years after the conclusion of *Requiem for Harlem* and tell the story of Ira's courtship with the young composer named "M," whom he will marry. Given the profound differences between the first four volumes and these final two (there are no longer two narrators, for example), the decision has been made that these two books will appear eventually under a different title.

While still alive, Roth received two honorary doctorates, one from the University of New Mexico and one from the Hebrew Union College–Jewish Institute of Religion. Posthumously, he has been honored in November of 1995 with the Hadassah Harold Ribalow Lifetime Achievement Award and by the Museum of the City of New York with Manhattan Borough President Ruth Messinger having named February 29, 1996, as "Henry Roth Day" in New York City. More recently, *From Bondage* was cited by The National Book Critics Circle as being a finalist for its Fiction Prize. And in September of 1997, Henry Roth won the first Isaac Bashevis Singer Prize in Literature for *From Bondage*, an award put out by *The Forward* Foundation.